T0165423

BY THE SAME AUTHOR

A HEARTBEAT AWAY

SAVING GRACE

CAFÉ NEVO

CHANGING STATES

ROWING IN EDEN

A NOVEL

BARBARA ROGAN

SIMON & SCHUSTER

SIMON & SCHUSTER
Rockefeller Center
1230 Avenue of the Americas
New York, NY 10020

Designed by Jeanette Olender.
Manufactured in the United States of America.

1 3 5 7 9 10 8 6 4 2

Library of Congress Cataloging-in-Publication Data
Rogan, Barbara.
Rowing in Eden : a novel/Barbara Rogan.
p. cm. I. Title.
PS3568.0377R68 1996 813′ .54—dc20
96-4918 CIP
ISBN 978-1-4391-3575-4
ISBN 1-4391-3575-4

ACKNOWLEDGMENTS

Like Blanche DuBois, novelists always depend on the kindness of strangers. I am grateful for the generosity of several people good enough to share their expertise. Dick Van Egghen, veteran firefighter and fire chief in the trivillage region of Old Chatham, New York, taught me all I know about firefighting and the crime of arson. The staff of Old Chatham's charming Shaker Museum and its associated bookshop were invaluable in directing my research into Shaker furniture. Rabbi Robert Marcus was a helpful and humanizing force in the creation of my defrocked rabbi, Haim Malachi. My thanks to Allen Stanton for permission to quote from Tim Hardin's song "If I Were a Carpenter," and to Robert Osterberg for his kind help in obtaining that permission. Finally, I owe a debt of gratitude to Emily Dickinson, two of whose poems are quoted herein.

For my sons, Jonathan and Daniel

CHAPTER 1

Even though she'd asked for it, Sam Pollak could not help feeling guilty the day he killed his wife. The act took longer than he had expected and involved several false alarms, but in the very last moment something startling occurred. Lou's eyes flew open and she gasped, a seemingly endless sucking in of air. "What?" Sam cried, for it seemed she was determined to speak; why else such desperate effort? But she did not utter a word. The gasp ended without exhalation and the light went out of her eyes. Sam glanced instinctively at his watch. Like a ship's captain navigating a strait or a doctor recording a birth, he felt compelled to log the exact time of passage. It was 10:45 A.M.

For fully half an hour, he lay beside Louise on the Shaker-style bed he'd built for them when they first bought the house. Though her body bore no mark of violence, it had acquired an inhuman stillness, a positive, almost aggressive absence that could not have been further from the peaceful sleep he'd envisioned. He murmured to her, brushed her long black hair, arranged her gown, and tucked the thick down comforter tight about her cool shoulders. The tension had drained from her face, leaving it smooth and unlined. In death as in life she looked younger than her thirty-six years. Kissing her lips, Sam felt a stray shaft of desire, which he thrust from him in disgust.

When he was quite sure she was past any hope of resuscitation, he gathered up the bottle, glasses, vials, and other paraphernalia from her night chest. Shutting the door gently, as if to spare her nerves, he padded barefoot down the hall to the kitchen. He piled the dishes into the sink and turned on the hot-water tap. Brown water sputtered out in short staccato bursts. Louise had been after him for months to fix the blockage, somewhere deep in the system. He kept promising to do it but postponing the job, hoping the problem would just go away. By profession and by nature, Sam was a carpenter. He could lay pipe in a pinch, install a faucet or a float—but wood was his natural element. He loved the clean hard lines, the fixed properties of wood. Wood was predictable, whereas water followed its own mutable laws. Dew appeared out of thin air, like manna on the hill. Rain seeped into hidden cracks and crannies, snaked across rafters, and manifested arbitrarily in the form of distant, untraceable drips. And wells: anytime he needed an extra dose of anxiety, Sam thought about the fact that their water came from a well. Even after ten years in the country, wells made him nervous. There was a line in some Diane Keaton movie Louise had dragged him to at the Wickham Playhouse. In the movie Keaton played a smart city businesswoman who bought a picturesque lemon of a country house. When the plumber informed her that her well had run dry, she broke down in hysterics. "I just want to turn on the tap and have water come out," she screamed at the man. *"I don't want to know where it comes from!"* Sam had laughed and laughed, until people in the row in front of them turned around to glare and Louise elbowed him in the ribs. But beyond his city-bumpkin facade, Sam found something unsettling, something magical and deeply feminine, about wells. They required too much faith: dig deep in the earth and water will flow.

The stream from the tap steadied and cleared. Slowly the temperature rose to scalding. Sam held his hands steady. Although the pain registered, his hands felt foreign, like a stranger's hands grafted onto his body. He turned them over, examining palms that outwardly looked unchanged. They were large, callused hands, the right traversed by two thick sickle-shaped bands of scar tissue, one across the palm, the other across the thick pads of his fingers.

Turn off the water, Lou said, her voice perfectly distinct and clear, unaltered by death. Sam wheeled around, but the hall was empty. When he called her name his voice echoed into silence. He shut the tap. Stiff-legged against the current of his fear he walked down the hall toward the bedroom. Was it possible? Would he have to do it again? *Could* he do it again? He flung open the door. Louise lay as he had left her, smiling slightly. Oh, *you* can smile, he thought, bushwhacked by anger. You're out of it now, aren't you? I'm the one left holding the goddamn bag. He sat on the edge of the bed, lowered his head to his hands. Though he knew it couldn't and wouldn't happen, his neck anticipated her soft touch, fingers rising to burrow in the unruly curls along his nape.

Later he sat on the porch rocker, waiting for his new life to begin. The porch wrapped around the front and side of the old farmhouse, which sat atop a hill in northern Columbia County. To the west, visible only on the clearest days, loomed the Catskills; to the east, the Berkshire range. Behind the house and to its left there was a deep pine forest, where sunlight, filtered through millions of pine needles, shone green. One hundred yards to the right was a densely wooded bird sanctuary. What saved the site from closeness was its elevation and the unexpected expanse of its eastward prospect. From the porch and the principal rooms of the house, the view stretched over miles of gently rolling hills, forests, and tiny hamlets. Ten years ago they had stood for the first time on this deck, and Louise, reaching for his hand, had said, "This is it." Closing his eyes, he conjured up the moment: saw her leaning over the railing, black hair drawn back in a loose braid, slender body clad in white linen. Spring then, the apple trees smothered in sweet white blossoms, wildflowers sparkling across the lawn, air leavened with the golden scent of honeysuckle. Beneath their feet a county lay unfurled, valleys and gentle hills framed by distant green mountains. At the sight of such opulence and expanse Sam felt dizzy. The most frightening part was that this house was within their price range. They could be the people who owned this property, possessed this view. Sam could hardly believe it possible. Lou had no such difficulty. She fit this picture like the missing piece of a jigsaw, looked as though she'd lived here all her life.

She was twenty-six then; he was thirty. They had been married for three years, living in Manhattan. Louise stood just two inches under Sam's six feet, an elegant woman whose beauty owed nothing to mere prettiness; stunning but not dainty, no china doll. Lou was a tender but solid armful of female flesh, and it was that solidity that first attracted Sam to her, the feeling that here was a woman who would not melt away or break if he held her tight. What attracted her to him he didn't know and would no sooner ask than he would shake a sleepwalker. When they walked together in town and people they passed glanced from one to the other, he always assumed they were wondering what a woman like her was doing with a man like him. Not that there was anything repulsive in Sam's looks. He had a chiseled face, Slavic cheekbones, hooded eyes. Women found him attractive, though usually on second glance. The disparity between him and Louise was not in the realm of looks but rather of class; that difference, though, had seemed definitive. It never ceased to astonish him that this woman was his.

Earl Lassiter was searching for the key, patting his pockets, lifting the mat outside the kitchen door with the tip of an enormous black shoe. "I could have sworn . . ." He left them on the porch while he tried the garage.

Later, after he got to know Lassiter, Sam would suspect the realtor of purposely misplacing the key, leaving them to wait out on that deck, exposed to that killer view. And it worked, because the moment they were alone Lou turned to him and said, "This is it."

He knew as well as she did that this was the house they'd been looking for; but looking and finding are two different things. Suddenly their dream had taken on a frightening reality. Sam was a competent man, but he'd never owned a house before. The imminent prospect scared him. He temporized: "You don't think we should look at the house before we buy it?"

She smiled indulgently. "If you insist."

He ran his hands along the deck's railing. The thick cedar rail was straight and true, well planed. Underfoot the deck was solid as a rock. Through the curtainless kitchen windows he glimpsed burnished, wide-board oak floors: a well-built house, lovingly maintained. *Take me or leave me,* it declared. *I was here before you, and I'll be here after you.* Oh, Sam wanted it all right, but couldn't keep from fretting. "A lot of land means a lot of upkeep," he said. "And the driveway's in bad shape."

"The *driveway*!" Lou, laughing, swept her arm in a wide arc that embraced valley, hills, and forest. At that moment, a large buck emerged onto the lawn from the wood not forty feet away. The beast swung its massive antlered head their way; its eyes met Sam's; a signifying look passed between. Sam was struck by a sense of déjà vu, although, city boy that he was, he knew he'd never seen such a creature outside of a zoo. Presently the buck turned its head and resumed its solitary procession across the lawn, across the driveway, and into the woods on the other side, where it disappeared instantly amid the foliage.

"See?" said Lou. "It's an omen."

"An omen of what?"

She waggled her eyebrows like Groucho Marx. "Great changes. Infinite possibilities."

Infinite possibilities. If God Himself had spoken then, if God had told Sam what lay ahead for them, Sam would have laughed in His face. Because even in the range of infinite possibilities, some things are impossible.

The wind chimes over the kitchen door, one of Lou's priceless yard-sale finds, tinkled dully. Sam opened his eyes to bleakness, the flip side of picturesque. Barely mid-September, yet already winter was knocking at the door. Dead leaves danced across the wide sweep of frost-bit lawn, eddying about the trunks of ancient oaks. Giant maples, prematurely bared, bowed and swayed as if to cover their nakedness. A lone hawk swooped and soared, battering its head against the gray sky. What remained of those infinite possibilities now? Sam didn't know what his new life would entail but could foresee several alternatives, none of them good.

Time passed, a chill wind blew through him; he was a hollow man, a tunnel, a ghost. He felt nothing but a dull internal ache, like a Novocained tooth: more a promise of pain than pain itself. Pain waiting.

A gray Plymouth station wagon appeared, driving slowly along the dirt road at the bottom of the hill. It passed the Muellers' driveway, paused at Sam's mailbox, then turned up the drive. Sam expected no one but the doctor, and that wasn't his car. The Plymouth climbed uncertainly, weaving between ruts and jagged stones. Got to do the driveway again, Sam thought, before the ground freezes. Their fall ritual. But Lou was gone. Panic seized him suddenly; his thoughts grew disordered and dreamlike. One thing only was clear to Sam: that anyone looking at him would know at once what he had done.

The car stopped out of sight in the parking area behind Sam's workshop. The motor died and two doors slammed, sharp cracks echoing in the valley. A woman and a boy, strangers to him, came into view on the path. The woman had a sharp-featured face capped with short black hair, a compact body covered by a trench coat. She was short, but it took a while to see that because she had the stride of a tall woman. Her son—if it was her son, for the boy looked nothing like her—was a rawboned youngster of twelve or thirteen, half a head taller than the woman, as fair as she was dusky, with a forelock of straight blond hair that slanted across his brow. Even through the haze of his confusion, Sam noticed the boy's strange, watchful eyes, wary as a deer in hunting season, the irises a crystallized blue, fractured, like marbles plunged first into boiling water, then into ice.

The woman had one foot on the bottom porch step. Sam rose, not to welcome but to forestall. "Mr. Pollak?" she said. "I'm Jane Goncalves, and this is Peter. I've brought something for your wife."

Can't she see? he marveled, though of course he realized she could not. Neither the walls nor his head were made of glass. Louise was dead and apart from Sam not a soul knew.

The strangers exchanged a look. She climbed up a step; the boy stayed behind. "She ordered this book," the woman said. Her voice collided with his silence, faltered, and rose again. "I work in the Wickham Bookstore, and when the book came in I said I'd run it by for her. We live just in the village." She nodded back toward Old Wickham, half a mile away but hidden from view behind the hills. When he said nothing, she peered into his face. "Mr. Pollak?"

Her words reached him from across a great distance. Sam backed up to the rocker and sat down, his large hands splayed across his knees like a pair of helpless babies. He knew he had to speak, but the effort of bridging that vast chasm was beyond him; besides, what could he say? If he opened his mouth the truth would fly out: *My wife is dead. I killed my wife.* How would they look at him then? In horror, no doubt. He felt he could accept that, he could be the thing he was. It was the first part he found himself incapable of saying: that Louise was dead. As if the words would seal the deed.

"My wife can't see you now," he said.

His voice sounded unlike itself. The words emerged with unreal, icy clarity, hailstones from the frozen interior, and hung in the space between Sam and the woman.

The boy had been eyeing him suspiciously. Now he reached around the woman and grasped her sleeve. "Jane. Let's go."

She paid no attention to the boy, but produced a small paper bag from the pocket of her trench coat and held it out, advancing slowly up the steps, while the boy worried the foot of the stair. Sam was struck with a sudden vision of Louise, proffering handfuls of birdseed to brazen chickadees.

"Jane," the boy called softly.

"It's okay," she said. Her eyes were watching Sam.

Sam couldn't utter. He felt as if a great gray blanket had fallen over him, cutting him off from the world. The void in his head was echoed or perhaps induced by the unaccustomed idleness of his hands, for he was a man who thought, spoke, and felt through their agency.

The woman kept coming. He could not bear the thought of her looking through the living room window behind him, violating his privacy and Louise's. To fend her off, he reached into his pocket for his wallet.

The woman shook her head. "Your wife paid." She had reached the top of the porch; in two steps she was before him.

Sam rose. It was only then he saw how small she was, barely up to his shoulder.

She held out the book. "She was anxious to have it. Called the store twice to ask if it came in yet." Her speech was city-seasoned, inflected with a musical Hispanic lilt.

He took the book with a mumbled word of thanks. His eyes, like bricked-up windows, repelled light. Still, something must have shown in those eyes, for Jane Goncalves retreated more quickly than she had approached. Halfway down the path, though, she hesitated, looked back.

"The thing is," she said, "I had another reason for coming by."

The boy tugged her arm. "Let's just *go*."

"I understand you're a carpenter."

Sam nodded.

"I bought the old Atkins place," she said. "Do you know it?"

And suddenly, like a movie coming into focus, he realized who these people were. He'd have seen it long before this if he hadn't been so sunk in himself.

It had been the talk of the country store for months when Earl Lassiter finally unloaded the Atkinses' place, that sprawling old Victorian that abutted the village pond. It wasn't the sale but the buyer that got people talking, for Lassiter had sold the house to a city woman who harbored foster children, and not just any foster children but the hard-to-place kind, problem kids. "Bad seeds," Frank Gower called them, but that was Gower for you, always looking to pick a fight. Sam remembered him butting heads with Earl Lassiter in the back room of Whitehill's country store, a laughable mismatch, like a Pekinese baiting a mastiff. Lassiter was 6-foot-4 and weighed 240 pounds, and if he'd lost any muscle since his football days it didn't show; whereas Gower was a wiry shrimp, 5-foot-5 on tiptoes. The minute Lassiter walked in for his morning cup of java, Gower was in his face. "What are we," the little man squealed, "the city's goddamn garbage dump?"

"Now, Frank," Lassiter said soothingly, "they're only children." Gower was blocking the coffee pot. Lassiter took him by the shoulders and moved him aside, as effortlessly as a man shifting a hat stand. He poured coffee into a large Styrofoam cup.

"Bad seeds!" Gower said. "You son of a bitch, how many pieces of gold did you sell us out for?"

Gower didn't let it go. He got up a petition to block the sale, and Sam had heard he even went to the zoning board, but nothing came of it. Several months had passed since then, and the house stood empty. Sam had forgotten all about the pending bad-seed incursion, which had never worried him to begin with. But of course, as Frank Gower would have been the first to point out, the Pollaks too were city transplants; wandering Jews, and childless to boot.

So this was the woman, and this light-footed, wary-eyed boy one of her waifs. She didn't look like any foster mother Sam had ever known, and he'd known quite a few. If he'd thought of her at all, it had been to picture someone like the matron in the last place he'd lived in before lighting out for good: Old Bertha Potts, buttery, overflowing, pillow-breasted, sentimental female who kept a collection of Mother's Day cards from "her" children in a heart-shaped candy box to show visitors. The polar opposite, in fact, of the woman before him. This gal looked tough as beef jerky, her clever, dark features incapable of sentimentality.

"I've seen the house," he told her. "Never been inside."

"It needs some work."

Sam dropped his eyes to his hands. What could be built with such corrupted instruments? His eyes shut and he swallowed hard against the bitterness that flooded his throat. Louise's death, it was already clear, worked like a divorce, in that certain things went with her. His hands, for example. No longer his.

The woman shrugged and jammed her hands into her pockets. The corners of her mouth turned down. "So I guess you're not interested, either."

"Forget it," the kid said. "Let's go."

Sam wanted to explain. He understood the "either," and it didn't sit well, being lumped in with the likes of Frank Gower. But everything was tied to everything, and the task of unraveling it all was beyond him.

"It's not about that," was all he could say.

Jane looked at the house, then back at him. She said, "Maybe I picked a bad time."

"A real bad time," he said.

When they were gone, he looked at the book, a slim leather-bound volume of poetry by Emily Dickinson. He rubbed the leather, new but supple; he opened to a page at random and felt the paper, a thick ivory stock. His eye fell, with no expectation of understanding, on a cluster of words. Give him a blueprint, a diagram, the most arcane set of instructions, and Sam would instantly perceive the underlying design. But poetry was and had ever been a foreign language to him, despite Louise's periodic efforts at educating him. He read:

> There's a certain slant of light,
> On winter afternoons,
> That oppresses like the weight
> Of cathedral tunes.

The words entered him with a jolt, as effortlessly comprehensible as an old friend's elliptical remark. For didn't he know that very slant of light? Didn't its bleak glow bathe him now, inside and out?

Roused by the sound of a car shifting gears, he looked up in time to see a black Land Rover barreling up the driveway. It passed the workshop parking area and climbed the rough track to the house. As Sam walked around the corner of the L-shaped porch to meet the doctor, the deck seemed to sway beneath his feet. His body felt disjointed; he needed to think about how to move his feet, where to put his hands.

Dr. Martin Lapid started talking as he climbed out of the jeep. Stretched on a rack he would have had an inch or two on Sam, but years of bending over patients had taken their toll. He sported a full head of wavy gray hair, of which he was quite vain, and his face, plump, pink, and clean-shaven, belied his age of fifty-five. Thick, wire-rimmed specs magnified his blue eyes.

"Sorry, Sam. I got your message, but I was tied up. Twins," he said, rolling his eyes. "Where's Louise when I need her?" He reached the top of the porch and with a practiced move shifted his bag into his left hand and thrust out his right. Sam shook his hand. Lapid strode past him into the house.

Sidestepping quickly, Sam blocked the way. Lapid was Louise's doctor and her employer; he was also their friend. Sam couldn't let him walk in unprepared. He opened his mouth. "She's gone," he meant to say, but once again the words caught in his gullet, wedged like stones he could neither swallow nor spit out.

His face said enough. Lapid's eyes widened; he bolted around Sam and into the house. Sam followed slowly. When he reached the bedroom he saw the doctor standing beside Louise. Dappled red light from the setting sun, splashing through the bare window onto the bed, lent a false bloom to Lou's pallid face. Lapid was stroking her cheek.

Sam used to while away the hours waiting for Louise with lurid fantasies about the two of them, Lapid and Lou. He would imagine them emerging from the hospital after a late-night delivery, rumpled, weary, and exhilarated; imagine them climbing into the doctor's Land Rover, Lapid slipping the key into the ignition, then letting his hand fall away. Their eyes would meet; he would reach for her . . . That's where it ended. Sam knew his fantasy was born of nothing but fear. His wife was an honest woman. Lapid's marriage looked rock-solid. Still, it was hard for him to imagine any man not wanting Louise or, given the chance, failing to act on that desire.

Lapid's eyes closed, and his lips moved. It occurred to Sam that he was praying. The doctor stepped back from the bed and turned toward him.

"When?" he asked.

"This morning. Ten forty-five."

"You were with her?"

"Yes."

"Why didn't you tell me? You know I'd have gotten out sooner."

"There was nothing you could do."

There was a silence. The doctor said slowly, "It doesn't seem right."

"Of course it's 'not right,' " Sam said, with the first emotion he'd shown.

"I meant I didn't think it was imminent."

Sunlight glanced off Lapid's glasses, hiding his thoughts. He knows, thought Sam. Next he would ask about the medication, the morphine; and then life as Sam had known it would cease and a new life would begin. Anticipating this moment, he'd expected fear, prepared for it; but now that it was upon him he felt only a strange serenity, almost relief. No decisions left to make, his future out of his hands. Everything depended on what questions were asked. He would not lie. He hadn't promised to lie, only not to tell. In any case, what happened to him was immaterial. Lou was safe: that's all that mattered.

Then Lapid took off his glasses and their eyes met.

"You did the right thing, Sam," Lapid said. "You gave her what she wanted."

The inside of Sam's body seemed to shrink away from his skin, leaving a hollow space between, as if even he couldn't bear to touch himself. "How do you mean?"

"You kept her out of the hospital. Let her die at home."

Let her? Fateful words hovered on the tip of Sam's tongue. Only a lingering sense of Lou's presence blocked their utterance. Surely the truth was plain to see: but if Lapid saw it he gave no further sign. He went out to the kitchen to make some calls, and Sam crossed the darkening room to stand beside his wife.

"Now what?" he asked. She didn't answer. Her voice had gone to join the silent chorus that sang to him each night. It was the central fact of his life: everyone he loved died.

He sank onto the bed. Something pinched his hip: Lou's book, which he'd thrust into his back pocket when Lapid arrived. Sam took it out, let it fall open, a small, fine object in his rough hands. Louise had called twice to ask for this book, that woman said. Why? True, Louise had always been a great reader. In health she favored novels, in sickness short stories and poetry. "No point starting a good novel . . . ," she'd said one night—then, seeing his face, had failed to finish the sentence.

The ever-tactful Louise. So unlike her, he thought bitterly, to desert him this way. Even as her appetite for food declined, her hunger for books grew. "So many books, so little time," she joked one night; he hadn't laughed. In the end even reading was too hard for her. So he read to her. Some of the stories were not bad. There was this one writer, name of Raymond Carver. Carver wrote like a man who knew how to fix a car engine, gut a fish; like a guy you might have a beer with out on the porch. The poetry, on the other hand, seemed to Sam deliberately obscure, and offensive on that account. Sam strove for straight clean lines in his own work and admired it in that of others; personally he'd have taken more pleasure in reading a well-written instruction manual. But it was Lou's pleasure he served, not his own.

He thumbed through the new book as if it might hold the answer, a message from Louise; but if it was there, it was Greek to him. Gibberish, word stew: a sprinkling of God and nature, a dash of eternity. Then his eye snagged on one poem. He read it, squinting against the dying light, and the words seemed to bypass his brain and strike straight at his heart, or what was left of it. A chill traveled through him, taking a long, slow route. This was the poem, this was Lou's parting message. He read it again, aloud this time, for though she was gone it seemed to him that she was not too far to hear.

Wild nights! Wild nights!
Were I with thee,
Wild nights should be
Our luxury!

Futile the winds—
To a Heart in port,—
Done with the compass,
Done with the chart!

Rowing in Eden!
Ah, the Sea!
Might I but moor
Tonight in thee!

CHAPTER

2

"What I hear, ain't no white people left in New York City, just niggers, spics, and kikes," Walter Gower remarked at lunch.

"And faggots," Butch Hubbell amplified. Walter and Butch were best friends, as close as a boy and his shadow.

From over at the girls' table Marta Kimball called, "You guys got a mouth like a garbage truck, you know that?"

"Park it in your garage any day, babe," Walter shot back, attracting the attention of a lunchroom monitor. For a few minutes everyone hunkered down over their congealing pizza. Then the monitor, like a passing cloud, floated on.

"So which are you, city boy?" Walter asked the new kid. "You a nigger?"

Peter Quinn shoved the blond hair out of his eyes. "I look black to you, asshole?" he inquired, cool as cool; for Peter dwelt in a place where no loudmouth schoolyard bully could reach him.

"Kike?" asked Walter.

"Nope."

"Faggot, then."

"You wish."

A low titter ran down the table, quelled by a look from Walter. "Must be you're a spic, then, huh? Or maybe just a spic-lover."

"Walter, you're a pig," Marta called from the girls' table. She was the alpha girl, leader of the pack, Walter's property to his way of thinking, though not to hers.

"Ain't no pig, baby," he protested. "I'm a sensitive guy. I write poetry. No, really," he said as his audience roared. "Wanna hear my poem, Marta?"

"No," she said.

Walter cleared his throat and recited:

"Peter, Peter, pussy-eater,

"Had a ma and couldn't keep her,

"Now he's eatin' Puerto Rican,

"Never mind what Peter's drinkin'."

The raunchiness of young adolescent males being equaled only by their ignorance, Walter's ditty was greeted by a moment of silence while his listeners worked it out; then a great wave of laughter rocked the seventh-grade boys' table. Even Billy Mueller, who until Peter's coming had served as Walter's primary victim, couldn't suppress a high-pitched squeal.

Peter didn't hold it against him. He, too, was impressed. If Walter had spent half as much time on his schoolwork as he spent devising torments, he wouldn't be fifteen years old and still in seventh grade. Peter could afford to admire Walter's jingle because he knew that, after today, he would never have to hear it again. Fighting with Walter was already on his schedule for recess. He'd held off as long as he could, in deference to Jane's wishes, but waiting just made things worse.

Everyone was watching, expecting, willing him to take a swing, but Peter was no dilettante. If you fought in the lunchroom you had thirty seconds, tops, before the aides and teachers broke it up. Outside, if you picked your spot, you could get in a solid five minutes. Peter reckoned five minutes would more than do it. He finished his pizza.

Outside in the schoolyard he took up a position on the section of blacktop he'd fixed on. Hidden by the equipment shed, the spot was invisible to prying eyes within the school and to the recess monitors who, during cold weather, congregated in doorways. Billy Mueller trailed after him. He liked Peter, who never teased him or made fun of him the way the others did, and was ashamed of having laughed in the lunchroom. He was explaining that he hadn't meant to, the laugh just burst out of him by accident before he could stop it, when Peter cut him off.

"Go tell Gower I'm crying."

"Crying?" Billy shoved his glasses up his nose and squinted through the thick lenses. "You ain't crying."

"Just do it, Billy. Tell him he better lay off, 'cause I'm back here bawlin' my eyes out."

Billy took a few steps away, then returned, his full moon face eclipsed with worry. "I don't know," he said doubtfully. "Walter's kinda mean. Telling him that be like waving a red flag front of a bull."

"Do it!" Peter said. Billy scampered. Peter removed his jacket, folded it neatly, and laid it on the ground beside the shed. He lit a cigarette, and hunkered down. Hadn't taken five puffs before Walter's voice reached him. "I ain't gonna hurt the little crybaby. I'm just gonna wipe his snotty nose for him." Peter stood and crushed the butt beneath his heel. The moment Walter's smirking face appeared around the corner, Peter jumped him.

A crowd gathered quickly, concentric circles, boys on the inside, girls on the outside, like a country dance. Butch Hubbell made to shuck his jacket but a couple of eighth-graders grabbed his arms: "Fair fight, fair fight." Already they were on the ground, Peter kneeling on Walter's chest as he pummeled his nose. When Walter raised his hands to protect his face, Peter kneed him in the belly. With a roar of outrage, Walter heaved himself up. Peter flew through the air, landing hard on his hands and knees. His jeans split; blood welled to the surface.

Blood and mucus streamed from Walter's nose. He drew back his foot to kick at Peter's head, but Peter rolled away, sprang up laughing.

Walter stepped back, striking a defensive karate pose.

"Very impressive," Peter said. "Saturday morning cartoons?"

"You're dead, you know that, asshole? You are totally dead meat."

Peter laughed. Walter still had no idea who he was playing with. "Yo, Gower," he taunted. "Your mama's so ugly, when you were born the doctor slapped her instead of you."

With a roar Walter rushed him. Peter was ready and they traded blows. Walter had two years and twenty pounds on Peter, but Peter had one unbeatable advantage: he didn't care what it cost to win. Pain didn't scare him. He didn't like it, but he knew how to handle it. Walter had a good punch but he did his best work with someone holding his victim. One on one he was slow, much too slow for Peter, who'd grown up in a tougher town than this and knew a trick or two. Peter hooked a leg behind Walter's knee, put the palm of his hand to Walter's chin, and shoved hard. The big boy toppled like a hewn oak. Peter dropped to his knees on Walter's chest and grabbed him by the ears. "Loved your poem," he said, slamming Walter's head against the blacktop. "Read it again some time."

He sat tall in the penitent's seat. Perched behind the counter in the main office, Mrs. Primworthy, the principal's secretary, pecked away at an old black Smith-Corona while sneaking glances in his direction. Peter felt good, he felt fine. Power surged through him. His knees burnt a bit—the school nurse, malicious old biddy, used iodine on the cuts when Bactine would have done just as well—but he didn't care. Tomorrow they'd have righteous scabs on them. His knuckles tingled and the muscles in his arm ached pleasantly. Walter was such a gratifying enemy: pure bully, unrelated to Peter, thus lacking any possible claim on forbearance. Beating *his* ass was a virtuous act, its own reward.

Walter had been driven to Albany Memorial's outpatient clinic in Valatie. No one was telling Peter anything, but he overheard the nurse on the phone mention a possible concussion. If Walter had a concussion, it couldn't make him any stupider than he was already; it might even smarten him up some. Why not? There had to be a limit to stupidity. Eventually, Peter reasoned, you'd hit the final barrier and rebound.

Jane entered the office, not exactly sauntering but not hurrying either. She wore her bookstore outfit: denim skirt and blouse. She didn't look at Peter. Her gaze took in Mrs. Primworthy and beyond her, the principal's closed door.

Primworthy peered over her glasses. "Miss Goncalves? Mr. Lightfoot will see you immediately."

Jane nodded but took a seat beside Peter. "Talk to me."

"I got in a fight."

"Tell me something I don't know."

"I won," he said.

"Oh, Peter."

"Couldn't be helped," he said by way of apology.

"They're watching us, you know. We talked about this. What you do reflects on the others."

"That's right," the boy said. "And it didn't help them any, me pussyin' out."

"I hate that expression."

"Sorry."

Mrs. Primworthy cleared her throat. "He's waiting."

George Lightfoot sat behind his desk at the far end of the room. The junior-high-school principal was a man of medium build with small, well-kept hands. In his bearing and appearance—bristle-cut gray hair, pencil-thin mustache, deep furrows about the mouth, square jaw, ice blue eyes—he looked every inch what he was, an aging ex-Marine. His desktop was bare but for a box of Kleenex, a cylinder full of pens and pencils, and an open file. He waved Jane forward without looking up from his page. Unbidden, she took a seat and waited. Lightfoot finished the page and immediately took up another. The fractured rhythm of Mrs. Primworthy's hunt-and-peck typing filtered in from the outer office. Somewhere a phone rang on unanswered. Jane extracted a paperback from her pocket and started to read. Lightfoot looked up at once, scowling.

"Miss Goncalves," he said icily.

She finished the paragraph and marked the page before shutting the book: *A Prayer for Owen Meany*. Jane was in a John Irving phase, making her way through his books.

"Mr. Lightfoot," she said.

They eyed one another. Lightfoot licked his lower lip. His tongue was unusually long and narrow, reptilian. White man speak with forked tongue, she thought. According to Paul Binder, her boss at the bookstore, Lightfoot had been dean of discipline in the high school during a period when corporal punishment was allowed, a policy Lightfoot apparently endorsed with excessive enthusiasm. There was an incident—Paul was vague on the details—but a boy ended up in the hospital. No one blamed Lightfoot, precisely. There was no way he could have known of the boy's prior medical condition. But the policy was changed in a hastily called board meeting, and it wasn't long after that that Lightfoot was transferred, booted upward into the middle-school post. He brought his paddle with him; it lay now on a shelf behind his desk, a well-worn trophy.

Jane looked at it, and a small frown furrowed her brow. Lightfoot ought to be warned against raising a hand, or anything else, to Peter. Coming now, though, a warning was bound to be taken wrong. Better to say nothing.

Lightfoot produced a grimace of sympathy as convincing as a wax apple. "I regret to inform you that Peter has been suspended one week for fighting. Naturally this will appear on his permanent school record." It was at this point, in his experience, that the tears commenced to flow. He nudged the box of Kleenex closer to Jane.

She nudged it back. "And the other boy?"

Lightfoot blinked. "The other boy?"

"I presume he wasn't fighting alone."

He picked up the paddle, started tapping the edge against the palm of his hand. "The other boy was taken to the hospital."

"Who was it?"

"Walter Gower."

She didn't laugh but she did smile. Lightfoot drew his eyebrows together till they met over his nose: Look #28 from the Principal's Arsenal. She'd seen worse.

"Nothing serious, I trust?" she asked.

"The boy was looked at and released."

"And is he, too, suspended?"

"By all accounts, including his own, your foster son started the fight."

"Peter was provoked," Jane said. "We both know that. Since the day he started school here he's been harassed and assaulted, and you have done damn-all about it."

Torn shirts, bruised knees, buttons missing off his jacket, here a scrape, there a bump, every day something, and every day a new explanation. He fell off the bus, tripped on the playground, walked into a door: this from a boy with the grace of a panther. Peter didn't even expect her to believe his stories, he just produced them with a look that said, clear as day, *Don't mess with this. Keep out.* With another child she might have forced the issue, with Peter she would not. He was desperate to exert control over his own life and it was not her place to stand in his way, though it went against her grain to sit and do nothing.

Peter didn't talk, but her other kids did. Old Wickham's elementary-school and junior-high kids shared a school bus into Wickham; Walter Gower and his band of junior-high rowdies picked on Jane's little ones, too. No wonder, with a father like Frank Gower. First time she saw that name it was on top of a petition to bar her purchase of the Atkinses' house. The petition was three pages long. A lot of the people she now saw daily had signed it, but Gower was the only one who still went out of his way to be nasty. Every time they met in the country store, Gower started talking to anyone who'd listen about city brats and hoodlums. If Walter was picking on her kids, no doubt his father was egging him on.

Jane was a great believer in letting kids sort out their own battles, but Peter's hands were tied. During his nine months in juvenile detention Peter had been involved in several fights. In the city school Jane put him into, he was suspended twice, both times for fighting with larger, older boys. When they moved up to Old Wickham, Jane had coerced a promise from him: a new start, no fighting. She'd tied his hands; the way she saw it, this made the Gower kid her problem. Four weeks into the school year, she called the principal.

"It's the nature of the beast," had been Lightfoot's response. His voice oozed as if forced through too fine a strainer. "There's always a certain amount of rough-and-tumble when a new boy comes to town. Sort of like hens, working out their pecking order. Boys will be boys," he'd said.

Now, sitting in his office, she reminded him of that conversation.

"Peter went way too far," Lightfoot said. "He deliberately set about to inflict maximum damage."

"Did he tell you that?"

"The teacher who broke it up told me your kid was totally out of control."

"You just said he acted deliberately. Now you're saying he was out of control. Which was it?"

"Don't bandy words with me, Miss!" Lightfoot took a few deep breaths. "Is there anything you can tell me to explain this behavior? Anything we should know?"

There was everything to explain the behavior and nothing they should know. Peter, the last child in the world who could afford to sit still for abuse, had done what he had to do to end it. But Jane was no virgin; she'd worked in the school system and knew that anything she said about Peter could and would be used against him.

Not that she knew much, only the bare bones of his story, and even that came from Portia, the boy's social worker. Peter himself didn't utter a word. To hear him talk you'd think he'd sprung to life full-blown, a twelve-year-old orphan without a shred of history. It was only by looking into his eyes that you saw the damage.

"No," she said. "There's nothing."

"Then there's no excuse." Lightfoot smiled; she'd confirmed his expectations. He leaned forward, pressed his palms on the desk, and spoke in a voice as smooth as lotion. "Tell me: Do you really think those children will ever truly feel at home here in Wickham?"

How quick the transition: in a blink of an eye, the problem had changed from Peter to *those children.* Why was she not surprised?

"So," Jane said, "you think I should toss the rejects back into the urban slime from which they arose?"

He sputtered. "How dare you? You know nothing about me. See here, Ms. Gonzales—"

"Goncalves."

"—Your ward beat the living daylights out of another student. *That* is the issue."

"It's one of the issues. The other is that you and your staff deliberately looked the other way for weeks, while Walter and his gang tormented my kids. You knew and you did nothing. So who's really culpable here?"

Lightfoot, his attention now ratcheted up to combat levels, studied her closely. It crossed his mind that Goncalves might have done well in the Marines. Not that he was generally an advocate of women in the military, but this particular woman had that in-your-face quality that distinguished the Corps. Under the circumstances, though, and directed as it was toward him, her attitude was intolerable. He thrust his balled fists into his armpits, narrowed his eyes, and glared.

Jane let the silence work. She could see the wheels turning in his head as clearly as clockwork in a transparent casing. Lightfoot leaned across the desk and negotiations commenced in earnest, ending fifteen minutes later with a curt handshake. Peter's punishment was commuted to two days' suspension, no mention to appear in his school record; and the same would be accorded to Walter Gower.

The principal walked Jane to the door and watched her leave with her son. Foster son, he reminded himself, for in attitude if not by blood the two seemed related. Summoned to Lightfoot's office, Peter had made no excuses, offered no explanations. He had called the principal "Sir," but with a look in his eyes that cost him an extra two days' suspension. And the woman! Suddenly Lightfoot remembered whom she reminded him of. A few years ago, after his youngest son joined the Navy, he brought home a dog so his wife wouldn't be alone all day. Got it from a breeder friend of his: a little brindle boxer bitch, ugly as sin but feisty, absolutely loyal, and the best damn watchdog he'd ever owned. They had her for three years, till one day the dog got out and mauled the paperboy. Luckily the kid had the presence of mind to protect himself with his sack; still it took eight stitches to close the gash on his forearm. Lightfoot had wept when they put the bitch down.

Goncalves reminded him of that boxer bitch, not in appearance but in character. The resemblance tempered his dislike. He had every reason to detest her, that insolent outsider with her insolent city ways. Sitting in his office, telling him his job. But after she was gone, he startled Mrs. Primworthy by laughing out loud. Say what you would, the goddamn woman had balls.

It was Peter's week for KP. As a matter of principle he tried getting out of it, limping around the kitchen, groaning loudly and clutching his knees, but Jane didn't seem to notice. She was lost in her thoughts, hunched over the big old cast-iron stove like a storybook crone, stirring the soup with a wooden ladle. Presently, without looking up, she said, "Knock it off, Peter, and get on with those potatoes."

When he first came to live with Jane, ten months ago, Peter was amazed at how much work he was expected to do. At that time she'd had five foster kids, all squeezed into a brownstone in Brooklyn's Cobble Hill. In that tiny kitchen, a quarter of the size of the one they had now, a big, laminated, erasable chart with columns and rows hung on the wall beside the fridge. Each kid's name headed a column, and a list of chores ran down the edge: Help with Dinner; Laundry; Set Table; Clean Kitchen; Sweep; Vacuum; Take Out Garbage; and on and on the list went, to the very bottom of the chart. Every week the names were rotated, so everyone had to learn every job, except for the littlest ones, who always got the easiest tasks. "Cooking!" Peter had scoffed, checking out his name that first night. "Guys don't cook!"

"Guys eat, don't they?" Jane had replied, pulling a saucepan and a cutting board out from under the sink.

"Yeah, but they don't cook. Women cook."

She took a large bunch of broccoli out of the refrigerator and laid it on the cutting board. "Cooking's a survival skill, like changing flat tires. Survival skills are not gender-specific. First rinse, then cut, then drop in the pot." Jane demonstrated on a single stalk, then handed the knife to Peter. It had a sharp, serrated blade and a wooden hasp. He took it gingerly, eyeing her. How much did she know?

"Cut," she ordered.

When his mother was alive, things were different. All Peter had to say was, "I'm hungry," and before the words were out of his mouth she was in the kitchen fixing him a snack. His mother used to peel his apples, pour milk in his cereal, butter his toast. The first time Peter said to Jane, "I'm hungry," she looked up from her desk with a little frown of distraction and said, "You know what *I* do when I'm hungry?"

"No, what?"

"I eat." Then she went back to writing checks.

Peter hung in the doorway for a while, not knowing what to do.

Was this some kind of joke? Finally he said, "Well, could you get me something?"

Jane's eyebrows rose so high he thought they were going to fly off her head. She took him by the hand and led him to the kitchen. He sat at the table. She pulled him up and over to the counter.

"Silverware," she said, opening a drawer, then a cabinet. "Plates. Food." She opened the fridge. "More food. Feel free." Then she gently touched his cheek with the back of her hand and went back to her study.

Jane's golden rule: Don't ask people to do for you what you can do for yourself. And it wasn't just him. The others, too—Keisha and Carlos and even Luz, plus the kids who'd come and gone, adopted or sent back to their families—they all had their assigned tasks, which had to be completed before they could play. At first Peter thought Jane acted so strict because she didn't care about them. Since his mother was the only adult in the world whose affection he had been sure of, her cosseting was all he knew of love. Gradually he figured out that Jane had her own way of loving, a way that had more to do with propping kids up than clutching them to her bosom. She wasn't stingy with hugs—Luz in particular demanded and received about fifty a day—but Peter didn't like being mauled, and Jane respected that. She allowed him his space, giving respect but demanding it, too. Peter had long since gotten past resenting the chores, and, though he'd never admit it even to himself, he'd actually come to enjoy cooking. For one thing, the rewards were immediate and tangible; for another, on his cooking days he got to spend time alone with Jane, working in the kitchen while the others did homework or chores.

The thing he respected about Jane was that she didn't pry. She'd made it clear from the start that if he wanted to talk, she was willing to listen; he made it equally clear that he didn't and wouldn't, thanks all the same, and that was that. Their talk ranged far afield but stayed anchored safely in the present. They drifted easily, like old friends, between silence and conversation.

Tonight, however, silence filled the kitchen like a dense fog. Jane brooded and stirred her soup and would not look at him. Peter stood at the butcher-block countertop with his back to her. He finished peeling the potatoes and started cutting them into chunks. Jane sighed heavily; he glanced at her, then quickly away. Jane's "little talks" were famous; kids had been known to beg for beatings instead. Tonight, however, Peter would gladly have suffered a lecture. This silence threatened. Was she planning to send him back to the court? Had she given up on him?

Who cares? he said to himself. Who needs her? It didn't matter where he lived or who with. Yet at the thought of his impending exile, the lump in his throat grew and his eyes began to burn. And this in a boy who hadn't cried since a day in his seventh year when his mother lay bleeding on the kitchen floor and his father said, "I'll give you something to cry about, boy," and did.

Just then Peter brought the knife down on his left thumb—not entirely by accident. Blood welled from the gash, splashing onto the potatoes. Now he had a reason to cry but no tears.

Though he didn't see her move, Jane was suddenly by his side, grasping his wrist in one hand, reaching for the faucet with the other. She thrust his hand into the cold stream, muttering "Shit" as the water ran red.

Peter's real mother never cursed. Never. Even lying in her own blood, the worst she would say was "Lord, Lord," or "God help me." Jane, on the other hand, cursed like a longshoreman when anyone mucked with her kids. Despite her petite frame, her delicate features, and her fiercely held brood of runts and rejects, Jane wasn't Peter's idea of a feminine woman. He couldn't see her as anyone's wife—but then, he couldn't see her sprawled on the floor in her blood, crying "Lord, Lord," either. Not, as Carlos always said, in this dimension.

"You know what your problem is?" Peter asked.

Jane wadded up a paper towel and pressed it to the cut. "Hold this tight," she said. She crossed over to the cupboard beside the back door where the first-aid kit hung. "What's my problem?"

"Your problem is you expect people to be what they're not and never will be."

"Is that so?" She carried the kit to the kitchen table, straddled a chair, and beckoned him over. Rummaging through, she pulled out a half-used tube of antibiotic ointment, a cotton pad, a roll of gauze, and some tape.

Peter sat opposite her, averting his gaze from his outstretched hand. The paper towel was soaked through with blood. Jane removed it and peered closely at the cut, angling his hand under the light.

"You'll live," she pronounced. "What do I expect *you* to be?"

"A *good* boy," he sneered, trying not to wince as she squeezed ointment directly into the wound.

Jane laughed. She pressed a cotton pad hard against the cut and raised his hand above his head. "Hold it up there. Press tight. That's it. What do you mean by a good boy, Peter? Do you mean a kid who's been through a lot of bad shit but still retains the capacity to care for others, look after them? I'm not mad at you, if that's what you think."

"You're not?"

"Hell no. Keep that hand up."

"But you said—"

"I know what I said. Only how much shit is a kid supposed to take?"

"Really?"

"I'm supposed to tell you fighting doesn't solve anything, right? Okay. Consider it said. You know you've got to try and solve disputes through talking. But if that doesn't work . . . I'm just saying no one has to let himself be somebody else's punching bag."

"You got *that* right." Peter was not about to mention Walter's little piece about her. Wild horses couldn't have dragged that bit of filth out of him.

"If that's what it's about I can live with it," she said. "Everybody's got a right to defend himself. But you can't fight for the others, Peter. That's my job."

"Right," he drawled.

Jane shot him a look. Then she brought his hand down, removed the pad, and examined his thumb. Blood still oozed from the cut, but the heavy flow had been stanched. Suddenly the door between the kitchen and dining room swung open and Keisha appeared.

"Is dinner ready yet? I'm—what happened to Peter?"

"A little cut," Jane said. "Nothing serious. Dinner will be ready in fifteen minutes. Is the table set, Keisha?"

The little girl shook her head. Her huge brown eyes were fixed on Peter's hand. "Did Walter Gower do that? Carlos said you kicked his butt to Pizza Hut."

"Get on with your job, girl! That table's not gonna set itself." Jane turned back to Peter as Keisha disappeared. She put another pad on his thumb, wrapped it tight with gauze, and taped it.

"If you're not mad, how come you weren't talking to me?" Peter asked.

She turned her dark eyes on him. So serious, those eyes, they looked like they were listening. As though her eyes had ears.

"I wasn't not talking to you," she said. "I was thinking."

If there was one lesson Peter had learned in life, it was always to expect the worst. Quinn's First Law of Human Dynamics: No sooner do you imagine you're sitting pretty than someone's bound to pull the chair out from under you. The solution was to trust no one, a solution Peter had been well on the road to implementing when Jane plucked him out of the system. It was hard not to trust Jane, mostly because she generally said what she thought and did whatever she damn well pleased. Like moving them all out to the country, her latest stroke of genius. She and her social-worker buddy, Portia, just rammed that through the city bureaucracy. Jane kept saying how wonderfully cooperative everyone was being, and Portia kept telling her it wasn't cooperation. "Girlfriend, they just can't wait to get shut o' you," Portia said. "And these kids? Columbia County, shit. If you'd of said you was takin' them to the moon, they'd of said 'Bon Voyage!' "

Naturally nobody thought to ask the kids their opinion. Luz was too young, and Keisha and Carlos didn't care, they really would have followed Jane to the moon; but Peter was dead set against the plan. "Me move to the sticks? I don't think so," he told her. Sweet lot of good it did him. Not a day went by that he didn't swear to himself that one of these days he'd be off, back to the city where he could function on automatic pilot. Jane wasn't his mother, and this hick town sure as hell wasn't his home. Nevertheless there was no denying that when Jane said she didn't blame him, Peter felt a cold knot of fear dissolve in his gut. She's not mad, he thought. She's not sending me away. He could have kissed her. Hell, at that moment, he could have kissed Walter Gower.

"So what were you thinking?" he asked, as if it mattered now. "What were you thinking so hard about?"

Jane got up from the table and started packing the first-aid kit. Her face was somber. "That man we visited, Sam Pollak? I heard in town today, his wife died yesterday. Poor bastard. And I kept shoving that damn book in his face. What a jerk."

Peter thought back to the day before. He recalled the man's nervousness, the look on his face as Jane approached, the way his hands lay on his knees like foreign objects. He remembered the man squinting at Jane as if he could barely see her when she was standing right in front of him, and the air of desolation that enclosed him like an isolation chamber. With a shock of realization, Peter blurted out words he would come to regret. "He killed her!"

Jane gasped. "Oh no, Peter, no. The poor woman was sick. Cancer killed her, not him."

And though Peter said no more, it was too late. Jane was staring at him, and he could see what she was thinking. He knew how adult minds worked. After the trouble with his father, he'd been given over to the blunt probings of the shrinks and social workers. He'd learned their lingo the way a waylaid traveler learns the language of a country he'd never planned to visit. Projection, they'd call it, that sense of recognition he felt when he looked at Pollak; displaced guilt. And a bunch of other fancy words to justify their bills. As far as Peter was concerned, it was just a clear-cut case of takes one to know one.

CHAPTER

3

There was no air in the living room. Instead there were odors: the cloying scent of unseasonal flowers, the pungency of tobacco, the seductive aroma of fresh-baked pies, and underlying them all, a subtle, corrupt stench of singed hair and burnt wool. The room was crowded. Not only friends and neighbors had attended the funeral, but also people Sam had never seen before, Lou's patients, he guessed, for a disproportionate number of the women carried babies on their hips or strapped to their backs, papoose-style.

Two little girls in starched Sunday dresses shared Louise's chair, rocking and giggling behind their hands. On the sofa, Louise's mother was attended by Marty Lapid and Kate Mueller. The other women, having paid their respects, kept their distance. Old Wickham did not know quite what to make of the tall, tanned woman who had flown in from Palm Beach for her daughter's funeral. Blanche Mannheim wore a black pantsuit, tapered to emphasize her slender figure. Her golden hair was pulled back and gathered under a wide-brimmed black hat. Mother-of-pearl earrings adorned her lobes, and beneath the large sunglasses she wore indoors and out, her face was exquisitely made up. Scandalized, Old Wickham's ladies whispered among themselves: What kind of woman wears pants, jewelry, and makeup to her own daughter's funeral? What kind of woman looks like that at, what—sixty-plus, surely? Blanche's third husband, Harold, had been spotted the previous day in the country store dressed in lime green pants and a jaunty white golf cap—this in the middle of a cold northern autumn—but *he* at least turned up for the funeral decently attired in a charcoal-gray suit. Now he hovered about the funeral table, loading his plate with this and that, chatting with the little rabbi who'd read the Kaddish over Louise's grave.

In the middle of the room, a grim-looking bunch of men held court. In work clothes and slickers, muddy boots pressing into Lou's prized

Navajo rug, they spoke in voices muted for the occasion but taut with excitement. As they talked they punched the air for emphasis and touched each other's arms and backs. It was the country store crowd: Willem Mueller, Stan Kuzak, Tom Whitehill, Frank Gower, Earl Lassiter.

When Sam came over they fell silent. He asked, "What's going on?"

They exchanged a look, but no one answered. Sam realized with a sudden shock that none of these men had attended the funeral, neither the services nor the burial. Not surprising in the case of Gower, no friend of his, who for that matter had no business here in his house; but the others *were* friends, and not the kind of men to slight the dead. In his grief and exhaustion, Sam had felt their absence without quite registering it. It came to him that they'd stayed away because somehow they knew what he had done and could not stomach the spectacle of a murderer weeping at his victim's grave.

Metaphorically, that is. He hadn't actually wept. Sam never cried at funerals.

Willem spoke. "Didn't you hear the siren, Sam?"

Had he? Hard not to hear the fire alarm, designed to summon men for miles around. Now that Willem mentioned it, Sam recalled hearing it wail sometime early that morning. He'd paid no attention. He was not a member of Old Wickham's volunteer fire department, though he'd been asked to join.

The invitation came about five years after he and Lou moved to Old Wickham. Kate and Willem Mueller had walked up the hill one summer evening after dinner. They were each other's only close neighbors and had fallen into the habit of drifting together two or three evenings a week. While the women made coffee, Sam and Willem sat on the porch, watching the fireflies come out. They exchanged a word now and then but for the most part smoked in companionable silence. Willem, who wasn't much of a talker, had the odd habit of weighing each word he said. If someone asked him how he felt, he'd mull it over for a moment or two before answering, "Fine." Not that he would have said so if he felt bad; he wasn't that type. He just liked to think it over. This ruminating habit rendered his speech deliberate and, for the impatient, agonizingly slow. Sam didn't mind, even found it relaxing in a Zen-like way; but Lou, although she liked Willem, couldn't talk with him for five minutes without breaking into hives. She said it was like trying to jog with someone moving in slow motion.

As they sat, the sky darkened. An iridescent green hummingbird darted amid the honeysuckle vines that snaked along the railing. The coffee-scented murmur of women's voices drifted out through the kitchen window. The men made plans to work on Willem's roof next weekend if the weather permitted. Then Willem asked if Sam would care to join the fire department. Casually, as if it were no big deal. "We could use an extra hand."

Only it *was* a big deal, and they both knew it. The volunteer fire department was the village fault line, separating the locals from the city folk. What the hunt club was to the weekenders, the firehouse was to indigenous Old Wickham, the nexus of its social and communal life. Throughout the year there were cake sales, raffles, and car washes, and every July the ladies' auxiliary held a huge steak roast, with kegs of beer for the grown-ups and races and carnival rides for the kids. When the Whitehills' girl Margaret fell ill with leukemia and needed chemotherapy, when the Fallons' little Mikey developed cataracts in both eyes and needed surgery, it was the fire department that raised the funds.

Village society was split into separate spheres, of which the two main divisions were old Old Wickham—the natives—and new Old Wickham, city folks with second homes in the village. These spheres were not quite mutually exclusive. A few individuals, mostly professionals and real estate brokers, were able to travel between them, like bottle-nose dolphins who swim in both fresh and salt water. The Pollaks fell somewhere in between, which is to say nowhere. As a midwife, Louise worked exclusively with local women, yet city women regarded her as one of their own. Sam did the bulk of his carpentry and cabinetry for second-home owners but gravitated in his free time toward the local men who, like himself, earned their living with their hands. Thus the couple straddled the fence between locals and city folks, friendly with both societies but belonging to neither.

It wasn't what they wanted, which was to set down roots in this alien soil, but neither had much experience in setting down roots. Sam had spent the later part of his childhood in a succession of foster homes and institutions. Lou's path, though far more affluent, was no less nomadic, following the upward trajectory of her mother's successive marriages. They were Jews and city folk: tumbleweed, to local eyes. For four years Sam had been politely asked to contribute money to the fire department, and he did. Now Willem was asking him to join. The change was qualitative and the message clear. Old Wickham was extending its hand.

Understanding the significance of this unsought, off-handed invitation just made things worse. Sam smoked his Camel down to the filter and snuffed it out underfoot. Turned his palms up on his knees and studied the scars like a Gypsy fortune-teller reading tea leaves. Willem watched sideways, a little hurt, though nothing showed on his stolid face. He'd come prepared to slough off gratitude.

"Appreciate the offer," Sam said at last. "Wish I could accept."

Willem just looked at him, holding his cigar. Mueller ran a crew for the highway department. He was a solid man, square and heavy yet surprisingly mobile. Watching him trudge up the hill, Sam always thought of a boulder with legs.

Minutes went by. The last rays of light drained from the sky; the hummingbird departed. "Come in, come in," the women trilled. By mutual, unspoken consent, the men sat on.

"How come?" Willem asked. Years of shouting over heavy equipment and roaring fires had eroded his speaking voice to a rasp.

Sam flicked his lighter, lit another cigarette, then held the flame in front of him. Moths gathered around, flirting with fire. One flew too close: its wings flared and it lit up like a sparkler before disappearing in a puff of smoke.

Sam shut the lighter and returned it to his pocket. "Fire scares me shitless," he said.

Willem's eyebrows rose a quarter of an inch. "Fire scares everyone ain't got rocks in their head. Wouldn't want you if it didn't."

"I'd be useless to you. I see a fire, I run the other way."

Willem snorted. He turned his head away. In the set of his heavy jaw Sam saw that battles had been fought over this offer; it hadn't come easily. He knew a thing or two about the department, pieced together from comments Willem had let drop over the years. On the surface everyone was buddy-buddy, but underneath something was always seething. By law the department was open to all who were fit and wished to join, but new members were subject to secret ballots, and five negative votes were enough to scuttle any candidate. The department's balance of power teetered precariously on the fulcrum of village politics. Alliances formed and re-formed; candidates of each bloc were impeded by the other.

Lyle Fertig, for example. Lyle Fertig was Frank Gower's best friend. Every year for the past eight years, Fertig had applied for membership, sponsored by Gower, who was a longtime firefighter, nineteen years in the department. And every year for the past eight years he'd been voted down. Fertig's problem was that they all knew him. A fireman's life depends on the competence of the man beside him, and competent was not a word that had ever been applied to Lyle, a legendary fuck-up.

Then there was the case of Earl Lassiter's friend, Mark Hambro. Before he came home and took over his daddy's real estate agency, Lassiter had a distinguished twelve-year career playing linebacker for a succession of winning NFL teams. The year he left football, he came out of the closet.

It was a shock at first, but after the initial jolt no one really cared. It wasn't as if Lassiter was an outsider, one of those effete writers or artists from the city. His people had lived in this county for as long as anyone could remember. Lassiter was a volunteer fireman, a member of the Chamber of Commerce, a successful businessman; he wore a Superbowl ring. The tolerant indifference with which his coming out was greeted might have meant that Lassiter of all people turning out to be gay had altered people's perception of gays; or it might simply have had to do with size, Lassiter not being the kind of man you'd be likely to call a faggot. Most likely, though, people just made an exception. A guy like him, a football star in a county that took its football seriously—people figured he was entitled to his little idiosyncrasies. But it rankled the hell out of Frank Gower, for whom the sin of homosexuality ranked just lower than bestiality.

Hambro had been a professional firefighter in Boston till he quit to move in with Lassiter. As soon as he could, he applied to join the Old Wickham Volunteer Fire Department. Normally any professional would have been a shoo-in; but this was not a normal situation. Lassiter was in the department because he'd always been in it; his comrades knew him as a hell of a firefighter and there wasn't one of them, not even Frank Gower, who would have kicked him off the force. But they owed nothing to Hambro.

Lassiter waited downstairs with his lover while his fellow firefighters met upstairs. When they got to Hambro, Frank Gower, smarting over yet another rejection of his buddy Lyle, said sure, let's vote this guy in, and while we're at it why not paint the fire engines pink? That got a big laugh, and the candidate was voted down by a margin of twenty to eight.

Old Wickham's fire department had no women, no blacks, no Jews. Sam had counted on never being asked to join. But Mueller had asked him, and Mueller never spoke idly; he wouldn't have extended the invitation if he didn't have the votes. Which meant Willem must have called in some serious chits.

A great sadness came over Sam. He reached toward Willem, but let his hand drop. "I'm sorry."

Without looking at him, Willem shrugged. "Guess you've got your reasons."

He did; they were written in the palm of his hand. But if Sam hadn't told Willem that story during the five years of their friendship, he wasn't about to tell it now.

"No hard feelings?" he asked, though he knew there would be, had to be.

"Better you telling me up front than us finding out the hard way," Willem said, but he didn't wait for coffee, didn't even wait for Kate, just nodded good-bye and headed back down the hill.

Now he thinks I'm a coward, Sam thought. Well, I am.

Willem tried to keep up appearances. Their wives were close friends, and beneath his dour crust Willem was too kind a man to exhibit disdain. Nevertheless Sam sensed it, and their meetings, once full of ease and the mutual respect of hard-working men, grew fraught with awkwardness and restraint. The friendship would have died but for Louise. She made Sam tell her what had come between him and Willem, then did what he would not: she told Kate, who told Willem, what fire had done to Sam.

Willem never spoke of it, never indicated by word or look that he knew; but he started coming around again, to ask for help or offer it, or just to sit out on the porch, smoking and watching the sun go down. Thus Sam had understood that he was forgiven.

And now he understood why they'd missed the funeral, why they were here in his house booted and slickered, stinking of wet ash and worse things.

"Where was the fire?" he asked.

"Crawfords' barn," Willem said. The Crawfords were a retired couple, former teachers in the Wickham regional high school, who lived alone on ten acres or so outside the village. The old man was wheelchair-bound, but Sam often saw Mrs. Crawford in the country store, buying treats for the dogs and the paper for her husband. Willem plowed their drive for them.

"Anyone hurt?"

Willem pursed his mouth as if to spit. "Nope. But they lost that pony they kept for the grandkids. And one of the dogs."

"How'd it get started?"

Lassiter answered, his huge hands curled into fists. "Torched. Third damn arson in two months. Like to get my hands on the sonuvabitch."

"Why we didn't make the funeral," said the sheriff, Stan Kuzak. "Sorry, Sam. Would of seen her off otherwise, you know." Then the others remembered why they were there, and one by one they offered their condolences. Sam shook their hands.

What a hypocrite he was. His secret poisoned every offer of consolation; it stood between him and all hope of comfort like the angel with a flaming sword who barred the gates of Eden. When the old rabbi led him through the Kaddish, the words formed a bitter bridge that Sam crossed and recrossed in a kind of fugue state, flickering from this funeral to the last one he'd attended, at age eleven. Then too, they made him recite the Kaddish. Three times he'd said the words, once over each coffin. *Yiskadal veyiskadash:* the words curdled in his mouth. He'd had no use for religion then and now had less, although lately he'd come to feel a need of judgment. Someone, somewhere, had to know what he had done. Someone had to judge.

The men shifted, exchanging glances, inhibited by his presence. Seeing that they wanted to get back to talking about the fire, Sam drifted away. He felt distant from them, as much of an outsider as Lou's mother, Blanche, now ensconced on the couch, talking obsessively about the subject that had occupied her throughout the long drive from Albany Airport: the drugs she took to safeguard her pregnancy with Louise.

"How could I have known?" she appealed to Marty Lapid, who sat beside her on the couch. "They swore it was safe. And after two miscarriages . . ."

The doctor pressed her hand. "You couldn't have. Nobody knew, then."

"They still don't," Kate Mueller added briskly. Lou's best friend and a mother herself, she had her own opinion of Blanche, who'd stayed away through most of Louise's illness. "No one can say what caused Lou's cancer."

Sam could have told them then and there: *Cancer didn't kill her. I did.* The temptation was strong: get it out, get it over. But he'd promised Lou he wouldn't, a deathbed promise he'd keep if it killed him.

Kate noticed him hovering and smiled up at him. Kate had the most beautiful mouth Sam had ever seen, a luscious cupid's bow. A couple of years older than Louise, she possessed the kind of looks that made Sam wonder why men bother with young girls. It was a careless, country beauty: honey-colored hair swept back, often as not, in a ponytail bound by a rubber band, a wide brow, forthright gray eyes, and that heartbreaking mouth. Kate was his wife's best friend and his best friend's wife, doubly out of reach. Yet, safe within the confines of his marital state, Sam in happier times had thought about that mouth, indulging in the kind of pleasant speculation that carries no risk of fulfillment.

They had their own relationship, separate from the others. Kate ran the Old Wickham Country Furniture shop out of a converted barn just off the highway to Wickham. Over the past few years she'd become the sole vendor of the Shaker-style chairs, desks, armoires, and tables that Sam made in his spare time. Handcrafted of the finest local hardwood, his pieces were costly, but not nearly as much as their antique prototypes. The store was set back, well-signed but sufficiently off the beaten track that city women, wandering in, felt as if they'd discovered hidden treasure, and no doubt the men felt the same way about Kate. This was something Sam had always felt they had in common, he and Willem: they'd both married out of their league.

"Have you eaten, Sam?" she asked him now. He hadn't, but wasn't hungry. At Blanche's urging that morning he'd put a dutiful crust of bread in his mouth and choked on it. "I'm fine," he said. Kate started to say something else, but she was interrupted by a loud crash, followed closely by the clatter of breaking glass. At the refreshment table, the little rabbi stood wringing his hands and gazing around him at the floor. From his feet, shards of glass radiated outward, glinting against the hardwood floor. Tiny bits of fruit dripped from his trousers. The rabbi closed his eyes, and the light in the room seemed to dim a little. "Oy," he groaned.

"Whoa," a young voice said. "*Major* mess."

Glancing down at Blanche, Sam saw her white-lipped glare directed at the rabbi. He looked away before it could be turned on him.

In perfect accord, the countrywomen swarmed into action, performing their tasks as if they had practiced and rehearsed for just such a contingency. Within seconds mops were produced, sponges appeared; the owner of the broken bowl had declared it of no account, and Sam found himself propelled down the hall with the glass-studded, fruit-dripping rabbi in tow.

The rabbi's black woolen trousers were soaked through with fruit juice. "You'll have to change," Sam said.

"Into what? I go to make a funeral, I don't bring with me a change."

The rabbi looked up the length of Sam, then down at his own self: five-foot-two at a stretch, skinny and hollow-chested. "We don't exactly wear the same size, you and me."

Sam rifled through the closet. Louise's clothes had utterly disappeared from her side of the closet—the work, no doubt, of Blanche and Kate, who'd spent the morning cloistered in this bedroom—and his own clothes, sparse and lonely, colonized the rack. The only pants that wouldn't fall off the rabbi were an old pair of denim overalls with adjustable shoulder straps. He passed them through the bathroom door, with an armload of towels. "Sorry about the jeans. Best I can do."

Muffled thanks came through the door.

It was so quiet in here, so peaceful after the hubbub outside. With the door shut, Sam heard nothing but the sound of water running and a fierce chittering of birds. He'd forgotten to feed them again. Louise would be outraged. He could hear her. *So I died; does that mean they have to starve?* There was a little family of four or five chickadees who ate from her hand. Damnedest thing he ever saw. Living with Lou was like living inside a Disney movie. "When the mice start singing," he'd told her, "I'm moving out."

Sam sat on the edge of the bed, slipped off his shoes, leaned back, and put his feet up. He hadn't slept in this room since it happened. At first he'd tried bunking down in his workshop, but there too the cot was infested with memories of stolen hours, daring daytime seductions of his wife, so he'd ended up on the living room sofa. Now, lying on their bed with his head on Lou's pillow, Sam inhaled her lingering scent and stared up at the sky-blue ceiling. If he kept his eyes from straying, he could almost feel her breathing beside him.

The old man was muttering to himself in the bathroom. Over the rush of water Sam heard only a few scattered words. "Klutz . . . shame . . . *goyim.*" Then, raising his voice, the rabbi called through the door. "Mr. Pollak, are you there?"

"I'm here."

"I apologize. Such a mess, and that poor lady's bowl."

"An accident," Sam said. "Could have happened to anyone."

Though it struck him as odd that the rabbi had returned to the house. The funeral was over, his job done; why hang around? Bit of a vagabond, this rabbi. Knew his stuff all right, but a rogue for all that. Where exactly did Lapid find this guy? Sam couldn't quite remember; lack of sleep had turned the past few days into one long blur. They had needed a rabbi, that much he recalled. And the rabbi down in Hudson was on vacation, and the one up in that little one-room synagogue in New Galilee turned out not to be a rabbi, just a local pharmacist with two years of rabbinical school under his belt. Still, when the doctor turned up with this fellow on the eve of the funeral, Sam was taken aback. With his hollow cheeks, wispy gray beard, and doleful, deep-set eyes, the rabbi had the haunted look of an accountant for a failing firm. But what did it matter? The man could have been a one-eyed mongoose for all Sam cared, though it did occur to him, as he watched the rabbi drive away in a rusty, mud-splattered old Dodge, that Lou's mother would not be pleased.

As indeed she was not. The moment she walked into the funeral parlor, Blanche took one long look at the small man in his frayed black suit and battered hat, then turned to Sam and inquired, with faint horror, if *this* was the rabbi? Blanche's tone brought back to him her reaction on learning of Lou's engagement to the carpenter she'd hired to redo her kitchen. "Is this the man my daughter is to marry?" she'd cried, pressing manicured hands to throat. Every word received a separate emphasis, as if to show there was not a single element of that proposition that did not offend her.

The rabbi stepped forward, and proffered his card. Blanche held it by the edges. "Rabbi Haim Malachi," she read, peering down through her dark glasses. "Rabbi-at-large." This time her steely gaze bypassed the rabbi altogether and clamped directly onto Sam. Once again, the rabbi stepped into the breach. He snatched the card from her hands and turned it over to reveal printing on the back.

"'Better than nothing,'" she read aloud. And shut her eyes.

Sam stared at the rabbi.

"Fancy I'm not," Malachi said with a sigh. "You want fancy, you go to that Jewish cathedral on Fifth Avenue, Our Lady of Emmanuel. Me, I'm available."

"I would settle for respectable," Blanche had muttered. Wait till she sees him now, Sam thought, as the bathroom door opened and Malachi appeared on the threshold. He looked lost in Sam's overalls, which even rolled at the ankle were far too long. Under the overalls he wore his white shirt and tie, and above them his now damp and fetid black suit jacket. The effect made even Sam blink.

The rabbi stretched out his hands. "So what do you think, a new trend in rabbinical wear?"

"It's . . . unusual."

Malachi shrugged. "An itinerant rabbi is not your usual everyday rabbi."

"You have no congregation?"

"I go where I'm needed. A bar mitzvah here, a wedding there, now and then a funeral. Once I had a *shul* of my own, with a *chazan* and an ark and red velvet chairs on the dais. And flowers, every week fresh flowers."

"Why'd you give it up?"

"I didn't. It gave me up." He crossed to the dresser and regarded himself in the mirror, frontward and sideways. Noticing a framed portrait of Louise in her wedding dress, he picked it up, carried it up to his eyes to study it closely, then replaced it with a sigh. "I'm not," he said, "a very good rabbi."

"What's the difference? A rabbi is a rabbi. You're all peddling the same line of goods."

The rabbi turned to face him, dark eyes gleaming. "And you, Mr. Pollak, you're not buying?"

"Please," Sam said with a dismissive wave. As if they were actors backstage; no need to pretend.

Malachi wore an air of humility as impermeable as a bullet-proof vest. "And yet, in my experience, it helps to say Kaddish, it helps to sit *shivah*."

"Empty ritual."

"When a man is drowning he don't look a gift lifeboat in the mouth. Faith is good," the rabbi said, "but not necessary."

"Faith in what? I'm supposed to believe Lou's an angel now, flitting around heaven in a brand-new pair of wings? Bullshit, man! You know and I know she's gone forever."

"I don't know about wings. Wings may be excessive. Still, a person can hope."

The old man sounded bleak, though. Sam looked at him. If Malachi was a salesman, he sure as hell wasn't working on commission.

"Hope," Sam said, "is for children and fools."

Muffled voices filtered into the room, people talking in the hallway. As the sounds from outside penetrated, the silence in the room seemed to grow deeper, Sam's lethargy greater. Very soon, he knew, he would have to face those people again, accept their condolences, smile and say thanks while every word of sympathy cut like a knife. He ordered himself to his feet, but sorrow sat on his chest like an elephant. He couldn't speak; breathing was a conscious effort. He shut his eyes, hoping Malachi would take the hint and disappear.

"You may be right. What do I know?" The rabbi sat on the edge of the bed, bouncing experimentally in the manner of a man accustomed to temporary lodgings.

"Aren't you supposed to know?" Sam taunted. "Isn't that your job?"

Me?" said Malachi, with a self-deprecating moue. "About God I understand nothing, which believe me for a man in my profession is a serious disadvantage. If He exists, if He don't, where He's been the past few thousand years—don't ask. But I'll tell you something I do know. People need to believe; this is how we're made. Something happens, a good thing or a bad, people got to figure out why. They got to praise somebody, or blame; they got to figure out a reason." Malachi nodded toward the picture of Lou on the dresser. "Beautiful young *maydeleh* gets sick, dies in her prime, where's the sense in that? A person believes in God, at least, worst comes to worst, he's got who to blame."

"God didn't kill my wife," Sam said. The old man looked at him and at last fell silent.

CHAPTER 4

In the weeks that followed the funeral, Louise's death proved to be not a singular loss but rather a myriad of separate losses, all lying in wait to ambush him. Again and again Sam would lose himself in some household task, only to find himself calling out to her. Rising in the morning he would make a pot of coffee and automatically pour two cups. Waking at night, he'd reach for her. Each time it happened it was as if she died all over again. Her absence was a black hole that sucked up all the life and energy from the house. Bulbs failed and were not replaced. Dust mottled the furniture, cobwebs obscured the corners of the rooms. The television lost its color and Sam didn't even notice.

The exigencies of Lou's illness had defined his days; the metronome of her pain gave shape and rhythm to their lives. Now, without the regimen of her medications, Sam's days grew indistinct. One blurred into the next, day grew indistinguishable from night.

Work might have helped, but he had no work to occupy him. That this flowed from his own decisions made it no easier to bear. Before Louise got sick he'd had as much carpentry work as he could handle, most of it renovation, old farmhouses, colonials and Victorians being updated by new owners. His clients were all city folks, since they had the money—with country people it was generally, "Do for yourself or do without." There wasn't much free-floating cash among the indigenous population of Columbia County, for the simple reason that there wasn't much work. No industry to speak of; that was further north, in Troy. Local women worked mainly in low-paying service jobs; the men worked for the railroad or the utilities, or they drove trucks. Every unemployed man who owned a hammer and a pickup called himself a carpenter, and for a while it seemed as if there was enough work for all of them. Columbia County, gloriously scenic and just across the state border from Tanglewood, had long enjoyed a reputation as a sort of unspoiled Hamptons among that class of city-dwellers, artists and intellectuals, who prided themselves on their essential down-homeness. The recent resurgence in the long-dormant real-estate market had set off a wave of renovation. Sam had offers enough to work year-round if he chose to, usually with another job or two in the offing. For a guy with no overhead, the work paid remarkably well. That income, together with Lou's salary and the occasional windfall from the sale of Sam's furniture, gave him a feeling perilously close to security: perilously, because Sam knew better than most that the only real security is false security.

Those were the good years, the best; their only sorrow then Lou's failure to conceive. An only child herself, she yearned for children of her own, lots of them, four at least, she warned him before they married. Sam cared nothing for children and could have spent his life in utter contentment alone with Louise, but whatever his lady wanted he was bound to do his damnedest to provide. When they bought the Old Wickham house, it was partially in the hope of filling it with children; but though they gave it their enthusiastic best, every month ended the same way, in blood and tears.

Sam had himself checked; the results showed normal fertility. Then Louise went in for testing, and that was when they found the first tumor.

It was as if some giant, malevolent prankster had reached down and plucked the wings off their life. Sam was sick at heart, furious at the doctors, scared to death . . . but not surprised. How could he be, when never for one moment had he trusted their happiness, never believed it could last? Didn't he know how quickly things can change? In no time at all, in the fraction of a second it takes for a ball to hit a wall and rebound, a man's whole world can shatter. Trucks appear out of nowhere, cells throw off all restraint, viruses invade the blood through cracks the width of eyelashes, bridges collapse, and tornadoes touch down where they will: Some are lost and some are saved, and no one, no one can say why.

Superstitious, Lou called him, and worse things than that, but Sam, though he didn't parade it, would not be talked out of his fear. Before they found the house in Old Wickham, they'd looked at a number of others. One in particular, a cedar-sided contemporary in the upstate village of Eden, had captivated them both. Surrounded by meadowland, the house, with its weathered wood, multilevel decks, and crow's-nest turret resembled nothing so much as a ship sailing on an undulating sea of green. The interior of the house was full of light; best of all, there was a separate skylit studio that would serve perfectly as a workshop.

"This is it," Lou said.

"This would have been it," Sam said, "anywhere else."

"Not that again! It's just a name, Sam. Lots of villages up here have biblical names: Canaan, Lebanon, Bethlehem."

"Ah, but Eden—don't you see, Lou? That's just asking for trouble."

"I can't believe you're serious," she said, though she could see he was. Her eyes filled with tears. "That house is perfect for us. And you love it as much as I do, I know you do."

Now Lou was not your weepy type of woman; in fact, Sam could not remember ever having seen her cry before. He felt terrible, but what could he do? When he tried to picture himself living in Eden, his imagination seized up and spat out the image. It seemed to him an act of sheer reckless folly, like waving a red flag in God's face and yelling "Come and get me!" and he couldn't understand why Lou didn't see this. Because what, after all, did they know of Eden? Two things only: it was perfect while it lasted, and it didn't last long.

"Ah, Sam," she said, putting her arms around him, "it's not the name, it's you. I know you. You think happiness is a lightning rod. You can't even laugh out loud without looking over your shoulder."

With good reason, as things panned out.

They didn't buy the place in Eden. Lou bowed to his paranoia; they settled in Old Wickham instead, made friends, made a good life. But Lou never forgot the house in the meadow; hence the poem. "Rowing in Eden, ah, the sea."

Might as well have bought that house, Sam thought now. God doesn't need a red flag. If He wants you, He'll find you even in the belly of the whale.

After they found the first tumor, Lou had tests and more tests, and then one day Marty Lapid called them into his office and shut the door, so that Sam knew instantly, before the doctor said a word, what the prognosis would be. Lou reached for his hand, he clasped hers tight, and they looked up at the doctor like little babes lost in the woods. Lapid had the habit of jiggling his right foot when he was nervous; that day, it rattled so hard the desk shook. Although he tried valiantly to project an attitude of optimism and calm, he was too fond of Lou by half to carry it off, and finally his voice trailed off into silence and he fell into a fit of furious blinking.

Sam cut back on work to stay home with Louise and take her to treatments at Albany Memorial. Money wasn't a problem, not yet. Her job carried comprehensive medical insurance, and they had built up enough of a nest egg during the fat years to carry them through the lean. As each successive mode of treatment failed and her cancer progressed, he quit working altogether. Thus it came about that after Louise died, he found himself with nothing but time on his hands. And that time hung heavy.

Kate and Willem asked him over most evenings; when he begged off, they sent their children up the hill to bully him down. They had two: Melissa, seventeen, flirtatious and pretty, though not quite as pretty as her mother; and twelve-year-old Billy, a slow-witted boy, but good-natured and biddable. Sam was grateful for his friends' kindness but would have been more grateful for less of it. Solitude seemed his natural state in this new and untried life of his. Louise had always been the sociable one; even if that were not so, Sam's awful secret would have stilled his tongue. Dwelling now on a vast and lonely tor, he found the simplest communication required the effort of shouting across a chasm. All he wanted was to be left alone, but he found it hard to refuse the kids, especially Billy. The youngster had been very fond of Louise and seemed devastated by her death. One of the few things Sam remembered about the funeral was the sight of the boy at graveside, sobbing into his mother's shoulder, while he himself stood dry-eyed.

He couldn't sleep at night. Sometimes, toward morning, he dozed off for an hour or two, only to wake with a start of guilt. He sat at the window looking out over the dark valley and smoked endlessly. His mouth tasted of ashes. What oppressed him was the sheer tedium of mourning, the endlessness of the pain, like a chronic toothache of the heart. For a while after Blanche flew away in a flurry of hugs and luggage and promises they both knew would never be kept, Sam spent whole days entombed in the house, puttering about unshaven and barefoot in an old flannel robe Louise had more than once threatened to burn. The silence of the empty house beat on him. He had never been aware of his house as a living thing until it died; now he felt as if he were living inside a cadaver.

Eventually the roar of silence drove him out. Sam took to walking, briskly, aimlessly, at all hours of the day and night. He roamed the wooded bird sanctuary, pastures and orchards carpeted with autumn leaves; he strode for hours and hours through the cold bright air until his muscles ached and his ears rang. The walking exhausted his body but did nothing for his heart, which beat but grudgingly and might have stopped altogether were it not for the demands of his body, which imposed its own agenda of warmth, food, and occasional rest.

Sam could cook—during Lou's illness he had cooked for her every night, overreaching himself to tempt her flagging appetite—but for himself he couldn't be bothered. After the funeral neighbors had brought over casseroles and quart containers of thick country stew. For a good while he lived off these. When they were gone, he would scramble an egg or open a can of soup, no more. Sam had a stash of marijuana left over from Louise's chemotherapy; it had eased her nausea, and he'd gotten into the habit of smoking with her. After dinner, if the Muellers left him alone, he'd light up a joint, put his feet up on the couch, and fall asleep to the late-night talk shows.

Kate, seeing his idleness, kept after him to make her some furniture. "With Christmas coming up, I can sell anything you give me," she said. "And don't tell me you can't use the money." He put her off. She was right, of course: he *could* use the money. Lou's insurance had not after all covered everything; bills were piling up alarmingly. But Sam had lost faith in himself, lost faith in his hands. His hands, corrupted instruments, were no longer his to command; he felt he had forfeited grace.

It takes a particular frame of mind to work wood the Shaker way; it takes a sense of harmony that Sam no longer possessed. The first time Sam visited the Shaker Museum up in Old Chatham, he was blown away by the furniture, a perfect meld of form and function, free of ornamentation for its own sake, its elegance derived from simplicity, utility, precision, and the natural beauty of fine wood. Furniture that spoke his own language, furniture he'd seen in his mind but never knew existed. The sect's buildings, both living quarters and workshops, were models of economy and order. "A place for everything and everything in its place" was more than an adage for the Shakers; it was a religious tenet, practicality elevated to sacrament. Lou used to say that it was lucky for her the Shakers, who practiced celibacy, had all but died out; otherwise Sam might have been tempted to join. A joke born of deep security.

He'd spent three hours touring the museum's building on his first visit. Before leaving he stopped in the office and wrote out a check for membership. Thereafter, whenever he had a few hours to spare, Sam visited the museum and studied the furniture. For Lou's birthday he built his first Shaker-style piece, the bed they were to share for the rest of their lives together. Kate saw the bed and immediately ordered one for a client. So it began.

Sam wouldn't sell his work but for a fair price, and that price, though far less than that of real Shaker antiques, was on the high end for reproductions. Every piece was hand-finished, perfectly fitted and jointed, made of the highest-grade hardwood. Barring fire, it would long outlive its purchaser. To Sam's surprise, though not to Kate's, quite a few people proved willing to pay his price.

To occupy himself during the interstices of Lou's illness, he'd started two new pieces. One was a tall, shallow cabinet of the sort the Shakers used for herbs and seeds. With two rows of a dozen drawers each, graduated in size, each of which had to be cut, jointed, and fitted precisely to its allotted carcass, the cabinet was the most ambitious piece he'd ever undertaken. No templates existed. He'd studied the seed cabinets in the Shaker Museum and grasped the principle, though the doing was something else again. The piece made no sense economically, could never be sold for anything like what it cost in labor to construct; but at the time he'd needed work difficult enough to require his full concentration. The other piece was a candle stand, a much simpler project that he undertook as a change of pace from the seed cabinet.

These unfinished pieces weighed on his mind. For twelve days after Louise's death, Sam did not touch his tools, nor did he enter his workshop. Yet his work called out to him in plaintive, muffled tones, mournful as an unfed dog waiting to be remembered. On the thirteenth day Sam awoke at dawn from a fitful sleep. Without stopping to think, he showered, dressed, and walked down the cobblestone path to his workshop.

The double doors—old barn doors, relics of the structure's previous incarnation—creaked as he shouldered them open. Cold, stale air engulfed him. He turned up the thermostat, hung his jacket on a hook, and moved to stand in the center of the room. The workshop, a converted barn, consisted of one large open space. Vertical strips of window, three to a wall, stretched from floor to ceiling. These and the vaulted ceiling drew the eye up toward what was once the hayloft, conferring a cathedral-like aura upon the room that Louise had called his sanctum. It is said of the Shakers that their churches looked like workshops and their workshops like churches, with arched ceilings and polished beams. And indeed, Sam had in what now seemed the distant past felt a peculiar grace to this studio, designed by him and built with his own hands.

Of that grace only memory remained, memory with a bitter aftertaste. The upward sweep of the room, the clean, vertical lines, the angles not merely right but righteous, all bespoke a view of the world that appeared to his unveiled eyes not merely optimistic but willfully, wickedly delusional. Now when Sam looked upward, it was only to inspect the beams, idly assessing their sturdiness. The laggard autumn sun was still low in the sky, and the light shining through the eastward windows had the gritty texture of sawdust. This very light which once elated now oppressed him. He remembered suddenly the poem by

Emily Dickinson in Louise's book: "There's a certain slant of light on winter afternoons, that oppresses like the weight of cathedral tunes."

The oak floors were clean-swept, the room all but bare. In his previous life this spaciousness had delighted him, but now he saw the shop as barren, sterile. A long worktable lined the northern wall, flanked by racks and boxes of wood on one end, a stationary cutting table on the other. A tiny, half-assembled drawer lay up-ended on the table, where he'd dropped it the last time Louise called. Sam's eyes rose to the combination telephone/intercom on the wall. She had cried out, waking to that old familiar pain; she had called his name, her voice a whisper, a remnant of her old voice. *Help me, Sam.*

Mounted on the wall above the table was a long rack full of glistening tools, and there Sam turned with a start of gratitude: nonsensical, of course, but he couldn't help it, for somewhere in the back of his mind he'd imagined the tools gone, taken for his sins. They were his treasures, these tools, his loyal friends, every one handpicked and saved up for, each with its own story. The oldest was a simple hammer, given him at the age of seven by his father. It was the only thing Sam had of his father's and it was a good hammer; he used it still. The second oldest was a screwdriver, the first tool Sam ever bought himself, a venerable Phillips. Looking at it brought back the year he'd spent living with his uncle's family in Borough Park.

Before the accident, Sam had never met his father's family. All he knew about them was that they were strictly Orthodox and had shunned Sam's father ever since his marriage to a woman who was worse than a *goy:* Jewish but nonreligious, a *shaygetz.* But they showed up at the funeral, where Sam's uncle Ezra, now by default his guardian, talked about God's judgment upon sinners, a eulogy that failed to endear him to his eleven-year-old nephew.

Uncle Ezra insisted on calling Sam "Shmuel" and enrolling him in the same yeshiva his cousins attended. Sam, ungrateful child that he was, neither answered to the name nor attended the school. He had, in those days, a doglike tendency to stray, usually ending up in his old neighborhood of Canarsie, playing stickball with his Italian friends and swimming off the pier. Uncle Ezra took to locking him in his room—for his own good, of course. The Phillips, Sam found, is an excellent tool for dismantling hinges.

The circular saw was bought with the proceeds of his first job, apprentice to a master carpenter. There were tools purchased as acts of faith, to be used in a task as yet undetermined, and others purchased because they were beautiful, elegant. In Sam's mind, a tool was not only a means to create something else but also a thing of value in itself. It was the Shakers' love of tools even more than their furniture that brought him to his knees. Many of the implements he saw displayed at the Shaker Museum had been invented and lovingly, intelligently crafted by the brothers themselves.

His most treasured tool was an antique rosewood plow plane with a set of eight blades given him by Louise as a wedding gift. He had opened the gift-wrapped box expecting some pretty but useless gewgaw like the gold locket he'd given her. When he saw the plow plane laid out in its case, tears sprang to his eyes. One by one he'd lifted each blade out of its black satin casing, holding it reverently in his rough palm. How she knew precisely what he most wanted and never thought to own was a mystery Sam never fully plumbed. She had given him a tool that radically altered the range of things he could do: a gift of possibilities. There was also a card, which he kept to this day in the strongbox along with the deed to the house and other vital papers. Written in her cool, sloping hand, it said, "To a Carpenter from his Lady: With love and trust, to build our life together."

Sam sat on his stool by the table and examined the half-made drawer. A spider had spun a web on the inside. He brushed it clean, then picked up a planing knife that lay beside it. This is what he was doing when Louise called that last time. The knife was cold. His hands began to shake. He shook them out and resumed his task, running the razor-edged blade along the rough edge of the drawer's upper rim; but again his hand trembled and the knife scored a deep scratch in the wood. Cursing, he tossed it aside and stood up. His eye fell on the cot in the far corner, covered by a Navajo blanket. He crossed the room and threw himself onto the bed. The blanket was another gift from Louise, who cared nothing for clothes or jewelry but had a passion for

Indian weaving. In their house, Zapotec and Hopi rugs lay scattered across the hardwood floors, colorful Mexican cotton weaves adorned the windows, and cushions made of red-and-black Navajo blankets softened the stern contours of Sam's Shaker benches and ladderback chairs. Theirs was an odd but successful combination of obsessions, the lush colors and clean lines of the Indian weavings perfectly complementing the austere grace of Sam's Shaker-style furniture.

Gathering up a handful of blanket, Sam pressed it to his face and inhaled her smell, not her perfume or shampoo, but the true woman-scent of her. He closed his eyes and she came to him.

She lay down beside him, her sweet round rear against his groin, and laughed as he nuzzled her neck. "Sam—dinner will get cold."

"Let it freeze." His hands cupped her breasts, felt the nipples harden through the denim shirt she wore. Gotcha, he thought.

Moments later, braced above him, she pretended to pull back. "Should we?" she teased.

He groaned but didn't really mind. Her shirt was open and the view was fine from where he lay. Lou liked to tease; she drove him to distraction but always paid off in the end.

"Absolutely," he said. "It's required. All the help have to."

"The help!"

"Come here, you."

She brushed against him. "It'd be like doing it in a synagogue."

"More like a church. My child: prepare to receive the host."

"Bad!" She laughed and smacked his mouth but Sam was ready for her; he pulled her down and then they were rolling in the blanket, joined at the hip, the lips, the heart.

The telephone shrilled, and Lou vanished with the first jarring ring. Sam sat up, hunched over, arms wrapped around himself. He considered answering, but couldn't summon the energy. Why bother when there wasn't a soul on earth he cared to talk to? But the phone continued to ring: ten, twelve, fifteen times. When he saw that the caller was not going to relent, Sam picked up. "Hello?"

Silence came down the line: but a familiar silence, more charged, more alive than Sam's deadened voice.

"Who's there?" he demanded.

No one answered. Sam could discern no background noise or sounds of breathing; yet he sensed, with absolute certainty, a taut, listening presence on the other end. A sudden thought shocked him.

"Lou?" he whispered, then quickly hung up, appalled at what he had said, but unable to dismiss the vision he'd had of Louise reaching out to him. It made no sense, the very notion was an offense to the orderly, rational mind of the carpenter—and yet this call, this silent listener, whose silence seemed born not of inability, but rather of refusal to speak, filled him with horror. He felt it as a reproach—but what right had she to haunt him? Hadn't he done what she asked, no, *begged* him to do? He was blameless. She'd said so herself, explained it a hundred times. It was her decision. Lapid had promised there would be no pain, but he lied. There was pain to spare. The remedies always lagged one giant step behind the beast, which, as it grew, devoured her from within. Sam couldn't bear her agony—but he didn't do what he did to spare himself. The choice was hers alone. He bent his will to hers; he made himself her tool. In the end she kissed the hand that poisoned her.

Why, then, did he feel like a murderer?

The telephone lay beneath his hand in ominous silence. The thought that it might ring again at any moment flooded him with a spurious energy. He ran out of the workshop only to pause outside, irresolute. There was plenty to do on the grounds. The driveway especially needed work. In a few weeks the ground would be frozen and then it would be too late. But the prospect of spending another interminable day in his own company sickened him.

Across the road, at the bottom of the hill, he saw the Muellers' red truck pull out and head toward the village. Creatures of habit, the Muellers; without looking at his watch Sam knew it must be 7:30. He set off on foot down the hill.

The back room of the country store was crowded, and it wasn't for the coffee which was tolerable at best. In a county whose only local paper came out weekly, the country store doubled as social hub and information center. Every chair around the six wooden tables was occupied, and a handful of men lounged around the pot-bellied wood stove. The room smelled of fresh-brewed coffee, donuts, and cigarettes. The anti-tobacco revolution had missed Columbia; perhaps people here tended to be more fatalistic, more resigned to eventual illness and death than sophisticated city folks. Several women clustered near the window, watching the children play while they waited for the school bus to take them into Wickham. Dressed in ski jackets, mittens, and stocking caps, the children squealed and whooped, wrestled and swung their back-packs, their colors as brilliant as the autumn leaves they tossed at one another. Their words came out in puffs of smoke, high-pitched laughter rising like smoke in the frosty air.

A gray Plymouth station wagon pulled up in front of the store. A woman and a boy emerged from the front seat, and from the back three smaller children spilled out. Inside, the women turned to each other, murmuring, "*Them.*" They had no name for this family, if you could call it a family when each of its members had a different last name and they had nothing, not blood, not even race, in common. Of the girls, the older was a deep chocolate color, the younger the color of a newly minted penny, with kinky, light brown hair. The little boy was Latino, while the blond kid who emerged from the front seat looked like a posterboy for Aryan youth.

Frank Gower left the table where he'd been sitting with Lyle Fertig to join his wife at the window. His truck was visible from the back-room window, a white van with an emblem on the side—a rat enclosed by a circle with a red slash across it—and the company motto: "We Know How to Deal with Pests!" The exterminator stared out the window, stroking a sparse ginger mustache that crouched above his upper lip like a whipped dog. Hilda Gower glanced sidewise at his face. Word in the back room was Frank beat her periodically, but to her credit she never complained, just went out to that Evangelical church back in the woods and prayed. She was a tallish woman with the broad bones of a workhorse, but her pallid skin hung loosely on her frame and she walked with a permanent stoop that brought her height down to her husband's. Her hair was the color of dirty dishwater, and her pink, rabbity eyes blinked rapidly when she was nervous. She was blinking now.

"Pack of mongrels," Gower said, pursing his mouth. He turned around, searching for a target. Found Earl Lassiter. "I hope you know I hold you personally responsible for this, this *infestation!*"

The realtor glanced out the window, then resumed an intense conversation with Willem Mueller and Stan Kuzak. Gower scowled. No doubt they were talking about the arson fires; it was all anyone talked about these days. Every man in the department was sick and tired of them, but to look at Mueller, Kuzak, and that faggot Lassiter all huddled up, you'd think it was their personal cross to bear. Goddamn typical, Gower thought. It was always like that. Everybody's created equal, but some are more equal than others. Gower had his own theory about the fires, not that their lordships would listen to him. He raised his voice to address the room at large. "Bunch o' damn misfits. I'm damned if I'll pay taxes to school someone else's odds and ends."

"Woman lives in the village, Gower," Lassiter said. "She's got a right to send her kids to school."

"They ain't even her kids is what kills me!"

And the country-store chorus sang the refrain: "Not her kids."

"Losers and rejects." Gower's mustache bristled; spittle collected in the corners of his mouth. He worked the room like a circuit preacher. "A nest of vipers, that's what you've brought us."

Willem Mueller raised his heavy head. "You're just pissed because that *loser* whupped your boy."

"The hell he did. Ain't got nothing to do with that anyway," Gower said, but as quickly as it had gathered behind him, the pendulum of consensus swung away. People laughed behind their hands, while Gower fumed. Walter's letting himself get beat by that pissant shanty-Irish white-trash city kid had robbed the exterminator of every trace of respect for his son. It wasn't just the fight; anyone could get decked by a sucker punch. It was the aftermath. He'd told young Walter he damn well better get his own back, and what did the boy do? Waffled, made excuses. Look at him now out by the bus stop, making like he don't notice the Quinn kid standing fifteen feet away. Walter was turning into a pussy, a goddamn mama's boy, and it was all thanks to that little prick.

Willem said, "Them kids are no problem. Walter just finally found someone who ain't afraid of him. Frank, you got to let that boy fight his own battles."

Gower glared at him. No love lost between these two, for all they worked together in the Old Wickham VFD. Before Peter Quinn displaced him, Willem's son, Billy, had been Walter's favorite whipping boy. Walter would trip him on the bus, punch him on the playground, spit in his milk carton. Slow and unsuspecting, with no one but a sister to stand up for him, Billy made an easy target. Finally Willem had had enough. He confronted Frank Gower in the back room of the country store, told him to call his boy off.

Gower laughed in his face. "Walter's just horsin' around. That's boys for you. My opinion, Willem, you got to let that boy of yours fight his own battles. I know the lad's a trifle slow, but it don't do no good coddlin' them. My old man sure as hell never coddled me."

"And look how you turned out," Lassiter chimed in.

"Least he didn't turn out no goddamn pervert," Fertig called out from his corner. Lassiter didn't even glance his way. He'd no sooner reprimand the likes of Lyle Fertig than he would wrestle a mosquito.

"The boy of yours's a vicious cur," Willem had said then. "I never blame a biting dog. It's the dumb sonsabitches let 'em off their leashes piss me off."

No, no love lost on either side. But how it works in cold northern villages: things get buried. Long, drawn-out feuds are not practical in a county where sooner or later everyone lands in a snow bank and needs a tow, where cars freeze up in the winter and lines go down in storms. They didn't have to like each other. When it came to fighting fires, Willem Mueller and Frank Gower worked together as well as any two men in the village.

Outside, the three youngest members of the infestation had dispersed and were now indistinguishable among the tumbling mass of children. The oldest boy stood to one side, alone and watchful. Billy

Mueller threw a handful of leaves and waited hopefully for a chase, but Peter didn't respond. The other children kept away. The woman stood on the porch of the country store, watching him watch them. She waited until the bus came and took them away. Then she went inside.

"Morning, Jane," said Tom Whitehill, who made a point of getting along with all his customers. "Can I get you something?"

Jane Goncalves drew a crumpled list from her jacket pocket. "Morning, Tom. Pound of Swiss, pound of ham, and three of chop meat, please." She took a basket and headed toward the back of the store. As she paused in front of the vegetables she heard raised voices from the back room.

" . . . crap and you know it. It's just that kind of stupid loose talk—"

"Mueller, when you gonna wake up and smell the coffee?" Gower's shrill voice was unmistakable. "It's a simple fact we didn't have no arson fires till *they* came to town."

Outside, Jane paused in the act of selecting a tomato. She replaced it carefully and moved over to browse the canned goods on a shelf just behind the back room door.

"Bullshit," Earl Lassiter said. "Remember Norwell's place last year?"

"That's a whole other thing, that's an insurance thing. John Crawford sure as hell didn't burn his own barn down."

A wake of agreement swelled up around him:

"No, he didn't."

"Somebody set that fire."

"Didn't set itself, no sir."

"*She* moves in," Gower said, "with her little criminals, her packet of bad seeds, and all of a sudden there's fires sproutin' up like daisies in the spring. Gee, Willem, what a freakin' coincidence."

The sheriff turned around. "You got any evidence, Frank, or you just generally shooting your mouth off?"

"Common sense is what I got," Gower replied. "Eyes in my head is what I got." Lyle Fertig laughed appreciatively. It was then Jane entered the back room. Marched right up to Frank Gower and stood too close, invading his space. If she'd been a man he would have shoved her back. Wasn't far from doing it anyway. Silence fell over them all.

"You talking about my family?" she said.

Gower flushed. Woman had a goddamn nerve, calling him out on his own turf. "I'm just saying what everybody here is thinking: that one of them little street rats you harbor is just a little too fond of playing with matches. And I've got a good idea which one."

Jane's right hand clenched and she drew her arm back. It was a very quick response, a gut reaction; she checked it, but not before Gower took a startled step backward. Stan Kuzak was at her side before anyone saw him move. Not for nothing was he known as the stealth sheriff. He grasped her arm. "Now, Miss—"

"Get your hands off me!" Jane sputtered, with cheeks as red as her scarf. She jerked her arm free and stepped up to Gower. "Walter got what he deserved. You know it, I know it, and he knows it. Those kids settled their account, they're quits. You're the one can't leave it alone. What bothers you so bad, Gower? Is it the color of our skins?"

"This ain't about me, lady. What I think's my own business."

"Not when you keep making it mine."

"The lady's right, Frank," Kuzak said, imposing his bulk between them. "So far all I've heard from you's a lot of hot air. Son, you gotta either put up or shut up."

Gower said, "Puttin' up's your job, Kuzak. That's what we pay you for, not sittin' around guzzling coffee. As for shuttin' up, 'son,' last I heard it's still a free country. Man's got a right to voice his opinion."

Jane stepped around Kuzak's broad back. "So's a woman," she said. "And my opinion, Gower, is you're full of—"

"Easy now," Kuzak said hurriedly. He cast an agonized glance back at Willem, who sat laughing silently. This Goncalves woman was a pisser, all right, a real hot tamale. She had Gower huffing and puffing and dancing on his toes, while behind him, Hilda soared to sixty blinks a minute on the anxiety scale.

"Gower, what the hell you stirring up now?" a new voice said. Sam Pollak had entered the room while everyone's eyes were on Goncalves and Gower. Unnoticed till he spoke, he appeared beside the coffee urn as if he'd materialized out of thin air.

Few people had seen Sam since the day of Louise's funeral, not to talk to, anyway, though he'd been spotted any number of times from afar, striding across a field as if some vital business drew him on, or emerging all disheveled from the woods. Half a dozen people called out greetings, and Kate and Willem beckoned him over. But Sam stayed where he was, eyes fixed on Gower.

"Nobody's talking to you, Pollak," Gower said. "Why don't you just sit down and shut up?"

"Why don't you come over here and sit me down?"

The back room had grown very quiet.

"Fuck you," said Gower, who'd had one go-around with Sam and wasn't burning for another.

It had happened a few years ago, when Bush was in the White House and Operation Rescue was riding high. Frank Gower had set out to organize his own personal antiabortion vigilante squad, drawing on members of his evangelical church. His target was Marty Lapid's clinic in Wickham. Lapid was a full-service ob-gyn, which meant that first-trimester in-office abortions were on the menu along with obstetric services and general gynecology. Not only did this make Lapid a baby-killer by Gower's lights, it made him something so bad it could only be whispered: a Jew who slaughtered Christian babies.

Gower's mistake was in failing to take into account that most of the women in his church were patients of Dr. Lapid, and though they heartily disapproved of abortion, they just as heartily approved of Lapid. Though many were called, only a handful appeared outside Lapid's office on the appointed day. Gower, humiliated, was determined to make up in aggression what his little group lacked in numbers. The demonstrators linked arms in front of the clinic entrance. Louise, arriving for work, could easily have used the unobstructed back door, but she wouldn't walk three steps out of her way for these people. As she shouldered her way through the small knot of protesters, Frank Gower emerged from the ranks to spit on her.

Sam wasn't there, but within six hours he had heard about the incident from three different people. Louise, who knew her husband well, was not one of his informants. The following morning, Sam strode into the country store and invited Gower to step outside. The exterminator mugged for the back-room crowd, pressing hands to cheeks in mock dismay. Despite his size (or because of it), Gower was a scrapper from way back, a famous Saturday night brawler in the days before he found God. Even post-salvation he was no turn-the-other-cheek Christian lamb but a bare-knuckled soldier of Christ, whereas Sam Pollak was a Jew—which in Gower's lexicon meant a coward and a weakling.

Gower was laughing as they walked out back, though not for long. Sam had broken his nose, fractured a rib, and was a kick or two away from irreparable damage to Gower's kidneys when Willem Mueller reached the end of a leisurely stroll over and plucked him off, saying, "I guess he's taken your point."

After Gower got out of the hospital he tried to bring charges. Kuzak told him not to bother. "You go spitting on a man's wife," the sheriff said, "don't come crying to me when he pays you a call." Gower's chastisement was generally regarded as well-deserved, and Sam's stature in the village did not suffer as a result. "Never knew a Jew could fight like that," Tom Whitehill said, which pretty much summed up local reaction.

Gower stole out of the store, shadowed by his wife. Jane, finding her adversary had vanished, left the back room and brought her groceries up to the front counter. She paid; Tom Whitehill counted out her change cheerfully, pretending to have heard nothing. Jane picked up the bags and shouldered her way out the door. Stowed the groceries in the back of the wagon; slammed the tailgate, muttering to herself. When she came around, Sam Pollak was leaning against the driver's-side door.

She looked him over. He was as tall as she remembered but somehow seemed less substantial. Thinner, perhaps.

"What?" she said, in a tone that gave him three seconds to get to the point.

"Gower's a jerk," Sam said. "Don't take it to heart."

"I don't give a flying fuck what Gower thinks of me or mine or anything else. I do care that people listen to him."

Sam felt a quick stab of nostalgia. Women didn't talk like that in Old Wickham. He said, "Gets dead boring around here, winters. People'll listen to just about anything. Doesn't mean they believe what they hear."

"Say anything loud and long enough, some people'll start to believe."

Sam shrugged. Couldn't argue with that.

Jane moved forward, dislodging him from the door. Opened it, looked back over her shoulder. "Yeah, well, thanks for the encouraging words, Mr. Pollak, though I notice you saved them till we were alone."

Sam blinked like a dog who's just been swiped by a kitten it could crush with one paw. "That's not why I came out here."

"No? Why did you come out, Mr. Pollak?"

"That time you drove up to my house, you were looking for a carpenter."

Suddenly remembering the circumstances of their last meeting, she turned to him with compunction. "Sorry about that. I had no idea—"

He cut her off. "Did you find one?"

"No. Seems no one even had time to come look. Lot of busy people around here."

"I've got time and I wouldn't mind taking a look, you still want me to."

Her tough little face relaxed a bit; she gave up a quick nod. "I'm home today," she said. Sam watched as she drove away without a backward glance.

CHAPTER 5

The afternoon sun was sinking when Sam parked his pickup at the curb of the old Atkins house. Like a monstrous, sea-battered ship, the white Victorian rode the crest of an undulating lawn strewn with golden leaves and fine old plantings. A pair of spirea framed the front door; honeysuckle vines, denuded by the frost, clung to the trellis like skeletal fingers. To the right of the house was the village pond, black and frozen. Sam sat for some minutes behind the wheel of his pickup. Did he really want to go through with this? The farther he got from Gower and his big mouth, the less inclined he felt to take the job. He would play it by ear, he decided, climbing out of the cab. He could always find a reason to turn it down.

He knocked on the kitchen door and right away she called out, "Door's open!" He entered to find Jane Goncalves perched on a stepladder painting a cabinet door. "Just let me finish this last one, then I can wash the brush," she said. "Coffee's on the stove. Help yourself."

Sam poured a cup and carried it to the rectangular oak table in the center of the room. He sat down, stretching his legs, and looked around the large country kitchen. The door to the dining room was ajar; beyond it he caught a glimpse of the front parlor. He could tell a lot about potential customers by the way they kept house. Goncalves's came as a surprise. Knowing she had four or five kids living with her, he'd allowed for a fair degree of chaos. Instead he found a clean house, perfectly if casually ordered. Beside the kitchen door stood a sturdy-looking coat rack and a row of pegs mounted at child-height: for book bags, he supposed. The wooden cabinets were old, but their paneled doors looked flush and solid. The walls were freshly painted the color of sunflowers. There was a deep, stainless-steel double sink, a modern refrigerator, and a big old cast-iron stove. What he could see of the wide-board oak floor, partially covered by a tarp, looked well-worn but still vibrant. Sam grunted approvingly. If there was one thing he hated it was seeing was a beautiful wood floor desecrated with linoleum.

Jane gave the door a finishing stroke and canted her body backward to inspect her work.

"Not bad," Sam said.

"For a female?"

He didn't bite. "You paint this whole room?"

"Sure." She climbed down the ladder with the brush and paint tray cradled in one arm. He noticed that beneath the paint-splattered flannel shirt and jeans, her body was lean and taut. This observation, born of long habit, carried with it no load of desire. Lust was one of the things he seemed to have buried with Louise.

Jane skirted him to get to the sink. She spoke over the rush of water. "I don't mind paying someone to do what I can't, but damned if I'll pay for painting."

"Thought you mentioned working in town, at the bookstore."

"Three days a week. Great job. Doesn't pay much, but I get to borrow all the books I want. We're reading our way through Narnia."

"We?"

"Me and the kids."

"You read to them?"

"We take turns. A chapter a night, after dinner."

He saw a sepia-toned image of a woman in an armchair, an open book on her lap, children gathered round. "Cozy," he said, but Jane took it wrong. She flushed, and her tone grew defensive.

"Where they came from, their lives didn't have much order to them. Kids like structure, makes 'em feel safe. They like knowing dinner will be on the table at six every night. They like knowing there's a time for chores and a time for play." She shut the tap, placed the brush and pan on the drainer, and dried her hands on a dish towel.

Sam shrugged. "I don't know much about kids."

"And didn't come here to learn. Fair enough."

They walked through the house, room by room. The building looked at least seventy years old, yet somehow it had escaped the aggressive modernization that so often befell these old Victorians.

Though the mechanical systems had been updated—lead piping replaced by copper, new electrical wiring, and an additional bathroom put in—the infrastructure was as close to virginal as he'd ever seen. Like most Victorians of its era, the ground floor was a warren of smallish connecting rooms, with solid walnut doors, oak floors, and fine detailing in the original woodwork. There were working fireplaces in the dining room and front parlor. The second and third floors contained no less than six bedrooms, four of which appeared to be occupied.

Everywhere he looked he saw water damage. The location of the stains and crumbling ceilings seemed unrelated to the plumbing lines, which meant the roof had to be leaking. No surprise there. John Atkins had prided himself on his parsimony; no way in hell he'd put money into a house he was planning to sell. "New roof?" Sam scribbled in his notepad. "Repair water damage." No telling till he opened up the walls how deep the rot had permeated.

When the tour ended, they sat at the dining room table. Jane unrolled a blueprint of the house and they anchored the corners with coffee mugs. The plans were dated 1927. "All I've got," she said apologetically. "These are the originals, I think. Though except for the extra bathrooms, nothing much has changed." Apart from the kitchen, half bath, and combination mud and laundry room, there were six rooms on the ground floor. Jane wanted only three: a dining room, a living room, and a library. "Always wanted a house with a library," she said. "Never thought I'd get one." Could they, she asked, break down some walls, make three large rooms out of six small ones? Sam studied the plans, located the bearing walls. Doable, he said, though of course they'd have to fix the floors and walls afterward. The walls were trivial but the oak floors, with their tongue-and-groove construction, were not. Upstairs she wanted no major structural changes, but none of the bedrooms had built-in closets and Jane hated the clunky wardrobes that took up half of each room. "Closets," he noted. She also wanted to convert the largest bedroom into a playroom with built-in shelving along the perimeter. "Shelves," he wrote.

Just about now it occurred to him, with considerable surprise, that he wanted this job. He cared nothing for the woman, it was the house itself that attracted him. Its neglected beauty and vulnerability aroused his protective instincts. The alterations she proposed were reasonable, in keeping with the spirit of the old house—but Sam was well aware that the art of renovation lay as much in the execution as in the planning. There wasn't a house in the world, no matter how beautiful, that couldn't be ruined by shoddy workmanship.

Nothing, so far, had been said about money. Everything about Jane Goncalves—her looks, walk, speech, the tough directness of her gaze—set her apart from his usual type of client. No silver-spoon baby, but a working stiff like himself. Would she have any idea what a job like this would cost? The floors alone . . . People talked about taking out walls as if that was all there was to it, as if the floors, walls, and ceilings would miraculously heal themselves. Sam figured that when they got down to numbers, the woman was bound to back off.

When at last she asked for a ballpark estimate, Sam found himself stalling. "Haven't seen the roof yet."

Jane grimaced. "Takes every damn pot I own to catch the leaks when it rains. Figure a new roof."

"Give me a few minutes?"

"Sure." She left him and went out through the kitchen. Moments later he heard the washing machine start up. He was just finishing his calculations when the kitchen door flew open and a horde of children clattered into the house. The little ones rushed to Jane in the laundry room off the kitchen, but the older boy came directly to the dining room.

Sam glanced up from his calculator. The boy stood like a sentinel in the open doorway, body rigid, fists curled. "Hey," Sam said.

Not a word from the boy. Not a smile, not a glimmer of recognition or acknowledgment. Just a stony stare.

"We've met. I'm Sam Pollak."

"I know who you are," the boy said. "What are you doing here?"

He spoke as if he'd known Sam all his life and hated him for cause; his tone was steeped in an intimacy that astonished the carpenter. For the first time he really looked at the boy, who zoomed into focus with a clarity Sam had not experienced since Louise's illness eclipsed the world.

Jane appeared behind the boy. She called his name softly.

The boy turned. "What's *he* doing in this house?"

They exchanged a look. Something passed between them that Sam didn't understand; then the boy bolted for the kitchen door.

Sam raised his eyebrows.

"So," Jane said, "how's it going?"

He had to smile. What a cool one she was. Ninety-nine out of a hundred women would have felt compelled to explain.

"Got a ballpark for you," he said. "Better sit down."

"That bad, huh?" She pulled up a chair opposite him. The smallest child, a chubby-cheeked little doll of five or six, climbed onto her lap, fixing Sam with huge brown eyes. Jane rubbed her chin against the girl's black hair. "Luz, honey," she said, "run in the kitchen and have your snack, then it's homework time. Teacher give you homework today?"

Luz didn't take her eyes off Sam. "Peter mad. This a bad man, Mama Jane?"

"No, baby, he's our friend. Keisha, Carlos, take Luz into the kitchen. There's milk and oatmeal cookies on the table."

As the children left the room, she watched after them with a light in her eyes that reminded Sam forcibly of Louise. "My wife loved children," he blurted, not meaning to, shocked that he had, for he had not reached, and never would, the stage of casually invoking her name. But Jane just turned her dark eyes on him and nodded as if it were perfectly natural and even expected. Sam cleared his throat and slid a piece of paper across the table.

"Very rough," he said, watching her face as she studied the figures. "I'm guessing on the extent of the water damage. I've seen houses where it goes right down to the timber. I don't think yours is that bad, but there's no telling till we get in there. And this doesn't include the roof."

"Why not?"

"I don't do 'em. House this size, though, figure a new roof's gonna run you anywhere from three to five thousand." Depending on who she got, he meant. Depending on who was willing to work for her and how bad they ripped her off. She ran her fingers through her cropped black hair. He tried to read her face but failed. "If it's too much, maybe you can live with the wardrobes and the small rooms for a while. The roof and the water damage, though, they need to be fixed."

"Before I bought this house," Jane said, "I had a contractor friend come up and take a look." She touched the paper. "I know this price is fair."

"But . . ."

"No buts. I can handle it."

He started to apologize. "It's okay," she said. "Don't exactly look like Donald Trump, do I?" In order to buy this house, she told him, she'd sold the house she inherited in Brooklyn. Her parents had purchased a dilapidated old brownstone when the Park Slope neighborhood was still poor, black and Latino. Little by little they'd fixed it up, filled the spare rooms with boarders, and paid the mortgage. By the time they died, the neighborhood had undergone gentrification, and the house, now owned free and clear, was worth many times what they had paid for it.

Jane didn't plan to sell. She gave the boarders notice and as they left, filled their rooms with foster children. She'd grown up in this neighborhood but it wasn't the same. Most of the old people were gone, forced out by higher rents and taxes, and the new ones objected to her motley brood. Juvenile Hall, they called it, but what could they do? The house was hers, free and clear. They had only one way to get at her, and that was through the children.

There Jane stopped abruptly. "Poor man," she said. "Comes to look at the house and gets bombarded with the story of my life."

Sam shrugged. They both knew he had nothing to go home to. Jane went into the kitchen to make another pot of coffee. He followed her with his eyes. The younger children had finished their snacks and were doing their homework around the old oak table. While the coffee brewed Jane passed from one to the other, bending her head down to theirs, offering each a word of encouragement, a bit of help. It was a scene radiant with domesticity: the children's plump hands clutching stubby pencils, the trim, dark-haired woman in the yellow lamplight. He registered the warmth, but where he should have sensed an answering glow he felt only an aching emptiness. No connection existed between what his eyes saw and his heart felt, as if the ligaments binding his thoughts and feelings had been severed.

Sam stood and wandered over to the window. Outside on the lawn, Peter raked leaves into piles of gold. Graceful and fluid, the boy moved like a natural athlete, but in the vehemence of his raking Sam sensed a terrible anger. For the first time he wondered if by some fluke Frank Gower hadn't stumbled onto the truth.

Jane returned bearing two cups of coffee and a sadly depleted plate of oatmeal cookies on a tray. Sam lingered at the window, gazing out. She followed his eyes.

"It's so fucking unfair," she said.

"What is?"

"I thought, you know, coming up here, people would be more tolerant."

Sam shrugged. "People are people, wherever you go. Takes time."

Jane snorted. "That or a good bleach job."

He gazed up at the ceiling, noticed the peeling paint. He wasn't about to dispute her. As far as Sam could tell, racism was a simple fact of life in America, as pervasive as bacteria in the water, salt in the sea. Though more concentrated in some spots than in others. "My opinion," he said, "less racism up here than down in the city."

"No offense, but how would you know?"

He looked at her then. "Grew up there. Lived most of my life in the city."

"Oh."

"Took me for a hayseed, huh?"

"No," she said. "It's just I've seen people around here treat you like one of their own, talk to you. How long does it take before they stop treating you like an occupying force from Mars?"

He laughed. "A while."

"They're wrong about my kids, you know. I do take hard cases, but there are limits. I don't accept kids who've tortured animals, because they're too damaged; there's no gettin' through to them. And I don't take firebugs."

"Scared?"

"You bet."

He nodded.

Jane ran her fingers through her spiky hair. "People think if a kid won't lie down and let the world steamroll him, that means he's bad. Personally I like a kid with a spark, some fight in 'em." She looked Sam up and down with a jaundiced eye. "Bet you were no angel as a kid."

He said, "I'm no angel now."

"Hey. You're here, aren't you?"

"That's business."

"Uh-huh. Still, I bet you were a hard-ass kid. Am I right?"

Was he? He could hardly remember. The man he used to be had a history, a childhood, however truncated. That man died the day he killed his wife; what took his place was a creature born of that awful necessity. There were things, Sam was slowly coming to see, that you do because you have to, but even though you have to, they're still wrong; but even though they're wrong you'd do them again, given the same circumstances, because they're necessary. Go explain that to a stranger. Go explain it to yourself.

He turned back to the window. Scar tissue contains no nerve endings; when he pressed his right palm against the cold glass, his scars were defined by their lack of sensation. Outside, the boy stopped raking, wiped his brow with his sleeve, and glanced toward the house. Their eyes met. Once again Sam was jolted by a live current of hostility.

He returned to the table. Jane slid a mug across.

"Tell me that boy's never been in trouble," he said.

She was silent.

"Who is he? How'd he come to be with you?"

"Found him under a cabbage leaf."

"Gotcha." He pushed his chair back, but before he could stand, her small, strong hand grasped his wrist.

"Hey," she said. "Tell you one thing. What Gower said? Peter's not capable of anything like that."

"No? What is he capable of?"

She let go his wrist in silence. Sam carried his mug back to the window. He ought to go; suddenly it was clear he'd lingered too long. Didn't want to get sucked into this woman's life. He had problems of his own. The coffee's what held him, strong and good. He'd been living too long on instant.

The sun sank behind the hills, and the yellow glow of lamplight within the room made translucent mirrors of the windows. Somewhere a door slammed. Through his own ghostly reflection Sam saw the boy drop the rake and turn toward the house . . .

Peter spun around and spread his arms wide. The other children came tearing across the lawn. All three leapt at him; Peter staggered and twirled and fell into a huge pile of leaves. Their mustiness tickled his nose. Sneezing, he jumped to his feet, grabbed a handful and tossed them at Carlos, who returned a salvo of his own. The little girls screamed with delight, burrowing through the pile to wrap their arms around Peter's ankles. They tugged; he windmilled his arms and toppled backward. All three children piled on top as he thrashed and bucked. When Luz's laughter turned to coughing, he set her on her feet and zipped up her jacket. Carlos took the opportunity to stuff a handful of leaves down his back. As Peter turned to chase him, his eye snagged on the tall, still figure of Sam Pollak silhouetted in the dining-room window. Abruptly all the play drained out of him.

Women were such fools. Even Jane, sensible, practical Jane. Peter stood motionless on the lawn while the children wrestled like puppies at his feet. His eyes locked onto the intruder's. I know you, Peter thought. Don't think I don't.

CHAPTER 6

Jane strode down the corridor, inhaling the familiar mingled odor of Lysol and sweat, chalk and wool. She'd started off in a school like this one, only bigger, of course; she was counselor to three hundred kids until she realized that the job was just a joke, a sop to the Board of Ed. No one except her took it seriously, and nothing she could do would make a difference. So she scaled down her efforts radically: not three hundred, but two, three, maximum five kids at a time.

This school was one-third the size. Outside each classroom hung student artwork: etchings of pilgrims and Indians, collages of fall foliage. Pretty but juvenile, which was her impression of the school as a whole: nice to look at, but soft in the belly. She found room 124. A young woman sat behind the teacher's desk, head propped on hand, reading from a typed composition. Jane tapped on the door frame. "Miss Brick?"

"Ms. Goncalves, come in." Spoken with a stab at the Spanish pronunciation. "Thanks so much for coming in."

"No problem." Jane flung herself into the chair opposite. On the blackboard was a parsed sentence: "[Jim (*subject*)] [drove (*verb*)] [his father's tractor (*object*).]" Miss Brick looked all of twenty-five. Sweet face, Botticelli hair, watery blue eyes a tad too prominent; an adolescent's wet dream in spiked heels, fluffy pink sweater, and black pencil skirt. She appeared nervous but determined. "What's up?" Jane asked.

"I wanted you to read this," Miss Brick said. "The kids all had to write a composition for Thanksgiving: 'I'm thankful for . . .' Kind of an awful assignment, from my point of view. You end up with seventy-five variations of 'I'm thankful for my mother, my father, my brother, my sister, my Sega Genesis.' I'm trudging along and suddenly I come to Peter's story."

She held out the pages. Jane took them and read:

I'm thankful for my two best friends. I know they'll always stand beside me. Even if everyone else in the world lets me down, I know I can depend on these two. They're always there when I need them, tighter than the tightest homeboys.

They can be gentle at times. They know how to tie a little kid's shoe so it stays tied, tuck in a scarf so no wind can get in. Alley cats purr at their touch; babies laugh. But don't be deceived: these two guys don't take crap from nobody. Get 'em mad, you'll wish you'd never been born. Mess with me, you mess with them: that's how we are.

My best friends, I called them, but they're more than that. Come right down to it, they're the only friends I've got. I call them Lefty and Righty. My fists: where would I be without them?

Deep inside Jane laughed, a sad laugh. Miss Brick said, "Two things. First of all, I don't know if you realize how very well he writes. Not just this essay, everything he's written for me. Even the mistakes, the double negative, the sentence fragment: he uses them deliberately, for effect. The *punctuation*—you know how often seventh-grade kids punctuate, correctly, with colons and semicolons? Does he read a lot?"

"Yes. All kinds of things, from 'Calvin and Hobbes' to *Huckleberry Finn*."

The teacher nodded, suspicion confirmed. "Most of the kids we get here, they're just punching the clock till they can go out and get a job. But we do get some college-bound kids, and Ms. Goncalves, I have to tell you that Peter's writing ability is just head and shoulders above anything I've ever seen."

Her face shone with the thrill of discovery. How often, in the year since Peter came to her, had Jane heard the same song? And not only from English teachers, but also math and science. Peter, surly creature that he was, always took them by surprise. They didn't expect what they got from him. One teacher, less tactful or more forthright than the others, said it was like kicking over a rock and uncovering a diamond, not a rhinestone but the real thing.

Of course, it didn't hurt that Peter was such a good-looking Lost Boy. He pushed that button in women marked SAVE THIS CHILD! located right next to the red one marked SAVE THIS MAN! If Peter didn't find his feet, Jane reflected, one day soon he would find dangerous paths opening up to him.

"You mentioned two things," she said.

"The content," Miss Brick replied. Her slightly bulbous eyes grew sorrowful. She read from the composition: "'Come right down to it, they're the only friends I've got.'" So clever, she said, and yet so sad. Miss Brick couldn't help wondering—of course strictly speaking it was none of her business—but with nothing but the boy's best interests at heart she did just have a peek at his school records and found them singularly uninformative, just a bare list of grades and courses completed, and of course that amazing IQ score, but no personal records at all—here she paused to draw breath and perhaps invite a confidence—but you know, Ms. Brick continued when none came, she couldn't help *wondering*: Didn't he have *anyone*, wasn't there someone in the boy's life, a loving presence of some kind? Not to imply, she hastened to add, that Ms. Goncalves herself wasn't . . .

Here she grew flustered and at last fell silent.

Jane smiled a measured smile. "I appreciate your concern."

Miss Brick wrapped a wispy blond strand around a pink-tipped finger. "But it's none of my business?"

"It's Peter's story, not mine."

"I've tried talking to Peter. He's not, he wouldn't . . ."

"He's not alone," Jane said gently, "and he knows it."

"But his composition—"

"Posturing. Macho muscle-flexing."

"But why would he . . . ?"

Jane raised her eyebrows and Miss Brick turned the color of her angora sweater.

They parted on friendly terms. Driving home, however, Jane found herself troubled by the conversation. He's not alone, she'd assured the teacher, but was it true? So often when Peter was with her, he seemed far away. She'd seen him sit and stare at a book for fully half an hour without turning a page. Other times he would be playing with the little ones, absorbed in some game or roughhouse, when suddenly he'd turn in on himself. His eyes would go vacant, his body quiet and still. The children knew to leave him alone then. But where did he go, her fair-haired boy, when he seemed to be there but wasn't?

Jane left Wickham behind and drove north on the narrow country road that led to Old Wickham. Though it was not yet five, night was closing in. Deep shadows fell across the road. She turned on her headlights, kept an eye out for deer. No cute little Bambis in Columbia County—they grew some monstrous deer in these parts, the rural equivalent, she figured, of muggers in Central Park. Last week her boss, Paul Binder, was driving home at dusk when his car was sideswiped by a buck that came crashing out of the woods. The car was deflected and smashed into a tree, crumpling the left fender. The buck kept running.

Peter, when he first came to live with her, was like an animal that had crawled off to lick its wounds. He mocked the psychologists who came to examine him, stonewalled his lawyer, opened up to no one. Jane gave him time, didn't crowd him. Gradually he seemed to emerge from his shell, falling with suspicious ease into the role of big brother to his foster sibs, adopting toward Jane an air of chivalrous condescension, appropriate to one who has been to the mountain top. He might like her, might grow fond of her, indeed she thought he had; but no way was this boy ever going to seek shelter beneath her wing.

Peter never talked about the past. Never mentioned his father, which in itself was understandable, but neither did he mention his mother. All Jane knew of her was that she had died when he was nine; yet she believed, by the tough, resilient sweetness of the boy's nature, that someone, sometime, must have poured a lot of love into this vessel. Stranger still that Peter never even asked about his little sister, although by all accounts the two had been deeply attached. Did he think about her? Miss her? Shocking, when she came to think of it, how little Jane knew.

Early on in their relationship, Jane and Peter had worked out a *modus vivendi* which, considered now in light of Peter's Thanksgiving composition, amounted to little more than "Ask me no questions, I'll tell you no lies." Her discretion had gained Jane his trust, but cost her his confidence. When they worked together in the kitchen Peter would chatter for an hour at a time about books, school, sports, current events—everything and anything except himself. On the rare occasions when she tried to breach that barricade, Jane was politely but firmly rebuffed. Peter made it clear he would deal with personal matters in his own way, in his own time.

Jane respected this. She believed, moreover, in the power of the human mind to heal itself. But was Peter really healing, or was he merely scabbing over festering wounds? It was too stupid of her not to know. Had she fallen into the same trap as Peter's teachers, gone mushy-soft over a boy who needed not hugs and coaxing but an immovable anchor, a firm hand on the tiller?

That night, after Carlos and the girls were tucked into bed, Jane went up to Peter's room on the third floor of the old Victorian. It was the only room on that floor and her favorite in the house: a turret really, octagonal, oddly shaped with cubbies and window seats. Not a convenient room by any means. Dead last in the steam-heating chain, located atop two long flights of stairs, the second particularly steep; no bathroom, so you had to run downstairs to use the john. With windows in all directions, the room was cold in the winter and hot in summer. It was only when it rained that the room's true virtue emerged—but then, oh then it was magical. One could lie on the big brass bed that the Atkinses abandoned because it was too heavy to move, and be at once engulfed by the storm and sheltered from it, caught up in the elements yet safe. When it snowed, white flakes fell silently in all directions, surrounding the room and filling it with an unearthly pale glow. It was like flying through clouds without a plane, or sleeping not under but inside the softest, thickest of white eiderdowns.

Or so Jane imagined, for in fact she had never spent a night in the room. It was Peter's room, and had been ever since they took possession of the house. She hadn't planned on giving him the room. From the moment she laid eyes on it, Jane had marked it for her own. Apart from everything else, the turret room was drop-dead romantic, the perfect place to bring a lover, should such a rare and exotic creature ever present itself. But when she casually floated the idea of her claiming that room, the little girls were aghast. "So far away," they cried, "so far from us!" Even Carlos, who would never admit to fear, looked bleak at the prospect; so Jane sighed to herself and let it go. "On second thought, someone's got to keep an eye on you wild things," she said. Luz and Keisha giggled to hear themselves so described, Carlos preened, and Peter said quickly, "I'll take it."

"You want that room?"

"No," he said. "I want to stay in Brooklyn. But since that's not happening, yeah, I want the room."

"It's yours, then," said Jane, not without a pang of envy. Peter smiled, a rare event, an almost-sufficient recompense. When he smiled he looked his chronological age, he looked like the boy he might have been under different circumstances. Jane knew very well you couldn't buy another person happiness, but with Peter, she couldn't help trying. Nothing else seemed to work.

She knocked, heard a rustle and a creak, and then his voice saying, "Come in." She entered, shutting the door behind her. Peter turned his book face down on the bed and sat up. His room was orderly, Spartan almost, more notable for what it lacked than what it contained. No photos, trophies, plaques, knickknacks, or posters, no mementos of any kind, no sign of a previous life. Plenty of books, though, on teeming, precarious shelves of planks and bricks. When Jane glanced at the paperback on his bed, Peter's hand slammed down on the cover.

"What's this," she said with a laugh, "adolescence kicking in? What are you reading?"

He shoved the book behind him. "Nothing."

Under the old policy Jane would have backed off at once. Policies change, however. She approached Peter; he straightened defensively.

She feinted to the left, dove to the right, and emerged triumphant. "*The Fellowship of the Ring,*" she read. She tossed him the book, drew over a chair, and sat down. "Tolkien. Hardly smut."

"Who said it was smut?"

"Why hide it, then?"

Peter scrunched up his mouth. "Kid stuff."

"No way!" said Jane, who had but recently discovered Tolkien herself.

"Not the way it's written, the whole . . . cosmology."

"The cosmology, huh?" It killed her, how this kid talked.

Peter shrugged. "It's a fairy tale."

"Yes," she said, struck by this. "That's what I like about it. You can tell the good guys from the bad. An orc is an orc is forever an orc. Elves are light made flesh, the seven horsemen are black holes. It takes courage, but you could navigate Tolkien's world; you could find your way." She looked at him slantwise. "Ever wish you could live in a world like that?"

He snorted. "I'm too old for make-believe."

"Still, you're reading the book."

"It's a good story. As a story it makes sense."

"Unlike the real world?"

He turned his palms up. Obviously, the gesture said.

"Our world has its share of saints and sinners," Jane said.

"Sure," said Peter. "Only here they come packaged, two for the price of one."

What could lead a boy to such an extraordinary statement? Peter had gone where no child ought to go, had drunk from bitter waters. Now he was stuck, with no way back and no way forward. An awful pity seized her but Jane forced it down. Pity was not needed here.

"Who are we talking about?" she asked. "Who is part saint, part sinner?"

Peter narrowed his eyes at her. "Did you actually want something, Jane, or did you just lose your way?"

"Don't you be dissin' on me, boy. As a matter of fact I've been thinking about your sister."

Peter's face drained of expression. He sat as still as if any move might be his last.

Jane waited. He didn't speak. She said, "Holidays coming, her being your sister and all, it's natural. Okay, amigo?"

"No," Peter said. "Not okay."

"You must miss her."

"I don't think about it."

"What's her name?"

A long pause. "Maura."

"She's your sister. How can you not think about her?"

"Hard work and self-discipline," he said.

Jane didn't smile. "Where is she?"

"You've been talking to the Brick, haven't you?"

"What makes you say that?"

"She's been nosing around, too. Never should have written that goddamn essay."

"You ungrateful pup! At least the woman cares."

"Why we call her the Brick," he said.

"Besides which," Jane said, "what if I have? Isn't that my job, isn't that what the state pays me to do, look after you?"

"Wouldn't do it, wasn't for the money, would you?"

"Hell no!" she said. They leaned back, smiled at one another. This was their old routine, a sure-fire tension breaker, a way out when the talk got too personal. Peter yawned elaborately and glanced at his watch. "Ten-thirty already! Past your bedtime, Janie."

"So where's your little sister, anyway? How do we contact her?"

"We don't," he said. "We don't call, we don't write, and we don't visit."

Jane leaned over and touched his arm, taut as a violin string. He jerked it away. She said, "You don't want to, or you can't?"

"What's the difference? Give it a rest, why don't you?" Peter pressed a pillow to his stomach and turned his head aside.

"Can't or won't?"

"Can't, goddamnit! Terms of her adoption. Satisfied?"

"What, no contact at all?"

"*Nada.* It's cool, though. They're good people. And she's better off without me."

"It's cool, huh?" She shook her head slowly, not at him. "How come she's better off without her brother?"

He squeezed the pillow so hard feathers burst out of the seams. "How the—what kinda dumbass question is that? Don't you know what I did?"

"I know what you did and why. Nobody blames you, Peter. It wasn't your fault."

"Yeah, right."

"So losing your sister, too—that's some kind of punishment?"

"Maybe."

"Did you ever stop to think maybe *she* needs *you*?"

Suddenly, shockingly, tears burst from Peter's eyes. They streamed down his cheeks, soaked his face in seconds. Jane was amazed. One minute she's thinking this is useless, he'll never open up, I'm tormenting him for nothing; the next minute this. She yearned to reach out to him but kept her hands firmly on her knees. Peter held the pillow in front of his face and cried for some minutes, a raw, painful, helpless sobbing that was horrible to hear. When she could stand it no longer, Jane crossed to his side. She put her arms around him. For a moment he suffered her embrace, his body stiff yet full of longing. Then he shoved her away.

From the doorway she asked, "Lights on or off?"

"Off," he growled, yearning for darkness.

She opened the door and switched off the overhead lamp. Starlight flooded the room; the moon cast shadows. Her voice spoke out of the darkness. "We'll talk again," it said.

More a threat than a promise, and what exactly had come over Jane? Peter listened to her footsteps receding on the stairs and groaned to think of how he had betrayed himself. Blubbering like a baby—stupidest thing he could have done, letting her get to him. She took him by surprise is why. They'd had an arrangement, or so he'd thought: she stays out of his business and he stays out of trouble. Maybe that was it:

maybe his fight with Walter had broken the pact, so that she felt free to prod and pry with impunity. Much as Peter deplored her interference, he had, as one street fighter to another, to admire her technique. The woman knew how to hit below the belt; she had an instinct for the soft spot that would do a nose tackle proud. Peter hadn't known he had a soft spot till she kneed him in it. He'd thought he had things under control, by which he meant separate.

For Peter, it must be understood, had two worlds, and those worlds were divided by an iron curtain. In his shared world he lived with Jane and Carlos, Keisha and Luz in a white house beside a pond in the god-forsaken one-horse town of Old Wickham, New York. Prior to that they had all resided in Brooklyn. And what came before *that* was irrelevant, didn't pertain. How, then, could he think of Maura when Maura didn't exist here?

Peter's private world was a vast and barren land, a desert of stony cliffs and precipices, echoing canyons, raw winds that scrape across the desolate plains and whisper down narrow passages. This was his true home, his dreaming place, his natural habitat. This was the place that drew him in when he was by himself, and sometimes when he wasn't. Here he wandered alone, though not quite alone, for this world was populated by ghosts, living and dead, by presences sensed not seen, by cries and whispers carried on the winds.

Kneeling to drink beside a faint, shimmering pond, Peter once saw a face reflected in the water, not his own. The watery image spoke to him. "My son," it said, "what have you done?" Another time, seeking shelter beneath a ledge, he heard all around him the plaintive weeping of an inconsolable child. The wind, the wind—oh, let it be just the wind! But in his heart Peter knew whose voice was crying for a mother, a father, a brother who did not come. Did she cry still, or had she forgotten him?

Better, a thousand times better for Maura to forget: so Peter believed with all his heart. For himself no forgetting was possible, no forgiveness existed. He had become the thing he did; a single word stood for both deed and doer, for it was a defining act. Jane meant well but didn't understand that for certain crimes, it is childish to speak of justification. Just as some diseases have no cure, certain acts have no justification.

Where else should an outcast go, then, but the wilderness? When Cain slew Abel his punishment was lifelong exile, and Abel a mere brother. The desert Peter inhabited was as real to him as the world he shared with Jane, and far more demanding. That's why he protested the move to the country, not for the reasons she thought. What difference did it make where he lived? What mattered, desperately, was the waste of precious energy entailed in the move, energy he needed to survive in the other place.

Though he could not place it on a map, Peter's wilderness was neither imaginary nor metaphorical. Sometimes it sucked him in, other times he got there by closing his eyes and setting his mind adrift. But it was always the same *there*, no airy-fairy fantasy, but rock-hard, sere and dangerous. A person could die of thirst in such a "dream"; he could fall to his death. One false step was all it took.

CHAPTER 7

He is skiing with Lou, and though neither of them are skiers, they seem to know how. They pause atop a snow-covered slope, ringed by mountains, utterly alone. Lou's face glows in the cold bright air. Red cheeks, sparkling eyes, black hair escaping around her forehead: he's never seen her lovelier, more alive. "Race you," she says, and without waiting for an answer launches herself off the crest of the hill. He starts to follow but his pole is wedged in the snow. He tugs; it won't come loose. "Wait," he calls after her. "Wait for me!" But Louise is halfway down the slope already, a distant figure the size of his hand.

She looks back; he sees a flash of white teeth, red scarf-ends swirling. Her voice takes several seconds to reach him. "Can't stop," she is shouting. "Catch up!"

The telephone pealed. Shuddering awake, Sam found himself lying, fully dressed, uncovered on the couch. He sat up slowly; his body ached all over. The room was dark, the iridescent display on the clock radio read 1:15. The phone had settled into a patient, rhythmic ring. He knew that ring. Sam picked up the receiver but said nothing.

The whispering voice could have belonged to anyone, male or female, living or dead. "I know what you did," it said, in a tone neither accusatory nor conspiratorial, but rather matter-of-fact, like a wake-up call.

"What do you know?" Sam said.

"I know what you did."

"What did I do? Tell me what I did."

"You know."

"Who the fuck is this?"

Click.

Sam hung up, cursing. He'd lost track of how many calls he'd received; six or eight, anyway. First few times the caller didn't speak at all. Then the whispering began. "I know what you did," over and over. "I know what you did."

He was sick of the calls. He was sick of everything, but these calls were exquisitely painful, a kind of mental root canal. They occurred unpredictably, day or night, so that he could never be easy but lived in a state of perpetual dread and slept only fitfully. It came to him, not for the first time, that there was one sure way of ending the torment. Actually there were two, but in Sam's current state of mind, changing his phone number seemed far too complicated. As he huddled in a corner of the couch with his knees pressed to his chest, thoughts of suicide, never far since Louise's death, jostled to the forefront.

Since she died, he'd been going on and going on. Six weeks had dragged by with glacial speed and still it got no better. His body felt like dead weight he had to haul around. Time had turned to sludge; the future was an endless tunnel, no light ahead. With all the flavor gone from life, why linger at the table? He wasn't a glutton for food, or punishment either. There was nothing to keep him, no obligations. The Goncalves job was on hold, pending her getting the roof fixed. She could find another carpenter. He had no family, and his friends would survive.

Of course, Louise wouldn't like it. Once, when she was very sick, he'd let slip some thought about going out together. She got so angry, even her pain was banished. "Don't you dare!" she sputtered, struggling to sit up. "None of that Romeo-and-Juliet bullshit. Don't even think of it, don't dare!" She started to cough. The thing had captured her lungs by then (for thus he conceived the cancer, as an alien creature, all teeth and claws, feeding on her substance), and her cough sounded like death rattling the door. "Promise," she gasped.

He'd promised. At that moment, he would have said anything, promised anything to calm her agitation. Such is the power of the dying. But later, in the clear cold light of mourning, he wondered: Was it fair to deny him what she demanded for herself? Why was she free to end her pain, and he not?

And then Sam remembered his dream, and remembered the last words she called to him, and it came to him then that this dream about Louise was more in the nature of a visit, or at least a message. He thought of that moment when Louise, on the cusp of death, had opened her eyes and drawn breath as if to speak. Too late—she died without a word. But perhaps the message lingered. Sam despised the Hallmark comfort of life-after-death theology; he knew his bereavement to be utter and endless but at the same time wondered: How could any force as vital as Louise be wholly extinguished? Where would all that energy go?

"Catch up," she had cried. What was that but the clearest of summonses, an acknowledgment that she had erred in extorting that promise; what else but permission?

Sam was not a careless or impulsive man. A carpenter can't be. A carpenter has to think before he cuts, not after; he has to plan ahead. By nine that morning Sam was seated at his bench in the workshop, planning his death.

He had written a note, lest anyone else be blamed for his demise. The note was in the pocket of his shirt. "I did this myself," it said, "of my own free will. Because I'm tired but I can't sleep. Because I can't live with what I did, though it needed to be done and I'd do it again in a second. Because life without Louise is not worth the effort. Because there's no reason not to."

A thick coil of rope lay at his feet like a faithful dog, ready to do his bidding. Now he was almost but not quite ready. Certain concerns remained. One was aesthetic. Somewhere Sam had read that at the moment of death, people void themselves. Didn't matter that he'd be beyond knowing or caring; the thought of being found in that condition still disgusted him. He wasn't sure how long it took for food to clear the digestive tract, but he figured that if he fasted for twenty-four hours, that ought to do it. His last meal had been around eight o'clock last night.

His second concern had to do with the discovery of the body. He had to find a way to control that, because if he left it to chance, it might very well be Willem or worse yet one of the kids who found him. Sam wouldn't hurt them like that for the world. Who should it be, then? Briefly he considered Marty Lapid, a doctor and so not unacquainted with death. But Lapid was too close a friend.

It came down to Stan Kuzak then. Sam felt bad for Kuzak. Finding Sam's body was bound to spoil his day. As sheriff, though, he'd be called in anyway; might as well let him make the discovery.

Kuzak was divorced. He lived alone in a small house in the village of Old Wickham; Sam had been over once or twice for poker games with Mueller and Lassiter. He decided to call Kuzak's home during work hours, leave a message on his machine. To make sure there were no mistakes, Sam jotted down the text of the message. "Kuzak, something's come up. Need to see you right away. I'll be out all day but come tonight if you can, anytime after nine. Sorry to screw up your evening but it's important. I'll be in the workshop."

Then a problem occurred to Sam. For Kuzak to get in, Sam would have to leave the door unlocked, which meant anyone might wander in. What if he locked the door? Would the sheriff be worried enough to break in?

He would lock the door but leave a note: "Kuzak, come in." That ought to do the trick. Sam glanced at his watch. It was too early to call now. Kuzak often went home for lunch; Sam couldn't chance him getting the message and swinging by early. He'd call after 2:00.

It proved something to Sam that he could think this way, work things out, show concern for his neighbors. It meant he was acting rationally, sanely, not out of despair or depression.

Finding himself with time to spare and feeling strangely invigorated despite his fast, Sam decided to spend his last hours working. He could actually feel his hands again; they ached for work, the texture and solidity of wood. He glanced first at the tiny, disjointed drawers of his seed cabinet that lay scattered across his workbench like poor aborted fetuses, but quickly turned his eyes from them. That piece required more time than he had to give; it would never be finished. The candle stand, however, was nearly done. He had only to plane and finish the top and attach it to its stand, a few hours' work. He could finish it this morning and leave it as a gift for Willem and Kate.

The idea pleased Sam. He stood up, kicking the coiled rope aside, and started assembling his tools, so intent that he didn't hear the car chugging up his driveway. He jumped at the sound of a rap at the door, accompanied by a voice he'd never thought to hear again.

"Mr. Pollak, are you there?"

Sam kept silent, but was not surprised to see the door open. First to appear was the rim of a battered black hat, then the tip of a gray beard, and finally the rabbi's long, mournful face, which brightened fractionally at the sight of Sam. "So here you are." He shouldered the door open and advanced into the shop, so laden with bags and bundles that he could not see the floor beneath his feet. Just as he reached Sam, Malachi tripped over the rope and would have fallen flat on his face had not the carpenter jumped up and caught him.

Sam set the rabbi upright and relieved him of his burdens. "*Vos iz dos?*" asked Malachi. They both glanced down at the rope. Sam had been experimenting with slipknots. The rabbi shook a loop off his ankle.

"A rope on the floor," he said. "You know how dangerous is a rope on the floor? A person could accidentally break his neck."

"I was just—" Sam said.

"You was just . . . ?"

"Putting it away."

"Good idea," said the rabbi. "Put it away. We don't want anyone should be hurt." He waited without speaking until Sam did as he was told, tossing the rope into the wood box. Next Sam noticed Malachi eyeing the message to Kuzak that lay on the bench. He crumpled the paper and stuck it in his pocket.

"This is a very fine room," the rabbi said, looking around. "You built this room?"

"Yes."

"Mr. Pollak, you should excuse a personal remark, but this is not the work of a man of no faith. You see, I remember our little conversation."

"Rabbi, what are you doing here?"

"What am I doing here? What are any of us doing here?" Lowering himself onto Sam's stool, the visitor rooted through one of his bags. At last, with a snort of triumph, he unearthed a neatly folded pair of denim overalls.

"I apologize it took so long."

"You shouldn't have bothered. But thanks for stopping by." Like a man who's given up on catching a horse but thinks perhaps it might be induced to follow, Sam took a step toward the door.

"Sit, sit," the rabbi said, though he had just appropriated the only seat. Sighing, Sam propped himself against the workbench while the rabbi extracted from yet another bag a lumpy brown paper sack. "Give a look," he urged. "You won't believe: bagels! Real bagels, not some *goy-ishe* imitation." He pulled one from the bag, plump and smothered with poppy seeds, and held it out. As if by magic, the scent of fresh, warm bread permeated the room. Sam's treacherous mouth watered.

"No thanks," he said. "I'm not hungry."

"What hungry? You gotta be hungry to eat a bagel?" Malachi pressed the bagel into Sam's hand. "Eat," he said. A veil had been dropped: his voice was stern, the tone not one of invitation but rather of command.

The bagel was warm and crusty, the voice compelling. Before Sam knew it he had taken a bite, and after that he couldn't stop. It tasted like manna from heaven. Malachi watched, dark eyes glistening in his aged face like black pearls in a bed of wrinkled tissue paper. But no sooner had Sam swallowed the last morsel than the spell was broken, and he grew angry at himself and at Malachi. "Weren't you supposed to be the itinerant rabbi?" he said. "The prayer-peddler, here today, gone tomorrow?"

"You hired me," Malachi said, restored to mildness. "I didn't hire you."

"I hired you to bury my wife, not feed me bagels."

"You think burying the dead is such a simple thing? As for the bagels . . ." The rabbi shrugged. "With me you get a bargain."

Sam groaned. "Why are you here? You're supposed to be gone."

"I'm staying for now in Wickham. Sometimes even a wandering Jew gets tired."

"This is no place for a rabbi."

"Why not?"

Sam cast about for reasons. "There isn't a kosher deli for miles around."

Malachi rolled his eyes.

"No Jews, either."

"The good doctor is a Jew," the rabbi said. "And what are you, chopped liver?"

"Told you before: I'm not much of a Jew."

"It don't come in degrees, Mr. Pollak. It's like being pregnant: you are or you aren't. Besides which, I'm not much of a rabbi." Malachi leaned toward Sam, and a whiff of dust and age and poppy seed bridged the gap between them. "In fact," he murmured, "I'm what you might call a defrocked rabbi. Here, have another bagel, they shouldn't go stale."

What the hell was a defrocked rabbi? Sam absently accepted another bagel. "I've heard of defrocked priests. Never of a defrocked rabbi."

"You think it's easy? How they gonna defrock you, they never frocked you in the first place? In my case, though, an exception was made."

"Why?" asked Sam, and as he asked the question there came a tiny click of engagement, inaudible to Sam, though the faintest of smiles crossed the rabbi's face.

"Don't ask," he said.

"*You* brought it up."

Malachi hooked his heels a rung higher and rested his forearms on his knees. Sam was reminded of a picture in a book his mother used to read to him: the mournful griffin of Alice's Wonderland. "You really want to know?"

"Actually . . ."

"I'll tell you. But I warn you, the lady in this story—"

"The lady!"

The rabbi winced. "Please. This poor lady, you think you've got troubles, you should only know what happened to her. I know, because I was her rabbi. This is back when I had my own *shul.* This woman, a good, pious woman, every Shabbat they walk to services, her and her husband and the children. Fine children, a boy maybe fifteen and a beautiful little girl, six years old. One day the woman comes to my office. 'Rabbi,' she says, 'such trouble we have.'

"'What trouble?' I ask her.

"'Sari, my baby—the doctor says it's leukemia.' She cries and cries, and I have to comfort her. What can I say? I say what comes to me, I don't know what. She goes away. I pray for the little girl, every day I pray. Two, three months later, back she comes. 'Oy, Rabbi, such *tsuris.*'

"'Now what?'

"'Sari every day gets sicker, and my husband can't take it. He's left us, run away.'

"'Do you need help?' I ask. God forgive me, I'm happy because here finally is something I can do. 'Do you need money, food, a ride to the city? Tell me what you need, I'll get for you.'

"'Answers,' she cries. 'I need answers. I want you should do your job. Explain to me, Rabbi: What did I do so bad in my life that this should come to me? What evil thing did I do?'

"'No evil,' I tell her. 'Trouble comes is all. Look at Job: a blameless man, look how he suffered.'

"'I can't go on,' she tells me.

"I say all what they taught me to say. 'Pray for strength,' I tell her, and I pray with her. 'Yea, though I walk through the valley of death I shall fear no evil, for Thou art with me.'

"That far we get, then she breaks down. 'It's no use,' she cries. 'God *hates* me.'

"'He don't hate you,' I tell her, but to myself I'm thinking it's worse: He don't even know you exist."

Malachi paused. He sighed deeply, he tugged so hard at his beard that strands came out in his hand. "I ask you, Mr. Pollak, is this a thought for a rabbi to think?"

"Is this a true story," Sam said, "or are you just trying to cheer me up?"

"You want cheer, you get a cheerleader. I'm just telling you what happened. A month or two later, the little girl dies. I make the funeral, say Kaddish by the graveside. The mother, she don't cry. She watches me, all the time watches with such eyes the words turn to dust in my mouth. Afterward she comes to me.

"'Rabbi,' she says, 'it's finished. My life is over.'

"'You can't give up,' I tell her. 'You still got your son. For his sake you got to go on.'"

Sam's hand shot out, palm outward. An unplanned gesture, defensive in nature. "Stop right there."

The rabbi stopped. His chin dropped to his chest, his shoulders sagged; he seemed exhausted. Silence enclosed them, no telling how long.

Sam broke it with a string of curses. "Go on, let's hear it: The son dies."

"Car crash," Malachi said faintly.

Sam groaned.

"I go to her home. I don't want to go, but I go. She's sitting on the floor, a ghost of her old self. Her clothes are torn, not just a symbolic little slit but great jagged rents, as if an animal had clawed her.

"I sit down beside her. She takes my hand. I can see right through hers, nothing there but grief and bones.

"'Rabbi,' she says. 'Why?'"

Again Malachi paused. Cleared his throat, pounded his chest.

"'Why?' she asks. Do I know why? The answers they taught me in the seminary I would be ashamed to give this woman. My honest opinion is who knows why? It could happen to anyone, that's all I know. *He's* up there playing Russian roulette with the gun to our heads, and *we're* down here searching for reasons. 'Why,' she asks. I should answer such a question? The Almighty himself should give her an answer."

"So that's what you told her?"

"God forbid."

"Then what did you say? What did you tell her?"

"Nothing," said Malachi. "What could I say? I sat there and wept like a lost child, and this woman, this saintly fool, she patted my hand and stroked my back. She comforted me." He sighed and fell silent.

"That's a horrible story," Sam said presently.

Malachi scowled. His fatigue seemed to have lifted, for now he sat tall and still, a small, solid man covered in black, a narrow erect figure like an obelisk or a finger pointing upward. "The world is full of horrible stories," he said coldly. "Bad things happen every day to good people."

"That's comforting."

"I'm not here to comfort."

"What are you here for?"

The rabbi didn't answer. Silence settled over them. Against his will Sam's thoughts returned to the story. It felt incomplete. What had become of the woman? Did she die of sorrow?

"She survived." Malachi answered his thoughts. "She lived. Last time I went back I heard she'd married again, a widower from the congregation. This to me is the deepest mystery. You could possibly call it a miracle."

"Some miracle," Sam sneered. "Hallelujah."

Outside a cloud covered the sun and the room grew dim. Mist clouded the windows. They might have been in a spaceship, light years from earth.

The rabbi's voice seemed to come from far away. "Broken hearts mend," he said. "Not without scars. But they mend."

"So that's the moral of the story," Sam said in sudden rage. "Broken hearts heal?"

"There is no moral! This is not Aesop's fables here, this is not the children's hour. This is just a thing that happened, how Malachi lost his calling. Because you asked how come I'm not a real rabbi anymore."

"Then what are you?"

"I am what I am," the rabbi said.

A little while later Sam walked Malachi to his car, then climbed the path to the house. Something had come over him. He felt so sleepy he could hardly make it up the steps. All he wanted in the world was to fall into bed, not the couch but his very own bed. He would pull the phone out of the wall, he would sleep for a week. Why not? Malachi and his goddamn bagels. The candle stand would have to wait.

CHAPTER 8

Thanksgiving was not a holiday Sam needed to celebrate. The very word *thanksgiving* made him crazy, made him itch to do something bad, bust up a church, burn a flag or something. He knew a man whose son had died on Father's Day. Driving down from Buffalo to see him, the son fell asleep at the wheel, or so they figured afterward; anyway he lost control and hit a concrete abutment head-on at 65 mph. Sam used to wonder how the man got through subsequent Father's Days, with all the hype and hoopla that had helped get his son killed. Now he knew, because that's how he felt this Thanksgiving. *Thanks for what?* he wanted to ask, though he didn't, because he knew how little patience people have for mourning that goes on past the funeral.

You'd think people would understand, you'd think they'd know to leave him alone on this of all days. But no one, it seemed, wanted Sam to spend Thanksgiving alone. Invitations poured in; he'd never been so popular. The Muellers, first and foremost, Kate insisting she wouldn't take no for an answer. Earl Lassiter, a bit shyly, because he and Mark Hambro were discreet about their union, not denying the relationship but not flaunting it, either. Tom and Mary Whitehill. Jane Goncalves, though once he turned her down she backpedaled all the way to the next county. Marty and Mildred Lapid. That one surprised Sam. A few weeks ago he'd run into Lapid in the Wickham Quickmart, face to face in the frozen-food section. The doctor blushed, and seemed to hesitate a moment before offering his hand. Then he squeezed extra hard. "Sam, how are you? Jesus, I keep meaning to call." But no words could mask the stricken look in his eyes.

It was disheartening. They'd been close, and had grown closer during Lou's illness. Mildred Lapid visited nearly as often as her husband. On the Sunday before she died, Marty and Mildred came over together. Marty opened his black medical bag and pulled out a bottle of French champagne, Louise laughed with pleasure, and Sam asked the occasion. "None," Marty said. "Put it down to the principle that good things should never be postponed." Sam filled their glasses and they drank a toast to friendship, then killed the bottle.

These days, though, Lapid rarely called, and when he did his voice had the strained quality of a filter holding back more than it was letting through. So maybe he did know, maybe he'd figured it out. Lou's pain meds had disappeared from the house, and reckoning back, Sam figured it must have been the doctor who took them the day she died. But if he knew, why didn't he speak up? And if he suspected, why didn't he inquire? Lapid had asked no questions, but signed the death certificate with what seemed to Sam indecent haste.

Even Marie Pellagio, Lapid's receptionist, called to invite Sam. After Lou died Marie came to the house three times, reeking of Shalimar and bearing homemade lasagna. Makeup so thick Sam was tempted to carve his initials in the layers of pancake and powder. It was funny but depressing too, because Lou wasn't there to say *I told you so.*

They'll be lining up with casseroles, and Marie will be first on line.

Lou, give me a break.

Bet you ten bucks, Sam. She always thought you were hot. I told her looks can be deceiving, but I don't think she bought it.

Which led to one of the few fights of their marriage, the only one during Lou's illness. "Don't fall for the lasagna," she'd said, propped up on pillows. "You can do better."

"Better than what?"

"Better than Marie Pellagio. Did you know that on the days she works, she tapes the soaps?"

"No, actually, I didn't know that." He fell silent then, held back as long as he could, then said, "Have you picked her out yet?"

"Don't be like that, Sam. Life goes on." Tears in her eyes because she's still struggling with the concept, but her voice was steady. "You're young. Of course you'll remarry eventually."

"Eventually?" he said. "Why wait?"

"Sam . . ." She tried to calm him but something had burst in Sam; he was unstoppable.

"Who's the lucky girl? Do I know her? In fact, why wait till you're dead? If you really cared about my welfare you'd free me now, cut me loose to find a healthy broad to fuck. 'Cause that's all men really need, isn't it, Louise? Something to fuck, that's what it all comes down to. You know," he said, "this could turn out to be a blessing in disguise. Maybe I'll get me a young one, tits out to here. Shit," he said, "I can hardly wait."

He stormed off to sleep in one of the spare rooms. Couldn't. Crept back at 2 A.M. Lou was awake. They made it up then, kissed and cried and for the first time in many weeks made love. Terrified of hurting her, Sam held back at first, propping himself on knees and elbows, but Lou would have none of that. She pulled him down and ground her hips into his, wrapped her arms around him and squeezed so hard he thought they'd merge into one. She was hot inside and out. Fire sped up into his loins and Sam lost all control; he cupped her ass in his hands and thrust harder and harder until with a moan she came and he came with her.

He stayed inside. For a long time they lay wrapped together, limbs entangled. After that night there was no more talk of remarriage. Whatever Lou thought she kept to herself.

So no, he was not inclined this year to thank anyone for anything, nor did he look kindly on those false comforters who pointed out how much he had to be grateful for. Ten years with a woman he'd never for a moment stopped loving, who loved him back. Wasn't that cause enough? But the way Sam saw it, he'd been set up, tantalized, slapped down and taunted, and not for the first time. He'd be damned if he'd kiss the hand that did it.

"No one's asking you to," Kate Mueller said when he tried to explain. "All we're asking you to do is haul your ass down here and eat some turkey and trimmings like you did last year, and if that's too much to ask, then to hell with you, Sam Pollak."

Between her not-so-subtle blackmail and the inconvenience of devising excuses for other friends, it finally proved more trouble to refuse than to accept. Thanksgiving evening found him trudging down his long driveway beneath a starless, overcast sky. A dank blanket of air, heavy with the threat of snow, grew denser with every step downhill. All around was darkness, but the Muellers' house, blazing with light, drew him on. From fifty yards away he could smell roast turkey mingling with the sweet aroma of burning logs. Exactly one year ago today he had stood in this very spot, arm in arm with Louise. A red wool scarf had encircled her neck; she wore no hat, and the moon shone down on the fundament of her long black hair. From inside the house came bursts of laughter, conversation, children's voices. In unspoken accord they paused on the threshold. Their eyes met, and Sam was nearly overwhelmed with a feeling of love for his wife and wonder at the way his life had turned out. Lou was healthy then, or so they thought; he'd had no reason to fear. And yet at that moment of deepest contentment, the old fear struck. Something will happen, he'd thought. This can't last. And it hadn't.

Now the door flew open and Melissa Mueller appeared on the threshold. Sam greeted her. Instead of moving back to let him enter, she stepped out onto the porch, wrapped her arms around his waist, and rising up on tiptoes kissed him full on the lips. Nothing neighborly about this kiss, nothing childlike about the body pressed to his. Even through his jacket Sam felt more than he needed or wanted to feel. He grasped her by the shoulders and set her at arm's length. "Whoa, girl," he said.

"*Whoa?* Am I a horse?"

"I know exactly who you are: Kate and Willem's little girl."

She didn't like that, but before she could reply her mother appeared in the doorway.

"Sam," Kate said, "come on inside, it's cold out there." She took the wine he held out to her and kissed him on the cheek. Sam kept a wary eye on Melissa as she took his coat, but in her mother's presence the girl was chaste as new-fallen snow. Kate led him into the living room where a fire leaped in the hearth. The room was cozy, a bit overfurnished with solid country pieces gleaned from Kate's shop. An eclectic assortment of upholstered chairs and an old settee clustered around a low coffee table; hunting prints lined the walls; an oval hooked rug set off the oak floor.

Footsteps clattered on the stairs and seconds later Billy ran into the room. He flung his arms around Sam's waist. Over the past year the boy had shot up four inches; peach-fuzz now adorned his upper lip, but in the violence of his affections Billy seemed half his age; unlike Melissa, Sam reflected. He'd seen her every now and then being picked up by dates, husky high-school athletes with pickups, who held their caps in their hands and called her parents "sir" and "ma'am;" and he'd wondered how Kate and Willem could let her go. How they could fall for the old polite routine? Didn't they know that before the truck was out of sight those young bucks would be all over their daughter? Sam surely would have been, at their age. Melissa had inherited her mother's womanly figure, slender but full where it counted, and her style of dress seemed calculated to inflame. Tonight she was outwardly demure in schoolgirl clothes of white blouse and navy skirt, only the skirt was a bit too short and the blouse a bit too tight, so the effect was of a woman in little girl's clothing. What did Kate and Willem think? Did they, for example, suppose her a virgin? Perhaps, Sam thought, being a parent requires a degree of blindness, more than a touch of amnesia.

Billy was tugging at Sam's arm, vying for his attention. "I knew you'd come. *Melissa* said you wouldn't, but *I* knew you would."

"Who could resist your mom's cooking?"

"Is it true what they say, that the way to a man's heart is through his stomach?" Melissa asked sweetly.

Kate whipped her head around and stared.

"Shut up, stupid," Billy said. He rolled his eyes at Sam. "Girls."

Kate took Sam's arm. "Willem just got home. He's upstairs showering. Come keep me company in the kitchen."

Kate mashed the sweet potatoes with more rigor than they may have needed. "I swear I'm going to have that girl spayed. She is too much for me."

Sam had no comment on Melissa. "Willem was out this morning?"

"Fire."

"*Another* one?"

"Another arson." She looked at him. "Stan Kuzak's joining us. He just went home to change."

"What's going on?"

Kate shook her head, tight-lipped. She poured them each a glass of wine, then turned her back and busied herself with the meal: basted the turkey, tossed the salad, blanched almonds for the string beans. For five minutes Sam sat at the kitchen table and sipped his wine without once hearing her voice or seeing her face.

"Can I do something?" he asked.

"No thanks." Her voice taut, pitched too high.

"Kate?"

She didn't answer, wouldn't look at him. Wrapped her arms around herself and stood very still. Sam crossed to her. Kate averted her face but her ragged breathing gave her away.

"What is it, Kate?"

"The onions," she mumbled.

There were no onions in sight. What the hell was keeping Willem? Women crying did Sam in. He patted Kate's shoulder, feeling useless; comfort and advice had been Lou's bailiwick, not his.

"It's just something she's going through," he said. "Don't take it to heart."

"What?" Kate said, lifting her head and staring at him. "Oh. Melissa."

"Not Melissa? What's wrong, then?"

Tears on her cheeks. "I miss her, Sam."

As if he didn't. Blood rushed to his head; he put his hands on the counter, leaned on them.

"I'm sorry," she cried. "It's just, last year we did this together, and it was the best Thanksgiving of my life. We never stopped laughing. I loved her, Sam."

"I know."

Kate wiped her eyes on her sleeve. "Damn. I swore I wouldn't do this."

"It's okay."

"No, it's not." She came over and hugged him, burying her face in his shoulder. Sam stared over her head. He felt nothing. His body was leaden, lifeless.

Melissa appeared in the kitchen doorway. Cheeks paled under her blusher. "Charming," she said. "Does Dad know?"

Kate stepped back. "Don't be an idiot. Go away."

Melissa disappeared.

"I went to the cemetery this morning," Kate said, "put some flowers on her grave. The old wreaths were still there, from the funeral. Don't you visit her, Sam?"

"She's not there," he said.

"Where do you go to mourn her? What do you do?"

"Nothing," he said. "There's nothing I can do."

Then, to Sam's great relief, Willem came downstairs, and a few minutes later Stan Kuzak arrived. The sheriff was a robust man of sixty-odd years, with a red, weather-beaten face furrowed around the mouth, a shock of wiry gray hair, and heavy jowls that gave him a fierce bulldog look. He greeted Sam cordially, with so much warmth in his handshake that Sam felt a stab of guilt, though he hardly knew for what.

Kate commandeered the children for a final assault on dinner and sent the men away. They lit cigars and cigarettes in Willem's tiny den, protected by a sign on the outside of the door: CHILD-FREE ZONE. Willem passed out cold beers and turned on the football game. Amazingly, the Jets were leading Miami 17 to 14.

"Heard you're working again, Sam," Kuzak said, with one eye on the game. "The old Atkins place."

"Supposed to be, she ever gets her roof fixed." Sam hadn't told anyone of the Goncalves job, but it didn't surprise him Kuzak knew. Kuzak had spent his whole life in the village, except for a three-year stint in the Navy. He knew every resident, first- and second-homers both, and what he didn't know of their affairs was not worth knowing.

"Heard she's got herself a roofer," Kuzak said.

"Oh, yeah? Who?"

The sheriff paused for effect. "Lyle Fertig."

Willem laughed so hard he sprayed beer on the screen. "Fertig? Oh, Lord. Poor lady."

"Ah, well," Kuzak said, "maybe he's changed."

"Right. And maybe tomorrow the sun'll rise in the west."

Mueller and Kuzak started swapping Fertig stories. Kuzak told the one about the house he roofed down in Hillsdale. Fertig finished the job but neglected to replace the rain gutters. The owner came back from Florida to two feet of water in the basement. Then Mueller reminisced about the time Fertig got himself hired onto an Albany crew as a backhoe operator. First time out he knocked down a telephone pole, severed a water line, and flooded the site. Kuzak and Mueller howled at each story. Not Sam, though. He wasn't laughing at all. "How the hell'd she end up with that fuck-up?" he asked.

Kuzak shrugged. "Couldn't find anyone else, most likely." But when Mueller left the room for some more beer, the sheriff turned to Sam and said, "Woman on her own, with kids . . ." He shook his head. "Person would be doin' her a favor, he tipped her the wink on this guy."

"What person would that be?" Sam asked.

"Any interested party," Kuzak said. "Personally I wouldn't invest my work in a house with one of Fertig's roofs overhead."

Roast turkey, sweet-potato pie, cornbread, cranberry sauce, string beans, squash, chestnut stuffing. Everyone held hands while Billy said grace. "Thank you for the food we eat, thank you for the world so sweet, thank you for the birds that sing, thank you, Lord, for everything." Melissa, sitting to Sam's left, rubbed his palm with her forefinger. He stared at his plate and kept silent when they all said Amen.

Kate was to his right, Stan Kuzak beside her, then Billy, then Willem at the head of the table. If by separating Kuzak from her husband Kate hoped to inhibit discussion of the fire, she was disappointed. Though they'd showered and changed, the scorched smell clung to them, and fire sat at the table like an unwanted guest. They tried to talk of other things but the conversation kept drifting back to this latest outrage. This fire had been different from the others. The arsonist—for both Mueller and Kuzak were convinced that the series of five was the work of one person—had started out by targeting billboards, then escalated to sheds and barns. This time, for the first time, he'd burned a house. The house on Ravens Road in the Old Wickham countryside belonged to two city women who lived and worked together; one wrote, the other illustrated children's books. The house was five hundred yards from its closest neighbor, set back in the woods. The owners were away, the house unoccupied; by the time neighbors noticed the flames, the structure was fully involved. Willem had his men lay some water on the fire, but that was just to be doing something. They'd known from the moment they arrived that the house was a dead loss.

"What worries me is how he keeps upping the stakes," Kuzak said. "Maybe the next house won't be empty."

"Oh, poor Lydia, poor Karin." Kate knew the women well; they were customers as well as neighbors. A pair of beautiful carved blanket chests, a pine sideboard, an antique maple school desk: those too must have gone up in flames. She had pitied the Crawfords with all her heart for the loss of their animals and their barn, but this time the loss felt personal. Sitting in her own dining room, surrounded by her possessions, children, husband, and friends, Kate shuddered as if someone had stepped on her grave.

"Did you reach them in the city?" she asked Kuzak.

"Tried to. Must be out celebrating Thanksgiving, poor souls. Left a message for them to call."

"I don't envy you your job."

"Times like this, I don't either."

"All those beautiful things," Kate said mournfully. "All their hard work."

Melissa sniffed. "Things can be replaced," she said. "It's not like they're homeless or something. It's the Crawfords' pony and dog that kill me."

Billy spoke through a mouthful of turkey and stuffing. "You should catch the guy and put *him* on fire. See how he likes it."

"You're sure this was arson?" Sam asked Willem.

As always, Willem took his time replying. "Multiple origins," he said. "Identical burn patterns in each downstairs room. Window busted inward. Strong smell of accelerant. Yeah, I'm sure."

"They're such nice women," Kate said. "Who would do a thing like this?"

Kuzak let out a harsh laugh. "If we knew, would I be sitting here?"

"Those two women, they're . . ." Willem seesawed his hand.

"So what?" cried Kate. "Who cares?"

"Not me. Live and let live. There's plenty do, though." He was looking at Kuzak, who replied with the readiness of one resuming an earlier argument:

"Trouble with that is there's no pattern. Arsonists make choices like anyone else. Where's the connection between the Crawfords and these two women? How's he picking 'em?"

"You're looking at it so logically," Kate said. "Maybe it's random, like an act of God or a tornado."

The sheriff shook his head. "This is no act of God. This is a man, and men do what they do for reasons. Twisted reasons, maybe, but you can bet the ranch these burnings make sense to *him*."

"Opportunity," Willem said. "That's all. This bastard likes to burn. Anything. Gives him a kick."

"Then you'd expect him to show at the fire," Kuzak said. He exchanged a look with Willem, who nodded but did not speak.

A small hand brushed the outside of Sam's left thigh. He moved his leg, but the hand followed. Melissa, sitting next to him, said, "Walter Gower said his dad says it's those new people in the Atkinses' house."

Willem glared at his daughter. "Did you ever hear any Gower say anything worth repeating?"

"No."

"Then don't go quoting 'em at this table. Frank Gower's full of—" he caught a look from his wife "—stuffing."

Billy's fork was frozen halfway between the table and his gaping mouth. He looked from his father to his sister. "That's Peter Quinn's house."

"*Duh*," said Melissa.

Billy's fair skin flushed to a deep red. "Peter's my friend."

"And you really know how to pick 'em."

"Hush, Melissa," Kate said sharply. "We don't spread malicious rumors about people just because they're newcomers."

"I didn't say it was true," the girl drawled. "I just said I heard it."

"They're decent people," Sam said, and though his voice was mild there was something in his tone that drew Melissa's eyes to him. She subsided into silence, and the hand that had been inching its way up his thigh dropped away.

"Peter's my friend," Billy said. There was a dab of cranberry sauce on his nose, and behind his thick glasses his eyes glistened with tears. "He stands up for me. He likes me."

"We know, honey," Kate said.

"I'd be real surprised if it turns out to be anyone new," Kuzak said. "Whoever's doing this knows the area as well as I do."

Willem grunted. "Knows fire, too."

"Probably knows the people involved. He's laughing at us. Thinks he's real smart."

"You sound like you know him," Sam said.

"Oh, I know him," said Kuzak. "I just don't know who he is."

CHAPTER 9

"But he had references," Jane said. "I checked them."

"Remember the names?" Sam asked, looking up at her. Once again she was perched on a ladder, shelving books in the overstock section of the Wickham Bookstore.

Her eyes grew distant. "Weigert and what was it? Richards, Roberts, something like that."

"Mary Weigert is Lyle's mother's sister. Bob Richards is a hunting buddy." Sam gave a short laugh. "Man's got to be long on faith or short on brains to go hunting with Fertig."

"How do you know all this?"

"Told you: small town, long winters, gossip's the main pastime."

Jane sank down onto the top of the ladder. "So you're saying I'm fucked." She put her fist to her mouth, dislodging a book.

Sam snagged it one-handed. "Not necessarily. How much did you pay him?"

"Half."

"Then we've still got some leverage."

He passed up the book. She noticed the "we" and despite herself, her spirits lifted.

"How much do you know about roofing?" Sam asked.

"Nothing."

He nodded, thought for a moment, hesitated, then said, "Got a dollar?"

Her eyebrows rose but she asked nothing, just reached in her pocket and pulled out a bill.

Sam took it, folded it and stuck it in his shirt pocket. "You've just hired yourself a general contractor. Now your roofer answers to me. No more payments till I sign off on the job."

Jane descended four rungs, till they stood eye to eye. "Why?" she asked, and if there was gratitude in her voice there was also a deep wariness.

"No point putting good work under a bad roof."

She smiled. "Thanks, Pollak."

"*De nada*, Goncalves."

Lyle Fertig was taking a well-earned break, smoking a joint and soaking up the rays on top of the old Atkins house, when trouble loomed in the form of Sam Pollak's head breaking the plane of the roof. Lyle sat up sharply, extinguished the joint, and pocketed the roach.

"Yo, man," he said, "fancy meeting you here."

"How you doing, Lyle?" Sam hoisted himself up onto the roof.

Fertig was not pleased to see him. Pollak had a real critical way of looking at things, an attitude directly opposed to Fertig's philosophy of life, which was encapsulated by the bumper sticker on his truck: "Don't sweat the small stuff." Pollak took things too personal, acted like every house he worked on was his own. Nor was he a man to be lightly crossed. Everyone knew what he did to Frank Gower on account of Gower spitting on his wife—not that the guy didn't maybe have it coming, okay, but the point was, Sam Pollak was not your typical New York City faggoty Jew. He was a big, strapping guy who knew how to handle himself, and there was not the least percentage in riling him.

"Not bad," Fertig said. "Yourself?"

Sam poked around among the untidy piles of asphalt shingle. "You working alone?"

"Hey, why share the loot when I can keep it all for myself?"

"Uh-huh." Sam squatted by a new-laid patch of shingle. With the blade of his pocketknife he started prying at one of the nails.

Fertig ambled over to watch. "You mind telling me what you're doing? 'Cause somehow this don't feel like a social call."

"Not exactly, Lyle." The nail slid out cleanly and Sam palmed it. "Tell me something. Do you use a hammer on these nails, or do you just shove 'em in with your hand?"

Fertig scowled. "I was gonna go over them."

"Don't bother."

"What's that supposed to mean?"

Sam stood up. "Means you've got to pull 'em all anyway."

"The fuck I do! Who died and made you boss?"

"I'm the GC now, and *this*," Sam opened his fist to reveal a shiny silver nail, "this don't fly. Man, don't you take any pride in your work? What kind of moron uses nongalvanized nails on a roof?"

Fertig advanced till he stood chin to chin with Sam. Sam was taller but the slope of the roof evened things up.

"You calling me a moron?"

"Yeah. Why?"

Fertig saw one thing clearly enough: forty feet up and Pollak wanted to tangle. He backed off, put some daylight between them. Lyle's mama didn't raise no fools. If there was one thing he knew, it was how and when to pick his fights.

"Look, man, you got to cut me some slack here. What happened, I didn't have no galvanized nails, so I used what I had. Waste not, want not. Right, Sam?" Fertig winked. "It ain't like *she'll* ever know."

Sam smiled. Fertig had seen friendlier smiles on crocs down in Florida.

"Let me make this real clear, Lyle. Either you pull all those nails and start from scratch with the right ones, or you're off the job, in which case you don't see another dime."

"Hey, man—that money's spent already!"

"Then I guess we know which way it's gonna go."

Fertig removed his shades, unveiling his powerful eyes just long enough to turn Sam's smile to dust. He flashed a Heil Hitler. "You the boss, Mr. Boss Man, sir. On your head be it."

"Anytime at all," Sam whispered. "Anytime you're ready."

By the time he was halfway down the ladder, Sam was shaking with rage. That goddamned little shit with his Nazi salute and his insolent eyes. Fertig had read him right; he *was* hoping the little prick would swing on him. A fight would have done his heart good, but he knew all along it wasn't going to happen. Fertig didn't have the balls. Sam knew the type. Lyle was a stalker, a back-stabber.

He reached the bottom rung and swung off to find himself face-to-face with Peter Quinn. Tried to go around, but the boy planted himself squarely in Sam's path.

"What?" Sam snapped. "Spit it out."

"I heard you up there."

"Yeah, so? You want a medal for hearing?"

"So when did you start giving orders around here?"

Sam had to laugh. Welcome back to the world, welcome back with a vengeance. First the roofer from hell, now this beardless wonder. Still, he couldn't help contrasting Fertig's craven bob-and-weave with Peter's heads-up stance, visored cap tipped back to reveal unwavering eyes. This stripling had an attitude bigger than himself, but it was in some ways an attitude familiar to Sam.

"Since Ms. Goncalves hired me as general contractor," he said.

"Making your move," Peter drawled with mock admiration.

"Is that what you think? You think I'm putting the moves on your mother?"

"Jane's not my mother."

"Foster mother, whatever. The person who looks after you."

Peter stared into his face. "We look after each other."

"Fine," said Sam. "Then you and me have got no beef, because I am here to do a job and that's all I'm here for."

"Better be," Peter said, and before Sam could muster a reply, the insolent pup had nodded and walked away.

There was one thing about Sam that even Louise hadn't known, the only thing he ever kept from her. Sam didn't like children.

There were exceptions of course, particular kids whom Sam could not dislike. Billy Mueller, for one: a soul without a speck of malice. Melissa when she was younger, though not in her current Lolita mode. And, strangely enough, this new boy, Mr. Attitude himself, Peter Quinn. Despite the hostility, if not because of it. The boy had guts, you had to give him that. Like those little terriers that take on dogs three times their size. Something about Peter reminded Sam of himself as a boy. All that free-floating bravado, perhaps.

Generally, though, Sam gave children a wide berth. Maybe it came from losing his parents so young, or maybe he just poured all his nurturing instincts into wood; whatever the reason, he felt uncomfortable around kids. When he spoke with them, his voice rang false in his own ears. His wife had felt no such constraint, had lacked the slightest self-consciousness. Lou used to plunge into conversations about dinosaurs or Barbie dolls the way she'd plunged into swimming pools, head first and full speed ahead; but that facility seemed to Sam a woman-thing, an instinct they had that he could admire but never emulate.

Babies alarmed him. You could never tell if they were going to laugh or cry, and if they cried in your arms then you felt like a criminal and the women laughed at you as they took the baby away. Toddlers were no better. They had a kind of opaque innocence, were horribly trusting, knew nothing of the world and would believe anything you told them simply because it came from a grown-up. And the older ones . . . Working in people's homes, Sam had had ample opportunity to observe their children. You had your lazy, pampered creatures, more like lap dogs than the kind of rough-and-tumble Brooklyn kids Sam had grown up with. You had your crybabies: one little spill off the monkey bars or a playful shove from another kid and off they'd go, whining to their mamas. "Wah, wah, wah." How could anyone love a kid like that? Generally speaking, the richer the parents, the more obnoxious the kids. But there was one incident that Sam never forgot, a kid who came to represent for him all the dangers of child-rearing. Sam was remodeling a kitchen in a second home, an Old Chatham estate. The owners had one kid, a boy of fifteen who played heavy-metal rock at full volume. Sam tried to ignore the noise but it got to him. When it reached the point where he couldn't cut straight, he approached the mother. "Could you get your son to turn it down a notch?"

She went up to the boy's room. Moments later, the volume increased. It was a solid house, but now the walls were vibrating. The mother came down.

"Teenagers," she said, with a rueful smile.

"Ma'am," Sam said, "I can't work like this. Either he lowers the volume or I'm out of here."

The woman went back upstairs. Over the music Sam could hear the kid scream at her, "Get the fuck out of my room!"

She came down. "He doesn't want to," she said. Sam packed up his tools and walked out. The woman followed him out to the truck, sputtering with rage. Not at her son. At Sam. "How dare you walk out! We won't pay you!"

"Keep your money," Sam told her. "Lady, I feel sorry for you."

Lou said a monster like that was the parents' fault; they raised him that way. Sam wasn't sure. What if you did everything right, and the kid still came out a bum?

But Lou's heart was set on children and Sam would do anything, take any risk for Lou. People said your own were different, and maybe they were; Sam knew some hard-hearted people who doted on their kids. But that merely posed a whole different set of problems. Loving anyone meant exposing a flank, but loving a child was pure recklessness. Anything at all could happen to a child. Every day you read about kids getting sick, hurt, kidnapped. You could put them to bed healthy and find them dead in the morning for no reason at all; crib death, they called it. Left to himself, Sam would just as soon go out on the lake in a lightning storm as father a child; still, for Louise's sake, he'd tried his damnedest.

Lyle finished the roof under Sam's close supervision, and in early December Sam started work in the house. The kids were in school most of the day, and when they weren't, they made themselves scarce. All except Peter. Peter hung around, often just out of sight. Kept a constant, oblique eye on Sam.

At first it grated on Sam. He liked his privacy when he worked. He used to employ an assistant till he realized that the time saved in fetching and carrying was lost to jabbering. He wasn't antisocial, he enjoyed the conviviality of working with a crew on big jobs, like sheetrocking or framing. Still, for Sam, the best part of carpentry was undoubtedly the time spent alone, working on a task that demanded good hands and a bent for precision. Every job had a rhythm, and once he found that rhythm things flowed; he lost himself in work and the thing he was building took shape beneath his hands.

Thus it was odd how quickly he grew used to Peter's peripheral presence, how he began even to look for it. He discovered that the less attention he paid to Peter, the closer the boy would come, which reminded him of the way Lou had tamed the wild chickadees. Suspicious as he was, the boy was yet drawn to the work. It interested him, and though pride or distrust or some inner code of conduct prevented him from asking a single question, if Sam explained what he was doing, he listened.

He was hungry for something; Sam could see that, though he didn't know for what. Maybe just company. Young Billy Mueller hung around now and then, but that was an unequal friendship at best. Sometimes Peter's young foster sibs teased him into playing with them; otherwise, Peter seemed very much alone.

Nothing wrong with that, Sam told himself. A dose of loneliness in childhood can cure a boy into a man; it surely did for him. Goncalves was still mum on Peter's background, but Sam knew the look of a boy jolted prematurely out of childhood; he knew an orphan when he saw one. It was something they had in common. Only Sam as a kid had gone through half a dozen foster homes before giving up on family life and striking out on his own, while Peter had clearly hit the jackpot with Jane. Dumb kid probably didn't even know his own luck. Or maybe he did. Who knew? Peter was not the confiding type.

One day Sam was in the middle of framing out the closet in Jane's room when he ran out of framing nails. He was about to make a run down to Dugan's hardware store on the edge of the village when a better idea struck him. School was out for parent/teacher conferences or some such thing, and Peter had been hanging around. Boy might as well make himself useful. "Hey, Peter!"

The boy, loitering in the hallway, popped his head in.

"I'm out of nails. How about taking a run down to Dugan's for me?"

"Jane's out," Peter said.

"So?"

"So I'm watching the kids."

"I'm here," Sam said.

If the boy found this reassuring, he managed to conceal it.

"Got a bike?"

"Yeah, but—"

"Fifteen minutes total, there and back."

"I guess," Peter said reluctantly.

Sam handed him a twenty and told him what to buy. "And don't let Dugan palm anything else off on you. Tell him they're for me." The boy stuffed the bill in his jeans pocket and ran.

Sam carried the ladder down the corridor and into the girls' corner bedroom. While he was waiting for Peter to come back he would measure the room, block out a space for the closet. Larger than Jane's bedroom, this one had two large windows facing front, two more overlooking the pond with a window seat in between. It was a cheerful, sunny room, with orange curtains and a striped throw rug. Orderly, too. Goncalves, he'd noticed, ran a tight ship. Twin beds separated by a night table were covered with yellow quilts. A well-worn teddy bear lolled on one pillow, a Raggedy Ann on the other.

With so many windows in the room, the only space to put a closet was where the wardrobe now stood, to the left of the door. Sam shut the door and opened his ladder, and as he did this he was startled to hear something move, a slithering sound. He spun around, expecting to see a mouse. Instead he glimpsed a small brown face peeking out from beneath the farther of the two beds. It disappeared immediately.

"Jesus," he said. "Who is that? Keisha, Luz? Come on out of there."

No response.

"You kids playing hide-and-seek or something?"

Still no reply. He couldn't even hear her breathe. Felt the onset of that peculiar unease children always roused in him. What was he supposed to do now?

"Okay, honey, you just go on with your game. I'll be out of your way in a minute." He climbed up the ladder and started by measuring the distance from floor to ceiling, checking several different spots. Like many old houses, this one had settled unevenly, which complicated what ought to have been straightforward work. Seven feet, ten inches. Sam took a pencil from behind his ear, rested his notebook on the platform of the ladder, and sketched the room. He had altogether forgotten the little girl when a muffled sound reached him from under the bed. It was a sound he hadn't heard in years but recognized immediately: the sob of a child with its hand pressed to its mouth.

Maybe the kid was sick or hurt. Whenever he felt bad as a kid he used to hide. Brilliant stroke, sending Peter out. Sam hopped off the ladder and the child fell silent.

"Keisha? Luz? Who's under there?" Sam knelt beside the bed and peered into the dimness. At first he could make out nothing, but then he saw the whites of her wide-open eyes. It was Keisha, curled into a ball in the farthest corner from him.

"What's the matter, Keisha? Why're you hiding under there?"

She covered her eyes with her hands.

"It's me, Sam, the carpenter. Come on out and let me have a look at you." He reached under the bed. His hand touched an ankle and closed on it. He tugged gently.

Keisha shrieked, pulled back sharply. Sam heard a crack as her head hit the bed frame.

"Oh, Jesus," he said. He let go of her ankle, stood, and in one swift movement upended the bed.

Keisha screamed. She jumped up and backed away from him. There was a lump on her forehead that grew larger even as he watched. Wincing in sympathy, Sam reached out.

She screamed again. For a moment he saw himself through her eyes: a great big white man reaching out to grab her. Sam backed away but Keisha kept screaming, a shrill, undulating wail like a car alarm that just won't quit. Then the door flew open.

He should have been gone by then. Would have been, if his bike hadn't seized up as he pulled it from the shed. He'd had to carry it to the driveway, where he hunkered down for a look. The chain was fouled, entangled in the spokes of the back wheel. Peter took off his gloves and started working the chain free. It had just come loose in his hand when Keisha screamed.

It couldn't have taken more than a minute and a half to run into the house, through the kitchen and the dining room, up the stairs to Keisha's room, but the trip seemed to last forever. Plenty of time for self-reproach. He should have stood up to the man, not run to do his goddamn bidding. Should have known better than to fall for the carpenter's line of goods. Hadn't he heard it all before, hadn't he been there? It was like this line in a play they were reading in English. "Men were deceivers ever." Old Shakespeare knew a thing or two.

At last he reached Keisha's room. He tried the door; it was unlocked but impeded by something heavy. He put his shoulder to the door and heaved. There was a loud crash and suddenly the door gaped open. Peter ran in and saw a toppled ladder, an overturned bed, Keisha cowering against a wall and Pollak facing her.

A stab of déjà vu sharp as an icicle split Peter's world in two. One moment it was Sam and Keisha who stood before him, the next, his father and sister.

A great calm descended upon him. This scene would play itself out. Peter would do what he was moved to do. What would be would be, and he could no more affect the outcome than he could stop the tide from flowing in.

He stood between them. Keisha was quiet now but the silence rang with the echo of her screams. Peter looked her over carefully. Saw the bruise on her forehead. Turned to Sam. "You bastard."

The carpenter's face was as pasty as day-old oatmeal. He was sweating through his shirt. "She was hiding; she banged her head. You want to put some ice on that bruise, keep the swelling down."

"Why was she hiding?"

"I don't know," Sam said.

Peter's eyes narrowed. "You waited till Jane was out. You sent me away. You barricaded the door."

"I didn't barricade the door, for Chrissake! I was measuring the room."

"Yeah, whatever." He took a step forward. Sam's eyes flickered toward his hand; only then did Peter realize he was still holding the bicycle chain. The chain was black and oily. He looped it around his hand and snapped the loose end.

Sam said, "Don't wave that thing at me unless you plan to use it, boy."

His father's very words. Last words, almost. There was a rushing sound as the present poured into the past. Peter cocked the chain behind his head.

"Put it down," the carpenter said. "You've got it wrong. I don't want to hurt you, son."

Son? There was a loop, a kind of temporal echo; time folded in on itself. It was all happening again. Looking at Sam, Peter saw his father's gleaming red devil-eyes, heard his whiskey voice.

Drop it, you little bastard.

Maura crouching in the corner where the old man had flung her. Peter, don't!

Leave us alone, Peter said. Get out or I'll kill you.

You'll kill me? His father laughed. I'll kill you, you little son of a bitch.

Small arms encircled his knees. Peter looked down. Maura. No, not

Maura; Keisha, ebony-skinned, staring up with eyes like silver dollars. "Peter, no! Don't hurt Sam!"

"Let go," he said.

Keisha clung to his leg. "He didn't hurt me. He didn't do nothing to me."

"I heard you scream."

"I just got scared," she whispered.

The bicycle chain descended slowly. Peter's eyes remained fixed on Sam's. With his free hand, he fished the twenty from his pocket and flung it at the carpenter's face.

"Run your own fuckin' errands," he said.

Sam remained in the house until Jane came home. Not to wait would seem an admission of guilt. At first he busied himself with the closet in her room, but his mind was not on his work and besides, without framing nails there was little he could do. After a while he sank into the wing chair beside her bed and thought about who he could get to finish the job. Save for the soft hiss of the radiators, the house was perfectly silent. He had no idea where the children were or what they were doing.

At 2:00 a car pulled up the drive and stopped. Sam stood and peeked out the window. He saw the top of Jane's head as she stepped out of the car. Keisha appeared, coatless, hurtling toward Jane, who knelt to catch her. Jane's arms engulfed the child. Words were exchanged. Sam couldn't hear them. Suddenly Jane looked up at the window in her room. Sam retreated to the chair and sat back down. He could feel his heart pounding; he was sweating again.

He had done nothing wrong. He tried to help an injured child, that was all. And yet from the moment young Peter burst upon the scene and leapt with lightning speed to the wrong conclusions, Sam had felt guilty.

Now voices floated up from downstairs. The little girls' twittered like sparrows. Peter's tone was sullen, Jane's comforting, calm. Sam couldn't make out the words. What were they telling her? What evil act did Peter think he interrupted when he burst into the room? *You waited till Jane was out. Sent me away. Barricaded the door.* What did the boy think? Impossible to say it even to himself, but Sam knew. And although he felt disgusted and sorely abused by the accusation, this was not the same as feeling innocent. He couldn't make that leap. Innocence and self were incompatible concepts in Sam's mind; for wasn't it true, hadn't he proven beyond the shadow of a doubt, that he was capable of anything?

One thing at least was clear: The situation was untenable. He'd have to abandon the job: a decision reached with relief but also a surprising pang. Still, any fool could see this wasn't going to work. Probably after today's incident Jane would be glad to get rid of him, but even if she wasn't, his mind was made up. When the door opened and Jane peered in, Sam was ready for her.

She came in, shut the door behind her. He opened his mouth to quit. Jane raised a peremptory hand.

"You can't," she said.

"Did it scare you, when she started to scream?" Jane asked.

"Scare me?" Sam lit a cigarette. They were sitting on her front porch. A light snow was falling, the winter's first, and the porch had become an in-between place, suspended between the cold outside and the warm house. Inside, the two girls and Carlos were cutting pictures out of magazines at the kitchen table. Peter was down by the pond, a dark silhouette casting pebbles into the water. A half-pint Heathcliff, Sam thought, in a spasm of irritation. "Let's just say my life flashed before my eyes."

Jane gave a low, sad laugh in reply.

"Keisha's okay?" he asked.

"She will be if you stay. If you quit she'll think it's her fault."

"That's blackmail."

"Hey. Whatever works."

"Tell her I had another job."

"I don't lie to them. The bitch of it is, this was all my fault. I had no business leaving you alone with them without warning you about Keisha."

What about Keisha? The question hung between them. Jane got up, wrapped her arms around herself, and paced up and down the porch. She'd changed into jeans and a fisherman's sweater that hung down to her thighs. Sam watched from the settee. He was through asking questions she wouldn't answer.

Jane stopped in front of him. She opened her mouth.

Sam said, "Don't bother. None of my business."

"It is if you stay. And you have to stay." She sat opposite him in a weathered wicker chair. The porch was so narrow, they were almost knee to knee. Her voice took on a flat, dry quality, as if to let any emotion through would be to risk a flood. A tone familiar to Sam.

Keisha and Luz, Jane told him, were the daughters of a Brooklyn woman named Georgia Jackson. Never married, Georgia was nonetheless a woman of strong commitment; unfortunately that commitment was to crack cocaine. When she wasn't getting high she was hustling for money to get high. Now and then she brought some food home. When she didn't, Keisha knew which of the neighbors were good for a meal or a handout. Georgia was rarely around. One night, though, she came home early, just as Keisha was putting Luz to bed.

She was carrying a big red box tied with a white ribbon. "Happy birthday, Keisha, baby."

"My birthday was a month ago, Mama."

"Mama been saving up. Open it, baby."

Inside the box was a frilly white dress, like the Communion dresses Keisha had seen on church-going girls. It was like nothing she'd ever owned or dreamed of owning. Brand new, with the price tag still on it, the dress was also (and Keisha, young as she was, knew this) wildly impractical, a dress she would never in her life have occasion to wear. Somehow this made it all the more valuable. Reverently, Keisha lifted the dress from its bed of tissue paper. Beneath the dress was another garment, a pair of silky, snow-white panties.

"Put 'em on," Mama said.

Keisha tried on the clothes, the only new clothes she'd ever owned. They fit fine, just a little tight. Mama looked at her and sighed. Then she told Keisha to get her coat, they were going to a party.

"What about Luz?" Keisha asked.

"She's too little."

"We can't leave her here alone. She'll be scared!"

"She be fine. Just a couple hours and we be back."

"No, Mama."

Smack. The edge of Mama's hand whipped across her face.

They took the subway. Keisha counted eight stops before they got off. They emerged from the underground into a neighborhood she had never seen before. Towering shade trees lined the streets. The houses were large, with wide green lawns in front and behind, and lots of space in between. There were basketball hoops facing the street and shiny cars in the driveways. Mama held her hand tight. They walked up a gravel drive beside a big brick house and slipped through a gate. Mama knocked on the back door. A huge white man opened the door.

("All right," said Sam. "I get the picture." It wasn't the first time he'd tried to interrupt. But Jane, having started the story, seemed incapable of stopping.)

At first the man was nice to Keisha. He sat her on his lap and read her a story about three little pigs and a big bad wolf who said "Let me in!" After that, he carried her into a bedroom and undressed her like a doll, taking great care with the white dress. Keisha cried out for her mother, but her mother didn't come. The white man was enormously fat and heavy, and when he hurt her Keisha thought she was going to die.

She didn't die. On the train going home, Mama shook her for whimpering. "You think that was easy for me?" Mama said. "You think I liked that?" She gave Keisha a Hershey bar and explained that if she ever told what happened that night, no one would believe her. The police would take her and lock her up in a home for little liars, and she would never see Luz again.

Keisha believed her. Afterward, she never knew when her mother would come to take her to the brick house. Not knowing made it worse, because there was never a time when she could feel safe. She kept the secret locked up inside her until one day a policewoman came to her first-grade class and explained about good touch and bad touch. The woman said that if it was bad touch children should tell a grown-up they trusted, like a parent or a teacher or police officer. She said the grown-ups would believe the children and help them. She said the children would be safe.

Safe: the word beckoned like a door into a world she'd never known, a world she longed to enter. Keisha was powerfully tempted, but that policewoman didn't know Mama. Mama would be real mad if Keisha told, and when Mama got mad, watch out. For the rest of the day Keisha worried over what to do. She thought so hard that at lunch time she forgot to eat, and alone in the midst of three hundred laughing talking shouting children she fell into a kind of waking dream. In the dream, she saw her mother enter the apartment carrying a big red box tied with white ribbon. Keisha cowered in a corner, but Mama's eyes passed right over her. "Luz," Mama called. "Come on out, baby. Mama got a present for you."

Jane fell silent. She leaned back in her chair with a sigh and pointed to Sam's cigarettes. He gave her one, lit it. They sat for a while without talking.

"It would've happened, too," Jane said in a conversational tone. "Sooner or later the bitch would have sold Luz, too."

"Keisha told, then."

Jane nodded. Smoke spiraled out of her nostrils; she looked, for a moment, like a fierce she-dragon. "She told the teacher. She told the principal. She told the police, and she testified in court. My friend Portia—she was the social worker assigned to the case—she said the lawyers and the judge were amazed. Said they never heard a kid her age testify like that. You hear about children repressing things. Keisha remembered everything, down to dates and times. Jury took less than an hour. Mama got fifteen years."

"And the man in the brick house?"

Jane's smile was cold as ice. "They got him too. Keisha saw to that. She knew the subway stop, you see. She knew the way to the house. She described it inside and out, down to the pattern on the sheets. She remembered a birthmark on his chest. He had three prior convictions. Her testimony put him away for life."

"Gutsy little girl," Sam said.

"She's a goddamn hero," said Jane.

As if on cue, the front door opened and Keisha slipped out onto the porch. She climbed onto Jane's lap, turning sideways to avoid Sam. "Is it dinner time yet?" she asked.

"In half an hour, Keisha. Did you set the table?"

"Uh-huh."

Jane kissed the top of her head, gave her a hug, and set her on her feet. "Go on, baby. I'll be in soon."

"You gonna read to us tonight?"

"Don't I read to you every night?"

Keisha nodded, satisfied. She edged past Sam and into the house. They watched her go.

"She felt trapped," Jane said softly. "She was scared. You can't hold it against her."

"I don't! It's not her at all. It's me. I'm not ready for this." He was weakening, and they both knew it.

"I'll keep the kids off your back."

"You're making me sound like an ogre."

When she smiled, the skin around Jane's eyes creased and laugh lines appeared around her mouth. He wondered suddenly how old she was, and why she had no man or children of her own. If Lou was here she'd have the story in no time flat. Lou asked very few questions but she had a way of listening that made her a magnet for other people's stories.

"You're not an ogre," Jane said. "I have weird kids."

Sam laughed, and with that there came a palpable easing of tension, a sense that something had been decided, an agreement reached. Though the sun had set behind the old clapboard church, Jane made no move to turn on the porch light. Lamplight filtered through the windows, bathing the porch in a pale yellow glow. Outside snow swirled through the air, settled in lacy filigree across the lawn. Jane watched Peter, who sat hunched on a log by the pond's edge, his stubborn back to her. She willed him to come home, though she knew he wouldn't. He was waiting for the sound of Sam's car.

Sam knew he should leave. For people who lived by the clock it was coming on dinner time. But a great lethargy had gripped him, making it hard to move. It was not so much that he wanted to stay as that he had nowhere to go, nowhere but a house whose emptiness mocked and tormented him. In the depth of his loneliness he had come almost to welcome the nameless caller, who, though he/she rang less frequently these days, still had not deserted him.

I know what you did.

At least someone knew.

CHAPTER 10

"That you, girlfriend?" Portia asked.

Portia was one of those who believed viscerally that if you were talking long distance you needed to shout. Jane moved the receiver away from her ear. "Live from the country," she said.

"How you doing, darlin'? I been meaning and meaning to call. How those children doing?"

"Come see for yourself."

"Sugar, you know how I feel about the country. Gives me the creeps."

"You and Woody Allen," Jane said. She leaned back in her chair, stretched out her legs. Steaming mug of coffee on the oak table. Talking on the phone to Portia was a city luxury, like the *New York Times* in bed on Sunday mornings. "Next Friday's Peter's birthday."

"You don't say. Having a party?"

Jane's smile was grim. Of course she'd offered him a party. Invite some friends, she'd said. I'm not talking pin-the-tail and ice cream. We could do a movie, bowling, pizza—whatever you like.

He'd looked up from the sled he was waxing. A party? he'd replied, polite but puzzled, as if she were offering him the Ganges River. Why?

It's your birthday, isn't it? You're officially a teenager? It just seems an occasion to be marked.

I'll go out and steal some hubcaps, he'd said, and went back to the sled.

"Not a party," Jane told Portia. "Just family. The kids, me, you if you'll get off your ass and make the trip."

"Friday, huh." Jane could hear her riffling through her desk calendar. "Lord, what I do for you."

They planned it out. Portia would arrive early Friday so they could have some time together before the kids came home from school; she would stay for the birthday dinner, sleep over, and return to the city on Saturday. After that they tried to have a normal conversation, but circumstances were against them. Portia was in her office: phones ringing, people shouting, constant interruptions. "Gotta run, girlfriend," she finally said.

"Just one thing," said Jane.

Portia bayed a laugh. "Once in my life before I die, I'd like to end a conversation without you saying 'One more thing.'"

"Peter's sister."

"Hang on." A chair scraped; then came the sound of footsteps, the click of a door latch, and a sudden diminution of background noise. When Portia spoke again it was in her professional voice: clipped, precise, official. "No can do."

"It's his birthday."

"Don't start with me, Jane. I'm so far out on a limb with you already, one more step and we both crash."

"Doesn't have to be a visit. A phone call."

Silence.

"A card, even," Jane said.

"How 'bout I just hand you my head on a platter?"

"Come on, Portia. What harm could it do?"

"Anyway it's out of my hands. The adoptive parents—"

"He's hurting," Jane said. "And you know what? A million to one she's hurting too."

"Jane . . ."

"He was never charged. This is a good kid, Portia."

"I know he's a good kid."

"Never should have split them in the first place."

"Shit," said Portia. "And what were we supposed to do, hold her in limbo till his case was disposed? She's with good people. They wanted her. They didn't want him. Under the circumstances, can you blame them?"

"If they knew him—"

"They don't want to know him."

"Portia," Jane said, pitching her voice to slide under the barbed wire of Portia's professionalism. "She's all he's got."

"He's got you."

"Not enough, not by a long shot."

Portia's long fingernails clicked against the receiver. Jane counted the clicks: five, six, seven.

"I ain't promising a goddamn thing," Portia said.

On Thursday it snowed. Friday, Peter's birthday, dawned clear and cold. Frost on the windows lent a translucent glow to the kitchen as Jane puttered about making French toast. Peter never admitted to any food preferences, but she'd noticed that when she made her cinnamon toast he always took double helpings. She was standing in front of the cast-iron stove in her slipper socks and long flannel nightgown when the birthday boy walked yawning into the kitchen.

"Good morning," she said.

"Morning." He took a seat at the table and poured himself a glass of orange juice. Carlos, Luz, and Keisha followed in various stages of undress. Over breakfast they talked about Portia's visit and about school. No one mentioned Peter's birthday or showed him any particular attention. After clearing their plates, the children went their separate ways to dress for school, and at 7:45 they assembled once again in the kitchen. Jane handed out lunch money and grabbed her car keys. Peter, looking peeved though trying not to show it, was the first out the door.

"Ready?" Jane asked softly.

The children nodded.

"Oh, Peter?"

He stuck his head in the door. "What?"

"Happy birthday!" they hollered in unison.

He couldn't keep from grinning. Gotcha, Jane thought. Made you smile, crocodile. They piled into the station wagon and Jane backed down the drive. Old Wickham looked like a picture postcard, with the frozen pond encircled by snowy pines and the naked limbs of majestic oaks, and her own great yellow house adrift on a white sea. She dropped the children at the bus stop, returned home to let Sam in, then headed south on the Taconic toward Hudson and the train station. Jane was thankful for the glorious day, sunshine sparkling on pristine snow. Not even Portia could resist such beauty. Though, come to think of it, if anyone could it was she. From the crown of her cornrowed head to the tips of her scarlet nails, Portia was a city girl born and bred.

This would be Portia's second trip up to Columbia. The first had been last spring, when she came with her husband, Ike, a New York City contractor. Jane had just found the house and wanted Ike's opinion on its soundness and the cost of putting it to rights. The three friends drove up together from Brooklyn—Jane behind the wheel, Portia beside her, and Ike in the back. "Oh my Lord," Portia kept saying, "would you look at that?"

Jane finally bit. "At what? There's nothing there."

"My point exactly. Miles and miles of nothing. Girlfriend, how you gonna live out here in the wilderness?"

"Come on, Portia, it's not exactly the far side of the moon."

"Might as well be. Do you realize we haven't passed a restaurant or a movie theater in fifty miles? And what the hell are *those*?"

"Cows," Ike said. "Steak on the hoof."

"What a stench," cried Portia, to whom exhaust fumes were as mother's milk. "Shut the window."

This time she was coming alone, and as much as Jane longed to see her, she never for a moment forgot the dual nature of this visit. Portia was Jane's oldest and closest friend, but she was also the social worker in charge of Jane's foster children; so much for maintaining a professional distance. On the whole their friendship had worked to Jane's advantage. Portia, a front-line child-welfare worker for twelve years, knew the system inside out and was not averse to fiddling with it for a good cause. City policy was that black children went to black foster homes, white to white. Hispanics could be either black or white but were not supposed to be both. Jane, with skin the color of café au lait, could pass as either. The way the two friends set it up, Jane's racial identity was pegged to that of the child she was trying to obtain.

Which is what Portia meant about them being out on a limb. She relied on the city's left hand not knowing what its right was doing, a fairly safe though not infallible assumption. So far so good; but even Portia had her doubts about the move to the country, and it wasn't because of the cows. "Like calls to like," she'd argued when Jane first broached the idea. "They'll never fit in."

"But isn't that the American dream? Anyone can live anywhere?"

"Sure," Portia said. "In dreamland."

Jane's mission this visit was to show her friend how well they'd settled in. She made it to Hudson half an hour early and was waiting on the platform when the New York train pulled in. The doors opened, a few dozen passengers got off, but not the one she was waiting for. A knot formed in Jane's stomach, but just as she was about to go search out a phone, a black conductor laden with shopping bags emerged from the last car, followed by a vision in turquoise and gold. Portia was a broad-beamed, dark-complected woman who never sought to disguise her size, but rather flaunted it with bright caftans and wild dashikis. Five-foot-ten-inches and never went out without three-inch heels. "Girlfriend!" she bellowed, enveloping Jane in a meaty hug.

"Hey, darlin'," Jane replied, falling with ease into the cadence of the city.

The conductor laid the bags down on the platform and wiped his brow on his sleeve. "Thank you, Henry," Portia said. She tried to tip him but he waved her off. "You girls have a good visit now," he said, and hurried back to the train.

"What's all this?" Jane asked, laughing.

"Life support," said Portia. "Don't just stand there, girl, grab ahold!"

A mouth-watering, garlicky odor emanated from one of the bags. Jane couldn't help peeking as she loaded the back of the wagon; she saw a huge salami, Saran-wrapped packets of corned beef and pastrami, a jar of pickles, and a loaf of seeded rye. Half the social workers in Portia's department were Jewish, the other half black; a certain degree of culinary cross-pollination was inevitable. Another bag contained an array of Indian and Caribbean spices, a bunch of plantains, fresh chili peppers. "They do have food up here, you know," Jane said.

"Sure they do, sugar," Portia replied. "White bread and mayonnaise."

Back in the house Jane showed off the renovations. The ground floor was finished except for painting, six small rooms converted into three great spaces. Portia stood in the middle of the living room and stretched out her arms. "Me, I'd feel lost in a house this big," she said. Jane smiled but said nothing. To her this house felt exactly right, fit like a second skin. Or maybe it was she who'd expanded to fit the house. All her life she'd wanted a big house full of children, and now she had it.

On the second floor they came upon Sam, building shelves in the playroom. Jane performed the introductions, Sam proffered his hand, and Portia, with her usual subtlety, held onto it while she looked him up and down. "So you're the miracle worker," she said.

"Didn't take a miracle. It's a good house." He smiled but stood awkwardly, waiting for them to leave.

"Mmm, mmm, mmm," said Portia in the kitchen. "That right there is why God created Levi's."

"Down, girl."

"Now I *know* what you been up to. Married?"

"Might as well be. Recently widowed." Jane put a fresh filter in the coffeemaker and measured out four scoops.

Portia settled into a chair, arranging her caftan around her. "How recently?"

"Couple of months."

"Couple of months! What you waiting for, girl? This one ain't gonna last."

"Come on, Portia, the man's still in mourning. Anyway, I'm off men. Waste of energy, most of 'em." Jane poured water into the machine and switched it on. "Guy's a hell of a carpenter, though. I know people say you always end up hating your contractor, but this one's a godsend."

"I bet he is," Portia leered. "Just don't wait too long, darlin', 'cause you know there's only one way to a man's heart and it ain't through his stomach."

"Portia."

"Tell me it never crossed your mind."

"It never crossed my mind."

"Liar."

Jane took two mugs out of the cupboard.

"Nothing wrong with it," Portia said. "Matter of fact it would ease my mind. Can't stand the thought of you cloistered up here, Our Lady of the Sticks."

"Hardly cloistered. I've got the kids."

"Kids don't keep you warm at night. Leastways I hope not."

"Which is why we have electric blankets," Jane said. "Portia, darlin', butt out."

"Well, what am I suppose to think, my best friend runs off to join a Norman Rockwell painting?"

Jane couldn't help but laugh. It was true, the scene outside her kitchen window had a certain paint-by-the-numbers quality, essence of distilled Americana, pretty but two-dimensional; whereas Portia in the flesh was a breath of city air, harsh but in-your-face invigorating. Jane ducked under a wave of homesickness, came up the other side. Maybe settling here was an impossible dream, but it was her dream, wasn't it?

"Emilio's been asking about you," Portia said with a sideways glance. "Said be sure and give you his love."

"That and a token'll get me on the subway."

"I believe the man still cares about you, girl."

"Tell me something, Portia. What would you do if Ike ordered you to quit your job and never work again?"

"You mean after I fell to the floor and kissed his feet?"

Jane smiled. She happened to know that Portia had twice turned down promotions that would have raised her salary but taken her off the street. "Seriously."

"Seriously? I'd tell him to take a hike, Ike."

"So how come you're giving me grief? These children are my vocation, which I am not about to give up for any man."

"Did I say give them up? Person's got a right to a life of her own is all I'm saying. 'Specially in our business, you got to draw a line. Everywhere you look there's children hurting. You can't save 'em all."

Jane poured two cups, left hers black, and fixed Portia's the way she liked it, plenty of cream and don't spare the sugar. She sat opposite her friend and looked into her broad, brown, supremely practical face, a face as familiar to Jane as her own. Somehow, until this moment, Jane had managed not to realize how much she'd missed soaking in the warm, affirming waters of a friendship built up over years. The distance she'd moved couldn't be measured in miles. Nobody here knew her from Adam, nobody knew her people; she was an immigrant on foreign shores, with an immigrant's bright and willful blindness.

Portia reached across the table, engulfed her hand. "I'm just saying what your mama would say if she was here to say it."

Jane remembered a story she heard somewhere. A big storm blew up over the ocean. Next day a woman went walking on the beach and found thousands of starfish stranded on the shore. Each one she came to she picked up and tossed back into the water. A man came along, watched for a while, then caught up.

"What's the point?" he asked. "You can't save them all."

"I've saved these," she said.

Jane told the story to Portia. Portia's long red nails ticked against the table, once, twice, three times. She sniffed. "Who you preachin' to, girl?"

"The converted," said Jane. "Forget it."

Mollified, but constitutionally incapable of ceding the last word, Portia raised her cup in a toast. "Mother Teresa," she drawled, "with attitude."

Jane had planned a simple lunch of omelets and salad, but Portia's deli offerings smelled too good to resist. She was just setting the food out on the kitchen table when Sam walked through.

"I'm off to lunch," he said. "Back in an hour."

"Have lunch with us," Portia said.

Sam, mistaking this for an invitation, declined.

"We insist," Portia said. Behind Sam's back, Jane shook her head vehemently. "Don't we, Jane?"

Jane, having no choice, issued the required invitation.

"Another time," Sam said, although he couldn't help glancing at the platter of meat whose spicy aroma reminded him of distant childhood feasts. "Thanks anyway."

Portia set her hands on her formidable hips and fixed him with a look like a tractor beam. "Corned beef or pastrami?" she said.

Sam glanced at Jane, who smiled through clenched teeth. He took off his cap. "Are those half-sour pickles?"

If Jane had not forgotten Portia's dual role, neither, it became clear, had Portia. Over lunch she set out shamelessly to pump Sam dry. First she put him at ease, talking about the house and praising his work. Married to a contractor, she knew just what to admire. But as the conversation swung slowly and inexorably around to the children, Jane's heart sank. She'd planned this visit down to the quarter hour but hadn't planned on this. Should have known. Portia in her professional mode was the 007 of caseworkers, licensed to snoop; friendship was no barrier to her eagle eye. Not that Jane planned to deceive, but surely there was no need to trouble her friend with every piffling incident and rumor.

"Portia," she said brightly, "is the children's case officer."

Sam looked at Portia. "Our paths don't cross much. Seem like nice enough kids."

"Happy?" Portia asked.

At once Jane envisioned Keisha cowering under her bed, Peter brooding by the pond. She felt a stab of anger at Portia. All things considered, happy was a hell of a lot to ask.

The carpenter surprised her. "Real happy," he said firmly. "As well they should be. I saw plenty of foster homes when I was a boy, but never one like this. These kids have it good."

Jane stared at him. It was the longest speech she'd ever heard from him, and the most personal. "Amen to that," said Portia, and the interrogation was over.

Stark black branches capped with snow framed the sky, a taut canvas of robin's-egg blue. Portia stared upward through narrowed eyes. "What's that? A vulture?"

"A hawk. The vultures come out at night, with the werewolves."

"Don't mess with my head, girl. You know the country give me the creeps. All them weird little insect noises where there oughta be horns and boom boxes and people yelling in a thousand languages."

"And gunshots, and sirens."

"Got to take the good with the bad, darlin'."

With each step Portia's high heels pierced the snow's crust. She held Jane's arm and leaned a little on the smaller woman as they strolled down the lane, the air bright and cold against their cheeks. "City mouse and country mouse," Jane said. "Remember that old story?"

"You ain't no country mouse, Jane. You just wish you were."

"People here leave their doors open. They never lock their cars. A woman can walk out any hour of the day or night without looking over her shoulder."

"And once a year," Portia said, "regular as Christmas, some old farm boy takes his daddy's shotgun and shoots his family as they sleep."

They turned the corner onto Main Street. Thirty feet ahead, young Walter Gower was walking toward them with his buddy Butch.

Why aren't they in school? Jane thought. Her arm tensed in Portia's. Portia glanced at her but Jane stared straight ahead. A dreamlike sense of inevitability had descended upon her.

The boys stared at Portia as if she were an alien life-form. Walter whispered something in Butch's ear, and Butch smirked. As they approached, the boys swung wide, bracketing the women. Two steps beyond them, Walter Gower murmured distinctly, "Nigga."

Portia spun around with a speed that belied her bulk, but the boys were already racing down the street, uncatchable. "Morons!" Jane screamed after them. They laughed over their shoulders.

Portia's ponderous face looked carved in flint. She stared straight ahead. They waded through silence thick as mud toward the country store, where a bunch of women stood waiting for the school bus to arrive. Portia muttered something under her breath. It sounded like "Pillsbury heaven."

"Who was it said you got to take the good with the bad?" Jane said defiantly.

"Girl, you know there's some shit a person can't afford to take."

"That's one thing I miss about the city. No assholes there."

"So those two are just a couple of rotten apples, huh, Jane?"

"That's right."

"You and me," Portia said, facing her at last, "we're big girls. We can take care of ourselves. But the children—"

"Those bums don't bother my kids."

"Do tell." Elaborate sarcasm.

Jane sighed. "Peter talked to them."

"Did he," said Portia with a slow-dawning smile. "Very persuasive boy, our Peter."

For dinner, roast leg of lamb with mint jelly, rosemary potatoes, fresh string beans, and salad. For dessert, a whipped-cream cake big enough for "Happy Birthday, Peter" in blue script and fourteen candles, one for good luck. Peter, looking sheepish but pleased, blew out the candles. They sang "Happy Birthday," then Carlos, Luz, and Keisha rose from their seats and bolted from the dining room. Peter pretended not to notice. A few moments later, back they came, giggling, bearing gifts.

Peter opened the smallest package first. It was from Carlos: six of his best basketball cards, each in its own clear plastic case. Carlos skipped forward. "That's a Magic Johnson rookie card, mint. That's a Alonzo Mourning Holojam, worth a real lot, five dollar maybe. This an Ultra Fleer Shaq . . ."

Peter didn't collect cards, but he knew, they all knew, what Carlos's collection meant to him. "Thanks, man," he said, drawing the younger boy into a headlock and rubbing a knuckle into his scalp. "Shouldn't of given me your best cards."

"It's cool, man," said Carlos. "I wanted to." His eyes lingered on the cards, and he flicked an invisible speck off Shaq's face. "Take care of them, bro."

Keisha's present was a framed picture, a crayon drawing of two large people bracketing three small ones, all holding hands. "Magnificent," Peter declared. "Keisha, baby, tell me you didn't steal this from a museum!"

Giggling, Keisha pointed to her signature. "I made it."

"No!"

"It's us. See, there's you and Mama Jane, and that's me and Luz and Carlos in the middle."

Peter announced his intention of hanging the picture on his bedroom wall that night, then turned to the next present: from Luz, a hardcover edition of *The Adventures of Sherlock Holmes.* "Excellent taste, dudette," he said.

Luz flushed with pleasure. Luz was a hoarder. Food, clothes, string, flattened dimes, books she couldn't read—didn't matter. Giving was hard for her, a skill undeveloped in her old life and still of questionable value in her new; and yet giving to Peter was an unalloyed joy. Peter was good to them, never teased like Carlos did, taught them cool stuff like how to whistle and catch a ball and make a yo-yo come back up to nestle in your palm. His rusty, raggedy smile made her happy.

Jane's present was a pair of hockey skates. Black boots, glistening blades. Surprise his first reaction; here was something he'd never thought to own, never thought to want. Jane, who retained vivid, envious childhood memories of watching the skaters in Rockefeller Center, wasn't sure whose wish she was fulfilling but hoped it was his. She'd seen him watching the skaters on the pond.

He lifted the skates from the box, ran a thumb and forefinger along the thick steel blades. Color flooded his face. "Jeez," he said.

"That the best you can do?" Portia scoffed. "Get off your lazy butt and give her a kiss, boy."

"He doesn't have to," Jane said, but Peter complied without protest. His lips brushed her brow like butterfly wings. First time ever.

"It's nothing much. Talk about your anticlimax," Portia grumbled as she handed over her gift, a blank book with a tartan cover. "To write down all that stuff you don't talk about." She laughed at his look, ripe with suspicion. "Ain't nobody gonna read it, you don't want 'em to."

"Shouldn't say ain't," Carlos piped up. "Teacher said."

Portia sniffed. "Teacher white?"

"Yeah."

"Portia," Jane groaned. "Like white folks don't say 'ain't'?"

Portia ignored her, concentrated on the boy. "That's why. She's teaching you white English. Nothing wrong with that, Carlos. When in Rome and all that. Just don't go thinking white English's the only kind there is."

"Grammar doesn't come in colors," Jane said. "There's a right way and a wrong way, and I for one prefer the right way."

"That's because you are a victim of cultural imperialism."

Jane couldn't help grinning: such a well-worn argument it was, smooth as a stone washed in the river of their long friendship. "So saying 'ain't' is a blow for liberation."

"Girlfriend, I believe you are beginning to see the light."

"No, I ain't," Jane said, and they rocked with laughter while the children watched with puzzled, willing smiles.

It was all too much for Peter. Last time anyone celebrated his birthday was back before his mother died. Better that way. All this unwarranted kindness choked him. Soon as he could he slipped away, climbed the wooden stairs to his eagle's nest. Opened the Sherlock Holmes, tried to hide inside but couldn't. He looked up to see his father lurking in the far corner of the room, beside the wardrobe.

Which father? Peter had two: drunk and sober, bad and good. His good father took him to ball games, bought him a glove, ran alongside Peter's first two-wheeler till his face was the color of the raw beef he purveyed. That father never raised a hand to Peter except to straighten his collar or pat his cheek. His other father beat the shit out of him. Beat him with fists, belts, boots, straps, whatever came to hand. Called him a worthless shit, bounced him off walls, cursed the day he was born.

A person can get used to abuse. A person can learn to work around it, make himself invisible. There are ways to cope when you know what's coming. What's hard is when you never know from day to day which father to expect. Then everything depends on telling them apart.

Peter stared at the father in the shadows.

Hear it's your birthday, the father said. His black mouth gaped in silent laughter. *Good to be alive, ain't it, boy?*

Peter shut his eyes. When he opened them, his father was gone and heavy footsteps were clomping up the stairs. A tap on the door; "Come in," he called.

Portia, breathing hard. "Here you are."

"Here I am."

She plopped down in his desk chair, which groaned but held. Peter willed her to leave but her bulk was impervious to thought waves. She settled in.

"So, Peter, how does country life suit you?"

"It's okay."

"You don't miss the city? Your friends?"

He shrugged. He might bitch and moan to Jane about this old hick town, but Peter was far too well-versed in keeping family laundry from public view to complain to Portia.

"I wish you could trust me," she said.

"You're not my enemy."

"But not your friend, either, is that it?"

"Friends are equal," he said gently. "You have power over me."

"You got that right, baby. Lucky thing I care. Lot of people care about you, Peter."

Sure, he thought. People who didn't know him.

Portia sighed. "You ran off so fast, I didn't get to give you this." She extracted a square white envelope from the folds of her caftan.

His name, carefully printed; no return address, but as soon as he saw the writing Peter knew it. Had to grasp the bed frame to keep from levitating. She tossed the envelope into his lap; he picked it up, looked at her.

"All right, all right," she said, levering herself out of the chair. "I'm going." At the door she looked back. "You can answer her. It'll go through me and yes, it will be read. But you can answer." She shut the door behind her.

Opening the envelope, his hand shook so badly he gave himself a paper cut under the nail. Blood dripped onto the card. On the front a rainbow. Inside, a printed message: "Follow your heart." On the facing page a note in a child's block lettering. "Dear Peter, Happy Birthday. I am fine. My new famly is nice to me. I miss you very much. Love, Maura." A heart beside her name, pierced by an arrow.

CHAPTER 11

Sam was lying on the couch in sweatpants and a T-shirt, dozing to the news, when a knock at the kitchen door woke him. He glanced at his watch. Eleven-fifteen on a miserable Saturday night—who the hell could it be? Opened the door to find Melissa Mueller, half-drowned by the look of her. She stepped in out of the freezing rain, shut the door behind her, and leaned against it, breathing hard. Her red and gray Wickham High jacket hung open; underneath she was soaked to the skin. White blouse clung so tight a blind man could see she wore no bra. Gorgeous tits, he couldn't help noticing, plump and perky. "Jesus, Melissa, what happened to you?"

Wrapped her arms around herself; shivered. "Can I come in?"

"You *are* in. Come on, I'll get you a towel."

He gave her two and a dry sweatshirt. She disappeared into his bathroom. He spoke through the door. "Want me to call your folks?"

"No!"

He retreated along her wet trail. Turned off the TV, paced the floor like an expectant dad. Coffee, he thought. Does she drink coffee yet? Didn't have any cocoa. He put up a pot. She took her time. Came out, finally, bare-legged, wearing his sweatshirt, which came down to mid-thigh. He averted his eyes.

She laughed. "It's okay, Sam, I'm not gonna bite you."

When did she start calling him Sam? Country kids, Melissa and Billy had always called them Mr. and Mrs.

"What happened?" he asked.

"I went out with this octopus from the football team, couldn't keep his tentacles off me? Every time I peel one off my tit there's another one crawling up my skirt?"

Sam, trying his best not to picture this, broke into a sweat.

Melissa curled up on the sofa. "I'm like, 'Chill, asshole,' and he's like, 'Come on, baby, you know you want it,' and I'm like, 'In your dreams, Junior.' So finally I just got out and walked home."

"Only you didn't."

She rolled her eyes. "Right. If my father saw me all soaked and all, he'd kill that creep, which I wouldn't exactly mind except then *he'd* get in trouble."

Sam grunted. Like a lot of quiet men, Willem had a hell of a temper when he cut loose. Wouldn't be overly pleased if he could see her now, either.

"I thought maybe I could dry my stuff here? That way they'll never know I had to walk." She looked up at him, smiling her Lolita smile. "You don't mind me hanging out for a while, do you?"

Sam remembered the kiss bestowed on him Thanksgiving Eve, the hand beneath the table, and suffered a faint unwelcome stirring in his loins. "I'll throw your stuff in the dryer." He retreated to the bathroom, where her clothes lay in a puddle on the floor. Blouse, skirt, panties. So what was she wearing underneath the sweatshirt? Wicked little tease. A moment's pity for the football octopus, then he wondered if she hadn't made the whole story up. He picked up the panties, lacy, pink, moist and warm. Felt himself harden. Shameful: he'd known this girl forever, watched her grow up under his nose. He could hear her moving around the living room. Now what was she up to?

"Got any matches, Sam?"

"Kitchen. On top of the stove. Coffee's made," he added, but she didn't answer. The washer and dryer were in an alcove of the bathroom, hidden behind louvered doors. He tossed in her things, turned on the dryer. Glanced at himself sideways in the full length mirror on the back of the door. Maybe she wouldn't notice. Fat chance.

He smelled the weed the moment he opened the door. "Damn. What the hell do you think you're doing?"

She held out the joint. "Want a hit?"

"You shouldn't be doing that!"

"Come on, Sam. I know you smoke. I've smelled it a million times. You might have offered me some."

He laughed incredulously. Wasn't that a picture, him turning on his best friend's teenage daughter. "Melissa, you're way out of line."

She got up from the sofa, crossed the room to where he stood. Came so close her nipples brushed his T-shirt. Put her arms around his neck, blew smoke in his face. Sam, unmoving, barely breathing, said, "You're a very naughty girl."

Her mouth went to his ear. Her hair smelled damp and sweet, like wet grass. "If I'm so naughty," she whispered, "why don't you spank me?"

Line from a B movie, he thought. A saving notion, that plus the thought, What would Lou say? He backed away into an armchair. Melissa followed, plumped herself into his lap. Wriggled. God Almighty, he prayed, give me one fucking break. The sweatshirt rode up. Another inch and he wouldn't be responsible. How long had it been? Too long. His hand had to go somewhere; he laid it flat against her smooth bare thigh. Why not, why the bloody hell not? What sense did it make, a man who'd done what he had, balking at sex with a willing ripe girl? Seventeen wasn't so young. If she was a virgin he'd eat his boots. She turned around, held the joint to his lips, leaned into him. The soft mound of her breast nudged his chest. The inside of her wrist pale and smooth, blue veins delicate as thread. He summoned Lou, who refused to appear; he pictured Willem's righteous wrath. Like a man setting a back fire, he invoked the image of Kate: fight lust with phantom lust the idea, but with Melissa's buttocks pressed against his erection it was an uneven match. A whole separate dialogue going on below. His groin on fire, resistance bleeding out.

The phone rang.

Sam jumped up so fast Melissa slid off his lap onto the floor. Ran to the kitchen, snatched the phone like a drowning man seizing a life preserver. "Hello!"

"I know what you did."

The spell broken, he succumbed to feckless gaiety; greeted his tormentor as an old friend well-met in the wilderness. "How are you? Good to hear from you again."

Puzzled silence on the other end; then came the ominous whisper, not untouched this time by indignation. "I *know* what you did."

"Hey. Nobody's perfect," Sam said, then hung up and did a little war dance in the kitchen. Melissa watched from the hall, open-mouthed. He glanced over, saw her, with infinite relief, once again as a child, skinny legs and all. "Saved by the bell."

"Sam!"

He made her get dressed. Clothes still damp but dry enough. He drove her down the hill. Her house was dark, but the porch light was on. Melissa refused to get out. Sat in his car staring straight ahead, shoulders rigid, tears on her cheeks. "I love you," she said. "I've loved you since I was fourteen years old."

"Honey, you're breaking my heart. I'm an old man."

"You're forty."

"Old enough to be your father."

"But you're not."

"Melissa, please."

"You didn't think I was too young back there."

"I'm not saying I wasn't tempted. Can't deny it, can I? But it wouldn't be right."

"You're in love with my mother!" she cried.

"I'm in love with my wife."

That stopped her. She turned to look at him. "Your wife is gone."

"I know that here." He pointed to his head. "But not here." His heart.

Which, though true as far as it went, begged the question of his obvious response to the girl. A purely physical response, no element of tenderness or sentiment. Another thirty seconds of her writhing on his lap and he'd have forgotten who she was, forgotten who he was, just said damn the consequences and stuck it to her good and hard. A strange and unexpected development. For thirteen years Sam had been married to Lou and for thirteen years he'd been faithful, an effortless fidelity derived neither from principle nor lack of opportunity, but rather from the fact that once he met Louise, the separate streams of love and sexual desire had merged into a single driving force. While she lived, he could not uncouple one from the other. He might admire other women, might even speculate idly, as he had with Kate; but the switch that transformed thought to action had seemed permanently disabled.

When he buried Louise he'd said good-bye to those parts of himself he'd invested in her. Good-bye to love, desire, and hope for the future. To the grace inherent in his hands, sullied forever by what they had been forced to do. To his heart, that broken, useless appendage. But not, apparently, to his dick, which had proved to have a life of its own.

The incident with Melissa continued to infect his thoughts long after they'd parted. Lust was a genie that once uncorked could not be contained. Sam went about his business as usual—worked on the Goncalves house, shopped in Wickham, drank his morning coffee in the country store and his evening beer in the bar of Jessup's Steak House—only now he saw the world through a red haze of horniness. Noticed for the first time women he'd seen a thousand times before: the checkout clerk in the supermarket, the barmaid at Jessup's, the flirtatious postmistress (Mistress Come-Hither, Lou used to call her), the horsey city women who stopped by the country store for their *New*

York Times, the young mothers who strolled down Main Street with their baby carriages. Women hazy with long familiarity sprang into sharp focus; at the same time the world fragmented and re-formed along impressionistic lines. Like Picasso in his Cubist period, Sam saw women as assemblages of breasts, asses, monumental thighs. Interactions he'd previously overlooked—lingering glances, private smiles, hands that rested a moment too long on a pliant shoulder—were also laid bare. Gossip, he perceived, was not all that kept the town going through the long winter months.

Like a newly pubescent pup, Sam went about semi-erect, perfectly indiscriminate, ready at the slightest provocation to spring to full attention. And not just his prick; his head also throbbed with endless speculation. What would those legs feel like, wrapped around his back? Was she a crier, a moaner, a screamer, a scratcher? How would that one taste, feel, smell? As it was all mere fantasy, nothing was forbidden, no barriers existed. Safe within his head, he indulged himself; yet it seemed as if his thoughts leaked out through his eyes, for everywhere he looked, women were looking back at him. Smiling at him, raising their eyebrows, running their hands down their hips. Was it all in his imagination? Sam didn't think so.

One night, a little while before Christmas, Marie Pellagio came over. The sacrificial offering this time a platter of home-baked Christmas cookies. Sam asked her in, suggested coffee. While it brewed they sat at the kitchen table and made conversation about the clinic. She wore a V-necked sweater dress of some clingy woolen material, sheer stockings, high heels despite the falling snow. Leaned forward and touched him frequently as she spoke. "Poor boy," she said, "so skinny." Fed him cookies, traced his mouth with a red-tipped finger, offered up a generous display of uplifted cleavage. Sam's free-floating lust found a focus; he stared, didn't trouble to hide it. Marie drew a deep breath, inflating her chest. She'll be first in line, Lou had said. But talk is cheap and where was she when he needed her?

"Come here," he said. Marie wrapped her gum in a napkin and with a little smile of triumph posed before him. He slid his hand up the inside of her thigh. When she threw back her head, he noticed that a smear of lipstick had come off on her teeth. Tugging her panty hose down to her ankles, he pulled her close. She smelled of Shalimar and damp wool. "Sam," she cried breathily. "Oh, Sam, take me." Lou had said she liked the soap operas; probably read those trashy romance novels, too. Sam shut his eyes and laid her on the table amid the green- and red-sprinkled Christmas cookies—crumbs, by the time they'd concluded, which didn't take long. The coffee had just finished brewing.

"Thank you," he said politely. "Milk and sugar?"

The Goncalves job was done. Jane, ecstatic about the changes in her house, asked Sam to a celebratory dinner the following Thursday. He, in his present unscrupulous state of mind, wondered if he couldn't parlay that gratitude into something more substantial. For now Sam was on a mission, out to ball as many women as he could as efficiently as possible. Romance the furthest thing from his mind; the very thought of a relationship, a girlfriend, a lover, made him gag. He'd felt no more emotion screwing Marie than he would have banging a nail into a piece of wood; maybe less, if it was good wood. Climax was all he sought, not the prelude, certainly not the aftermath, just the thing itself, that fleeting moment of release and forgetfulness. Love and sex, he saw now, were two distinct tributaries of the heart; sometimes they flowed together, more often apart.

Still, it was different this time around. Something had gone out of him, something was missing. Before he met Louise, he'd slept with dozens of women. He didn't love them, but he was grateful and as kind as he could afford to be. Now his desire was laced with contempt; anger animated him, and he was as cold-blooded in pursuit as he was indifferent afterward.

Cruel, Marie called him, when he refused to let her spend the night. As if he would allow that gum-chewing, soap-watching, scent-doused sow to lie in Lou's place! "You never used to be mean," she pouted. True enough, he admitted, but clearly he wasn't the same man now as then. It amazed him that people couldn't see this transformation. Would the old Sam have played upon the sympathy women felt for his bereavement? The new Sam didn't think twice. Would the old Sam have had sex with a woman, then run out without a word? The new Sam took to carrying condoms in his wallet. Two days after the Pellagio encounter he stopped by the post office to buy some stamps, stayed to nail the postmistress in the sorting room. Couldn't get his pants on fast enough, after. Picked up his mail and left her mewling on the table.

Why? He did wonder, was not beyond shame. Sam tried to look into his heart but couldn't find it. All that remained was a burnt-out core, a ball of hardened scar tissue. And anger, that mysterious anger. Serves them right is what he thought, though he had no idea for what.

He accepted the invitation.

Peter and Jane stood on ladders, painting opposite walls of the dining room. The color was the same daffodil yellow as the kitchen walls, with white for the ceiling, moldings, and trim. A strong color, but the room, which incorporated the old dining room and what had been the breakfast room, was large enough to handle it. Full of light, too, with four sets of long double windows overlooking the front of the house. While she worked Jane whistled, well content. Peter worked steadily, silently.

"Done," he said at length.

She turned to look. A fine job, nice and even. "Thanks, Peter. Why don't you go rinse out your brush and roller? You've done enough."

"Aren't you gonna quit, too? You've been at it all day."

"I want to finish this wall, then tomorrow I can knock off the moldings and the trim."

"What's the hurry?" he asked.

He had to know sooner or later. Better sooner, she thought; give him time to get used to the idea. "Thursday night Sam Pollak's coming to dinner."

Peter had been gathering up his paint tray, brush, and roller. Now he put them back down and turned to look at her. Didn't say a word, just looked.

"What?" she demanded.

"Do you think that's a good idea?" His patient, Father-knows-best tone of voice.

"I think it's an excellent idea. Man deserves a lot more than dinner for the job he did."

"I believe he was paid for his work?"

"Nothing wrong with saying thank you." Jane leaned against the top of her ladder.

"Depends on how you say it."

"Peter!"

"You ought to listen to me, Jane. I know his type."

"Oh yeah? What type's that?"

Peter gazed down on her from the heights of his experience. He recognized Sam's brand of charm because his father had possessed the same brand. Sean Quinn had quite literally charmed the pants off the ladies; not for nothing was he known inside and outside the ring as "Hands."

"All I'm saying," he said to Jane, "is you don't need what he's got."

"And all I'm saying is, he's coming to dinner and you'd better be civil."

Sam came to the kitchen door. As Jane left to hang his overcoat in the mudroom, Peter strode in. He checked out the wine on the counter, the flowers in the vase. He turned his blue marble eyes on Sam, who wore a sports jacket with his jeans.

"Don't we clean up pretty," he said.

"Hello, Peter," Sam said.

"Flowers and everything."

"Glad you like 'em." Sam was cool, amused. No way was this munchkin going to spoil his plans. It was none of his business anyway. Was the boy's devotion purely altruistic, Sam wondered, or did he covet Jane himself? Worse luck for him if he did. Some women prefer men, others boys; still others don't like males in any form. Sam had a fair idea of where Jane fitted in. No proof; they'd spent days and weeks alone in the house together and never got a step past proper. But all that time he'd sensed a low-grade current running between them, a field of attraction unacknowledged but not unfelt. Goncalves seemed possible; and if so, well worth the tumble. That he happened to like the woman seemed to Sam regrettable but basically irrelevant. As for Peter: let him eat cake.

Jane returned and produced a corkscrew for the wine. Handed it to Sam, though she was no doubt perfectly capable of opening the bottle herself. It seemed a promising sign. Sam inserted the glistening tip into the top of the cork and twisted. The corkscrew penetrated smoothly. The act seemed to him, as so many did these days, overtly sexual. He glanced at Jane and caught her watching his hands. When their eyes met, her dusky skin turned duskier. Sam smiled to himself. Doable.

Peter, standing to the side, saw this exchange. Fools, he thought. What fools women are. If women could be men for one single day, men would never get laid again.

Every time she looked up from her plate, Sam's eyes were on her. The length of the table separated them, the children spread out between. Peter hugged her side like a guard dog, bristling at the slightest approach. The other kids showed off, competing for the attention of their guest, a most reluctant pied piper. He'd seemed surprised, entering the dining room and seeing the table laid for six. But what had he expected, Jane wondered irritably, a cozy little tête-à-tête? The man had changed somehow, in just the week or so since he'd left them.

And yet she felt warm under his gaze, and aware of his size, the bulk of his body compared to hers. He could, as they say, make two of her. Emilio, her last lover, had been a small man, though *muy macho.* Jane preferred large men, who didn't always need to show off how tough they were. A large man could afford to be gentle. How long had it been since any man had looked at her that way? Emilio hadn't seen her, really seen her, for a long time before the end. All he could see those last few months were the children. Always underfoot, he complained. Everything they did or said seemed to irritate him. "How can you stand it?" he'd asked, until one day Jane couldn't; she told him the truth, that he was more difficult and demanding than any of her kids, and that was that.

Not his fault really. Men just aren't wired that way. But given that knowledge, what was the point of banging her head against a wall? Portia was right about one thing: Jane moving to the country was the equivalent of a gunslinger hanging up his guns.

After dinner they moved to the living room. This room too had been enlarged, the old carpets taken up to expose oak floors in need of sanding, the walls primed but not yet painted. In one corner, a large Christmas tree covered with tinsel and strings of popcorn, underlain with gaily wrapped packages. Lou, visiting so close to Christmas, would never have forgotten presents for the children. Sam never even thought of it until this moment. Too bad. A large brick fireplace dominated the room, and around it Jane had arranged her furniture: a well-worn tweed couch, an eclectic collection of armchairs, straight backs, and child-sized rockers.

"Why don't you start the fire while I get the kids to bed?" she said. "Coffee'll be ready in a few minutes."

Peter stayed behind. Sat in a chair, said nothing, watched with glowering disapproval every move Sam made. Sam got the fire started, then moved over to the stereo, an old-fashioned console with a turntable, and a stack of LPs and 45s on the shelf below. Felt the boy's eyes on him as he flipped through the albums. Pawing through a person's music was like rifling their drawers, but what else could Sam do? He was on a mission.

The records were an odd mix. A bunch of kids' music, Mr. Rogers, Raffi, and the like. Some cool jazz, bebop. A few salsa bands. An impressive collections of female blues vocalists, mostly black but including Piaf and Janis Joplin. Lou had been a die-hard fan of Joplin's. It occurred to Sam, not for the first time, that Louise would have liked Jane Goncalves. He put that thought out of his mind and turned to the 45s, a jumble of vintage rock and roll. Thumbed through some Elvis, Supremes, early Beatles, till he came upon one disc that stopped him cold. Tim Hardin's "If I Were a Carpenter." He slid the record out of its sleeve and heard the song in his head as clearly as he'd heard it the day he married Louise. It was their song. It was playing on the car radio the day he asked her to marry him. They danced to it at their wedding. He closed his eyes and Lou was in his arms, a tall drink of water in white satin, his wife now, to have and to hold forever, till death did them part.

If I were a carpenter
And you were a lady,
Would you marry me anyway?
Would you have my baby?

Her faith in him was greater than his own; yet he resolved on that day that he would either give her a life better than the one he took her from, or die trying. Even as his heart cried out with gratitude for the unexpected gift bestowed upon him, a corner of his soul cringed in fear. For did he not know, had it not been proven to him in the most direct and incontrovertible manner, that what God giveth with one hand He taketh away with the other? "In the midst of life we are in death," the old rabbi had intoned at the funeral, perhaps the one true thing he'd said.

Behind him a voice said, "Put it on."

Sam turned. It was Peter, standing at his shoulder.

"Play it again, Sam," the boy said.

"Bogart fan, huh." Sam replaced the record in its sleeve, buried it in the box. "Don't you have homework or something?"

"Did it."

"She let you wear that in the house?" For a new growth had blossomed on the boy's head, a Yankees cap worn backward, tough-guy style.

Peter's eyes flickered toward the door.

"Guess not," Sam said.

"No offense, Mr. Pollak, but what's it to you?"

Sam's eyes lanced him. If this were his boy, Sam would straighten him out in a hurry. A mouth on this kid the size of the Battery Tunnel. Some might call it spunk. He called it attitude.

Jane backed into the room, holding a tray with three mugs and a plate of coffee cake. Was the boy then to be a permanent fixture? She laid the tray on the coffee table and handed out the cups: coffee for them, cocoa for Peter. She sat on the couch with her legs tucked under her. Sam went to sit beside her but Peter got there first. Sam took a facing chair instead. The kid was starting to piss him off.

Jane waved at the room. "What do you think?"

"I think it came out fine," Sam said. "House is yours now."

Peter snorted. Jane shot him a look. He kept his eyes on Sam.

"So," he said, "I guess we won't be seeing much of you, now that your job here is done."

"It's a small town," said Sam.

"Peter." Jane waited until he faced her. "Good night," she said.

"Good night?"

"Good night."

They listened in silence to his footsteps slowly mounting the stairs. Sam blew out air, leaned back in his seat. "Boy's half Doberman," he said.

Jane laughed. "Exactly. Loyal as hell to his pack and menacing toward strangers."

"Am I a stranger?" Carrying his cup, he took Peter's place beside her. Not too close, not too far.

"You're a man. Generically untrustworthy."

"That's your opinion or his?"

"His."

"Why's that? Old man beat on him?"

Jane didn't answer.

"You planning to adopt him?" Sam asked.

"I foster kids, I don't adopt. If I adopted one, then all the others would feel rejected, like they didn't make the grade. And if I adopted them all, I'd have to stop taking in other kids who are just as needy."

"So these kids, you take them in, invest in them, get attached, then give them up?"

"Goes with the territory."

"Must hurt, though."

"Breaks my heart sometimes," she said matter-of-factly.

"So?"

"It heals." She leaned forward, turned those dark eyes loose on him.

"They do, you know. Anyway it comes down to the old question: Is it better to have loved and lost than never to have loved at all?"

He gave it some thought. Better to have loved and lost Louise, or never to have known her? Louise had been his salvation, but what good was salvation without her?

The fire crackled and flared. Jane's face was cast in shadows. "Anyway," she said, "much as I love Peter, he's the last kid on earth I'd think of adopting."

"Why?"

"He needs a man in his life. A good man."

"Thought you just said he distrusts men."

"Still, it's what he needs. Kind of a homeopathic cure."

"Get him a Big Brother," said Sam, who had by now lost what little interest he had in the subject.

"I suggested that once. Peter swore he'd run away, and I believe him."

Just as well, Sam thought. Pity the poor man saddled with Peter. The fire was dying down. Jane got up, grabbed a log from the stack, and tossed it into the fire. Embers flew up like fireflies. He watched with interest as she took a poker and bent to shove the log into place. Nice ass. He felt the urge to pounce. But Goncalves was no Marie Pellagio, he told himself, no Mistress Come-Hither. Easy does it.

Jane straightened, turned toward him. "Would you like some more coffee? I made a whole pot."

"What I'd really like is some more of that wine."

"Good idea."

While she was out of the room he put a Billie Holiday album on the turntable, turned the volume down low. Jane came back in, holding the wine and two clean glasses. She stood just inside the doorway, taking in the music, looking at him. He went to her, took the bottle and glasses from her hand, and poured the wine. He handed one to her.

"To your new home," he said.

"To your good work," she replied. He took her arm, led her back to the sofa. This time he sat within striking range. Now there was no mistaking which way the wind blew. She frowned into her wineglass. Sam took it and set it down with his. He reached for her. Jane met him with a straight-arm to the chest.

"Back off, Pollak."

"I don't want to back off, Goncalves."

"You know, I finally realized what's different about you. All night long I've been trying to place it. You've got the look."

"What look is that?"

"The tomcat look. Divorced men get it. That 'Gotta get laid tonight' look."

"Ouch."

"Tell me I'm wrong."

She was right on target, but he wasn't about to say that. "I'm here, aren't I? Not somewhere else."

"You're here 'cause I invited you. You're like, 'Hey, if it's available, I won't pass it up.'"

He winced. "So, you're saving it for your one true love?"

"Let's just say I'm holding out for someone who wants *me*."

Her resistance didn't harm her in his eyes, rather made her more desirable. He cupped his hand behind her neck, ran his fingers up into her hair, and tugged lightly. "*I* want you."

Jane reached back and removed the hand. "For more than an hour."

CHAPTER 12

Mildred Lapid led him into the front hall. She brushed the snow off his coat, raised a cheek to his kiss, then cupped his face between her palms and studied it. "Sammy, sweetheart, it's good you came."

The doctor's wife was a round-faced woman with a halo of gray curls, frankly wrinkled, with good humor stamped all over her face. An avid gardener, she babied her plants, bringing so many indoors for the winter that her house resembled a nursery. Her human children were similarly raised, though what seemed zealousness in horticulture appeared rather casual when translated into the realm of child-rearing. They were fed and watered, sheltered and given space to grow. Mildred enjoyed but didn't fuss over her children; it had never once occurred to her to send them to private school in Albany, as most local professionals did. Benign neglect was her policy, and the young Lapids thrived on it. They were living away from home now, the boy at Cornell, the girl at Harvard medical school.

"I was starting to think you were avoiding us," Mildred said.

He squeezed her arm in apology, glad he hadn't stayed away, as he'd thought of doing even at the last moment before leaving his house. In Sam's mind there was only one possible explanation for Lapid's strange behavior the last time they met: the doctor knew his secret and despised him for it. Yet he would not come out with it and voice the accusation. So much of import left unsaid will poison the closest friendship.

Now the man himself emerged from the living room, arm outstretched, voice hearty. "Come on in, Sam. Nasty night out there. Old Santa's gonna get a soaking tonight." He ushered Sam into the living room, Mildred returning to the kitchen. Rabbi Malachi looked up from his seat by the fire and smiled. The Lapids' Christmas Eve dinner for Jews and other outcasts was an annual affair with a variable cast, as the Lapids invited every misplaced stranger or wayfaring Jew in town. Sam was not surprised, though neither was he pleased, by Malachi's presence.

A girl's face peered around the corner of a high-backed chair. Then Jennifer, the Lapids' daughter, jumped up to meet Sam halfway across the room. As they converged there was a momentary awkwardness; were they to kiss, or shake hands as always before? Jennifer settled on a firmer-than-usual handshake and a few murmured words of sympathy, no less sincere for sounding thought out. She blinked hard when she said Lou's name. They'd known this girl since she was in braces; Jennifer had looked up to Lou, even considered midwifery as a profession before deciding she couldn't bear taking orders from doctors.

As Sam sat down, Jennifer and Malachi resumed what seemed to be an argument about religion. Jennifer had always been a contentious child—more suited, according to her father, to law than to medicine. Her thoughts arranged themselves in outline form; her words emerged in paragraphs. Other little girls had tea parties with their dolls; Jennifer held debates—which she always won—with hers. From the age of fourteen she'd been a devout atheist with a tendency to proselytize. Try as she would, she could not get a rise out of Malachi. Fighting with him was like sparring with a snowman.

"The more we learn about evolution and biology and physics," Jennifer declared, "the less we need to posit a supernatural force. Primitive people believed in multiple gods only because they had no other means of explaining the natural forces of the world. Today we know that thunderbolts are meteorological phenomena, not the weapons of some pissed-off Olympian. As science expands its territory, religion will continue to recede. I'm not saying that the religious habit will atrophy entirely; no doubt it serves some sociological need. But certainly it will lose sway."

"Oh dear," the rabbi said, though in rather a humoring tone.

Jennifer heard it and flushed. "'Oh dear'? That's it? You're not holding up your end, Rabbi. Not one word in defense of religion?"

Malachi made a dismissive motion. "What do I know about religion?"

"You're a rabbi!"

"Defrocked." Malachi winked at Sam. "One thing only I know, *maydeleh.* A person takes out of religion what he brings to it. The charitable man finds support for his good impulses, the evil man finds justification."

"What is a defrocked rabbi?"

"A rabbi what goes cold in the winter," Malachi said, and giggled at his own joke. Jennifer, suspecting she was being made fun of but not quite sure how, stared at him unsmiling. He composed himself and said, "A rabbi is a teacher of Jewish law and understanding. So a defrocked rabbi, that's a teacher who can't teach what he don't understand himself."

Jennifer looked over at Sam, who smiled and shook his head; he was staying out of this. The girl turned back to Malachi. "But you still officiate at funerals and things?"

"Yes, I still do that."

"Don't you think that's kind of hypocritical, seeing as how you've lost your faith?"

"Jennifer!" Lapid remonstrated, but Malachi was unoffended.

"Oh, I still believe in the trappings of religion," he said mildly. "It's the substance that eludes me. Which for a rabbi is not very wonderful but also not the worst thing in the world, since Judaism, thanks God, has more to do with a person's actions than his beliefs."

"But do you or don't you believe in God?"

The rabbi shrugged. "You know that philosopher what said, 'I think, therefore I am'? About Elohim I say: We argue; therefore He is."

"That doesn't follow!" the girl cried, vexed beyond proportion. "That's totally illogical."

"So what do you think, Malachi is a crazy man, Malachi argues with himself?"

Jennifer clapped her hand over her eyes. Just then Mildred emerged from the kitchen wearing an apron over a long, embroidered Bedouin dress. There would be a slight delay with dinner, she announced. Mildred's culinary excursions were notable more for their adventurous spirit than for their expertise. She was the Admiral Peary of cooking, determined that win or lose, she would go down in style. Lou and Sam used to have a bite before coming to dine, just in case.

"In honor of our neighbors' holiday," she said, "we're having a Middle Eastern feast; only for some reason the couscous came out hard and the hummus runny. Not to worry. But why don't you all have a drink and relax?"

Jennifer cast a baleful look at the rabbi, then followed her mother from the room. The doctor took orders and fixed drinks, scotch for himself and Sam, a glass of wine for the rabbi. "Let's take these into my study," Lapid said to Sam. "Rabbi, you're all right here?" It was not really a question, but Malachi answered it anyway.

"Go with my blessing. I'll just sit, rest my eyes a *bisl*." He put his head back and rubbed the bridge of his nose.

"Headache," Lapid diagnosed with barely a glance. "Jennifer takes a lot of people that way. Come, Sam."

"I guess you've noticed I haven't been around much lately."

"I've noticed," Sam said. The doctor's study was fine wood and leather, the only plant-free room in the house. They sat on opposite ends of a leather settee, half-facing each other, holding their drinks.

"Something's been weighing on my conscience."

"Your conscience?"

Lapid stared into his drink. "It wasn't right, the way she went. I'm not easy with it, Sam."

Sam had the feeling of a sleepwalker who suddenly awakens in a strange place. He saw ordinary objects with extraordinary clarity. The glass of cut crystal, the amber liquid, the scruffed brown grain leather of the sofa, like an aviator's jacket—all seemed charged with significance, as if he were seeing them for the first or last time.

An unearthly calm had fallen upon him. He said, "You do what you've got to do, Marty. No hard feelings."

"Do?" The doctor's brow furrowed. "But it's too late."

"Too late?" They stared at one another in perplexity. From another part of the house came a murmur of women's voices. For a moment Sam thought he heard Lou's laugh, high and wild, but it was only the wind rushing through the pines. He said, "What are we talking about here?"

"I thought she might have told you."

"Told me what?"

The doctor sighed. "Lou asked me for help. And I refused her."

Sam looked down at his hands, traced the sickle-shaped scars in his right palm. The words he'd just heard failed to converge into a meaningful statement.

"Help?" he said. "What kind of help?"

"Sam. I know you understand me."

"Louise asked you to help her die?"

"Yes."

"And you said no."

"I said no."

"She asked *you*," Sam repeated, still struggling to process the information. Lapid's voice reached his ears from a great distance. Inside, old jealousies stirred like sea monsters looming in the deep: senseless, but how could Sam help it? Such an intimate request felt like a betrayal. And why was Marty telling him? It was like telling a man you'd fucked his wife. He couldn't assimilate this turn of events, couldn't marshal a reaction or move on. It felt as if time itself had ebbed, stranding him on a temporal island.

"Why you?" he asked, though with only the faintest hope of being heard, as a castaway might launch a bottled message.

"Well, I had the means, didn't I? I had the knowledge. And we were friends." Lapid wiped his glasses on his shirttails. His pale blue eyes looked naked. "It happens. Happens all the time, as a matter of fact. You don't talk about it. You play the game. Everyone looks the other way."

The room was overheated. Sam kept forgetting to breathe, then needing to gasp. Amid a welter of confused and conflicting emotions, one clear thought was beginning to emerge. If Lapid hadn't said no, he, Sam, wouldn't have had to say yes.

"Why'd you turn her down?"

"Squeamish," Lapid replied in a tone of bitter self-contempt; what good, it implied, is a squeamish doctor? "Bad enough I couldn't save her. Didn't want her death on my hands. I cared about the woman, damn it. If I'd cared less I might have done it."

Sam looked down at his own hands, splayed on his knees. "And if you'd cared more?" he said.

Lapid's eyes met Sam's, then dropped away. "God spare me such a choice."

"Amen." Sam got up, walked to the window. It was dark outside and light within, so that both worlds fused in the glass, and Lapid's study appeared carpeted with snow. The two men remained for some time unspeaking, each occupied with his own thoughts.

At last Lapid said, "Nothing against it in principle," and Sam understood him at once, as if they'd been conversing all this time. "Situation like that," the doctor went on, "it's whatever you can bear to do. What matters is getting the most out of the time you have. Sometimes people who are dying take great comfort in knowing there's a way out when they're ready. That can't be a bad thing."

Sam saw what Marty intended and felt a distant gratitude. But Lapid's words were mere philosophy, while Sam, with the advantage of experience, saw the matter as pertaining more to physics, specifically to the principle that for every action there is an equal and opposite reaction. Call it an act of mercy, call it love or whatever you will: The fact is, no matter what you call it, there is no free pass.

Sam's mind seemed to him like a murky pond, full of darting, invisible fish. He took no solace in the information that had just been forced upon him. He saw no possible response to Lapid's declaration short of a reciprocal confession, and *that* he was barred from providing. Louise, fearful of the law, had extorted his promise not to tell, which Sam interpreted as meaning he would not volunteer the information that he had killed his wife. If asked, however, he did not hold himself obliged to lie, and if Lapid asked would not.

But Lapid had quite pointedly not asked.

Sam, focusing on his own reflection in the glass, saw hollow cheeks and sunken eyes, the face of a lost man, a ghost. He shuddered.

"Are you all right?" the other said.

Sam kept his face to the window, his back to Lapid. "Why'd you tell me? What good could come of it?"

"I've lost Louise. I don't want to lose you."

"Lose me how?"

"By lying. I failed Louise. I left her to grapple with her problem. I failed you too. I couldn't keep pretending otherwise."

"How does that work? Do I blame you for refusing to kill my wife?"

"I was her doctor. She had every right to expect my help."

"You passed the buck," Sam agreed, without quite saying where it landed.

"Yes. I'm sorry. But you know, it's remarkably easy to be sorry afterward. It's knowing what to do at the time that's hard. Tell you the truth, Sam? Given the chance to choose over, I'm still not sure I could have done it."

Sam said tersely, "Don't blame you. Not a thing you want on your hands."

There was another long pause, again broken by Lapid. "Mildred keeps *hocking* me to hire another midwife. God knows I need the help. But I still think of the job as Lou's. Can't quite get it through my head that she's never coming back. Which makes me wonder if all this fretting over how she died isn't just a way of avoiding the crux of the matter."

Their eyes met in the glass.

"Which is?" Sam said.

"That she's gone," Lapid said. "That's the real nut, isn't it, Sam? Not how she went, but that she's gone."

When Sam and Lapid emerged from the study, they found Malachi dozing in his armchair in front of the fire. Lapid tiptoed past with exaggerated care, but as Sam drew level with the old man, his eyes popped open and gazed directly into Sam's face. Sam halted, rebounding slightly like a fly caught in a web. Malachi's eyes directed him into the facing chair, which Jennifer had previously occupied.

"So, Mr. Pollak," he said. "What about the stone?"

Sam looked at him and drew a blank. "The stone?"

"Your wife's monument. You ordered it yet?"

"Sure," he said. "Sort of."

"What sort of? A stone is something either you have or you don't."

"Drop it, Malachi," Sam muttered. "This isn't the time."

"'If not now, when?' You know who said that, Mr. Pollak?"

"I don't give a shit who said it."

"You need a stone for the unveiling," the rabbi said, and now he was using the voice without the velvet glove, the same voice that had ordered Sam to put away the rope and eat a bagel. "You need the unveiling because it's part of the process."

"What if I don't want to be processed?" Sam whispered.

"Want don't come into it. Certain things just need to be done. Like burying the dead."

"We did that."

"I did. You still haven't. Want to tell me why, *boychik?*"

"No."

Silence fell between them then, and they stared at one another. Malachi's eyes burned with a terrible patience. Sam thought of beacons on a rocky coast, luring sailors to destruction. What did this awful old man want from him?

Mildred's voice broke the spell, calling them in to dinner. Sam tried getting up, but the rabbi's eyes held him pinned like a butterfly to a mounting board. "You got nothing to say to me, Mr. Pollak?"

"Yeah, Malachi, as a matter of fact I do. Mind your own fucking business."

"Which is what, in your opinion?"

Just as they were sitting down to dinner, the telephone rang. Mildred groaned. "Oh, no. No babies tonight."

Lapid took the call in the kitchen. They heard his side of the conversation. "Yes. That's okay. Calm down, now, I can't . . . Uh-huh. How much blood? Is she still . . . ? Yeah. Okay. No, I'll meet you at the office. Right."

Back he came, cringing under Mildred's steely eye. "Sweetheart . . ."

"Don't sweetheart me." But this was said with resignation. Mildred, wife of a solo practitioner for thirty years, was used to holding dinner, not grudges.

"Poor thing's had two late misses," Lapid told them as Mildred buttoned his overcoat. "Looks like she's headed for a third. I won't be long. Eat, drink, and be merry. I'll be back by dessert."

He wasn't. Mildred did her best, but without Lapid conversation at the table sputtered and stalled like a dying car. Jennifer made a halfhearted attempt to provoke the rabbi with pronunciations on religion in general and Judaism in particular; but Malachi appeared impervious. He ate with his head lowered, sighing occasionally as if a great weight pressed down upon his shoulders. Sam longed to be home alone but didn't feel comfortable leaving Mildred before Lapid's return. After dinner they regrouped in the living room, where Malachi sat down in an armchair and promptly fell asleep. He slept like an old man, snoring slightly, with his head thrown back, mouth open. Mildred covered him with an afghan. She telephoned her husband's office and got the service; if he was there, he wasn't picking up. "Probably on his way," Jennifer said. But another half-hour inched by and still Lapid did not return. Sam, seeing his opportunity, offered to stop by the clinic on his way home.

The snow had stopped falling, leaving just enough for a nominally white Christmas. The Lapids' house was just outside Wickham, on a piney hill overlooking the town. Walking to his truck, Sam thrust gloveless hands in pockets, hunched his shoulders against the chill wind. He inhaled the odor of fresh snow, pine needles, and wood smoke, and lit a cigarette. His head began to clear.

Car wheels spun on ice before gaining purchase. Slowly Sam maneuvered the hill. The snow clouds had dissipated, and a full moon shone down upon the earth. The road into town wound between woods on one side, apple orchards on the other. Rounding a bend, Sam's headlights reflected off the eyes of an animal poised on the woodside shoulder: something bigger than a cat, smaller than a dog. When he glanced into his rearview mirror it was gone. The road was empty of cars on this frigid Christmas Eve.

As he drove he reflected on Malachi, the most irritating man he had ever met. The rabbi knew, or thought he knew, what Sam had done. But if Malachi imagined Sam was ever going to spill his guts to him, he might as well climb into that battered old Dodge of his and head for the hills. Confession is said to be good for the soul, but it's mostly cops and clergymen who say it, and surely they have a vested interest. In the beginning, when the wound was raw, Sam had suffered a pressing need to admit what he'd done. As time went by, though, he came to see that some things don't bear talking about; that to seek comfort through confession is to trivialize acts that are without remedy.

The entrance to Lapid's clinic was a narrow road just off Main Street, between the Wickham Savings Bank and Lassiter Realty. This alley led to the clinic's parking area with space for half a dozen cars, beyond which was the clinic itself, a converted wood-frame ranch house. The first thing Sam noticed as he entered was Lapid's Land Rover alone in the lot, parked in its usual place by the front door. The second was the Christmas lights flickering red and yellow through the waiting-room windows. Which was strange, because Lapid never had Christmas lights in his office. The instant Sam opened the car door the smell engulfed him, the worst smell in the world—the stench of nightmares, pain, and terrible loss, the odor of his first failed trial of manhood. The smell of burning gasoline.

Before Sam's eyes a vision arose: a burning car, a face, a silent scream. He thought, No, it's too much. Not again. He ran to the nearest window and peered inside. Tongues of flame slithered up and down the curtains and the room was full of smoke.

"Marty!" he cried, banging on the glass. "Marty, you in there?"

No response came. Sam vaulted the railing to the front door landing. Smoke billowed out from beneath the door. He knew better than to touch the knob. He leapt off the stoop and ran to the back of the building. No flames, but a strong reek of gasoline. He upended a garbage pail, jumped up, and peered into the window of Lapid's office. It too was engulfed in smoke and flame. There could have been six people in that room and he wouldn't have seen them.

Again he shouted and banged his fists against the glass, which rattled but didn't break. When Frank Gower started his campaign against Lapid's "abortion mill," the doctor had put in an alarm system, installed cameras, and replaced all the windows with reinforced glass. Sam jumped off the pail and approached the back door. He was reaching for the doorknob when his hand felt the heat and rebelled, stopping dead. He couldn't force it into the heat. The scars on his palm began to burn.

He pleaded with the rebellious hand. Smoke kills faster than fire, he told it. If I go for help, Marty's dead before it gets here. Right now there's still a chance. It's me or nothing, poor bastard. He took the wool cap from his head, wrapped his hand, and reached for the knob again. This time he grasped it. The knob turned in his grip. Then the heat penetrated the hat and his hand sizzled. He jerked it away and recoiled. Fifteen yards back he fell to his knees, cradling his twice-burnt hand. Now he knew the door was unlocked. Be a man, he ordered himself; but what could a man do against the malevolent beast that occupied that building? Impossible not to sense it as something alive, a fire-breathing dragon, a dedicated mankiller. The dragon exhaled—Whoosh!—and blew out all the windows at once, showering glass onto Sam's bowed head. The dragon belched fire; it licked the outer walls of the building with its ardent tongue; it tossed its head like a flirtatious girl and shot flames out the gaping maws that had been windows.

As Sam crawled back toward the door, pieces of roof fell like Lucifer through the darkness, landing all around him. Again he retreated, batting embers off his coat and hair. When he looked up, the back door itself was engulfed in blue flame.

Now wailing sirens pierced the night.

Willem was the first to arrive. The Muellers had spent Christmas Eve at Kate's parents' house in Wickham, just a few blocks away. He found Sam kneeling in the dirt behind the house. His coat was singed; his hair smelt of fire. Willem bent down to see him better.

"You hurt?"

Without taking his eyes off the fire Sam shook his head.

"Anyone in there?" Willem asked.

"Lapid came to meet a patient. That's his jeep up front."

More sirens. Two more engines and a great many private cars arrived. Mueller moved away, took command. Pumper trucks were directed front and rear, streams of water laid on. A great hubbub arose on the outskirts of the fire, a babel of shouting men, squawking radios. For a while longer Sam knelt still as a rock, while men and machines eddied around him. Then he got up and went around front in search of Willem.

The chief was standing by his engine in the parking lot, strapping on a tank. Sam hardly knew his neighbor. Dressed in his gear, framed by the fire, Willem's bulk took on significance. He was a mountain of a man, a fire warrior to whom other men deferred. The moment he saw Sam, he spoke to him. "You said he was meeting a patient. So there could be two people inside."

"Maybe three," Sam said. "I doubt she'd have driven herself." Another section of the roof collapsed inward. "Three bodies," he amended.

Willem squeezed his shoulder and spoke in the tone he reserved for children and victims of shock. "You never know. We'll take a look." He started to turn away.

"Wait," Sam said. "I have to tell you something. I smelled gasoline."

Willem's steady gaze shut out, for the moment, the world around them. "Of course," he said.

A panel truck screeched into the parking lot and jerked to a stop beside them. Painted on the side of the truck was a rat with a red slash across it. Frank Gower jumped out of the cab, fell to his knees, and crossed himself. "Hallelujah! Talk about your power of prayer."

"Power of prayer my ass," growled Willem. "Get your gear on, we're going in."

"He's in there? The baby-killer's in there? It's an act of God."

"Grab a tank. Let's go!"

"What for? Man's burning in hell by now."

Sam took a step forward but Willem slid in front of him. He grabbed a fistful of Gower's ski jacket. With one hand he raised the small man up, held him with his feet dangling inches off the ground. It was a prodigious feat of strength, but Willem didn't seem to notice what he had done. He just said calmly, face-to-face, "No acts of God on my watch, Gower. You do what you're told or you're out."

The instant his feet touched ground, Gower flew in the chief's face. "You expect me to risk my life for a goddamn abortionist? Fuck that, Mueller."

"You don't get to pick your fires, Gower. Don't work like that. You treat this blaze like any other or so help me God, you'll never work another."

Earl Lassiter had drifted over during this exchange. Stan Kuzak, incongruous in a suit and tie, hovered right behind him. Gower's small eyes shifted from one implacable face to another. Then, muttering under his breath, he turned and snatched his gear from the truck.

Feeling useless, Sam drifted away. Behind the barriers set up by Kuzak's men, a small crowd had gathered out of nowhere, an oddly festive group in their holiday finery. One man caught Sam's eye because he alone wore work clothes, like someone on his way home from a job site or out for a beer. It was Lyle Fertig and indeed he was holding a beer, which he raised in mocking salute to Sam when their eyes met. "Burn, baby, burn!" Fertig hooted. "Bring on the marshmallows."

"Asshole," said a gravelly voice beside Sam's ear. It was Stan Kuzak and he was staring at Lyle. "Wait here a sec, Sam." Kuzak lumbered over to a *Wickham Courier* reporter who was snapping pictures of the fire. He spoke in her ear. She nodded, turned around, and starting shooting the crowd. Kuzak returned to Sam, took his arm, and led him away from the spectators, toward his Cherokee. Settled inside, he lit a cigarette, offered one to Sam, who refused.

"Willem said you smelled gasoline," Kuzak said.

"That's right."

"When did you arrive?"

"Left the Lapids' house around 10:15. Marty was late; Mildred was worried. Cold car, icy roads . . . say fifteen minutes to get here."

"Ten-thirty, then."

"Pretty near."

"Report came in at 10:45," Kuzak said. "Was it you called?"

"No."

The sheriff raised an eyebrow, waited.

"The fire was spreading too fast. I figured by the time I found a phone, called, and got back . . ."

Kuzak nodded. Sam couldn't tell what he was thinking.

"Seen anyone?"

"No."

"Any vehicles?"

"No."

"What'd you do?"

"Tried to get in."

Kuzak reached abruptly for his wrists. For a moment Sam thought he was about to slap on handcuffs, but the sheriff just turned over his hands and examined his palms. The scars on his right palm gleamed palely against blackened flesh. Strands of scorched wool adhered to the burn. Kuzak winced. "Ought to get that cleaned up, Sam. That's a nasty burn."

"I will."

"Where'd you get them scars, anyway? Look like old burns."

Sam wrenched his hand free. He crossed his arms over his chest and leaned into them. Kuzak sat on for a while. Presently his heavy hand descended on Sam's shoulder. "I don't know if you did the right thing, son, but you sure as hell did the brave thing."

"I blew it," Sam said.

"You did what you could."

"Cost the poor bastard his life."

"Not unless you set the fire."

Sam shrugged.

"'Sides which, he may not even be in there. If he was, fire like that, fumes and all . . . wasn't much you could've done for him." Kuzak levered himself out of the Jeep. "Stay put, Sam. I'll send someone by to look at that hand."

Alone in the Jeep, Sam leaned back in the passenger seat. A despairing peace had descended on him, a distant calm. Through half-closed eyes he viewed the efforts of the men outside as if watching a drive-in movie.

Most changes in a man's life are a gradual accumulation of smaller shifts, like an ocean liner slowly changing course, one degree at a time. Virtually undetectable, the stately undertow of time. Every now and then, though, a man knows the very instant in which his life is transformed. Some men say it happens to them with the birth of their first child: one moment they're watching their woman suffer through some primitive, bloody female ordeal, then comes the sound of a newborn's cry and suddenly they're fathers. Sam's epiphanies were of a different order, their lines of demarcation etched in fire. Despite the sheriff's consoling words, Sam had not the shadow of a doubt that if Kuzak had been the one to happen upon the scene, Lapid would be out of there. Dead or alive, he'd be out, which showed once and for all what stuff Sam was made of.

Though tired to the very marrow of his bones, he could not rest. His mind raced; fragments of conversation, sensations, images glimpsed during the night looped through his consciousness. He saw Gower on his knees, Fertig raising his beer; again and again felt the knob turn in his hand while his flesh sizzled. He tried to banish these visitations but his resistance was low. Perhaps he would have escaped into sleep were it not for the pain in his hand. The new burn overlaid the old; present pain met remembered pain. This convergence, along with the smell of burning gasoline that had lodged in his nostrils, raised an irrepressible tidal wave that swept Sam back to the place he least wanted to go.

He stands in his driveway, throwing a handball against the cement-block wall of the garage. Eleven years old and pissed as hell at his family. At his mother, who just pulled him out of the best street stickball game of his entire life, just so they can go as a family to Coney Island. Not even the amusement park, which would be halfway cool, but the aquarium, for Chrissake. And at his father, who naturally backs her up, even though he knows perfectly well which is more important. And Joey, that little traitor, acting like butter wouldn't melt in his mouth, as if he wasn't the one who engineered the whole thing just because they wouldn't let him play. Who ever heard of a six-year-old playing stickball with the big kids?

His mother calls. Sam ignores her. His father starts the car. Sam keeps slapping the ball against the wall. He hears the car, an old VW Beetle, start backing down the driveway. Like they're really gonna go without him. He wishes.

At the bottom of the drive his father leans out the window, hollers, "Get down here, young man!" in the voice that cannot be disobeyed. Sam pockets the ball and starts ambling down the drive, taking his own sweet time about it. In a burst of annoyance his father swings onto the street.

The truck comes out of nowhere. Later they would say it swerved wide around the corner, but Sam doesn't see that. To him it just appears, a big shiny van the color of summer lightning.

For a moment, just like in the movies, time slows. Sam's vantage point shifts to a point outside himself, high above the ground. He sees himself running in slow motion toward the street. The truck lifts the Beetle onto its grill, carries it almost tenderly fifty yards across the Morellis' lawn, mowing down two plastic Jesuses and a Virgin Mary along the way. Sam is thirty yards away when they reach the end of the line. Beetle slams into cinder-block garage; truck slams into car. Truck rebounds, backs onto the street, and stalls. Car looks like mashed potatoes.

Sam is back in his body now, running full speed toward the car. The air reeks of gasoline. Small blue flames spurt under the chassis. From somewhere behind him a voice cries, "Get away! Get away from the car!" but Sam keeps running. He's nearly there when the gas tank explodes. The impact reaches him before the sound. Sam is hurled backward into a picket fence.

The inside of the car is burning. Through waves of heat and fumes, Sam sees movement at the back window. Joey's face appears. His gap-toothed mouth is open wide. His fists beat against the glass.

Using the fence, Sam pulls himself up onto his feet. He lurches toward the car. There's a sharp pain in his side and the heat's like a huge hand on his chest, pushing him back. He lowers his head, forcing his way forward. Somehow reaches the car. The smoke so thick he can't see inside. The driver's-side door handle glows red. He grabs it. Pain explodes in his hand. He can't hold on. He tries but his hand just won't. Pain blots out everything.

The burn was his salvation; it kept him from thinking, it blocked all other sensation. At the funeral, whacked-out on painkillers and tranquilizers, he swayed as he stood, like an old man praying. They made him throw dirt at the coffins; they made him speak meaningless words.

His friends were there, the Italian kids he played stickball with. They were all crying, those boys, snot and tears mingling on their tough little faces. Sam didn't cry. He felt a despair so encompassing that nothing penetrated.

Over and over he heard it was a miracle he survived. Some miracle, Sam thought. More like a reward for bad behavior. His last words to his brother: "I hate you, you little shit." It had taken him thirty years to get over that, and now, sitting in Kuzak's Jeep, he realized that in fact he never had; he'd just got further away.

The driver's door of the Jeep opened, jolting him from his thoughts. Stan Kuzak leaned in, a strange smile on his face. "Brought someone by to look at that hand," he said. He stepped aside. Another man took his place. "Hey, Sam."

"Oh my God," Sam cried. "Oh Jesus." With his left hand he reached for the other's hand. Only when he felt solid flesh and bone did he dare to believe. He pressed the hand to his cheek, then let go and punched Lapid none too gently in the shoulder. "Where were you, you bastard?"

"Hospital. My patient needed emergency surgery. I rode with her in the ambulance. By the time we finished and I got a ride back, it was all over." He nodded toward the house. The fire was out now but the building was a wreck. Nothing left to save. Lapid climbed into the Jeep, set his bag on the floor, and switched on the interior lights. "Let's see that hand."

Sam still could hardly believe the doctor was alive and well, here with him. In his mind, Marty had been dead. This felt like a resurrection, a reprieve.

Once, visiting the dentist for a root canal, Sam was given nitrous oxide. For an hour he sat in the chair in a state of perfect, passive bliss, which had no connection at all to the rather unpleasant things being done to him. Sam liked an occasional high as much as the next man, but this disassociation so spooked him that he never again consented to take gas. Now, with Lapid returned from the dead and himself absolved of murder through cowardice, he felt the same sensation of untethered delight sweep over him. Lapid reached for his right hand; Sam put it behind him and said, laughing, "Get away, man! Damned if I'll be treated by a gynecologist."

"Is the big strong man afraid of a few girl cooties? Don't worry, Sam, they're not contagious." With that, Lapid seized the hand and turned it over. At once the humor drained out of his face. There was an almost audible click as he shifted into doctor mode. He angled Sam's hand toward the light and examined the wound closely.

"Probably not as bad as it looks," he said presently, "but it's full of fibers. What'd you do, wrap something around your hand?"

"Wool cap."

Lapid nodded. "Also, you've reinjured some of that old scar tissue, and I'm not quite sure how that's going to pan out. I can clean this up and put on some antiseptic, Sam, but you'll have to see a burn specialist. I know a good man in Albany."

That didn't sound good. Should've used my left, Sam thought, but really what difference did it make? A carpenter needs two good hands. He asked Lapid if there would be any loss of function.

"Shouldn't think so," Lapid said as he tweezed fibers out of the wound. "You're showing good mobility in it now. May be some additional scarring, though."

"Fair enough," Sam said faintly. Lapid's cleansing of the burn was sending renewed shock waves of pain roiling through his system.

The doctor peered up at him. "I'm hurting you. Sorry, Sam. We could do this in the hospital under local anesthesia."

Sam at this point wouldn't have minded a jolt of Novocain, but he'd spent enough times in hospitals with Louise to want never to return. "Go ahead," he told Lapid. "Finish the job."

Lapid did. With his right hand wrapped in layers of gauze, Sam got out of Kuzak's Jeep. The firemen were coiling the hoses, packing up their gear. The doctor came to stand beside him.

"You covered?" Sam asked.

"For most of it. Have to find another office, though. Replace all the equipment." Lapid grimaced, then turned his eyes on Sam. "Kuzak told me how you got burnt."

"Yeah, well." The elation of Marty's reappearance had ebbed, leaving behind a bitter sludge. Nothing, really, had changed.

"What do I say? Half my kingdom and my daughter's hand in marriage?"

A fleeting smile crossed the carpenter's face. "I'll pass on the princess, if you don't mind."

"You risked your life, Sam."

"I did nothing," he said. "Never made it inside. If you'd of been in there, they'd be picking your bones out of the ashes now. No thanks to me they're not, just pure dumb luck."

CHAPTER 13

Bad things were happening to Peter. It started with his voice. One morning he woke up with a frog in his throat, a deep raspiness in his voice. When it didn't go away, he told Jane he needed to see a doctor. Did it hurt? she asked him.

No.

Don't worry, then. It's just your voice changing.

Like hell! Who died and made you a doctor? And he kept on complaining until finally she did take him to the clinic. Doctor looked at his throat, listened to his chest, and diagnosed puberty.

Puberty? More like possession: a stranger inhabiting his body, tampering with his vocal chords.

A few weeks later, taking a shower, he raised his left arm to soap his armpit and discovered a thatch of foreign hair. Sprouted overnight, seemingly. Before this there'd been a little fuzz, nothing he couldn't ignore. Now a rain forest was growing. In the locker room at school, kids with body hair ran around shirtless, hands clasped behind their heads.

Some eighth-graders cultivated mustaches. Peter loathed these hormonal excretions, symptoms of impending manhood. Not that he wanted to be a woman, God forbid. In his experience, women were nothing but natural-born victims; why else would they marry? He just didn't want to become a man—brutal, gross, and smelly. Nor did he enjoy the messy and exceedingly public process by which the transformation was accomplished. Hair, sweat, acne, breaking voices, growing up a part at a time, advancing, retreating, the self in disarray. Not that girls had it any better with their emerging titties, like trainer breasts. Some, like Marta Kimball, toughed it out, acted like they'd always had those things, you just never noticed before. Others, hobbled by shame, slouched around clutching armloads of books to their chests. Those were the girls that kids like Gower and Hubbell liked to pick on, sneaking up from behind to ping their bra straps. Snakes had it a lot better, in Peter's opinion. First they grew a new skin, then they slithered out of their old. Butterflies better still. People ought to spin cocoons when they feel the change coming on, crawl inside and stay till the metamorphosis was complete. Go in a boy, come out a man. If you had to change, that was the way; not this piece-by-piece, half-and-half bullshit.

He got out of the shower, wiped steam off the mirror for a closer look. No doubt about it: hair. Jane's little pink razor was on the shelf below the mirrored cabinet. For a moment Peter thought of shaving the offending hair. Then he was embarrassed at the thought. What a pathetic idea, shaving his pits. Like that would help, like that would stop the train or even slow it. This wasn't Neverland and he wasn't Peter Pan. Sooner or later it was all coming down. He'd wake up one morning craving coffee. Hairs would sprout on his upper lip. He'd start thinking with his fists. People said he already did, and him just a kid. He'd grow up, turn into a bruiser like his old man. Bound to; it was in the genes.

In school they had separate assemblies for the boys and girls. The school nurse, her square face shiny with sweat, lectured them on the changes wrought by puberty. While she spoke to the boys, Lightfoot stood on the edge of the podium, tapping his paddle against the palm of his hand. Not even his beady-eyed stare could quell the titters that ran through the room. As visual aids the nurse used a color diagram that showed the insides of a boy, and a chalkboard divided into two sections. On the right side, a heading in yellow chalk: PHYSICAL CHANGES; on the left, EMOTIONAL CHANGES. When her lecture was finished, she asked for questions. One hand went up. "Yes, Walter?" she said.

"Wet dreams," said Walter Gower. "Good or bad?"

The audience dissolved. The nurse turned as red as an exit sign. Lightfoot strode to the front of the stage. "Gower! My office, now!"

Walter got a week's detention. Next weekend, graffiti appeared on the front of the school. Big red letters spray-painted a foot high: LIGHTFOOT SUCKS DICK. On Monday the principal summoned Peter Quinn to his office.

"You've got to be kidding," Peter said.

"Do I look like I'm kidding?"

"Why me?"

"All the time I've worked in this district, which for your information has been eighteen years, we never once had a problem with graffiti. It is strictly a city disease."

Peter put his hands on the desk and leaned across confidingly. "Graffiti's for wusses. If I wanted to say Lightfoot sucks dick, I'd get right in your face and say Lightfoot sucks dick."

"I've got my eye on you, Quinn," the principal said. "You might have your teachers conned. You might have that poor misguided woman you live with conned. But I know a troublemaker when I see one. I've got my eye on you, boy."

"Is that it?" Peter said. "'Cause I'm missing lunch."

The pond was frozen solid. Every day after school kids gathered at the pond's edge, skates slung over their shoulders: boys with black hockey skates, girls with white figure skates. Half the pond was given over to a raucous, ongoing hockey game; the other half was for toddlers and girls who formed a chain and played snap the whip. Their laughter rose through the air, piercing the double-paned windows of Peter's room. He watched them wistfully, as an old man watches youngsters play. They flew across the ice, leapt and turned; they skated as easily as they ran, as if they'd been born with blades attached to the soles of their feet. Though Peter treasured the skates Jane had given him, he had yet to remove them from their box. In Brooklyn the kids were into Rollerblading. Peter had been a whiz at that, but he'd never ice-skated in his life.

One day Billy Mueller stopped by on his way to the pond. "Come play," he said. They stood in the kitchen. Billy's glasses fogged up with steam.

"Can't," said Peter.

"Why not? You can be on my team."

"Can't skate."

Billy's mouth fell open. After a beat he said, "I'll show you how. It's easy."

Peter looked past him, out the door. Walter Gower and Butch Hubbell were passing by, skates slung over their shoulders. "Nah," he said. "Thanks anyway."

"You can't not skate," Billy said earnestly. "Everybody skates. I'll come back later, after dinner."

"Tighter," Billy said. "Else your ankles get all wobbly."

"Any tighter and I'll cut off the circulation."

Billy slipped two fingers between the top of the boot and Peter's ankle. "Tighter."

When Billy was satisfied, he stepped out onto the ice. Peter followed, clutching at air. Two steps and his legs slid out from under him. "Goddamn!"

Billy gave him a hand up. "Hold your arms out like wings. It helps you keep your balance."

Peter spread his arms. Pictured the others swooping over the surface of the pond, tried to imitate the motion. But his steps were tiny; hobbled by fear, he inched across the frozen surface. The world rested on two thin blades.

"Don't walk. Push off and glide." Billy demonstrated.

It looked easy. Peter tried and fell flat on his face. "Shit."

"Get up."

"Easy for you to say," Peter grumbled, but he managed. "How thick is this ice, anyway?"

Billy skated in circles around him. "Thick enough to drive a car on. My dad checks it all the time."

Gradually Peter found his balance and his faith. The old Rollerblade rhythm clicked in. With Billy at his side chirping encouragement, his stride lengthened and his movements grew fluid. The pond was not at all smooth, as it looked from his third-story window, but rather bumpy and ridged, pitted with frozen debris. After an hour on the ice Peter's ankles ached and his ass was sore, but he made it all the way across the pond and back without falling. "That's enough for the first time," Billy declared.

They sat on the rocks unlacing their skates. It was starting to snow, fat white flakes light as kisses. Billy giggled softly. Peter said, "What's so funny? I look like a geek out there?"

"No, it ain't that. It's just weird: here you're the smartest kid in the class and I'm the dumbest, and I'm teaching you."

Peter punched his shoulder. "Says who you're the dumbest? Shit, boy, you've got more sense in your little finger than most of them do in their whole damn selves."

Billy looked at his hands. "I do?"

"Hell, yeah."

They parted on the sidewalk in front of Jane's house. Peter was halfway up the drive when Billy called after him. "Peter?"

"Yeah?"

"Which finger?"

They practiced nightly until Peter could go for an hour or more without falling. He learned to stop, turn, skate backward. After a week Billy declared himself satisfied. Peter, he said, was to come out the next day after school and join the game. Peter agreed, but that night it snowed again, this time heavy and hard. By the time the snow tapered off, around noon the next day, fifteen inches had accumulated. Schools closed early, and the students were bussed back home.

Jane had shoveled a narrow path from the road to the kitchen door. Peter took the shovel and widened the path. Then he attacked the driveway. He'd cleared about half when Jane came outside and took the shovel from his hand. "I'll finish up," she said. "Why don't you get out the sleds and take the kids sledding?"

"Where?"

"Billy Mueller called. You're all invited over there."

Peter had never been to the Muellers' house, but Billy never tired of pointing it out from the school bus. "He doesn't live on a hill."

"I guess they use Mr. Pollak's hill, the lawn in front of his house."

"Forget that!" Peter said, just as Luz and Keisha came running out of the house, bundled in bright red Kmart snowsuits and yellow vinyl boots. Jane he could defy but there was no resisting the little girls. He waded into the backyard and cleared the snow away from the shed door. The Atkinses hadn't bothered to clear out the garage when they sold the house. In the loft Jane had found two old Radio Flyer sleds with rusty runners and traces of red trim on the wood. Peter had scraped off the rust, sanded and varnished the wood, and waxed the runners. Now they looked as good as new.

Through a village transformed, made radiant by snow, he pulled one sled and Carlos the other, while Luz and Keisha rode like queens, clapping their hands and calling out orders. The plows had been out; the streets were packed hard. In front of nearly every house people were shoveling, calling back and forth to one another. Except for a few teenage boys going house to house with a snow blower, there were no kids to be seen. Peter understood why when he turned the corner onto Billy's dirt road. The hill leading up to Pollak's house was swarming with children on sleds of all kinds. Few were traditional sleds; most were improvised out of garbage-pail lids, slabs of curved corrugated plastic, flying saucers, tiny wading pools, even plastic sheeting. It looked like every kid in Old Wickham was there.

Billy waved from the top of the hill and rode his flying saucer down to meet them. His pudgy face was flushed, his snowsuit sleek as an otter's skin. He led them to the driveway, where a line of kids trudged upward with their sleds. Carlos followed willingly, but Peter balked. "This isn't your house."

"It's okay," said Billy. "Mr. Pollak always lets us sled here. He's really nice. Mrs. Pollak's nice too, only she's dead now. She used to make hot chocolate for all the kids, but she can't no more 'cause she died."

Carlos, with Luz in tow, was already halfway up the drive. Peter had no choice but to follow, hauling Keisha behind. He lowered his voice. "What'd she die of?"

"Dunno. She was sick a long time."

"Must have pissed him off, her being sick so long."

"Huh?" Billy's childish blue eyes were perplexed.

"Forget it," Peter said, looking away.

"He wasn't mad," Billy said after a minute. "He was sad. He took good care of her. Mr. Pollak's a real nice man."

"Whatever," Peter said. By the time they reached the top of the hill, Carlos and Luz were halfway down the hillside, racing toward a cluster of hemlocks that separated the lawn from the road. "Oh, no!" Peter cried, springing forward. But Billy caught hold of his jacket and said, "Wait, watch." The sharp slope of the lawn tapered at the bottom, leveling off for the last thirty yards. Carlos's sled coasted to a halt five feet before the tree line.

"See, that's what's so cool about this hill," Billy's voice said in his ear. "You always think you're gonna crash, but you never do."

Sleds were launched from the crest of the hill, just below the deck. Peter spotted a bunch of kids from his class: Joey Whitehill, Mike Rizzo, Walter and Butch naturally—no Eden without its share of snakes. Girls, too, Marta Kimball among them. Marta wore a sleek pink-and-black ski suit with racing lines. She was looking at him. When their eyes met, she smiled and waved.

"Well, look who's here," Walter Gower said, following her smile to its source. "Who invited you, city boy?"

"Yeah," echoed Butch, "who invited you?"

"I did!" Billy said. Walter didn't scare him with Peter around.

"Aw, ain't that sweet. Billy invited his little boyfriend to go sledding."

"Shut up, Walter," Marta said. "He's got as much right to be here as you do." No one said shut up to Walter except Marta, who never had a decent word to say to him. Walter told everyone that was because she was secretly hot for him.

Peter left the sled with Keisha sitting on it. He walked up to Walter and spoke in a voice pitched for his ears only. "I thought we settled this thing between us, dude. But hey, you want to try again, just say the word."

Walter took two steps back and fixed a scornful smile to his face. "Sled all you want, city boy. Hope you break your neck."

He sat on the lip of the hill, Keisha's arms clasped tightly around his waist. Pollak's lawn was steeper than his driveway, which was steep enough. From up here it looked a hell of a long way down. Peter had sledded in Prospect Park with his dad when he was very young, later with his friends—but the park had no hills like this. He took a deep breath, pushed off, and launched the sled.

They hurtled downward, skimming the surface of the hill. The wind battered his face, drawing tears from his eyes. Keisha shrieked joyously. Peter touched the steering bar with his left foot and the sled veered sharply. They reached the bottom flying still. Through a haze he saw a solid row of thorny brush and massive hemlocks rushing toward him. He yelled. The sled decelerated as quickly as it had accelerated and coasted to a stop a yard or two before the trees.

"Jeez," said Peter, wiping his brow.

"Again, again!" Keisha cried ecstatically.

At first he went down with Keisha and Luz, but in a short while the little girls drifted off to sled with classmates, and Carlos too found a friend his age. Peter went down alone. Lying on his stomach, he seemed to slide faster. The sled's runners carved grooves in the snow. Flakes of ice flicked back in his face, frosting his lips and eyebrows. Billy was right: no matter how many times you didn't crash, it always felt like you would. The effect was like riding a roller coaster.

He climbed up after a run to find a bunch of the older kids lined up side by side along the crest of the hill. "Yo, Quinn," Joey Whitehill called, "wanna race?"

Peter lined his sled up beside theirs. "No fair," someone said. "Quinn's alone." The others had two kids per sled. Peter looked around for Carlos or Billy, who were nowhere in view. Then he felt someone sit down behind him. He turned around. Marta Kimball smiled at him, a bold smile, not flirtatious. "Let's do it," she said.

Joey yelled, "On your mark, get set, go!"

Marta held him tight the whole way down. She buried her head in his back. Even through all their clothes Peter could feel her breasts like hard rubber handballs pressed against his back. It felt like nothing he'd ever felt before.

They won the race and walked back up the hill together. Peter pulled the sled and watched Marta obliquely as she chattered. Her cheeks were bright, and she spoke animatedly, her words encased in little white puffs of condensed breath. He wondered if she would ride down with him again.

She told him that some of the kids were coming over to her house after this. "My dad said he'll take us sleighing; we have this really cool old sleigh that we hitch up to the mare. And my mom makes cider. Want to come?"

For a moment he was tempted; then the absurdity struck him. Peter could just feature himself riding in a one-horse sleigh, holding hands under a blanket, drinking hot cider with the gang. This is your life, Peter Quinn—not. He was not one of the gang and never would be. He was set apart, an outcast; he occupied a different world from these children, and he was old, way too old for junior high romance. Not for him the little notes, musical chairs at lunch, whispered tales of "he said, she said."

"No, thanks," he told her.

"You sure? It'll be fun."

"I'm sure."

Her look of disappointment cost him a pang or two of regret; but he told himself it was for her own good. If she knew the truth she'd turn from him in horror, and who could blame her? Surely not Peter.

The last few yards passed in silence. As they neared the top of the drive, a truck turned into the driveway, climbing slowly between two streaming ribbons of children. The truck passed Peter to park at the top of the hill. Sam Pollak got out.

Marta waved and kept walking, but Peter froze. Felt like a thief caught with one leg dangling through the window of the man's home, like a prime-time fool. Instead of turning toward the house like he should have, Pollak came over. Peter steeled himself, certain that in two seconds he'd be ordered off the property, which in a way he wouldn't blame the guy after that business with Keisha. Peter no longer believed Pollak had meant the girl any harm; once he calmed down, he'd taken Keisha's word for that. But he never said anything to Pollak, and Pollak never said anything to him; so no way the carpenter didn't have it in for him. Peter figured he was just biding his time.

"How's the sledding?" Sam asked.

"Okay."

"Some hill, huh?"

"Way cool."

"Best in the county. Why we bought the place." He looked away then, and noticed the sled. "Genuine Radio Flyer, huh? Don't see many of these any more."

"It's old. Jane found two of them in the garage, really bad shape, all rust and splinters. I scraped 'em, sanded 'em, painted and varnished." Peter was mortified to hear himself babbling this way, sucking up to a creep like Pollak. Wasn't nothing but a goddamn sled, anyway. And yet, when Sam ran a critical finger along the edge of the wood, nodded, and said "Not bad," Peter could barely mask his pleasure.

It's hard enough to be an outcast, but harder still when the people you're cast out of don't seem to realize it. Something changed after that day on Pollak's hill. Suddenly kids who'd never said a word to Peter were acting like old homeboys. In gym he got picked first for teams. Kids sat next to him on the bus, talked to him at lunch. The girls called him Peter, the boys Quinn; nobody, except Walter Gower and Butch, called him city boy. Walter was still his enemy, but Walter had lost sway.

Meanwhile Jane was going through changes. She kept pushing: urging him to write to his sister, edging him out of the nest. Some kids started coming around, asking him to play. Jane made him accept invitations that, left to himself, Peter would have refused. He explained to her very clearly that this was not his thing, that he had no interest in these country kids and their pastoral amusements; that he wanted to be left alone. Jane would listen in perfect sympathy, then hand him his jacket and shove him out the door.

He wouldn't, otherwise, have joined in the hockey game. But there was nothing else to do in Old Wickham, and once he started playing he got into it. The games were fast and rough, but not undisciplined. Fighting for the puck, checking and being checked, racing, falling, all reminded him of an earlier time, an earlier self: the boy he'd been before his mother's death.

Yet even as they brought him back to himself, the games also drew him out. Lofty detachment is not a viable attitude at a moment when you're all alone with the puck, no one to pass to, and a Mack truck on skates named Walter Gower is bearing down on you. At times like these, a person forgets who he is. He forgets he is different and apart from all others. He concentrates instead on saving his skin. And if he should happen to sink the winning goal, slip it right between the goalie's feet and sweetly into the net, and if his teammates should surround him and pound his arms and back, a person might so far forget himself as to laugh aloud for joy.

But such lapses as these were few and fleeting, and when they passed, as inevitably they did, Peter reverted to the solitary creature that he was. Could he turn back time, bring the dead back to life? For some acts, he reminded himself, no remedies exist. He was a living example of Newton's law that for every action there is an equal and opposite reaction. The very blow that stopped his father's heart had sent Peter hurtling into exile.

It was a Sunday morning in the fall, two years after his mother died. Peter, making breakfast for himself and his sister, moved gingerly around their father. He would have taken Maura out to eat, but he had no money and this was not the time to ask his father for anything. Sean Quinn sat slumped in the armchair at the head of the table, his eyes open but glazed. He was an ex-boxer, an Irish middleweight nicknamed "Hands" for those appendages which, in contrast to the rest of his solid but compact body, were as big as meat cleavers and nearly as dangerous. Those battering rams would undoubtedly have made him a contender, had it not been for Sean's single solitary weakness: his nose. A nose that bled if you looked at it, cracked if you tapped it. A nose with all the stamina of fine china. The standing joke in the gym was that Quinn's nose had been busted more times than Darryl Strawberry. Every time it happened, the damage went deeper, till it reached the point that Sean couldn't fight anymore.

Now he worked in a wholesale butcher shop. He spent his days hauling carcasses and cutting meat, his nights watching TV and drinking. Beer on weekdays, which didn't affect him, and bourbon on weekends, which did.

The table held an empty fifth of Wild Turkey, three overflowing ashtrays and a dozen or so bottles of beer. Sean wasn't up early; he hadn't gone to bed. The children tiptoed around him. Maura was safe enough, but Peter took care to stay out of reach. This was the red zone, the tail end of a binge.

"Want coffee, Dad?" Peter kept his voice low.

"Hell with coffee," his father replied. "Gimme a beer."

Peter knew better than to argue. Sean was quiet now, but he could turn on a dime. Peter never fought back when he did. Resistance was not only useless but dangerous. Flight and a keen awareness of Sean's moods were his son's first and last lines of defense. If he couldn't escape, Peter just shut down into survival mode: took his licks and tried not to cry.

He took a bottle of Bud from the refrigerator, opened it, and passed it to Maura to bring to their father. But just as she reached him, Maura tripped over her own shoelaces and stumbled. In what seemed like slow motion, the bottle arched from her hand, somersaulted through the air, and landed with circus-precision right in Sean's lap.

The children froze. Sean gazed down at the puddle forming in his lap. He righted the bottle and set it on the table. Then, as casually as a man swatting a fly, he backhanded Maura, whipping his hand across her face. The little girl flew across the cramped kitchen, hit a wall, crumpled to the floor, and lay sobbing.

Peter had been beaten more times than he could count. Whipped, punched, and kicked, bounced off walls and choked till he passed out. Their mother, too; Peter's first memory was of her lying on the kitchen floor, crying into her apron. But this was the first time Sean ever hit Maura, and it was the last.

Something snapped in Peter. He charged head-first, ramming his father in the gut. Sean's chair toppled and they fell together to the floor. Peter pummeled his father's chest and belly till Sean, roaring with outrage, wrapped his thick arms around his chest and squeezed.

He was drowning in his father's fetid breath, the stench of ashes steeped in beer. Couldn't breathe. Black holes swarmed before his eyes, pulling him in. He heard screaming, but it sounded far away and too late. Drawing on the last of his strength, Peter slammed his knee up into Sean's groin.

A solid hit that would have laid a sober man out. It just pissed the hell out of Sean. Now Peter was scrambling away on all fours, trying to get the table between them. Sean lunged, snagged Peter by the ankle, and hauled him back. He flipped the boy over onto his back and jammed his forearm into Peter's throat. He raised his massive fist.

Maura screamed. As Sean looked up blearily, momentarily distracted, Peter cocked a leg and kicked his father in the face.

Sean sprawled backward. Blood spurted from his nose, now banked steeply to the right. He fingered it, and astonishment spread over his face. "Son of a fucking bitch. It's broke!"

"Serves you right, you bastard!"

"Boy," said Sean, more in sorrow than in anger, "you're dead meat."

This from a man who knew dead meat when he saw it. Peter stood up. Sean too, positioning himself between Peter and the door. When Peter tried to edge past, Sean shifted to block him. He moved forward, reaching for his belt buckle.

Peter retreated until he couldn't go any further. He reached behind his back, groping blindly for the block of knives that stood on the countertop. His hand closed on a wooden hilt. He pulled out the knife and pointed six inches of gleaming steel at his father's heart. "Keep away! Leave me alone."

Sean eased the belt out of his pants and held it with the brass buckle dangling. His lips retracted in a lupine smile. "Kid's got the fuckin' street sense of a fuckin' ballerina. You don't show a knife 'less you plan to use it, boy, and you ain't got the guts." He snapped the belt at Peter's face. Peter ducked, but not soon enough. The buckle caught him on the forehead. Blood dripped into his eyes. As Sean raised the belt again, Peter struck with the knife. There was a momentary resistance; then the blade plunged to the hilt into Sean's chest.

Sean looked down at the knife. He looked at Peter and swayed for a moment, as if debating his next move. Then his knees buckled and he crashed to the floor.

All of this Peter remembered vividly and often. Of the events that followed, however, he retained only fractured memories. Odd things, like the maddening shrill of a teakettle on the fire, which turned out to be Maura screaming. Or the sight of his father lying on his back on the kitchen linoleum, huge and immensely out of place, like a beached whale. To this day Peter didn't remember calling 911, though he knew he had: They played the tape at his hearing, and he'd listened in amazement to his own stricken voice pleading for help.

One image, though, he could never forget no matter how hard he tried. He was sitting on the floor with his legs outstretched and his father's head cradled on his thighs. The drunken rage was gone. In its place a look of wonder had come over Sean's pale face. His eyes locked onto Peter's. When he opened his mouth to speak, pink spume bubbled out.

"My son," he whispered. He laid a bloody palm against Peter's cheek. "Oh my son. What have you done?"

CHAPTER

14

An invisible line of fire cut across the center of Whitehill's back room, which had, like a divided cell, two separate nuclei. In the back, darker half of the room, among the people gathered in knots around the wood-burning stove, Kuzak and Mueller prevailed; in the light-splashed front, it was Frank Gower and Lyle Fertig. Kuzak's cell was compact, but Gower's was loosely bound, an uneasy suspension of people who for various reasons were pissed at Kuzak and Mueller. There were plenty of those.

Three months had passed since the first in this series of arsons and still no arrest had been made. Mueller and Kuzak, who respectively as fire chief and sheriff were responsible for the investigation, weren't talking. Nobody knew their thinking, not even the men in the fire department, who surely were entitled. One thing *was* known, or so generally believed as to pass for being known. It was that the arsonist lived in the area. They all felt it, a hard little seed of malice in the body politic, like a grain of sand lodged in the eye, a lump in a breast. The women admitted to fear, the men to anger. Hell of a thing, they said, having a neighbor who settled scores with a match. As long as he went unidentified no one could feel safe. Yet what were Mueller and Kuzak doing? Sweet fuck-all, as far as anyone could tell. Whispering, scowling, playing their hands close to their chest, keeping their thoughts, if they had any, to themselves. Every morning when the sheriff came in, Gower jumped on him. "So, Kuzak, caught him yet?"

On this chill January morning, Kuzak ignored him. Unshaven, his stubbly jaw and drooping jowls made him look more than ever the bulldog. He poured a coffee, carried it to the Muellers' table, and sat hunched over with the barest flicker of a smile for Kate. The two men at once began talking in low tones.

Lyle Fertig called from across the room: "Hey, Kuzak, got any leads?"

Kuzak looked at Fertig through pale, bloodshot eyes. "Got one," he said. "Our boy's a moron."

"How's that, ya figure?"

"Don't take much brain power to pour gasoline and light a match."

"Right," Fertig drawled with a wink at Gower. "Only, if he's a moron, what does that make you?" Derisive laughter erupted from that side of the room. Fertig, beaming, went from table to table repeating his witticism.

Sam Pollak was too regular a patron of the back room to have registered the gradual deterioration of its atmosphere. Just now, though, stumbling in bleary-eyed for his morning fix of Whitehill's brew, he had a sudden vision of the back room as a boxing ring. *In this corner, wearing white and pissed as all hell, we have Mueller and Kuzak, the Calamity Twins. Note the clenched fists and jaws, ladies and gentlemen; these boys are spoiling for a fight. And in this corner, in the black trunks, we have the Lord's Anointed Warriors, Gower and his faithful companion Fertig. Shake hands, boys, and come out fighting.*

Lines from a favorite poem of Lou's jumped into Sam's head, something about things falling apart, the center not holding. He poured coffee into a Styrofoam cup, tasted it and made a face. The scuttlebutt was that Whitehill used old dishwater to make his coffee, and Sam wouldn't put it past him, cheap as he was. A few years back, a freak October snowstorm had devastated the county, snapping trees like matchsticks. Electricity wasn't restored for days, which meant that everyone's food started spoiling. Whitehill had a generator in the store, which shone like a beacon to cold and hungry villagers and road crews. But Whitehill wasn't giving anything away. He bottled tap water and sold it; he rented out space in his big freezer.

Kate waved and Sam joined them, carrying the cup in his left hand. The bandages had recently come off his right, which functioned satisfactorily but was still sensitive to heat.

"Personally," Fertig needled with an eye on Sam, "I'd say the guy deserves a medal. You gotta admit, the man knows how to pick 'em. First the dykes, then the kikes. Hey," he said, "kikes, dykes: I'm a poet and don't even know it."

As usual Fertig had gone too far. Old Wickhamites were not anti-Semites, or not the kind who used slurs like *kike.* Most considered themselves tolerant people. Tough negotiators were commonly said to "jew people down" but that was considered a compliment. To the extent that Jews as a class were disliked in Old Wickham it was because they were quintessential city folk, who drove up real estate prices, treated the village like a quaint theme park that existed for their amusement, and regarded the locals as rednecks. Everyone knew Lapid was a Jew, but he'd lived in Wickham for twenty years and sent his kids through public school. He was well liked in the village.

Slurs aside, since most of the regulars were either firefighters or relatives of firefighters, Fertig's suggestion that the arsonist deserved a medal managed to unite the fractured back-room chorus in momentary harmony. "Shut up, Lyle," they called; "Put a sock in it, Fertig." Even Frank Gower looked uneasy. It was *his* ass out there on the line, not Fertig's. If Lapid hadn't turned up when he did, Gower would have had to go in after him.

"My idea," Gower said, "we catch this kid, we give him a medal and a big fat cigar, then we tie him to a stake and burn him."

"Kid?" Sam said to Kuzak, but it was Gower who answered.

"Stands to reason, don't it? Didn't have no arson fires before."

"Getting old," the sheriff sighed. "Getting real old. Give it a rest, Gower."

"I'll give it a rest when you do the right thing. Get off your fat ass, pick the little bastard up, and sweat him till he talks."

"Little bastard?" Sam said. "Is he still on about the Quinn boy?"

Kuzak said, "Gimme one reason, just one, why I should roust that boy."

"How's this? He did it."

"Bullshit," Sam said.

"Shame on you," Kate Mueller cried, pounding on the table.

Startled, the men fell silent. "That boy had nothing to do with those fires and you know it, Frank!"

"Oh no?" Gower said. "Then who did?"

"I wish to God I knew."

"I rest my case."

"Better rest your mouth," Willem growled. He squeezed Kate's leg under the table, taut as the haunch of a good hunting dog and quivering with indignation. Ever since young Quinn had befriended their Billy, Kate had extended her maternal umbrella to cover him—never mind that the boy didn't look for, respond to, or even notice her friendly overtures. Willem trusted his wife's judgment but in this instance reserved his own. The boy was kind to Billy, no doubt of that, and solicitous of his little foster brother and sisters, but Willem couldn't bring himself to encourage the friendship. For one thing he'd seen his poor Billy hurt too often, picked up and dropped with casual cruelty. For another he just didn't trust this strange boy. What did they know about him, after all? Where did he come from? Who were his people? Kuzak agreed with Kate that the boy was no arsonist, and Willem had no reason to doubt them; yet a part of him wanted to believe, like Gower, that their troubles could be laid at the gate of a stranger. Because if it wasn't the stranger in their midst, then it was one of them, someone they thought they knew but didn't. And if it was one of them, that meant there was a deep, basic flaw in Willem's understanding of the world he'd lived in all his life.

Outside the yellow schoolbus pulled up with a screech, opened its maw, swallowed the children of Old Wickham in a single gulp, and resumed its lumbering route. This was the cue for the back-room regulars to drain the last drops of tepid coffee from their cups. They stood and stretched, tossed coins into the mug that served as a till, and set off to work under a pale gray sky.

Across the street from the country store, Mistress Come-Hither threw open the shutters and unlocked the door of the post office. Sam kept his eyes straight ahead as he marched to his truck, but he felt the postmistress's moist warm gaze condense on him. He hadn't stopped in for his mail since the incident between them, weeks ago. Mutual amnesia had seemed to him the obvious course, but whenever they met accidentally, in the country store or on Main Street, she showered him with arch looks and meaningful smiles. Kate and Willem had taken to collecting his mail along with their own; they did this without comment, so he knew they knew. Sam felt no compunction or pity for the vampish postmistress, but he did feel slimy and painfully embarrassed, as if he'd got caught masturbating in public. He couldn't imagine what had come over him, but whatever it was had passed, and not just as pertained to the postmistress. Sexually he'd gone dormant again, notwithstanding his few errant fantasies about the lesbians whose house he was now working on. (Two attractive women sharing a bed: he wasn't dead yet.) Otherwise, since the fire, nothing. And good riddance. If the irresistible urge ever recurred, he'd drive up to Albany and rent himself a whore. One thing was for sure: he'd slit his throat before he'd ever love again. What Sam wanted now was what the Shakers had sought: celibacy, a clear head, and a simple life. Life pared down to the bone.

That was what he told the rabbi when Malachi tracked him down in his workshop that evening. His outside job on hold while they waited for new windows to arrive, Sam had spent the day working on the seed cabinet he'd put aside when Lou died. Hadn't stopped for lunch, barely to pee. Pulled the phone jack out of the wall, filled a thermos with coffee, and bent his whole mind to his work. The Shakers had imbued their furniture with the same ideals they cultivated within themselves: honesty, simplicity, utility, precision, and economy. The outer world, they believed, must be brought to reflect the inner. Sam, owning neither peace nor harmony, hoped to reverse the process.

He worked steadily, without hurry. By the end of the day he had finished six tiny drawers (dovetailed in front, nailed in back, with pine inside, curly maple outside, and fruitwood knobs) and fitted them to their carcasses. The drawers slid smoothly and silently on their rails. The fit was precise, the joints were sturdy. He saw that the work was good. His hands ached with a pleasant tiredness and his mind was empty.

Now the light was fading and Sam grew aware of his hunger, but he was reluctant to leave the studio for fear of shattering the fragile peace he'd found that day. And so the rabbi found him there, still seated at his bench, when he came to visit shortly after dusk.

"Mr. Pollak," he called from the doorway, "can an old Jew come in?"

"If I said no, would you leave?"

"No, but my feelings would be mortified."

"Come in, then." Sam shivered a little as he said it. Maybe it was the draft from the open door. Or maybe the odd intrusive memory that presented itself, a bit of lore gleaned from old B movies: that vampires cannot enter a house unless invited. Sam didn't think there were any Jewish vampires, but if there were, Malachi, with his instinct for the jugular, would surely qualify.

The rabbi stepped inside, pulling the door shut behind him. "So dark," he complained as he picked his way across the floor. "No more ropes lying around, I hope."

Sam switched on the overhead light. He'd forgotten the time he sat in this room planning his suicide, only to be foiled by a bagel. Even now the memory failed to surface.

Malachi looked around. Took in the cabinet and the candle stand, ran his hand along a maple-and-cane ladder-back chair, recently completed. "Beautiful. Not fancy-shmancy, but such lines, like Greta Garbo in wood! What do you call this style furniture?"

"Shaker," Sam said, against his better judgment. Talking to Malachi was like giving to panhandlers or feeding stray cats. Sam had no desire to encourage the man; yet somehow he found himself explaining about the Shakers, their communal living, celibacy, their elevation of craftsmanship to a form of religious rite. He even recited a Shaker proverb he'd read somewhere: "Man cannot hope to attain a spiritual heaven until he first creates a heaven here on earth."

Malachi listened intently. When Sam finished, the rabbi nodded, profoundly unsurprised. "*Tikkun olam*," he said.

"What?"

"'Repairing the world.' A Jewish concept also. When God made the world, he didn't finish the job. It's up to us to fix it. This is good honest work you do, Mr. Pollak. I envy you."

"Why?"

"You make things. You create. A piece of wood, a nail here, a nail there, and presto chango, ipso facto you got a cabinet. Which when it's done is done. Me, what do I make?"

"Funerals," Sam said.

"Funerals! You think you bury a person and that's it, case closed, the end? My wife, she should rest in peace already, died ten years ago. Three days after she passed, I'm lying in my bed, she comes to me. 'Haim,' she says, 'you wrap the leftovers in tin foil, you forget what's inside. How many times I got to tell you: use the plastic!' "

"She's got a point," Sam said, edging toward the door. It occurred to him that the old man wasn't merely strange, but mad.

Malachi caught him by the arm and pushed him back toward the bench, his bony fingers unexpectedly strong. "Just because a person's dead doesn't mean they don't got accounts to settle with the living, or vice versa." He settled himself on the ladder-back chair. "Am I right or am I right?"

"About what?"

"Please." The rabbi closed his eyes. Even his eyelids looked ancient, wrinkled bits of parchment. "What are we talking about? You, your wife, unfinished business."

"Ah, Jesus."

"Why call on him when you got me?"

"Why should I tell you anything?"

"The man who built this room, the man who makes such work as you, he don't want a canker in his soul."

"What do you want me to say?" Sam blurted. Malachi's eyes were deep, black holes, sucking Sam in with a force impossible to resist. "You want me to say I killed my wife?"

"Did you?"

There followed a silence so charged that the hairs on the back of Sam's neck stood on end. He could not lie and would not tell the truth. Malachi's dark eyes gripped him. The nice old Jew persona discarded, the Yiddishisms swept away. No give at all; like looking at a mountain or into the face of God. Sam covered his face with his hands.

A firm hand cupped the top of his bowed head. Shudders coursed through his body but Sam didn't look up.

"She asked the doctor," Malachi said. "Why? To spare you. But he said no, he refused. Where else is she going to turn?"

Sam opened his eyes. He still felt the imprint of the hand on his head, but the rabbi was sitting six feet away, erect in the ladder-back chair, knees together, hands folded in his lap. "How do you know she asked Lapid?"

"I know."

"Then why ask?"

"Like you, I start a job, I got to finish."

"You *are* finished here. Go away. Leave me in peace."

"You're not in peace," said the rabbi. "You're in pieces." With that poor pun the spell was broken and Malachi reduced to what he had been, a wizened old man in a dirty black suit.

Malachi stood, he walked to the door. Sam watched, leaning on his bench, weak as a baby. The rabbi touched the brim of his hat. "Goodbye, Mr. Pollak. I'll see you again."

"Not if I see you first," Sam muttered as the door swung shut behind him. But no sooner did it close than it cracked open again.

"What a *dummkopf!* What did I come for?" Malachi threw the door open wide. Beside him, tied to a length of rope, stood a large, black dog.

"What the hell . . . ?" Sam said.

"A stray. Poor fellow needs a home."

"No way. No way! Get it out of here."

The rabbi released the rope and the dog ran to Sam. Close up he could see it was still a pup, skinny but large-boned with enormous paws. A lab maybe, mixed with something a lot bigger. The dog sat before him and placed an enormous paw on his lap.

"Get off," Sam said. "Malachi, come take this thing."

"Look, he likes you."

The animal was nuzzling Sam's hand. He snatched it away. "I don't want a dog. What kind of stunt is this?" He swelled with rage. "Is this some kind of fucking consolation prize? 'The man loses a wife, let's give him a dog!'"

Malachi seemed shocked. "God forbid!"

"Why me, then?"

"Why not? You got a big place here. Besides," the rabbi lowered his voice, "I think this is a Jewish dog."

"What, is he circumcised?"

"Give a look his eyes. Jewish."

Sam looked. The dog, whimpering softly, gazed back with mournful brown eyes.

"Fleas," Sam said firmly. "Take him away." But when he raised his head, Malachi was gone.

CHAPTER 15

"Are we the first?" Jane asked; then, noticing Kate's apron, "We're too early."

"You're right on time," Kate said, ushering them into the living room. "The others are late. And I'm chronically behind myself."

Billy came clattering down the stairs. "Mom," he cried, "it's Peter, Peter's here!" He'd been told Peter was coming, but Billy had learned long ago never to count his guests before they arrived.

Kate put her arm around him, turned him gently toward the other guests. "Yes, and here are Keisha and Luz and Ms. Goncalves."

"Thank-you-for-coming," Billy recited.

Peter gave him a friendly punch and the sisters cried in unison, "Happy birthday!" Luz handed Billy his present, coats were hung, and Jane and her brood ushered into the living room. Then Jane offered to help, and Kate paused for a moment before this delicate turning; because it's one thing to ask a person into your living room and quite another to allow her into your kitchen. If Kate were to answer, "No thanks, everything's under control; sit down and have a drink," then things would go one way. If she replied (as she would have to Louise) "You bet," they would go another.

"Sure," she said. But warily.

In the kitchen Jane sniffed the air. "Chili?"

"Uh-huh. Taste?" Kate proffered a spoonful.

Jane tried it. "Not bad."

"Thanks a lot!"

"Hey, you have to understand I was weaned on this stuff. I love it, the hotter the better. Every time my mom got mad at my dad, she made a pot of chili so hot it singed his eyebrows. That chili talked!"

"What did it say?"

"Said, 'Better watch your ass, man, 'cause I am on to you.'"

Kate leaned against the counter, arms crossed over her chest. "And what does my chili say?"

Jane took another taste, swilled it around in her mouth before swallowing. "Yours says, 'Have a nice day.'"

Kate gasped, then burst into laughter. Ages since she'd laughed like this; not since Lou died. She found herself liking Jane Goncalves better than she'd expected or perhaps intended to. For it must be said that by inviting Jane to their party, Kate was acting more from a sense of duty that any expection of pleasure. She was grateful for Jane's kindness to Billy, who hung around Peter every chance he got, and bothered by her perception of Jane's isolation. Kate hadn't signed the petition but knew plenty of people who had. It was time the nonsense ended, she decided. She intended to send a message via grapevine, Old Wickham's natural medium—its fax, e-mail, and conference call combined. By tomorrow everyone would know who had attended the Muellers' annual party and who had not.

But Jane in the flesh was not what Kate had expected. She was funny; she was something new, a wake-up call. Of course, Louise had liked her, but then Lou liked nearly everyone. They'd met in the Wickham

Bookstore where Jane worked: Lou, mortally ill (though paradoxically feeling better since they'd written off chemo), and Jane, the new girl in town. They struck up a conversation, hit it off. Afterward Lou mentioned her to Kate. "An unusual woman. You ought to meet her, Kate, I think you'd like her." Busy, busy Louise, arranging everyone's life for the post-Lou era. As if friends were interchangeable. And maybe, Kate admitted to herself, she had felt a little jealousy then—because Lou was Kate's friend, wasn't she? Her best and closest friend; her special, not-to-be-shared-especially-as-time-grew-short friend.

Yet two minutes into the relationship and here she was, laughing like a fool. She was still laughing when Billy shot in, rickety with excitement. Ignoring his mother, he turned to Jane and demanded to know where Carlos was.

Jane sat, bringing her head level with Billy's. "Did you ask Peter?"

"I asked him but he wouldn't tell me, he just walked away."

She sighed. Kate turned around. Jane looked at her, then at Billy.

"Carlos doesn't live with us anymore," she said. "He's been adopted. He has a new home now, a new family."

Billy shoved his glasses back up his nose. His full moon face scrunched with confusion. "But I thought you was his family."

"We were for a little while. Now he has a permanent family, just like you do."

"But—"

Just then, to Jane's relief, the doorbell rang. Billy's face was instantly transfigured. He stuck a finger in the air like a man testing the wind—*Fee, fi, fo, fum, I smell presents!*—and scampered out of the room.

Jane stood up slowly. Her eyes met Kate's: one mother to another, neither laughing now. Kate winced in sympathy.

"Yeah, well," Jane said.

"How's Peter taking it?"

"Hard."

They left the kitchen, Kate carrying the chili and Jane the tortilla chips. The party was in full swing, half a dozen families having arrived at once. Willem stood in the center of the room, talking with Kuzak, Lassiter, and a couple of firefighters. Kate watched closely for a moment but turned away when she saw him laugh. She'd made him promise: no arson talk today. This was Billy's day.

The birthday boy was passing out hors d'oeuvres, pigs in blankets and little bite-sized pizzas. Next to opening his presents, serving the guests was the part Billy enjoyed most. Holding the tray with white-knuckled concentration, he circulated through the room, for once the center of attention. Billy used to have ordinary kids' parties: balloons and cake, party hats and games. But the older his peers got, the less tolerant they became. His eighth birthday was the watershed: six of twenty-six classmates showed up. After that, Kate switched to grown-up parties, with a smattering of reliable children.

Kate's entrance altered the constellation of the room, as guests gravitated toward their hostess. Jane tried to back off but Kate wouldn't have that; she linked her arm in Jane's and held her close. As exotic a bird in this denim-and-plaid gathering as a parrot at a backyard feeder, Jane wore a red cable-knit sweater that reached down to mid-thigh, black leggings, and high lace-up boots.

Earl Lassiter left Willem and ambled over to the buffet table. He hugged Kate, shook Jane's hand.

"Jane, great to see you. How are you adjusting? Folks treating you okay?"

"Couldn't be kinder," Jane said. "Not so much as a dead rat nailed to our front door."

"Ah," he said. "No welcome wagon."

"Not quite."

"Shame. Still, give it time. Kate here's the key, you know. And small towns can surprise you." He drew to his side the man who'd been hovering behind him. "Mark Hambro, Jane Goncalves. Jane bought that wonderful old Victorian by the pond."

Jane registered the lack of any tag. Not my friend, my colleague, my brother-in-law; just the bare name, Mark Hambro. Noticed, too, the way they stood like discreet lovers, close to one another, shoulders aligned, dangling hands almost but not quite touching. Quite unconsciously she looked a question at Kate, whose amused eyes confirmed her suspicion. Shaking Hambro's hand, Jane sighed a silent "Ah, well."

Other guests approached. Kate introduced them all to Jane, as if they hadn't all met countless times in the country store or at the bus stop. Few had acknowledged her previously with anything beyond the most cursory of good-mornings, but as Kate Mueller's guest Jane was greeted readily and spoken to with pent-up curiosity.

Kate heard the front door open and was instantly struck by the transformation in Jane's face. The woman froze, her cheeks flushed. Tom Whitehill was talking to her, and though Jane nodded now and then, Kate could see she didn't hear a word he said. Following Jane's eyes, Kate turned and saw Sam Pollak standing by the front door, handing his coat to Billy.

Oh really, she thought, swelling with indignation—though whether on Lou's behalf or her own Kate did not care to inquire. A murky area. Sam was Willem's friend, Lou's husband; he built furniture, Kate sold it. Those were the parameters of their relationship, and Sam had never by word or deed strayed outside them. And yet . . . there had been times, during their long years of friendship, when Kate had felt his gaze on her; and when their eyes met he'd quickly lowered his, but not before she glimpsed in them a certain look, speculative and instantly recognizable.

Offended? Kate was flattered. Not tempted, precisely, but flattered. Willem was the bearing beam of her life, the rock on which she'd built her house. She loved her husband, relied on him, and would not for the world betray him. Yet what woman, however happily married, does not long for a cavalier, a Lancelot to her husband's Arthur? Sam had adored his wife; what woman Kate's age, with a grown daughter, wouldn't take a secret pride in rousing such a man's unwilling desire? A striking man, tall and hard-bodied, with sinewy arms and those strong, scarred hands. If now and then Kate thought about those hands, surely such speculations, held captive in the heart, hurt no one. Kate didn't inquire into Willem's fantasies, and she didn't share her own.

Silly things anyway; she'd have been ashamed to own up to them. Getting stranded alone with Sam in a cabin in the mountains, snowed in, benighted. A fire, a bottle of wine, a night out of time: dime-store fantasy, schoolgirl stuff. She had no claim on Sam, no claim at all.

So Kate scolded herself, and yet she watched Sam closely as he checked out the room, taking his bearings. His gaze passed over Jane, then jerked back. Kate read nothing but surprise on his face. After a moment he nodded politely and turned away.

Kate noticed Peter standing alone in a corner of the crowded room. His eyes, too, were fixed on Sam, but it wasn't a friendly look.

She filled a bowl full of chili and carried it to him. "Eat," she said.

Peter took it with a look of surprise. "Thank you."

"I heard about Carlos," Kate said. "I'm glad for him but sad for you. You guys were close."

"Not that close," the boy said with a shrug.

"At least now he'll have people to belong to, a family of his own."

"Better him than me."

"You don't care for families?"

She'd gone too far. Instead of answering, Peter filled his mouth with chili. Bland compared to Jane's fiery stuff, but still tasty. Over Kate's shoulder he spied Sam Pollak approaching. Peter nodded to Billy's mother and walked the other way.

The thing was, Peter didn't want to be here at all. Wouldn't have come if Jane hadn't twisted his arm. "Poor Billy, he'll be so disappointed." Poor Billy his ass. So what if the kid was no Einstein? He had a pretty mother who doted on him, a sexy sister, a father who never raised a hand to him . . . though that was something that in Peter's experience you never knew for sure. *He* sure as hell didn't go bragging on it when his old man beat him. Covered up, in fact; lied about it. You never knew. Families look one way from the outside, quite another from within. Peter was lucky to be shut of his, lucky to live in his lonely arid world.

The atmosphere here was cloying, the air unbreathably sweet. Peter tried hanging in the hallway, but Billy's sister, Melissa, was there, making out with some high-school kid in a Raiders jacket. Guy had his hands all over her, which surprised Peter, who wouldn't have thought it healthy with her father just a room away. Romeo glared at him and removed his hand from Melissa's ass long enough to flash him the finger. Peter slunk back into the crowded living room.

Jane was in the middle of a group of people, talking and laughing, her face shining. Out of place but happy just to be there. He realized how rarely he saw her with other adults: hardly ever, since Pollak had finished his work and cleared out. His anger underwent a momentary thaw; but then he remembered how easily she'd given Carlos away: a hug, a kiss, and *hasta la vista*, baby, good-bye and good luck. She could talk all day about how it was for Carlos's sake, how they'd stay in touch and all that bullshit. Truth was, if she really cared she'd have kept him. But no: with Jane it was easy come, easy go. No doubt she'd do the same with Peter if she could find anyone fool enough to adopt him. So to hell with her. To hell with her.

Peter didn't need to search for Sam Pollak. He could feel him; he could trace the carpenter's progress by the prickling of his skin. Like the only two vampires in a roomful of mortals, they shared a dire affinity. Each looked normal but was not. Sam's movements were as palpable to Peter as his own.

Sam was playing it cool, biding his time, but Peter wasn't fooled. Wandering about the room, the carpenter ended up as if by accident next to Jane, who turned to him, smiling, and held out her hand. He grasped her hand but didn't shake it. Instead he leaned forward and kissed her on the cheek. Peter shuddered. Found he couldn't, after all, consign her to the devil.

Sam took Jane's arm and lead her aside to stand before the hearth. Jane's face was glowing. Peter had to believe that was from the fire. He couldn't hear them but it was clear Sam was trying to sell her on something. He talked, she shook her head; he talked some more, she shook her head again, but this time less decidedly.

Say no, thought Peter. Whatever he wants, say no.

Jane raised her hands in surrender, and Sam beamed. "Shit," Peter groaned.

"What's the matter?" asked Billy, appearing by his elbow. Peter looked at him. Billy's mouth was smeared with chocolate. Behind thick glasses, his eyes sparkled.

"Nothin'," Peter said.

"I'm opening my presents, wanna watch?"

"Sure."

Willem Mueller tapped a knife against a glass and called the room to order. "And now, ladies and gentlemen, the moment you've all been waiting for. Or should I say the moment Billy's been waiting for?"

Billy sat cross-legged in the center of the room, with the guests gathered around and his mother stationed by his side. He opened the presents while she read the cards. Halfway through the pile they came to a small box, Sam's gift. Billy tore it open. On a bed of white cotton lay a gleaming red Swiss Army pocket knife. Billy gasped. Sam tried to catch Kate's eye, but Kate didn't notice. She opened the card and read it aloud. "Dear Billy, Happy Birthday. This was Lou's. I know she'd want you to have it. Your friend, Sam Pollak."

An angel passed over the room. The men looked at the floor, the women at Sam. Billy went over and hugged him, pressing his head to Sam's chest. As soon as he could, Sam slipped out of the room.

Melissa was in the hallway with some young buck stuck to her like Krazy Glue. "Excuse me," Sam said; they were blocking the coat closet. The boy shifted aside. Melissa opened one eye, then both. She flashed him a triumphant little smile so perfect that he instantly envisioned her practicing before a mirror. *Eat your heart out, Sam,* the smile said. Sam made a pistol of his thumb and forefinger, pointed it at his temple, and pulled the trigger.

Wondrously quiet outside, cold and crisp. A Sunday like this, Lou would have had them out tramping. Sam crossed the road, started up the hill to his house. The dog heard him and came hurtling out of the woods. Didn't matter how often Sam told him to get lost, the pup kept coming back. Never should have fed or sheltered it, but what was he supposed to do—let it starve, let it freeze? Sam drew the line at naming it, though; called it "dog" if he called it anything. His first thought was to give it back to Malachi, but nobody, not even Marty Lapid, seemed to know where the rabbi was staying. Next he tacked a sign up in the country store, offering the dog for adoption. No response to that, which didn't surprise him: in these parts, everyone who wanted a dog had one already. Never occurred to him to try Jane till he saw her at the party, but then it jumped out at him. "You take in strays," he'd said; "Kids, not dogs," she'd replied, but in the end she gave in.

A kind woman. He hadn't thought much about her since the night he tried to fuck her and got shot down. Hadn't worried him at the time; he just figured you win some, you lose some. Seeing her unexpectedly at the Muellers, though, he felt a jolt of belated shame. Goncalves was a different order of being from Pellagia and Mistress Come-Hither. The woman deserved some respect.

Sam trudged up the hill, the dog at his heels, and the higher he climbed, the sweeter the air and the better he felt. At the door the brown dog whined softly and thumped its tail against the deck. He held the door open. "Last time," he told the beast. "Tomorrow you're outta here." The dog shot him a reproachful look. Sam took a beer from the fridge and stretched out on the living room sofa. The dog sat in front of him and stared at Sam's face. "What's your problem?" Sam growled. "Found you a home, didn't I, kids and all? You ought to be grateful. Every dog needs a family."

CHAPTER 16

Sam fell asleep right after work and woke to a dark room, a ringing telephone. He stumbled into the kitchen. "Hello?"

That old familiar silence. Then a transitional sound, a kind of amplified scratch, followed by music.

Sam knew the song from the very first guitar chord. Well, why wouldn't he? Wasn't it their song, as much a part of him as his own heartbeat?

If I were a carpenter
And you were a lady,
Would you marry me anyway?
Would you have my baby?

It felt like surgery performed without anesthesia. As if someone had reached inside his body, grabbed hold and tugged. Sam slammed the phone down and sagged against the wall. He shut his eyes and immediately a succession of images filled the darkness: a stack of dusty singles, an old turntable, crystal blue eyes watching. *Play it again, Sam.* He knew what he should have known all along.

Moments later he was rattling down the drive in his pickup, tearing down the dirt road, blasting through town. He pulled up with a screech in front of the yellow Victorian. Strode up the path, threw open the side door without knocking, and stormed in. There was murder in his heart and in his eyes.

Jane and Peter were sitting at the kitchen table. The moment Sam burst in, Peter jumped up and ran. Not a word spoken; he just ran, as if they were hard-wired to the same circuit. His chair skidded across the kitchen floor. Sam leapt over it. In passing he glimpsed Jane's astonished face. It didn't slow him down.

Peter sprinted through the dining room and out the front door, slamming it behind him. In the time it took Sam to wrest the door open, the boy was halfway across the lawn, heading for the pond.

Sam chased him. In the deep country quiet, the thud of feet pounding the frozen ground filled his ears. His eyes stung from the cold. He had no idea what was going to happen when he caught this kid. He cared even less. It was like the time he went after Gower and put him in the hospital. He just needed to lay hands on this bastard; the rest would take care of itself.

The boy bounded like a deer, barely skimming the ground. He reached the lip of the pond and glanced back, then, without flagging, veered to his left and put on a burst of speed. Sam understood that he was trying to put the pond between them. The pond, gone soft in the middle, had to be circled, couldn't be crossed.

Peter was fast, but in the long run Sam was stronger. Fifty yards separated them, then thirty. At the far side of the pond, with Sam trailing by only twenty yards, Peter tripped on the roots of the old oak tree and sprawled flat on his face. He jumped up immediately but by then Sam was on him; he'd launched himself in a flying tackle and brought the boy down.

The struggle was short, silent, brutish. Peter kicked, punched, butted, even tried to bite, but in less than a minute Sam had knocked him onto his back, yanked his wrists down, and knelt on them. Panting, Sam grabbed the boy's chin with his left hand and raised his fist.

Peter had quit struggling. His cheek was bloody where he'd scraped it on the roots. The look in his eyes was stoic, resigned. Sam saw that he knew what was coming, that he'd been here before. So what? he told himself. This time the little bastard has it coming.

He ordered his arm to strike. He wanted to hit this kid so bad it hurt; but he couldn't. His fist remained suspended; the hammer didn't fall.

To Peter this hesitation seemed a deliberate prolonging of his torment. "Do it," he cried. "Think I give a shit?"

Jane was shouting from the other side of the pond, yelling out their names. Though both heard her, neither one responded or even looked her way.

"Always knew you had it in you," said the boy.

Much to his disgust, however, Sam found that he didn't. No doubt but that Peter richly deserved a beating; Sam just wasn't the man to inflict it. It would have been different if he himself had been innocent, but as things stood it was hard for righteous indignation to gain much of a foothold. Anger receded, leaving a backwash of hurt and bewilderment. Sam let his fist drop but continued to kneel on Peter.

"Tell me why, you little prick."

Jane, pacing indecisively on the other side of the pond, swung her arms to keep warm. Out of earshot, she watched, waited, strained to hear but couldn't.

"Had to," Peter grunted. "Get off me."

"*Why?*"

"None of your fucking business!"

"You made it my business first time you picked up that phone. Those goddamn calls, that song—what the hell were you thinking, boy?"

Peter lifted up eyes of crystal blue defiance. "They didn't hurt you."

"Didn't hurt!" Sam echoed in amazement.

"Wasn't it better, knowing someone knew?"

"Better than *what?*"

"Better than no one knowing."

Sam lifted his head; he felt like baying at the moon. "I don't believe you. That's like shooting someone point-blank in the chest and saying, 'Gee, I didn't mean to hurt you.'"

"I didn't. Not exactly. It's like we were having this . . . conversation."

"Conversation!" Sam howled.

Peter's eyes changed. He blinked hard, looked away from Sam, then straight back at him. "Fine," he said, raising his jaw. "Go ahead. I guess you got one coming."

It was a serious offer, one tendered, moreover, in the currency of the boy's homeland. Seeing this, Sam recoiled. "I don't hit kids."

"Then get the fuck off of me."

"You gonna run?"

"Where to?"

Sam let him up. True to his word, Peter made no attempt to escape, though in fact Sam doubted he could have run ten feet. It was awfully cold and the kid was shivering in his shirtsleeves. Sam took off his own jacket and tossed it at Peter, who hung it around his shoulders. This act, acknowledged by neither of them, was seen from across the pond by Jane. She turned and walked unnoticed back to the house.

"Tell me one thing," Sam said. "What the fuck did I ever do to you?"

"You tried to do her." Peter jerked his chin sideways.

"So what? That ain't your business, pal. She's not even your mother. Besides which, you started calling way before that."

They sat hunkered on their haunches, facing one another. Peter picked up a stout twig and jabbed at the frozen ground. For once he looked his age, and sulky with it. "Couldn't just let it pass. Couldn't let *you* pass."

"What's that mean, 'let me pass'?"

The boy rolled his eyes with an impatience he had never shown to Billy Mueller. Explained, as if to an idiot: "It's like, you're all alone in this desert full of nothing but bare rock and steep cliffs, and all of a sudden someone else comes wandering by? Another outcast, another Cain. You see him, but he don't see you. What do you do?"

"You call out to him."

"Exactly!"

Sam stabbed a finger at Peter's face. "No way do I buy that."

"Don't have to buy it. It's yours for free. I know what you did."

"How?"

"I saw you."

Sam shut his eyes as the past rose up and obliterated the present. Lou once again lay dying in his arms, gazing upward with that last desperate look, opening her lips as if to speak . . . but now he saw it all through a window, through the eyes of a stranger, an adolescent Peeping Tom. In his helter-skelter rush to Jane's house, Sam had grasped at this thing as an act of random maliciousness, a boyish prank gone rancid. The truth was far worse. He felt violated to the core, raped in the heart. His throat seized up, as it had when Lou died. How could he begin to swallow this?

Peter peered into Sam's face. His last words echoing in the silence between them, he hastened to amend them. "I didn't see you do it. I saw it afterward."

Sam gasped. "What are you, some kind of freaking psychic?"

"I've got eyes."

"You saw—what?"

"I just saw it in your face, man."

Sam touched his brow, where in the early hours and days after Lou's death he'd believed his guilt to be written. How odd it had seemed, how perverse, when others failed to perceive his stigma. At first he thought they were pretending; later he thought they were blind. Finally, though, he accepted that the act had left no visible imprint, no mark of Cain. And yet now it seemed it had, for the boy had seen it.

Peter, with a stab at kindness, said, "I don't think it shows to other people. I think it's kind of like, takes one to know one."

Sam gave him the kind of look a man gives a boy. "One what?"

"What do you think?" As Peter shook the hair back off his face, the moon, caught in the branches of the ancient oak, struck his forehead. Surely it was a trick of the moonlight, Sam thought in horror, that glistening patch on his brow, smooth and pale as scar tissue. An optical illusion, yet it seemed so real: a subtle, circular indentation, as of something not applied, but torn away. "Can't you see?" Peter asked, as if he were asking, Can't you see the pond, the stars, that massive oak: things so immanent and clear?

On this dark winter's night no one was abroad. The villagers were tucked in at home, eating their Sunday dinners. Bullfrogs slept beneath the frozen mud, deer shivered in the forest, dogs dozed beside fires. Apart from the lone owl hooting in the old oak, the man and the boy were the only creatures stirring. They might have been sharing a fire on some desolate plain. Out here it was possible to say what could never be said indoors, in the light and the warmth.

Sam lit a cigarette, cupping the match in his hand. "What did *you* do?" he asked, and there was, in the asking, an unintended admission.

Peter didn't answer at once. He brought his knees up to his chest and wrapped his arms around them. He stared at the frozen surface of the pond. From the steeple of the church across the road, a colony of bats erupted silently, radiating outward like runs in the black mesh of the night.

"I killed my dad," Peter said softly. "I committed patricide, which makes *me* a patricide. Strange, ain't it? How you can become the thing you did? And how one moment changes you forever?"

Sam pulled on his cigarette and was silent.

After she settled the girls down and put them to bed, Jane lay on her bed with the door open and the lights out. She felt the house closing in around her, humming deep in its throat, sighing through the radiators.

From across the hall came Keisha's steady breathing, Luz's gentle snore. The room beyond theirs—still Carlos's room, in her mind—exuded a silence, a hovering sadness she'd not yet allowed herself to feel. Branches tapped at her window like disconsolate ghosts, the ghosts of children past. Sometimes she wondered if the good she did was worth the damage done in parting. But she consoled herself that the damage was mostly to herself. The ones who go on are the ones who forget.

Peter was outside, talking as if his life depended on it with Sam Pollak of all people. Jane had baited the kitchen with coffee and hot cocoa on the stove, fresh-baked chocolate-chip cookies on a platter on the table. It was cold outside and they had but one jacket between them. They would have to come in soon.

She switched on the reading lamp and opened her book.

Usually Jane read novels, but right now she was engrossed in a book Paul Binder had recommended. Entitled *Shot in the Heart*, it was an account by Mikal Gilmore of his family, particularly his brother Gary, who was executed by a firing squad in Utah for the cold-blooded murders of two young men. The Gilmore family was an American nightmare, the underbelly of the American dream. They drifted from town to town. The father, an itinerant con man and a drunk, alternately coddled and brutalized his four sons. The mother, a lapsed Mormon cut off from her roots, suffered bouts of depression and rage. The vicious beating of their sons became a form of dialogue between husband and wife, the medium through which they communicated. Between them they destroyed their children, several of whom went on to destroy others and to complete the job of self-demolition their parents had initiated.

It was the saddest book Jane had ever read, and the whole time she was reading it she kept thinking of Peter. Not that Peter was any Gary Gilmore, nor ever could be. But the Gary of his brother's recollection, a bright, artistically talented, erratic, and troubled boy, seemed to Jane one who *could* have been saved, if only someone had reached for him early enough. That was what reminded her of Peter, for he was another who she knew in her deepest heart could be reached. But how, and by whom?

More than a year had passed since he first came to her, and in that time they had become good friends . . . of the sort of who value good fences. Peter had never asked her in, never opened his heart, never spoke a word without weighing it first. Some children can heal themselves, needing only warmth, space, and security. Not Peter. He was a garden choked with weeds, an artery clogged with guilt. The boy functioned at 10 percent of capacity. Where the rest of his energy and intelligence went was anybody's guess, but Jane suspected that a lot went into fence maintenance.

Those fences not only separated Peter from the world, they also sealed off his past. He had yet to talk about his father. He had yet to answer his sister's card.

Jane had tried and tried to reach him. She had a light hand with injured children, a patient, coaxing touch. When that didn't work with Peter, she took a harder line, rattled his cage a little. Still nothing, *nada.* Maybe hers wasn't the right approach, but it's not as if others hadn't tried. Even Portia, who came on like a sledgehammer, had failed to dent Peter's barricades. As time went on, Jane had grown more rather than less worried about Peter. Something, someone had to break through that armor of his; but in all the time she'd had him, no one had come close. Jane had never once seen him fully engaged with any other person . . . until tonight.

That's why, once the threat of violence subsided, she chose not to interfere. Portia would have marched right up to Sam and Peter, grabbed them by the earlobes and demanded to know what exactly was going on. Jane considered that course, but rejected it. She left them alone at the pond, engaged in that tense, extraordinary conversation; she retreated to her room, where doubts assailed her. If this was a mistake, it was a huge one. And yet she had a gut feeling that Sam could be trusted.

Restlessly she put aside her book, turned out the light, and crossed to the window that overlooked the pond. Still there, still talking. As she watched, Peter sprang to his feet and offered a hand to Sam, who accepted it and hauled himself up. The carpenter tucked his hands into his armpits, stamped his feet. Peter gestured toward the house. They set off walking briskly around the pond.

What had Peter done to Sam? Bursting into the house, the man had looked so wild that Jane's first fearful impulse had been to call for help. What stopped her was Peter's reaction, the way he took off before a single word was exchanged, as if he was expecting Sam's incursion, as if he'd waited for it. In which case he must have provoked it. One thing was clear to her: something was going on between the two of them that she knew nothing about. Jane felt too certain of Sam's orientation to entertain suspicions of the conventional kind. Whatever their secret, though, damned if she wouldn't have it out of them tomorrow. She'd tackle Peter, Sam too if necessary.

Not tonight, though. Tonight she would let them talk.

She opened her bedroom door and presently heard the kitchen door open and shut. A faint rise-and-fall of voices drifted up. Moving softly in slippers, Jane padded down the hall to the top of the staircase. From there she heard them rattling about, lighting the stove, opening cupboards. But she couldn't make out a word they said.

Her foot on the top step, she hesitated. A voice in her head, suspiciously like Portia's, declared that parents, like spies, must gather their information where they may. Wasn't Peter Jane's responsibility? Didn't she owe it to the boy to find out what was going on? A different voice replied sternly that no harm would come to the boy tonight, and Peter had a right to privacy.

She compromised by descending to the half landing. From there she heard Sam's voice, faint but distinct.

"What I don't get," he was saying, "is what you think you did wrong."

"Some things," Peter replied, "it don't matter why you did 'em. You did 'em; that's enough."

Jane sat down abruptly on the steps. She'd seen them talking but couldn't believe how far they'd gone. Peter must have told Sam everything, but why?

"Still, under the circumstances—"

"Fuck the circumstances, man! He was my *father.* All that crap about self-defense, justifiable homicide: what they really meant is the fucker got what he deserved. They didn't give a shit about him."

"And you did?"

"I hated him. But just 'cause you hate someone doesn't mean you stop loving them. I thought about him afterward, in that place where they stuck me. Thought about him all the time. Tried to focus on the bad stuff; plenty of that. But no matter what, the good stuff kept breaking through. Like him teaching me to ride a bike, a two-wheeler. Him running alongside, his face all red and sweaty, and me knowing it was okay if I fell because he was there to catch me. Or how when my mom was in the hospital he quit drinking for three weeks. D'you have any idea how long three weeks is for a drunk? He didn't have a single drink till she died, and I guess you can't blame a man for drinking at his own wife's wake."

They were quiet for a moment. Then Peter went on. "The thing is, he was really two people. Inseparable, like Siamese twins joined at the heart, but not identical. One a complete shit, the other a normal father. Maybe nicer than normal, see, 'cause he knows about the shit. When I killed one, the other died with him."

Another silence ensued. Then Sam spoke, his voice subdued, pitched too low for Jane to hear.

"Sure," Peter said contemptuously. "But he'd threatened me before and I was still breathing, wasn't I? I was just sick of the whole goddamn thing, that's all. I'm thinking, Enough of this shit; no matter what, he's not hurting me again."

"Did you tell them that?"

Peter laughed. "Lawyers, man. I told mine. He goes, 'Keep your thoughts to yourself and your mouth shut, kid.' Which I did, 'cause even though I deserved it I still didn't want to go to jail.

"They turned me loose. Justifiable homicide, they called it. I'm like, 'Thanks a lot, Judge, and while you're at it could you tell me how to wash this blood off my hands?' "

During the long silence that followed, Jane had time to think, and the thought that occurred most forcefully was that she had no business listening to this. So she crept off to bed and heard nothing more, other than a distant murmur of voices talking late into the night.

CHAPTER 17

"Freeze," Jane said.

He froze with one foot out the door. Only his eyes moved, to the watch on his wrist. "Gotta run. Early bus."

"I've been chasing you around the house all morning."

"Really?" said Peter, all wide-eyed innocence.

Just then Keisha and Luz skipped into the kitchen and presented themselves to Jane for tucking, zipping, snapping, and buckling. She took her eyes off him for one second. "I cut you a lot of slack, buddy. Don't abuse it."

"Wouldn't dream of it." The words drifted back to her, disembodied. Peter was gone, loping down the drive.

Damn but that kid was getting cocky. After school he managed to dodge her all afternoon, but that evening she corralled him in his room. Might have interrogated the wall for all the good it did her.

"What happened last night?"

"Nothin'."

"Why'd Sam Pollak come busting in like that?"

"Dunno."

"Why'd you run?"

"Dunno."

"Peter!"

"What?" he said, looking at her with an arrogance that was pure adolescent male, the old I-ain't-talking-and-you-can't-make-me look. Jane stormed out, slamming the door behind her.

The next day was one of her bookstore days. During her lunch break she went into the back room and called Sam Pollak. No reply. She left a message on his machine. Out on the floor Paul Binder asked, "Everything okay?"

"Sure, why?"

"You look a little frazzled."

"Me frazzled? Don't you know you're talking to the Queen of Cool?"

"Whatever," he said peaceably, and went back to pulling returns.

Jane opened her door that afternoon to the stale ring of an unanswered phone. She ran across the kitchen and snatched it up, expecting to hear Sam's voice, but it was Portia on the line.

"How's it going, girlfriend, up there in the frozen north? Are we gettin' any yet?"

Jane sat in a kitchen chair and propped her feet up on the table. Her legs ached from standing all day. She sighed contentedly. "You said it yourself, babe, the frozen north."

"What, nothin' doing with that sweet old hunk o' white meat?"

"Only in your dreams."

"Honey, I don't need to dream," said Portia. "I got the real thing warmin' *my* feet at night."

They talked about the children. Girls were doing great, Jane reported. Luz hadn't wet her bed in two months. Keisha got all excellents on her latest report card. "Plus, get this, she wants to join the 4-H club."

"And Peter?"

Jane hesitated.

"Aha!" said Portia.

"No aha. I was just formulating my thoughts."

"Spit it out, girl."

"That awful politeness is gone," Jane said. "Suddenly he's rude. He's evasive. He's secretive."

"In other words, your typical teenager. Didn't I tell you to be careful what you wished for?"

"Yes, but there's more to it. Something's going on between him and Sam Pollak."

Now the silence was on Portia's end.

"It's not what you think," Jane hastened to say. "Sam's not that way."

"And you know this—how?" asked Portia, who after fifteen years on the job knew a thing or two herself. Like the fact that boys like Peter, lost and wounded, drew pederasts the way red meat draws flies.

"I know the man," Jane said, though when you came right down to it, what did she know? That he was a good carpenter. That he had a gentle manner—which proved nothing. That he waited to finish the job before trying to bed her. That he accepted defeat graciously (maybe too graciously, but that was another matter).

Portia sniffed. "I hear you, girl. Still, just as well I'm coming up."

"You're coming up?"

"Why I called, actually. Ike's cousin's getting married up in Albany next month. Thought I'd stop by, see how you all are doing."

After she hung up, Jane laughed and hugged herself for pleasure. What a sight for sore eyes Portia would be. Just hearing her voice reminded Jane of who she was and where she came from, things easy to forget when all a person saw in other people's eyes was the reflection of a stranger.

She was breading chicken cutlets for dinner when the truck pulled up. Jane glanced out the window and spied Sam Pollak walking up the drive, leading a dog the size of a small elephant. "Oh, fuck me," she groaned, wiping her hands on her apron. That could not be the pup he'd talked about at the Muellers'. The creature outside was the size of a full-grown Labrador, with paws so huge that at first glance she'd thought it was wearing snowshoes.

She opened the door, but blocked the entrance. "*That* is no puppy."

"Sure it is," Sam said. "Seven, eight months."

"You mean it's still growing? Forget it, Sam."

"A deal's a deal. Besides, I already told him."

Luz and Keisha entered arguing but fell silent when they noticed the dog. Luz reached for her big sister's hand. Keisha asked, "Does he bite?"

"Nah," said Sam, "he's a pussycat."

"That ain't no pussycat," Luz said, wide-eyed. "That's a dog. A *big* dog."

The dog slipped past Jane and ran to the girls, who showed no fear at all, but put their arms around his neck and laughed as he licked their faces with an enormous pink tongue.

"Is he yours?" Keisha asked Sam.

"Nope. Yours, if you want him."

Jane shot him a curdling look but by then the girls were all over her. "Please, Jane, please can we keep him?"

"Kids and dogs," Sam said with a shrug, as if he'd had nothing to do with it.

"Please, please, please!"

Jane sighed. "Guess I don't have much choice. Okay."

The children shrieked so loudly that Peter came running into the kitchen. He did not notice the dog, who had wandered off to nose the garbage, but focused instantly on Sam. Jane watched them closely. Peter's smooth cheeks flushed a deep red, and Sam looked down at the floor. Then each made a second effort; their eyes met, they nodded and said hello. Jane thought of lovers meeting the morning after their first tryst. The analogy was imperfect since, despite Portia's suspicious mind, Jane was convinced there was no sexual content here. But the look was similar. Not surprising, considering last night's orgy of confession.

Now the dog approached Peter. The dog's ears stood at full attention, and he didn't lick the boy as he had the girls. Instead, he sat before the boy and proffered his left paw.

"What's this?" said Peter, shaking the paw automatically, then letting it drop.

"Sam says he's a pussycat, but really he's a dog," Luz said.

"I see he's a dog, Miss Thing. I meant what's he doing here?"

"Sam brought him. Jane says we can keep him."

Peter turned to Jane with an incredulous sneer. "Taking in stray dogs now, are we? Makes sense, I guess. Carlos's room is empty."

Jane sighed. Peter still hadn't forgiven her for Carlos, but there was nothing she could do about that. It was how things were. "You disapprove?"

"You're asking me?"

"Of course I'm asking you."

"What's the point?" the boy said. "I've had dogs. You get all attached, then something happens. Not to mention our life spans are incompatible. It's a fool's game."

"But that's life," said Jane. "No guarantees, plenty of risk, but better than the alternative."

Their eyes locked. The others were forgotten; it was just the two of them. Jane felt a jarring sensation, as if, quite suddenly, they had reached their destination.

Reached it? Slammed into it, more like.

"Something always happens," she said. "Even in the best of cases. So what do you do, huddle under a rock?"

"You keep your head down and your visibility low," Peter said firmly.

"Now *that's* a fool's game."

"What's his name?" Luz asked over dinner, Sam having been persuaded without difficulty to stay.

"Doesn't have one," he said. "Why don't you name him?"

"Fluffy!"

Keisha shot her sister a scornful look. "What you think he is, a damn bunny rabbit?"

"So what you want to name him, then?"

She mulled it over. "We'll call him Blackie, 'cause he's black."

"So are you, dodo brain, and you wouldn't like it if people called you Blackie!"

Lately the sisters had taken to occasional squabbling. Jane took this as a sign of progress, but a little of it went a long way. "Peter," she said hastily, "any ideas?"

Peter looked down at the dog, which, having with evident and immediate partiality attached itself to him, now lay at his feet.

"Cujo," he said.

"Doesn't sound very Jewish," Sam ventured. They all stared at him. "I didn't tell you? The guy who left him with me, this old rabbi, he claims the dog's Jewish."

"Why?" Peter stared down at the animal. "Is he circumcised?"

"What's that?" Keisha asked.

"Eat your string beans, girl," Jane said. "Jewish, huh? We could call him Freud. Or Einstein."

"Moses," Peter said. The dog stood up at once, wagging his broom tail; so Moses he was named and Moses remained.

Jane walked Sam out. All the way down the drive he kept up a steady, preemptive patter about nothing. "Sam," she said, "shut up."

He shut up. In the silence the real issue surfaced.

"You owe me an explanation," said Jane.

"I owe you an apology. I had no business busting into your house like that."

"Apologies don't interest me. I want you to explain."

"It was a misunderstanding."

"Over what?"

He shifted his weight from one foot to the other, he gazed past her toward the pond. Jane could see he would rather have been anywhere at all right now other than here with her. Courtesy held him, and a grown-up sense of responsibility. Unlike Peter, he accepted her right to ask these questions; he just wasn't willing to answer. Way to go, girl, she thought. Way to drive the man away. But what choice did she have? Peter was her child now, her responsibility.

"Someone was playing games," he said at last, with the air of a man choosing his words carefully. "I thought it was Peter."

Implying that it wasn't, though of course it must have been. Why else would Peter have run? "What kind of games?"

"Ask Peter."

"I'm asking you."

"Don't matter anymore. It's all straightened out. We're cool."

By the set of his mouth Jane knew he would tell her no more. It wasn't important anyway. What mattered most was what came after the confrontation, that extraordinary conversation.

Sam reached for the handle of his truck, but Jane slid in front of it. He raised his hands in surrender, his brown eyes amused but wary.

"I saw you at the pond," she said. "I heard you gabbing till all hours in the kitchen. Peter talked to you."

Warier still now: "Yes."

"Told you where he came from, his whole story."

"He told me some stuff."

"Which makes you the sole recipient of Peter's confidence. Congratulations, Sam Pollak! To what do you attribute your success?"

He gazed at her without responding.

"In other words," said Jane, "why you?"

Still he did not reply, but stared past her at something she could not see. It was the same shuttered look he'd worn when they first met, standing on the deck of his house while his wife's body lay inside. Whose privacy was he protecting now, it occurred to her to wonder. Whose secrets was he guarding? Peter's, she had assumed, but suddenly wasn't so sure.

"Thanks for dinner," he said. "And for taking the monster off my hands." Jane didn't budge. Their eyes met and held. Something clicked in his, and she thought of tumblers snapping into place. Jane had the odd notion that, for the first time in their acquaintance, Sam was looking at her and thinking about her simultaneously. He moved closer; his arms closed around her. He bent down and kissed her on the mouth. Kissed her firmly, without hesitation, as if he had every right. Pushed her back against the truck till she was trapped between two adamantine surfaces. His body so hard it made hers feel soft. A surge of heat began in her belly and spread outward.

His hands slid down to the small of her back, stalled, and fell away. He took a step back.

Jane touched her mouth.

"Don't mention it," she said.

CHAPTER

18

In the weeks that followed, Sam often found himself thinking about Peter Quinn. He'd be in the middle of installing a window or planing a drawer when suddenly a sentence or two would sound in his head, resonant and isolated, ripe with hidden significance, like words spoken in a dream; then his eyes would glaze over and his hands fall idle by his side. That night beside the frozen pond, the boy's confession had swept over Sam like a great hurricane sweeping over a plain. Though he retained the substance of their conversation, the actual words were lost in the roar. When Jane interrogated him the next day, his unresponsiveness, which she attributed to unwillingness and reserve, actually sprang from bewilderment, for he could not then with assurance have repeated a single sentence of their talk. Only later did the words come back to him, and then they came back piecemeal, a sentence here, a phrase there. Often he could not even remember who had spoken them, himself or the boy. It hardly seemed to matter.

It was as if Peter had given voice to Sam's own secret thoughts, or crystallized feelings that had not yet cohered into thought. When the boy spoke of wandering alone in a wilderness, he was describing Sam's own state precisely. Ever since Lou died, Sam had lived in exile from his own life. His house felt hollowed out, like a stage set. Friends reached for him and he failed to grasp their hands; they embraced him, yet he remained untouched. His was a wound that had not even begun to heal. He felt the numbness in his heart, the slow progressive failure of vitality. What might have seemed to others signs of life—little sparks of lust or anger or even sympathy—he knew to be just the last glowing embers in a dying fire.

It wasn't Lou's death, bitter and untimely as it was, that festered inside him. No, Lapid was wrong about that. What brought Sam to his knees, what mired him in despair, was not Lou's death but his collusion in it.

It wasn't fair that he should feel this way. She was dying in agony, one organ at a time. You wouldn't let a dog suffer like that. You'd put it out of its misery. What he did, he did for love and for Louise; and yet nothing, it seemed, could ease the peculiar pain of knowing it was his hand that had measured out the fatal dose, his hand that drew it up into the hypodermic, his hand that injected it into the veins of his beloved. An act he could justify a thousand times over; and yet it had sent him reeling out into the void. Truly they had met in the wilderness, the lost boy and himself.

With all his heart Sam pitied Peter Quinn. He blamed him for nothing, least of all the phone calls: distant echoes now, forgiven and forgotten. In striking out at his father, the boy had acted in self-defense and in defense of his sister. That Peter suffered the most awful guilt Sam had no doubt; but that he was in fact guilty Sam refused to accept.

Not that it signified what the carpenter thought. What does the absolution of others matter to a self-convicted heart? It was true what the boy said: Some things—it doesn't matter why you did them—it's enough that you did. Certain laws are written in stone. They are not the product but the root of religion; they represent an order so ancient, deep, and primal that beside it, man-made notions of guilt and innocence are of little account, and lack of conscious intent is no excuse at all. If the branch of a tree were to delve into the earth and smite its own root, wouldn't that tree die, and with it the branch? When Oedipus slew the challenger at the crossroads, he did not know the man was his father; yet he was doomed to suffer the fate of all patricides.

Isn't it strange, the boy had said, how you become the thing you did?

Sam's encounter with Peter Quinn had torn a chink in his isolation, through which he glimpsed the distant possibility of return, even of redemption. But though he saw the path, he was loath to set out on it, having perhaps grown used to his solitude, which he wore like a tattered but still useful old coat.

A little distance after the recent intensity seemed to Sam a good thing; that Peter concurred was evidenced by the fact that he made no more effort to contact Sam than Sam did to seek him out. Things were not yet finished between them, but what form their relationship would ultimately take was far from clear. Certainly Sam didn't see himself playing a father's role. He'd had too little fathering himself to take to it naturally, and anyway, in light of the boy's history, it probably wasn't the healthiest role to assume. Eventually things would work themselves out; for now, whatever they had to say had been said. No need to dwell on a connection acknowledged by both, especially since, in a village as small as Old Wickham, chance meetings were bound to occur. Indeed, within two weeks of their talk, Sam had glimpsed Peter half a dozen times, enough to register a startling change in the boy's demeanor.

There came a day in early March so unseasonably mild that the frozen ground had warmed to slush, and all through the village windows were flung open and bedding hung out to air. The streets were full of people who had discovered or invented some essential business to draw them outside. Not even Sam was immune to the general restlessness. He drove into the village with the excuse of stocking up on some hardware, and was just loading up his truck outside of Dugan's when Peter Quinn strolled by.

At first glance Sam hardly knew him. For one thing, the boy was going through a growth spurt and appeared a good four inches taller than in Sam's laggard image of him; broader in the shoulders, too, his body still in the cusp but suddenly closer to a man's than a boy's. For another, he wasn't alone. Moses trotted unleashed at his heels, and beside him a pretty teenage girl was talking animatedly, using her hands to illustrate her words. The boy's head was bent toward her; he didn't see Sam. As they passed, Sam heard him laugh out loud.

He stood and stared after them, a pair of ordinary kids, indistinguishable from any other young couple. "I'll be damned," he said. A peculiar kind of pain started up in his chest, a tingling, prickly feeling, like frostbitten fingers coming back to life.

Peter had confessed to Sam, and thereafter the boy's life seemed to change. There was no proof that these events were related, but then again no proof they weren't. Sam tended to suspect a causal link.

Thoughts of confessing began to trouble him. He resisted them, of course. It wasn't as if admitting what he had done would change anything. Sam had a carpenter's practical view of life. You screw up, you go back and fix whatever's fixable. Cut a plank too long, you can trim it; cut it too short and that's all she wrote. Lou's life had been cut short. What Sam was up against now couldn't be fixed.

Every day he dismissed the idea of confessing, and every night it returned. Misery loves company precisely because it does not love itself. Sam was weary of his, and would be rid of it if he could. The old rabbi had said he had a canker in his soul. How do you cure a canker? You lance it, you drain the poison from the wound. Perhaps if Sam did as Peter had, he too could get past the thing that could not be remedied; perhaps he could retake his life.

But who to tell? Malachi sprang instantly to mind . . . but oh, that voracious, beady-eyed old harpy, that spiritual vulture—Sam was loath to give him the satisfaction. Others might mistake him for an affable, inoffensive elderly clergyman, but Sam knew better. Malachi was subversive, an ecclesiastic mole who burrowed beneath defenses, then attacked from inside. Anyway, even if he'd wanted to tell Malachi (which he decidedly did not) Sam couldn't have done it; for the rabbi had disappeared. Not even Lapid knew where he was. Early one morning Sam ran into the doctor in the country store and asked him, out of idle curiousity, if he knew what had become of Malachi. Marty threw up his hands. "Ah, the disappearing rabbi. Now you see him, now you don't."

"Doesn't he have a home somewhere? You found him for the funeral."

"Actually, he found me. Sorry, Sam, haven't got a clue."

Just as well, Sam thought. In his present vulnerable state another dose of Malachi was the last thing he needed. And yet the old man continued to loom large in Sam's imagination. Why this should be he had no idea; for what, after all, was Malachi to him? A hovering presence in the back of his mind, a thorn in his side, a minor prick in the cactus garden of life. Perhaps it was his false humility, so at odds with his air of secret knowingness, that got to Sam; or his penetrating black eyes, or that air of dire patience, the patience of a devil who knows he'll get you in the end.

Whatever. The fact was, Sam would have been happy never to lay eyes on Malachi again, which made it all the more infuriating when the rabbi started popping up in his dreams. Barging right in, night after night; shouldering his way into dreams that had nothing to do with him, like that damned Energizer bunny that keeps going and going and going.

Sam could not keep him out.

Often the rabbi appeared in disguise. Once, in a dream about visiting Italy with Lou (a trip they had planned but never taken), Malachi appeared as a nun; another time as a clerk in a convenience store, still another as a Coney Island hot-dog peddler. Not only his apparel but also his face, mannerisms, even voice changed from dream to dream, subsumed into the character he played. But Sam always knew him by his trick of answering a question with a question, and because he never said anything Sam wanted to hear.

Lapid telephoned one night. "Mildred has deserted me," he announced.

"Movie?"

"Bridge with the yentas. You busy?"

Sam was very busy, deciding between a frozen pizza and a Hungry Man's chicken pot pie. He drove over. They ate reheated brisket (excellent; when Mildred reverted to her culinary roots she was a very decent cook) at the kitchen table, then retired to the doctor's study. Marty lit a fat cigar, Sam a cigarette, and there in the very seats they'd occupied when the doctor made his confession, Sam came out with his.

Lapid listened carefully, then replied in a tone he generally reserved for first-year residents. "Nonsense. Cancer killed her. A malfunction on the cellular level, a glitch in the immune system, a defective gene."

"No, actually, an overdose of morphine. As you would have discovered, if you'd chosen to look."

The doctor scowled at the tip of his cigar. "Which would have told me exactly nothing. Wouldn't be the first time a patient trying to deal with intractable pain accidentally overdosed."

"Are you trying to convince me that I didn't do what I know I did?"

"No. I'm saying it's irrelevant."

"Irrelevant?" Sam said.

"Whatever the proximate cause of death, the *reason* Louise died is that she had incurable cancer."

"*Irrelevant?*"

"What you need to deal with is her death, pure and simple. And if you'll excuse an old friend's frankness, I don't believe you've even started doing that. Tell me Louise isn't as much a presence in your life now as when she was alive."

Sam glared. "You want to take that from me, too? You want me to forget her?"

"I want you back among the living." Lapid leaned forward, blinking hard behind his thick glasses. "You were the best of husbands to her, the best of friends. Because of you she fought as long and hard as she did. She died in her own bed, in your arms. Whatever you did, Sam, you did for her. No one in the world would blame you."

Marty was all sympathy, no comprehension, but it wasn't his fault, Sam thought. If their situations were reversed, then no doubt Sam would be pumping out the same bilge as Marty and thinking himself wise in the bargain. He wished for once he were a man of words, a writer or professor; maybe then he could explain this thing so Lapid would understand. But Sam was only a carpenter, with a carpenter's way of seeing.

"It's not a question of blame," he said. "*Why* doesn't matter." He held out his hands, scarred palms upward. "What I'm saying to you is simple. These were not the right tools for the job."

"No," Lapid said after a pause. "I quite see that. But they were the only tools available."

Nothing came of it. Sam waited for days, but there was no relief, no sense of delivery, no sign of forgiveness, internal or external. And in his heart he knew why.

Lapid was the wrong confessor. When a man feels the need to bang his head against a wall, it's not a padded wall he wants. Lapid was soft, Lapid was safe, Lapid was grateful. Telling him risked nothing, consequently gained nothing.

The compulsion to tell someone, far from being sated, had grown stronger. If penance was required (and although he still maintained that what he did was necessary and right, penance seemed to be what he sought), then Sam had to tell someone who would stand back to judge, not rush in to comfort. What he in his despair longed for was the chance to lay his burden onto another, to let someone else choose between the voice in his head that said "You did right" and the one in his heart that cried "You did wrong!" To be judged, to be punished or absolved: anything, only to silence those incessant voices.

He thought of the Muellers, Willem and Kate. But it seemed weak to confess to a woman; and as far as Willem was concerned, they had not the habit of that kind of confidence. Theirs was a pragmatic friendship, based on helping and doing, not talking. Sam wouldn't know how to tell Willem; he'd never find the words. And even if he could, what harm had Willem ever done him that Sam should lay this burden on him? If the situation were reversed, if it were Kate who was dying and Willem who helped her over the edge, Sam would willingly have gone to his grave without sharing that knowledge.

It occurred to him that of all the people he know, the one who would surely understand him was Peter Quinn; but Sam put that thought straight out of his head. A boy can confide in a man, but a man can't lay his troubles on a boy and still call himself a man.

It came down, as it had once before, to Kuzak.

Late one Saturday night, Sam drove over to the sheriff's house, an old stone structure on a bluff overlooking the state thruway. Kuzak answered the door in a gray T-shirt and sweatpants. He didn't appear surprised to find Sam at his door, but then Kuzak's face wasn't built for surprise. He looked sallow, tired; the hand that shook Sam's was flecked with age. The unsolved arsons were taking their toll. Months had passed since the last incident, but Sam knew from Kate that Mueller and Kuzak still took turns patrolling every night.

"Come on in," Kuzak said. The local news was on in the living room, which smelt of wood-fire and cigar smoke. When his wife left, she left in style. Kuzak had returned home from a day-long conference in Poughkeepsie to find his wife gone and his house stripped bare. Kuzak didn't try to find her. He'd borrowed Willem's truck, driven up to Albany, and gone shopping in the Salvation Army's second-hand shop. The results were dowdy but comfortable: a nubby brown couch, a green armchair, a Naugahyde recliner and a couple of mismatched end tables.

Kuzak turned the TV off. "Get you a cold one?"

"Sure."

"Miller or Bud?"

"Thought you drank Coors."

"Used to, till I found out they're owned by a bunch of fascists. Too bad. Good beer."

"Miller's fine. You're a cop, Kuzak. You're supposed to like fascists."

Kuzak answered from the kitchen. "People who live in glass houses shouldn't go around stereotyping other folks."

Meaning Jews in Old Wickham, and he had a point. Sam accepted a bottle. No glass came with it, Kuzak having reverted to full bachelorhood. Kuzak tossed another log onto the fire, nodded Sam over to the couch, and pulled up the armchair.

"So," he said, "what's up?"

At that moment Sam faltered. He thought about jail. Growing up rough, he'd gotten by however he could: nothing violent, but the odd bit of burglary. Cops nicked him once for b&e, once for auto theft. First time he got probation, second time six months in a youth facility. It may be said that he was one of the very few who actually benefited from prison, for it was there in the carpentry shop that he first discovered his feel for woodwork. A useful talent, a discovery that turned his whole life around; nevertheless, the six months had felt like six years. Sam didn't ever want to go back. He didn't want to do this. His mouth went dry, and his voice stalled deep in the tunnel of his throat.

Kuzak raised a bushy eyebrow. "Well, spit it out, son. I ain't gonna bite you."

"What would you do," Sam said, "if a man told you that he helped his wife to die?"

The sheriff seemed to take on a troll-like mass. He sank lower in his chair, turned his stony face toward the fireplace. The new log was burning from the inside out, its fiery core bound by a latticework of blackened wood. Sam lit a cigarette and studied him covertly.

The carpenter was not a jealous man, but where his wife was concerned he was observant. It had always been clear to him that Kuzak admired Louise. They'd met nearly every morning in the back room of the country store and often in the evenings as well, when Sam and Lou would stroll down the hill to call on the Muellers only to find Kuzak already ensconced in their living room. The sheriff's eyes lit up whenever Lou entered the room; he'd sit up taller, run a hand through his grizzled hair, look at her often with a kind of wistfulness. That time that Frank Gower spit on Lou, Kuzak turned a blind eye when Sam went after Gower. After he got out of the hospital, Gower had tried to press charges. Kuzak laughed in his face. "If Sam hadn't of had his little chat with you," he told Gower, "I would've."

Sam wondered how Kuzak's feelings for Lou would factor into this new equation. Would he be grateful to Sam for sparing her the agony of certain, slow disintegration? Or would he resent the premature snuffing out of a light that had, however indirectly, brightened his own solitary existence?

Kuzak didn't speak at once. When he did, his voice was guarded. "This man, are you saying he abetted a suicide?"

"I didn't say suicide. What if he did it himself, but only because she wanted him to? Because she asked and he couldn't say no."

"She wanted to die, this woman?"

"She wanted to *live*. But say that wasn't an option. Say she was dying, and it was just a matter of how and when."

Kuzak grunted. His chin sank to his chest; the lines on his face deepened. He was silent for a long time. Sam closed his eyes. As soon as he did, the muted ebb and flow of thruway traffic, always audible in the background, grew more pronounced. According to the back-room crowd, Kuzak's wife had left him on account of that thruway. They said the sound seeped into her nerves, they said she begged Kuzak to move, but he refused. He was born in this house, he told her, and he would die there, perched up over the thruway with all the world rushing by below him.

Sam didn't know if it was true. He doubted it. People told all kinds of lies. They made up stories to account for things they couldn't understand.

When he opened his eyes, Kuzak was waiting for him.

"I'd tell him to go home," he said, "and make his peace with God."

"What kind of pissant answer's that?" cried Sam. He should have been relieved but instead felt cheated, like a kid who's walked in on his father in the shower and seen his old man's privates all shriveled up and puny. "You're a lawman, Kuzak, not a goddamn preacher."

The sheriff raised a heavy shoulder and let it drop. "Got no grounds to act."

"No grounds! If the man came to you, confessed?"

"Grief'll mess with any man's head. All survivors feel guilty."

"You could find proof once you knew. The body—"

Kuzak scowled. "God forbid I should disturb the peace of the dead without good cause."

In a low voice Sam said, "What about the peace of the living?"

"Not my department, Sam. Like you said, I'm no preacher. Tell you one thing, though, since we're talking hypothetical. Kind of situation you're describing, that's your classic no-win situation. Damned if you do and damned if you don't. Man gets caught up in one of them crunchers, he's just gonna have to find a way to live with whatever he decides."

"Easy for you to say."

Kuzak's gaze was steady. "Didn't say easy. I said necessary."

Sam was between jobs. The lesbians' house was finished. He had a renovation lined up in Valatie, a couple of city architects who were buying a two hundred–year-old Dutch colonial, but that wouldn't start till they went to closing sometime in late spring. In the meantime he built furniture.

The seed cabinet, long since completed, stood in a corner of his workshop beside the long workbench. Kate Mueller had exclaimed over its beauty—"extravagant beauty" she called it with a worried look, as she knit her brow over the problem of selling it for what it was worth. "It falls into that gray zone," she told Sam.

He nodded with perfect comprehension. People who could afford this piece tended to buy originals, while people who bought reproductions weren't looking to spend what this one would cost. "No problem," he said, and meant it, for this was one piece he'd never intended to sell. Sam, like most artists and artisans, was adept at separating from his completed work, sending it out into the world to fend for itself. In this case, however, there was no question of letting go. Too much anguish had gone into the making of this cabinet, which spanned the period of Lou's death, for him to allow it to stand in some stranger's house. Instead he kept it in the workshop and used it to store hardware—nails, screws, hinges, pegs, and knobs. Kate was appalled but Sam pleased at this journeyman's use of a fine piece of furniture; it seemed to him that the Shakers, for whom beauty was a byproduct of utility, would approve.

He was working now on a two-drawer blanket chest for a city couple who'd bought one from Kate and wanted a matching piece. The lumberyard in Wickham had come up with some beautiful boards of cherry heartwood, which he planned to use for the top, front, and sides of the chest. For the back and bottom he'd selected a secondary grade of yellow poplar, cheaper than the high-grade cherry wood but still a lot more expensive than the plywood most cabinetmakers would use for the parts that didn't show. He had just started jointing the edges for the top and side panels when he heard footsteps on the gravel outside. Someone was approaching the workshop.

His hand began to shake. It could have been anyone, but the moment he heard the sound he knew who was coming. Hadn't he been expecting this visit, hadn't he been waiting for it? Twice since baring his soul to Kuzak he'd run into the sheriff in Whitehill's back room. Each time Kuzak had greeted him normally, showing no sign of what now lay between them; yet Sam had no doubt that sooner or later the man would have second thoughts. It stood to reason; it went with the territory. *Sam,* he'd say, *I hate to do it, man, but I've got no choice: You're under arrest for the murder of Louise Pollak.* And Sam would have no one to blame but himself.

The steps came closer. Sam laid down his tools and stood up.

Someone scratched at the door.

Sam yanked the door open and Moses bounded in, feathery tail wagging like a semaphore. "Jesus Christ, dog!" Sam sagged against the frame. "Where'd you come from?"

"He's with me," Peter Quinn said, appearing from around the corner.

"Should have known. Follows you everywhere, don't he?"

"Everywhere he can. It's a pain," Peter complained, with barely concealed pride. "I used to like being invisible. Now every place I go people keep coming up, petting the dog and talking and stuff."

Sam suppressed a smile. "Girls, too, huh?"

"They're the worst. They get all mushy. 'Aw, what a cute doggy, can I pet him?'"

"You could leave him home."

"No way. He'd hate that, wouldn't you, Moses?"

Moses thumped his tail. Sam noticed there was a bandage wrapped around it. "What happened to him?"

"You should see the other guy. This jumped-up no-account German shepherd next door thinks he's king of the road; only Moses here, he don't take shit from nobody."

"Kicked that shepherd's ass?"

"But good," Peter said emphatically.

Sam laughed. "Aren't you the guy who said he wanted nothing to do with the dog?"

"I don't. It's him, he just glommed onto me. One stray to another, I guess."

"Uh-huh. So what brings you up here?"

The boy pulled an envelope from his pocket and handed it over. "Message from Jane."

"Phone doesn't work?"

"It works." He didn't elaborate and Sam let it drop. He had not the least interest in parsing with Peter the possible reasons for Jane's choosing to write rather than phone. Holding took the envelope gingerly between two fingers, he dropped it into his shirt pocket to open later, if it didn't explode first.

She had good reason to be pissed. For weeks Sam had been avoiding her. He'd stayed away from the country store, done his shopping at dinner time, driven the back roads just to keep from passing her house.

It wasn't that he didn't want to see her. He did. Jane Goncalves was small but hard, a walnut of a woman he'd like to crack. But he wasn't ready and maybe never would be. This woman deserved a whole man. If Sam couldn't help his attraction to her, he could at least control his proximity.

It was strange. He could fuck the likes of Marie Pellagio and Mistress Come-Hither till the cows came home and never feel a twinge of guilt, because with them it was nothing personal; the transaction carried all the emotional resonance of a sneeze. But that brief moment when he held Goncalves in his arms, when he kissed her, he had forgotten all about Louise. She had utterly vanished from his mind, ceased to exist.

Afterward, for the first time in his life, Sam felt he had betrayed his wife.

A polite cough from Peter drew him back.

"Still here? What you waiting for, a tip?"

"Hell no," Peter said, offended.

"Right, then," Sam said, turning away. "Thanks, kid."

Instead of leaving, though, Peter followed him inside. He stood in the center of the workshop and looked around. He raised his face to the grainy light filtering in from the west windows. His gaze followed the vertical strip windows upward to the polished beams and vaulted ceiling. "Did you build this place, or did it, like, come with the house?"

"It was a barn. I converted it."

"What do you make here?"

"Furniture, mostly."

Peter walked around, conducted by Moses, who had assumed a proprietorial air. While Peter exclaimed over the lathe and examined the orderly row of tools hanging above the workbench, Sam turned his back and opened Jane's note. He'd had a few notes from women these past few months, all variations on the theme of "Why don't you call?" and ranging in tone from plaintive to furious. He steeled himself. But Jane's note was a model of economy. "Portia's coming, wants to see you. Dinner, Saturday night, 7:00? Jane."

"Yo, Sam," Peter said.

Sam turned around, stuffing the note into his jeans pocket.

The boy jutted his chin at the seed cabinet. "You build this thing?"

"Yeah, I did."

"No shit. Really?" Eyes tracking from Sam to the cabinet and back again, seeking the connection, wondering how something like that could have come out of someone like Sam. The carpenter was not offended, having wondered the same himself. The boy reached toward a drawer handle, then caught himself and looked at Sam.

"Go ahead. This isn't a museum."

Peter slid the drawer in and out, smoothly, soundlessly. He brushed the back of his hand against the burnished wood. "Where's a person learn to do this?"

"Other carpenters, mostly."

"Can anyone learn it?"

"More or less. You need decent eye-hand coordination and a feel for the wood."

"What's that mean, 'a feel for the wood'?"

Sam shrugged uncomfortably. If he had a philosophy it was "Do the work, don't jabber about it," a cautionary attitude particularly useful when it came to Shaker furniture. People talked a lot of mush about the Shakers; they romanticized them, blunting the hard edges of their beliefs, and imbuing their furniture and artifacts with such a weight of spiritual significance as would surely have amounted in the eyes of the Shakers themselves to idolatry. A chair is a chair, to Sam's way of thinking; and a good chair is sufficient unto itself.

But when he saw Peter run a reverent index finger along the gently curved plane of the cabinet front, a strange thing happened. For one moment his point of view seemed to shift, so that he saw not through his own eyes but rather through the boy's. The effect was as if a man slowly losing his eyesight to cataracts suddenly had his vision restored in full. The room pulsated with light. Stippled beams played across the surface of the wood, bringing out the residue of vitality. Thus had the room appeared to him when it was first built, in the good years, before Lou's illness.

Within him something stirred: an impulse of gratitude, a welling up of words. "You've got to know your wood," he said. "Every kind is different; each one possesses its own qualities. You could make a desk out of butternut and the identical desk out of oak, and they'd come out totally different. Now that seed cabinet there, that's curly maple; a good hardwood and to my mind one of the most beautiful. It was a favorite of the Shakers. Look at the growth rings, look at the grain, look at the way it gleams. That's not lacquer. That glow comes from inside."

Peter asked what he was working on now, and Sam showed him the panels of cherry heartwood and the plans for the chest. Taped to the wall above the work bench was a photo of a blanket chest, not one of his own, but a Shaker original. The picture wasn't necessary—by now Sam could look at a plan and directly envision the finished piece, just as an architect looks at blueprints and sees, not a two-dimensional grid of lines and measurements, but an actual house—but he found that the photo helped keep him focused.

"Heartwood being wood from a heart tree?"

This mild joke was strangely moving to Sam, for the fact that it was made at all brought home the distance they'd traveled. He smiled. "Heartwood's the oldest, deepest, hardest part of any tree. It's the essence of the tree, the core, what you get when you strip away the branches, the bark, the outer layers of wood. If a tree is sound, its heartwood is just about indestructible."

"As opposed to the human heart."

Sam stared at him, wondering once again at the boy's ability to articulate thoughts Sam had never shaped into words. Not only were Peter's words true, they were a truth that had shaped Sam's life. People die, and what's left is fit only for burying or burning. But chop down a tree and what remains is valuable, useful, even beautiful.

Peter knelt beside Moses and scratched his chest. He leaned his forehead against the dog, and the words he spoke were lost in the dog's fur.

"Say again?" Sam said.

"Could you teach me?"

No, Sam thought. He was no teacher. He liked working alone. Last thing in the world he needed was some kid breathing down his neck.

"You've got school," he said.

"I could come after," Peter said.

Sam gazed up at the beams. Suddenly he had a sense of Lou's presence, as strong as if she were standing right behind him. Her voice spoke to him. *Don't blow this now, Pollak. Get it right.*

Aw, Lou.

Peter, face averted, waited for his answer.

Sam sighed. "You learn by doing," he said. "You start with total scut work: sanding, scraping, hauling, whatever needs doing."

"I'm cool with that."

"I'm not offering to pay you."

"I ain't asking." Peter raised his face. Kid looked different, Sam thought. Couldn't put his finger on it, and then he did. Peter was smiling.

CHAPTER 19

Portia blew in like a psychedelic schooner, tottering on four-inch heels as yards of rainbow-colored chiffon billowed and swirled around her. "Good God Almighty," she cried, sweeping past Jane to envelop Peter in a maelstrom hug, "what have you been feeding this child?"

"Untalon me, woman!" he said, laughing. "Phew, what is that scent: Bordello Number Nine?"

"Fresh thing! Now where's my little girls at? Where's Keisha?"

"Right here," said Keisha, holding up her arms for a hug.

"No! I thought you were the baby-sitter. And Luz! Come here, darlin', and gimme some sugar. Jane, I swear, these children are so beautiful it hurts my eyes to look at them. And you, don't even talk to me. You so skinny I could spit."

Jane said, "Hello, Portia." Ike had stayed on in Albany after the wedding to visit with cousins; Portia planned on spending the night at Jane's before rejoining him. Combining pleasure with pleasure, she called it; Jane was amused, never fooled. The eye of this hurricane was steady as a rock.

Which was fine with Jane, who had nothing to hide. After a short while she left Portia and the children in the living room and repaired to the kitchen, there to baste the chicken and calm her nerves, on edge for no good reason. So what if Sam Kiss-and-Run Pollak was coming to dinner? Only reason she'd invited him was to let Portia scope him out vis-à-vis Peter, who was currently suffering a virulent attack of hero-worship, the inversion of his previous detestation. Personally Jane could care less. She'd written Sam's sorry ass off already.

An onion-scented cloud of steam rose to greet her as she opened the cast-iron oven. The chicken, a seven-pound roaster, was browning nicely. Using a pot holder Keisha had made for her, Jane tilted the roasting pan, sucked some drippings into the baster, and squirted them over the bird. Closing the oven, she rocked back on her heels. Thank God she hadn't invested much: one kiss, a few late-night fantasies, a day or two wasted waiting for the phone to ring. Could have been worse. Men were plunderers by nature; she hadn't lived thirty-four years without learning that. She knew at least one woman he'd slept with and dumped, though rumor had it there were others. The buck-toothed woman who ran the post office knew he'd worked on Jane's house; somehow she managed to drag his name into every conversation. "How's Sam doing?" "Have you seen Sam Pollak lately?" Jane tried not to encourage her but could no more help listening than she could keep from rubbernecking a car crash. One time, the postmistress told her: "We've got this off-and-on thing going, you know." Pathetic creature. Jane at least was left with dignity intact. The rest of her too, damn his sexy eyes.

In the living room Portia was reading out a letter from Carlos. He'd sent a photo, too: the young prince in the bosom of his new suburban family. The girls passed it back and forth till it was smudged gray with prints. Peter barely glanced at it. Soon as Portia's back was turned, he slipped out of the room. Didn't say a word; she just turned around and he was gone.

She hauled herself up the steep wooden stairs, pulling on the banister. By the third floor she was huffing and puffing. Strident rock music seeped through the closed door of his room. Portia knocked three times before he answered. Then he just stood in the doorway, looking.

"Can I come in?"

Reluctantly he stood back. Portia checked out the room, messier than it had been, though not by much. A hockey stick leaned into a corner, socks and pads littered the floor. "You play?" she shouted over the music.

"I did. Ice's melting."

She walked over to the desk and shut off the radio. She could see the sudden quiet made him nervous. He stood by the door, hand on the knob as if ready to bolt. Never mind what Jane thought; the old Peter was so close to the surface, scratch him and out it came.

"Thought you'd be pleased to hear from Carlos," she said. "You two were tight."

He shrugged.

"Gonna write him back?"

"Maybe."

Maybe meaning no way. Portia snorted. "Out of sight, out of mind, that it, boy?"

"More or less," he said. "Got a problem with that?"

Cocky was the word that sprang to mind. She looked him up and down. "Bet your skinny ass I do. You ain't alone in this world."

"Everyone's alone in this world."

"Thank you, King Solomon!"

"You're welcome. And now, if that concludes today's lesson . . ." He opened the door with a flourish. But Portia didn't budge.

"Not so fast, young man. I've got a bone to pick with you. Last time I came I brought you a card from your sister."

Peter didn't answer, just stared at her.

"She ast you to write back. You done that yet?"

"No," he said with savage mockery, "I ain't done that yet."

"Why not?"

He rolled his eyes; he studied the ceiling and sighed rudely. "Because," he said, "I am trying to keep my life in order, okay? Doesn't help anybody to go dredging up the past."

"Except life ain't like that, Peter. 'That was then, this is now.' Life don't work like that. It's all of a piece."

"Whatever," he said.

Portia regarded him with narrowed eyes. "Her mama called me," she said. "Her new mama. Says Maura's been crying at night. They ask her why, she says you."

Peter winced. He covered his ears but Portia's voice reached him anyway, inexorable as rising flood waters.

"They tell her your brother's fine, girl, why you crying over him? She says you're not fine. She says you're mad at her. She says it's all her fault."

His hands dropped. "*Her* fault?"

"She says if she hadn't of spilt that drink, her daddy would still be alive and you'd all be together."

"Bullshit. You're scamming me."

"They *tell* her it's not her fault," Portia sailed on. "They say no one in the world blames her for what happened. She says, 'Peter blames me. That's why he don't write.' "

Tears gathered in his eyes. Peter didn't seem to notice. He said, "How can she think that?"

"Boy, don't you know there's always enough guilt to go 'round?"

Peter turned his back on her. His shoulders hunched. He didn't make a sound. After a while he began banging his head rhythmically against the wall.

Portia watched with the clear, cold conscience of a surgeon. She didn't speak; she offered no comfort. Eventually the banging subsided. With his face to the wall he said, "I thought I was doing the right thing. I thought she'd be better off forgetting me."

"Sometimes," Portia said, "you think too much." She pushed up out of the chair and pointed downward. "Write."

Peter wiped his face on his sleeve and sat down at his desk.

Jane had a plan; she knew exactly how to protect herself from Sam Pollak. Blandness was the key, armor-plated blandness, no rough edges for him to catch hold of, no way in. She would emulate the invincibly perky housewives of detergent commercials and fifties sitcoms. She thought Donna Reed and June Allyson; she thought turtles and armadillos.

Why this should be necessary, considering that she'd written him off, was a question she chose not to ask. Because to address it she would have to admit that he'd gotten to her. That he'd speared her with that kiss and the look in his eyes afterward. That he'd brought home all that was missing in her life, altering her perspective so that a life half-full came to seem a life half-empty.

Jane was thirty-four years old. She had a houseful of children who didn't belong to her. She slept alone; she had no man, no lover, no prospect of a lover. She'd always known there was a price to pay for doing what she wanted to do, but she thought she'd made peace with the cost; she'd fancied herself content. Then along came Sam, with his hooded eyes, quiet voice, strong skillful hands. Jane had a weakness for lost boys dating back to Peter Pan. What a sap that Wendy was. In her place they couldn't have dragged Jane away from Neverland.

Lost men were even more dangerous. Not all at once, but little by little Sam's hands crept into her fantasies. She imagined them moving over her body, his mouth pressed to the hollow of her throat. Like rust on a car, these thoughts ate away at her contentment.

Was that his fault? Not really. Give a boy a stick and show him a beehive, and what happens next is genetically, hormonally predetermined. He'd roiled her world, opened her eyes, offered her hope and snatched it away. If he had come to her that night after they kissed, she would have taken him straight into her bed. He must have known; but he stayed away. He stayed away and didn't call, and his silence was more eloquent than words could have been. And if, as she sometimes thought, there was honor in his restraint, that served only to make her regret him more.

Thus Jane, needing to protect herself, called upon skills unused since high school but perfected back then, when she used to attend dances in the gym with girlfriends, late bloomers like herself. She brushed off the old abstracted stare, resurrected the smile that said, "Hey—I'd be dancing if I wanted to be." She built a brick house to keep out the big bad wolf.

Sam arrived at the appointed hour bearing wine and cake. He shook her hand and met her eyes with a sheepish, charming look that said *Don't hate me.*

Her eyes gave nothing back. "How nice of you to come."

Sam blinked. "You're pissed at me."

"Of course not," she said sweetly. "We've all grown very fond of Moses."

At dinner Jane presided over the table in an eat-your-heart-out dress the color of burnished copper. Clinging velvet, just this side of vampish. She surrounded herself with children, barricaded herself behind her perfect hostess smile. She'd meant for Sam to sit next to Portia at the far end of the table, but somehow he contrived to change places, ending up between Jane and Peter. As the others were settling in he leaned toward her and pitched his voice low. "You look beautiful tonight."

"Thank you," she replied without inflection, as if he'd just handed her the peas. "Peter, tell Sam about your project in shop."

"We're making our own tools. You should see the monster lathe they've got there—it's mint. And he lets us use it. I'm making a chisel with a carved handle." Peter rambled on, addressing only Sam. The carpenter responded automatically but his eyes kept wandering back toward Jane. Several times he spoke to her, and met with impenetrable politeness. Her coolness kindled his warmth; he seemed determined to provoke her, if only to anger. Jane stuck to her game plan. One time only was she rattled. Something brushed against her leg, and she jerked it back, blushing violently; but it was only Moses, prospecting for scraps.

Sandwiched between the two little girls, Portia didn't miss a thing. She ate and talked and laughed, she cut up chicken and wiped chins; but all the while her busy eyes darted from Sam to Jane. Her eyebrows telegraphed urgent messages to Jane, who refused to acknowledge, much less respond. After dinner Portia gathered up an armload of plates and followed Jane into the kitchen, kicking the door shut behind them.

"Let me guess. He's a psychopathic serial killer with fifteen bodies buried in his basement."

"Cute, Portia," Jane said. "Hand me a coffee filter out of that box, will you?"

"Then you been holding out on me, girlfriend. You did the deed with him."

"Wrong again." She measured five scoops of coffee into the drip filter and filled the reservoir with water. "Would you put that cake on a platter?"

"You tell me, then," Portia said.

"Nothin' to tell, Miss Nosy."

"Hell there ain't! This is Portia talking, girl. That Stepford wife routine sent shivers up my spine, I tell you that for free. Could have chilled the wine on that smile of yours."

"This is not about me," Jane said. "This is about Peter."

She stared at Portia and Portia stared back. Friends for ages, but their mutual fondness owed nothing to similarity of temperament. Portia, in Jane's eyes, was a cross between Janis Joplin and Aretha. She wailed out her pain, cackled her amusement, bellowed her rage and crowed her joy; she believed that anything worth doing was worth overdoing. Whereas for Jane, the stronger the emotion, the greater the need to contain it. If Portia's anger was a bucket of scalding water, Jane's was a laser beam. When threatened she fought; when beaten, she hid and licked her wounds in solitude, and nothing could induce her to come out till she was ready. She was the immovable object to Portia's irresistible force.

This time it was Portia who retreated. "Peter," she drawled. "Right."

"Did you see how he talked to Sam?"

Portia sniffed. "Am I blind? Boy never talked so much in his life."

"So what do you think?"

"You always said he needed a man in his life, make up for the nasty piece of work he called a father. Although . . ."

"What?"

"How's Sam feel? I didn't pick up much on his end. Of course," she added slyly, "he *was* distracted."

Jane raked her hands through her short hair. "You know, I'm not sure. For a while I thought there was a real bond there, though God knows what it is. And he did agree to teach him carpentry, which seemed promising. But I don't know . . ."

"Ever talk to him?"

"Premature," Jane said at once. "Didn't want to scare him off."

"Maybe he runs hot and cold," Portia said. Her shrewd eyes studied Jane, whose face was unreadable.

"Maybe."

"In which case . . ."

"We're better off without him."

Sam was leaving. Jane walked him to the kitchen door.

"Good night," she said, holding out her hand. "Thanks for coming."

Instead of shaking her hand he held it. "Why so polite? You make me feel like a stranger."

"I don't think of you as a stranger. I think of you as Peter's friend."

He laughed. "God, you're a hard-ass, Goncalves."

"Thanks. I do my best." She allowed herself half a smile.

"That's better," he said. "Not much, but better."

"Are you flirting with me, Pollak?"

"Sounds like it, don't it? To tell you the truth, I don't know what the fuck I'm doing."

"Go home," Jane said. "Come back when you know."

CHAPTER 20

He wanders through a vast necropolis, spotted with markers ranging from simple wooden crosses to huge marble monuments, laid out in a geometric grid transected by cracked and buckling cement paths. A desolate spot, dreary of aspect, a windy treeless plain without distinguishing features save the statues of Jesus and winged cherubs that intermingle with a few sparse Stars of David. He has come to visit Louise. Amid the graves (overgrown with weeds, littered with candy wrappers and yellowed scraps of newspaper) not a soul stirs; or so it seems until Sam, trudging against the wind, discerns a dark figure hunched and motionless on the ground beside what somehow he knows to be Lou's grave. Drawing near, he sees a man in a dark overcoat, with a wide-brimmed hat that hides his face. The man raises his head.

Sam says, "What are *you* doing here?"

"What do you think?" Malachi says. "I've come for the unveiling." He rises creakily, pressing a gnarled fist into the small of his back. "Oy," he grumbles. "A young man I'm not, Mr. Pollak, to wait out in the cold and damp."

"What unveiling?"

Malachi points to Louise's headstone, which Sam now notices is draped in a painter's drop cloth that snaps and buckles in the wind. He reaches for the cloth, but before he can grasp it the rabbi slides in front of him. "Allow me," and taking the drape in both hands, he whips it off with a magician's flourish. "Now, *boychik,* we pray. *Yiskadal veyiskadash . . .*"

There are letters carved into the stone but Sam's eyes, teary from the wind, cannot focus. He wipes them on his sleeve and the words come clear:

LOUISE POLLAK
1957–1995
Beloved Wife
Done In

"No!" he cries. "Oh you wicked bastard, how dare you mock me!" Leaping across the grave, he grabs the little rabbi by his lapels and shakes him violently. "Do you take me for a fool?"

Malachi's black coat comes away in Sam's hands, revealing a fool's gay motley. Sam is not surprised. It seems to suit the old man's gaunt, inverted frame. Besides, he remembers Malachi saying, "An itinerant rabbi is not your everyday rabbi."

"On the contrary," Malachi replies. "Here's a riddle for you: What do you call a defrocked rabbi?"

"Riddles at a time like this? Malachi, you fool!"

"Precisely." The rabbi has completed his metamorphosis into a tragic Pierrot, with a painted teardrop on each wizened cheek. He begins to rock on his heels. "Repeat after me, Mr. Pollak. *Yiskadal veyiskadash . . .*" The little bell on his jester's cap tinkles as he sways.

"Damned if I'll say Kaddish!" Sam cries.

"And damned if you don't," says Malachi, not without sympathy. "Please, Mr. Pollak, I got a wedding yet this morning, and a funeral in the afternoon. *Yiskadal . . .*"

"You don't fool me," Sam says. "I see through you." Again he lays violent hands on Malachi; this time, however, the rabbi fights back, and in a manner amazingly elusive and agile. No sooner does the carpenter get a grip on him than the old man breaks free with some unexpected but effective counter. After managing to capture Malachi in a bear hug, Sam tries to lift him but he finds that he cannot. How can it be that the carpenter, who carries a hundredweight of lumber half a mile uphill without breaking a sweat, cannot budge a wisp of a rabbi who looks as if one strong gust would blow him to Jerusalem? Malachi stretches out his arms, twists, and is free. Even as Sam stands, struck with astonishment, the rabbi seizes him by the shoulders and throws him down.

From Sam's abject angle Malachi looks ten feet tall. "Where'd you learn that move? What, do they teach judo in rabbinical school now?"

"Kabbalah." Malachi points to his forehead. "Judo of the mind. Give up?"

Sam lunges at the rabbi's knees by way of an answer; but his arms close on air, and before he can recover Malachi has him pinned to the ground. Those delicate little hands with their birdlike bones possess uncanny strength and the grip of a heavy-duty wrench.

For a long time they strive, so evenly matched that neither can vanquish the other, until at last the younger prevails. Malachi lies upon the hard earth groaning, his force spent.

"Let me go," he gasps. "I must go."

"Not so fast," Sam tells him.

"What, you want I should say uncle? Uncle, *tante,* the whole *mishpuchah*—just let me go!"

"I want answers. The truth, Malachi, none of your shtick."

"You want answers, you need questions."

"Are you a man?"

"Of course I'm a man." The rabbi raises his eyes to heaven. "This he has to ask? What do I look like, gefilte fish?"

"Where do you come from?"

"From where all men come: my mother's womb."

"Where do you live?"

"Here and there. You should excuse me, Mr. Pollak, but in my personal opinion these questions are not so interesting. You got nothing better?"

Sam rears back and looks at the rabbi, who is no longer clad in motley but rather in the same sober, soiled suit he wore when Sam first laid eyes on him. The belled cap is gone as well, though the white makeup and painted tears remain on his face, and below the dusty cuffs of his pants Sam spies the curled, pointy toe of the jester's slippers.

"Tell me," Sam says. "Did I do right or wrong?"

"Ask your conscience."

"I'm asking you."

"Right question, wrong address. All I know is what I don't know."

They are sitting face-to-face, cross-legged on rocky ground beneath a gnarled olive tree. The cemetery is gone. They are on a hilltop, and a broken-runged ladder lies beside them.

"Don't bullshit me, Malachi, we're past that. Just answer yes or no: Did I do wrong?"

The craftiness drains from Malachi's face. He raises his face to Sam. His eyes are wells of crystal water. "You took a life," Malachi says. "Are we children here?"

"Was I supposed let her suffer, then?"

The rabbi sighs and spreads his hands. A painted tear trickles down his face.

Sam awoke, suddenly and completely, to perfect darkness. He looked at the bedside clock and groaned. Four o'clock, and his night was over. His body ached all over and his sheets were soaked with sweat, but that discomfort was nothing to the misery that blanketed his soul. For the first time he had dreamed of Lou dead. Countless times he'd dreamed of her, but always alive. Now he felt his grasp on her loosening; she was slipping away, slipping away. Soon she would be altogether lost to him.

He rolled out of bed, groaning, and stepped into the shower. Raising his face to the water, he felt himself begin to revive. He got out of the shower, threw on a pair of jeans and a sweater, and went into the kitchen. Started a pot of coffee, then stepped out onto the deck. Goose bumps covered his arms. There was half a joint left in an ashtray on the railing. When he lit it he felt his lower lip, sore and swollen. The dream had not faded on impact of waking, but rather had shifted in its entirety, with no loss of clarity or detail, to his conscious mind, where it lodged in a place given more to memory than to dream; so that although Sam *knew* he had dreamed of fighting Malachi, he *felt* as if he really had, and feeling this he relived his relish at the blows he'd landed. Guilt-free blows, because if any man needed the truth beat out of him it was surely Malachi; and as for Sam, who was not prone to assaulting old men, what blame could attach to the act of a dreamer? For whatever ontological state the rabbi inhabited, Sam himself had most certainly been dreaming.

With an effort he turned his mind away from the dream, back to the real world. Closing his hands over the smooth deck railing, he looked out over the valley. The night was very still. From the direction of the thruway came the faint mechanical sputter of trucks shifting gears. Somewhere in town an engine started and stalled repeatedly. A sliver of moon, a sprinkle of stars, and to the east, where the village lay hidden behind the hill, a faint yellow glow in the sky. Dawn, he thought . . . but surely it came too soon. He bent and peered through the kitchen window. The illuminated clock on the microwave showed 4:35, a good hour and a half shy of sunrise. He looked back at the glow, stronger now.

Down the hill, a light blinked on in Mueller's house. A split-second later the firehouse siren sounded.

Seconds later and Sam was in his truck, barreling down the rocky driveway. He was wide awake, but a dreamlike certainty was upon him; he knew what was burning. As he turned onto Old Wickham Road, a pickup zoomed past him in the opposite direction. Though he barely glimpsed the driver, Sam knew the mud-spattered green pickup as well as his own Ford. What with Lyle Fertig living up in the woods a mile past Sam's place, he saw that truck coming or going ten times a week.

Scattered clumps of people milled about on Jane's lawn, silhouetted by a house that glowed like a giant ember. He spotted Jane talking to Kuzak. He parked down the block to leave room for the fire engines and ran back. The first truck had arrived; Willem Mueller was at the curb, deploying men. Sam ran past him.

"Jane!"

She turned her head toward him. Her eyes had receded deep into her face. Flames danced in the pupils. It took her a moment to know him.

"Oh, Sam," she said. "That beautiful house. All your work."

"The kids?"

"Safe, *gracias a Dios.*"

He followed her eyes. Keisha and Luz were standing twenty feet away with their arms around each other. Kate Mueller was kneeling before them, talking. As Sam watched, more neighbors came out. Mistress Come-Hither appeared in fuzzy slippers and a terry-cloth robe with a couple of blankets over her arm. She handed them to Kate, who wrapped them around the children and drew them to her.

"Where's Peter?" Sam asked.

Jane looked about distractedly. "Searching for Moses. He woke us up, you know, barking like a maniac. Peter and I got the girls out. Only now the dog's disappeared."

Sam took Kuzak by the arm and drew him a few steps away. "Is this arson?"

"What do you think?" said the sheriff.

"Fertig passed me on the road," Sam said. "Must have been doing eighty."

"Lyle always shows up at fires. What are *you* doing here, if you don't mind me asking?"

"I was on my deck. I saw the glow, heard the siren." After a short delay, indignation kicked in. "In case you forgot, I'm looking at three months of my work burning up in there."

"Just doing my job," Kuzak said equably.

"And Fertig was headed the other way."

Their eyes held. Kuzak didn't speak for a full minute. The lines on his face looked bottomless. "Cuttin' it close," he said at last. "Coulda run into Mueller on that road."

"Asshole couldn't get his truck started. I heard it from my place. Engine kept stalling."

"Shit, Sam, the boy hasn't got the brains."

"You said it yourself. How much brains does it take?"

Kuzak's eyelids drooped. He looked tired and old. "I'm gonna pay the boy a call. Tell Mueller." He didn't so much run as lumber in high gear toward the road.

Sam found Willem Mueller standing by the fire engine, talking into a radio. The fire chief nodded but signaled him to wait. Watching the men work, Sam couldn't help but admire the economy of their movements, their practiced coordination with the hoses and ladders. He knew them all—Earl Lassiter, Whiteside, the whole back-room crowd—but he knew them as individuals. Now he saw them as a unit, like a veteran construction crew or a football team. Hugging the side of the engine to keep out of their way, Sam felt painfully useless and out of place.

A second fire engine arrived, screeching up to the curb. Frank Gower jumped out of the cab and headed straight for Willem, fastening his coat as he came. "Everybody out, all them kids?"

"Yeah."

"You know we're gonna need more water on this."

"We'll draft from the pond. Pumper's en route. Take your guys round to the south, lay a couple streams on there. Get a ladder up on the roof." Gower nodded and ran off. Willem hung up the radio and turned to Sam. "What's up?"

"Kuzak's gone off to look for Lyle."

Willem blinked. "Why?"

But before Sam could answer Peter Quinn shouldered him aside. Barefoot and shirtless, dressed only in a pair of jeans, the boy barreled straight into Willem.

Willem caught him. "Easy does it, son."

"Moses is in there!"

Willem's voice sharpened. "Someone's inside?"

The firemen nearby heard him and stopped what they were doing.

"My dog. Please, you gotta get him out."

"How do you know he's inside? Did you hear him, see him? "

"He was running around the house, barking. I thought he came out with us but he's nowhere around." The boy was shaking.

The fire chief looked at the house. It was fully involved. Smoke billowed from the windows, sparks shot off the roof like stars falling upward. If it weren't so awful it would have been beautiful.

"Dog ran off," he said. "They do. Scared to death of fire. He'll show up, day or two."

"He's trapped in there, I know it!"

Willem put his hands on the boy's shoulder and turned him to face the fire. "Look at it. Sorry, Peter. I can't risk a man's life for a dog. "

He turned away. Peter cried after him: "He saved ours! You can't just let him die in there!"

It just about broke Sam's heart. He'd thought he was doing a good thing for everyone, giving them that dog. He of all people should have known. Yet how could he regret what he'd done, when it seemed that the dog had saved their lives? If Moses died, it was a better death than most men are privileged to achieve.

But what comfort would that be to Peter, who loved him? Like an infarction, the death of a loved one kills part of the heart. Toward Peter Sam felt all the pity he denied to himself . . . for all the good it did the kid. Sam might know exactly what Peter was going through, but his knowledge was useless to Peter.

Still, he had to try. Turning to console the boy, Sam found him gone.

An air of grim gaiety prevailed beneath flickering red lights; neighbors wandered about in nightclothes, clutching blankets and thermoses. A kind of mad tea party, or secret vernal rite. Dreamlike yet hyperreal: the smell, the stench of burning, the grit in the air, the confusion and din of sirens and radios and men shouting, but most of all the fire itself, now writhing and roaring like a trapped tiger, beset on all sides by streams of water.

Sam looked all over. He saw Kate Mueller talking with Jane, pressing a thermos cup into her hands. He saw a clutch of village women fussing over Keisha and Luz. But the only sign of Peter was a flash of blue denim disappearing behind the house.

The strangest feeling came over him, then, as he loped after that fleeting glimpse of blue. It felt as if this whole event had been scripted and he was following the script, animated by forces beyond his control in the trajectory of his own greatest fear. It felt like sleepwalking through a nightmare.

The firemen had engaged the enemy from the front and side yards of the house, leaving the back deserted, almost peaceful. The door to the mudroom stood ajar. It was much quieter back here. Quiet enough to hear a voice calling plaintively from inside the house.

"Moses! Moses, here boy!"

If this goes wrong, Sam thought, he'd be hearing that cry for a long time to come. The thought spurred him to action; he ran toward the mudroom. At twenty yards the heat came out to meet him like a helmet to the chest. He lowered his shoulder and pushed against it till he reached the door.

"Peter!" he shouted.

The only sound was the fire, groaning in its death throes. Then again, the faint cry came from within: "Moses!"

Sam felt the undertow tugging at his ankles. No, he told himself. Not this time. A whole fire department just around the corner. Don't be stupid.

He ran toward the front, tearing around the corner so fast that he collided with Kate Mueller. Thank God for Kate, level-headed Kate. He grabbed her.

"Tell Willem—Peter's gone back in the house, through the mudroom in the back." He watched her eyes for comprehension. When he saw it, he gave her a shove and turned back.

"Where're you going?" Kate yelled after him. "Don't go in there!"

Sam waved but kept running. He had no intention of entering a burning house; he wasn't that stupid. He was simply going to wait by the mudroom door to point the way for Mueller and his men. Trained men, with masks and equipment. While he waited, he just edged the door open with his foot. A cloud of smoke shot out. Instinctively he dropped to hands and knees.

"Peter!" he hollered. "Peter!"

He strained with all his might to hear. He heard the crackle of fire, the hiss of water turning instantly to steam. Suddenly there came a human sound, a harsh cough; or was it just a timber cracking? It came again, unmistakable this time, a desperate choking cough that sounded close, maybe just beyond the mudroom, inside the kitchen.

Sam looked around wildly. What the hell was taking Willem so long? But Kate would have to find him first, and he would need to gather up men and equipment. Bottom line: Sam was here, Mueller wasn't.

He had to try. He wouldn't enter the house, only the mudroom. It was possible the boy was right there, within arm's reach.

From a drying rack just outside the door, Sam took a dishtowel and tied it around his face, covering his mouth and nose. He took a few deep breaths and crawled forward.

No flames in the mudroom, only dense, acrid smoke. This was the fire's anteroom. Sam kept low. He could see, but it was like seeing underwater: the shapes of things without the colors. With every step the stone floor got hotter. He remembered that Jane kept slickers and boots in the mudroom, found a pair of galoshes on a low shelf and stuck his hands inside. The rubber was warm but not nearly as hot as the floor.

He crept forward. The door leading to the kitchen was slightly ajar. Sam kicked it open and peered into gray smoke so thick he could hardly see his own hands.

"Peter!"

Silence answered him. Then a gasping cough and a single croaked word, faint but recognizable. "Here!"

The sound came from his left, inside the kitchen.

Oh God, not again, Sam thought despairingly. But even as he thought it he was inching forward. What choice did he have? Could he endure another dead voice in the midnight choir, crying in the darkness?

He crossed the threshold into a different world. The difference was not just the increased heat, which was palpable, or the blinding smog of particulate smoke. It was the presence of fire, a watchful mocking presence which Sam could not see but felt all around him. It lurked behind doors, smoldered in cabinets. He was inside the beast now, in the maw of his old nemesis. The overwhelming feeling was one of familiarity. He understood that the fire had been waiting for him his whole life, or at least since the day he should have been in the car but wasn't.

As the smoke closed in behind him, Sam lost his bearings. He was a man marooned in a heavy fog, a sailor adrift at sea. Peter's voice was his beacon, but Peter's voice was fading. He'd stopped answering Sam's calls. He'd stopped coughing.

Time loses its properties in the heat. It stretches out, forfeits elasticity; each movement takes minutes to execute, and it's hard to judge distances. Sam felt as if he were swimming through a sea of oil. He thought he must be close to the dining room door but couldn't be sure. Blinded by the smoke, he might have passed within inches of Peter and never known it.

Suddenly he banged his head against something hard. He grabbed—but it was just a table leg.

"Peter!" It came out a gasp. Tears poured down his face. His nose and throat burned, and it was getting hard to breathe. A cool, detached voice inside his head ordered him back. He crawled forward.

Under the table was a trapped pocket of cooler air, slightly more breathable. Sam paused there. He was very tired, and his chest hurt. The heat had a density that resisted his progress. If he could just rest a moment he'd get his strength back. He closed his eyes.

Strangely, with his eyes shut he could see more clearly. Louise stood in front of him, dressed in jeans, a tank top, hiking boots, and a jaunty straw hat. She looked beautiful but anxious.

"Nice hat," he said. "Suits you."

She knelt beside him. He smelled her scent, White Linen. "Hey, Sam," she said.

"Lou, I've got a bone to pick with you."

"Thighbone? Jawbone? Pick a bone, any bone."

"Louise, be serious."

"Sorry."

"I loved you."

"Loved you too, babe."

"Yes. But what was the last thing you did?"

"I died?"

"By my hand. You made me kill you. The only person in the world I loved, I had to kill."

She was silent.

"Lou?"

"I'm sorry, love. Forgive me."

"I do. Comin' home to you, darlin'."

"No, Sam," she said. "Get up. You're almost there."

In a moment's inspiration the poem came back to him. "Rowing in Eden, ah the sea! Might I but moor tonight in thee."

"Poetry, at a time like this?!"

"It's from that book you wanted. Emily Dickinson."

Lou scowled. "Stow the poetry and move, Pollak. Get off your ass!"

This in her acclaimed midwife voice. Drill sergeants trembled at that voice. When Louise said push, women pushed; when she said move, Sam moved. Got to his knees and crawled, chin to the ground in obeisance to the fire. Chunks of burning plaster rained from the ceiling. He was tunneling through utter darkness, his only orientation to the fire. The stink of it filled his nostrils. The hair on his arms smoldered. Every breath seared his lungs. But he was crawling toward, not away from, the heat.

Some would call it beneficent fate. Sam wasn't a subscriber; he marked it down to a stroke of luck, random as a lightning bolt. Whatever it was, blind as a mole in the dark recesses of the earth, Sam put his hand down on a face.

It scared the shit out of him. He let out a yelp. Crawling around in hell, he'd lost track of where he was, nearly forgotten what he was doing. The face reminded him. He called Peter's name, slapped and shook him, but got no response at all. The boy's body had the utter limpness of death. Sam grabbed him by the waistband, turned his back on the fire and crawled. The added exertion of hauling the boy made him cough, and the gasping between coughs drew the smoke further into his lungs. Inertia, he would later say, was all that kept him moving. Whatever. He crawled and kept on crawling until he heard a voice shout, "They're here!" and human arms delivered him.

CHAPTER 21

By the time Peter was carried and Sam led from the smoldering ruin of Jane's house, the fire was in remission. Not dead yet—flame still pulsed through the interior walls, flaring out to consume the contents of a closet or cabinet, then receding sullenly from drenched floors and outer walls—but beaten back, circumscribed, trapped.

They were found in the kitchen, not ten yards from the mudroom door. Sam's blind reckoning, toward and away from the heat, had served him well. Earl Lassiter carried Peter out. Sam walked, with assistance but on his own two feet. Outside the house, he collapsed onto the lawn.

Hands grasped and lifted him onto a stretcher. He was carried, conscious but helpless as an infant, toward an ambulance in the driveway. At first his arms dangled off the sides of the stretcher; then someone came along and crossed them over his chest. Bumping and swaying like an Eastern potentate on the shoulders of his mismatched human steeds, he gazed away from the house, toward the treetops and open sky above the pond. Cool breezes bathed his burning skin. It was full morning now, and the contrast between the darkness inside the house and the light made him squint. It felt good to be alive.

But his lungs were clogged. Inhaling felt like sucking water through a punctured straw. Fresh air all around and not a drop to breathe; the harder he tried, the less he got. He had just begun to thrash when his bearers laid the stretcher down on a gurney beside the ambulance. A broad calm face appeared above him, ringed by light. Sam had a sudden flash, an image too fleeting for retention, of his mother's face appearing over the bars of a crib.

"Easy, Sam," Willem Mueller said, fastening a mask over Sam's mouth and nose. "This'll help."

The oxygen cut a fast swath to his brain. Within moments Sam felt better. He remembered Peter.

"Lay down," Willem growled. "It don't work as fast as all that."

But Sam had spotted Peter now, and he stayed up on an elbow. Two medics were working on the boy, one breathing, the other pumping. Jane hovered over them with such anguish in her face that Sam had to turn away.

Oh God, he prayed, let him live. Let him not have died for that dog. And it didn't strike him as strange to be praying to a God he didn't believe in. He remembered Malachi saying, "We quarrel; therefore He is." He, Sam, lacked even that contentious wedge of faith; yet the prayer came, a natural last resort.

It wouldn't work. It never had. The only answer he'd ever received to prayer was a resounding celestial raspberry. But then, Sam's were always prayers of desperation, and desperation invites cruelty. Sam's father, after renouncing his orthodoxy, had turned away from prayers of petition. Didn't believe in them. "You want God to answer," he used to say, "pray for rain on a cloudy day."

Suddenly Peter coughed. The medics rolled him onto his side, and he vomited a dark, turgid stream.

Jane knelt beside him. Stroked his head, spoke his name. Peter opened his eyes, knew her, and smiled wanly.

"He'll be okay," Willem said.

Sam was surprised to find him still there. "Will he?"

"Close call, though. Another five minutes without oxygen, kid's a cabbage." Willem hawked and spat on the ground. His phlegm was black. "Damn fool. You too, charging in after him. Think that helps us? That don't help. All that does is, we got two assholes to pull out instead of one."

"Sorry," Sam said. He'd never seen Willem so pissed.

"Dumb fucking move. Even if you did save his life."

"Save his—Yeah, right."

"Ten feet from the door, Gower said, headin' for daylight and dragging the kid behind. You'd a made it without us."

"Gower?"

"He's the first one got to you."

"Fuck me," Sam groaned.

They were lifting Peter into the ambulance. Jane followed him in. Her head popped out and she waved to Kate, who stood a short distance away with the little girls gathered to her.

"What was that about Kuzak?" Willem said.

Sam, having refused a ride to the hospital, leaned back on the gurney and removed his oxygen mask. "Gone to see Fertig."

"So you said. Why?" Willem's face was gray with ash, his hair matted to his head.

"He passed me on the road, haulin' ass outta town. Never of believed that old crate of his could move so fast."

"Meaning what?" another voice said. Sam craned backward to find Frank Gower looming over the gurney. "What's this about Fertig?"

Sam sat up and pivoted to face him, straddling the gurney. The world reeled, then settled. "All I'm saying's what I saw."

Gower tapped him on the shoulder, not lightly. "Who gives a shit what you saw? Where the fuck you get off accusing Lyle?"

From behind Sam, Willem said, "He's not accusing anyone."

They ignored him. Sam said, "Racing out of here at 4:30 in the morning, you tell me: Where was he comin' from?"

"Balling someone's wife." Gower spat the words. "Stealing chickens. How the fuck should I know? Tell you where he wasn't: He wasn't setting no fire!"

"Kuzak figured it was worth asking."

"Kuzak's an asshole. And you're the last one to go pointin' fingers."

"Yeah? How's that?"

"You ain't done bad off these fires. Fixed the dykes' house, didn't ya? Nice bit of change." Gower jerked a thumb at the smoldering house behind him. "How about her? Think she'll need some work?"

Sam was on his feet and swinging before the last words had left Gower's lips, but his body betrayed him. His legs felt loose, as if the bones had melted in the fire; his knees buckled and the swing went wide. Gower, laughing, poked him in the chest, and Sam collapsed like a lawn chair.

Willem Mueller's huge paw lit hard on Gower's shoulder. "Nice move, decking a stretcher case."

"I ain't about to sit around while they railroad that boy. And you, Mueller, you'd best remember where you come from, and who you're dealing with."

"Impossible," Jane said.

"Not even difficult." Kate appealed to Sam. "Tell her we have plenty of room."

Sam didn't answer.

"You've been kind," Jane said. "More than that. But there's a limit to how much we can impose."

It was late that same morning. They had gravitated to the Muellers' house; to Kate, its warm center. A quiet center she seemed, though was not. She had brewed coffee with a pinch of cardamom and served it in mugs, caused baskets of buttered rolls and heaping mounds of scrambled eggs to appear, answered phone calls, received visitors, hustled her own children off to school, bathed, comforted, and put Keisha and Luz to bed. And when Jane arrived from the ER, without Peter but with the solace of having heard him pronounced out of danger and seen him resting comfortably, Kate tried to mother her too.

Installed on the living room couch, Jane sat erect, weary beyond measure but afraid to lie down lest she fall apart. Now that Peter was safe, the awful reality and magnitude of her loss were setting in. Like a time-release capsule, every few minutes a new loss burst upon her consciousness. Her papers, Rolodex, bankbook. Her beloved Humphrey Bogart trench coat. Luz's stuffed elephant. Her parents' photos. And poor Moses. All gone forever, burned for spite.

She couldn't think about it now. Later, alone, she would mourn. For now she had to concentrate on practicalities. Difficult, with her thoughts swirling around like demented snakes. Looming over all was the phone call to Portia, already too long delayed. Without a home, Jane's hold on her children was suddenly imperiled. Whatever she ended up doing, she had to find a place to rent quickly. Earl Lassiter would know what was available in the school district; she'd call him soon. Kate was pressing her to stay with them, insisting they had ample room—an offer Jane, knowing they had not, firmly refused.

"But it could take weeks to find a suitable house! You have no people in the county. Where will you stay if not here?"

"In a motel," Jane said.

"A motel!" Kate turned to Sam.

Sam had been so far remarkably silent; had seemed preoccupied. Now, stirring in the depths of Willem's armchair, he looked at Jane and said, "Use my house."

A long, thoughtful silence while each considered the implications. Then all three spoke at once.

Jane, shaking her head, said, "Thank you, but—"

Sam said, "I'll move into the workshop."

Kate said, "It's the perfect solution."

A truck pulled up in front of the house. All morning long trucks and cars had been stopping as villagers, hearing the news, came round to commiserate and leave care packages for Jane and her kids. But Kate recognized the chug and clatter of her husband's truck and hurried out to meet him in the hall.

Left alone, Sam and Jane allowed their eyes to meet.

"I haven't even thanked you for Peter," she said softly. "Wouldn't know where to start."

"No need."

"Yes need. Only it's too big, what you did."

Sam shook his head. "I gave him the dog. I felt responsible. It was more . . . self-preservation than anything."

"You call it that if you like. I call it something else. You're a stand-up guy, Pollak."

"Thanks, Goncalves."

He smiled and she felt a lurch in the pit of her stomach. Their eyes held, the silence stretched out, his offer hung in the air between them. The thought of living in such proximity to him stirred feelings that penetrated even her carapace of benumbed misery. Dangerous feelings, not good; premonitions of pain. Timing is all in human relationships; *when* matters as much as how, even who. Theirs, from the very first meeting, had been disastrous.

She looked down. "Appreciate the offer, but you know I can't put you out of your own house."

"The workshop's fine for me. House is too big anyway. Motel'll cost you a fortune."

Jane said, "Why are you doing this?"

He'd been wondering himself, hoping his motives were okay. As far as he could tell they were. As far as he could tell, he was just doing the neighborly thing. They were a family without a home; he had an empty house.

"It's no big deal. What's it cost me?" He shrugged. "Wouldn't mind a home-cooked meal now and then while you're in residence. Get sick of my own cooking. Not a condition, though."

That drew a smile; as if she would begrudge him a meal. They were like two people meeting after a flood. She was tired, tired, sick at heart and tired. The things he offered them—shelter, privacy, a chance to regroup—were the very things she longed for.

She accepted. Just for a day or two, she said; just till she found a place to rent.

"As long as it takes," Sam said.

"The bastard confessed?" Sam asked. He had, on Mueller's entry, ceded his host's chair and now sat beside Jane, a foot of sofa between them.

"Confessed?" Willem mulled the word over. "You could call it that."

"What would you call it?"

Another pause while the fire chief downed half a mug of coffee. "I'd say he bragged on it."

Jane looked from one to the other. "Who?"

"Lyle Fertig," Willem said.

"Are you saying Lyle Fertig burned my house?"

"Yes ma'am."

She pressed her hands to her temples. "Why?"

Mueller studied her through gritty eyes. He was unshowered and unshaven and the stink of fire clung to his skin. He was missing a day's work he could ill afford. Now it fell to him to explain to this woman who had just lost everything she owned why Lyle Fertig had seen fit to burn down her house with herself and her children in it.

He wasn't up to the task; found it hard just to look her in the eye. Willem knew of no reason why he should feel that way, unless it was Fertig's harping on *us* and *them* that made him feel like somehow he was to blame. Whereas in fact, even knowing Fertig as well as he did, Willem could not begin to understand why he set those fires. Much less explain to her.

He stuck to the facts: what he had seen, what Kuzak had told him. After leaving the fire, the sheriff had driven straight to Fertig's mobile home in the woods. Fertig's mangy yellow dog barked and snarled at his approach, but cringed when Kuzak showed his own teeth. Despite the noise, no one stirred inside the trailer. The pickup's hood was still warm. Four empty jerricans lay in the back of the pickup. Kuzak snorted. Lazy bastard hadn't even bothered to dump them. He climbed three cement block steps to the trailer, heralded by renewed howls of protest from the dog. The door was unlocked. He knocked and entered. Fertig was in bed, faking sleep with his pants and boots on. The boots, the bed, the whole trailer stunk of gasoline.

"Lyle," Kuzak said, not raising his voice above the conversational, "you've really done it this time."

An hour or so later, in the sheriff's small office, a strangely clubby atmosphere prevailed. Fertig had been read his rights and had waived them. He had done nothing to be ashamed of, he declared, so no way was he blowing his hard-earned stash on a shyster. They had passed quickly and rather amicably through the stages of denial and bargaining. By the time Mueller and Gower arrived, Fertig was instructing Kuzak on the finer points of motive.

They sat facing each other, a tape recorder on the desk between them. Entering the room, Mueller at first glance suffered an odd displacement. If he hadn't known better he would have mistaken prisoner for captor, for it was Kuzak whose chin drooped to his chest, whose face was hard and weary, and Fertig who sprawled, at ease and voluble, heels propped companionably on Kuzak's desk.

Willem Mueller had every right to sit in. He and Kuzak had worked this case together from the start. Gower was there uninvited and on sufferance, because Kuzak knew he'd never believe this if he didn't hear it for himself; also because Fertig was on a gloating jag and might well double his efforts to win Gower's approval, hanging himself in the process.

Certainly Lyle didn't mind the company; the more the merrier as far as he was concerned. He was especially pleased to see Gower, having dreamt of the day Gower found out who Lyle Fertig really was. Of the four men in the room, he was surely the happiest, and why not? It hadn't been easy, keeping his mouth shut when what he wanted was to shout it from the rooftops. At last he was free to take credit where credit was due.

It seemed very strange to Willem, who leaned against the wall, his hands stuffed in his pockets lest he be tempted to use them. Here was Fertig exposed as the torcher, and yet they were the ones who felt ashamed. At least he did, and judging by Kuzak's face, the sheriff wasn't feeling too great either. All this time, right under their noses: How could they not have seen?

"Truth of the matter," Fertig expounded, in the replete tone of a man who needs only a cigar to top off his happiness, "I was doing a public service. Sheriff here had any balls, he'd toss the cuffs and pin a medal on my chest. Everybody complained. Nobody wanted 'em here. Lots of talk, yakkity yak. But nobody *did* shit, 'cept me."

"Did shit about what?" Kuzak said.

"All the city scum invadin' our town is what! Jesus, Kuzak, where've you been? Movin' in, driving prices up to where a working stiff like me, five generations in this county, can't afford no better than a fucking trailer." He rolled his eyes at Frank Gower, whom he took for a certain ally.

Gower didn't look at him. He spat in the wastebasket.

The slightest flicker of doubt crossed Fertig's face. "Ain't like I did none of ours," he said. "I chose my missions carefully."

"That right?" Kuzak said, lighting one cigarette off the butt of another. "What about old Crawford's barn? Ain't he 'one of us'?"

"Shit, that's different. That's personal." *Personal* meaning, clearly, none of Kuzak's business. "Son of a bitch flunked my ass three times. Wasn't for him I'd of graduated. I owed him. Frank here knows; tell 'em, Frank."

Gower sat in the chair beside his friend. His face was a caved-in building with nothing moving in the rubble except his Adam's apple, which jerked spasmodically. Kuzak was right: Gower would never have bought this story if he wasn't hearing it from Fertig's own lips. Even hearing it, he didn't believe.

"You're full of shit," he said. "You're dreamin'. You never did nothing."

Fertig's expression was a cocktail of righteous indignation and contempt. He'd prepared for this day of reckoning, he'd rehearsed his lines. If today he was to emerge in his true colors as the Scarlet Pimpernel of Columbia County, the secret warrior, the torch-bearer, so too would others be revealed for what they were and what they were not.

Fertig said, "*I* never did nothing? What'd *you* ever do? Whined and complained for years about that baby-killing Jew doc up Wickham way, but what'd you ever *do*? Spit on a nurse: big fucking deal. *I* closed the shitheel down."

There was a silence. Mueller and Gower stared at the floor.

Kuzak doodled on a pad: crosses in a graveyard, neatly lined up. "Nearly killed four people tonight," he said neutrally. "Three kids and a woman. Dog hadn't woke 'em, they'd've burned alive."

"Wouldn't of happened, they hadn't been there," Fertig said with triumphant logic. "People set themselves down in the line of fire, can't complain if they get hit. What you gotta realize, men, this is war. This is Us against Them, all the way." Us, his expansive wave made clear, included Kuzak, Mueller, and Gower.

"But you don't use fire." Frank Gower's voice emerged from the rubble. "You don't use fire."

Fertig examined his wrists for cuff marks. "Hey, all's fair in love and war."

"You don't use fire." Gower half rose, leaning toward Fertig: nothing sudden or alarming in the motion till he wrapped his hands around the other man's neck and began to squeeze. "I could of been killed! You stupid fuck, I could of died in one of them fires; ever think of that, asshole?"

Willem took his sweet time getting there. But he did, and pulled Gower off.

Fertig fell back in his chair, rubbing his throat with a martyred look. "That's the thanks I get. That's what I get for taking care of business."

"Taking care of business my ass!" cried Gower. "Public service my ass! You wanted what you always wanted, to get into the company. Thought with all them fires we'd need more bodies, didn't you? Figured you'd finally make it."

Fertig's lips curled back, revealing long yellow teeth. The skin at his temples pulsed. He said: "They had no cause to exclude me. I'd of made a great fireman."

They looked at him.

"Only it ain't about that," he muttered. "It ain't about that at all."

Still they studied him, Willem in particular deeply perplexed. Given that Fertig was an idiot, given he was a racist, given his frustration and festering resentment and the natural tendency of unhappy people to seek out scapegoats for life's disappointments—given all that, it still made no sense. His mind drifted to other recent acts of inexplicable malice: terrorist bombings, parents killing children and children killing parents, random slaughter in post offices and fast-food joints by men with petty grievances. Gradually he began to see a connection. What linked these acts, Fertig's included, was the incongruity between provocation and response. There was in each case an imbalance, a disparity, an unbridgeable gap between cause and effect; and right there in that cavity, it seemed to Willem, was where evil resided and malice bred.

Frank Gower passed a hand over his eyes and said, more in sorrow than in anger, "Fuck you, man. I wash my hands of you." He thrust back his chair and Fertig flinched; but Gower just nodded curt thanks to the sheriff and stalked out, slamming the door behind him.

"I hired him," Jane said, studying her laced fingers.

"Well, yeah," Willem said, with a beseechful look at Sam. He saw where this was going.

"I hired the man who burned my house." She laughed, her eyes appalled. "What does that say about my judgment?"

Willem and Sam spoke as one: "He fooled us all."

"And we knew him," Willem added. "Or thought we did."

"How could he destroy a house he'd worked on himself?" Sam wondered aloud; for that was of all things the one he found most incomprehensible. "Roof a house and burn it down? Who would believe that, much less anticipate it?"

"Never mind killing us," said Jane, "but to destroy his own work!"

He looked and saw her laughing at him, and it struck him as an essentially female laugh. Sam believed women had a gender-specific way of looking at a man and seeing in him things he would never in a million years see in himself—then of keeping their knowledge to themselves, locking it away behind their eyes. It was part of their power, this secret knowledge and the laughter it engendered.

Kate, too. Even now he felt her watching him, watching Jane, wondering, speculating, thinking her own thoughts. You couldn't stop them doing that, saying one thing, thinking another. "The perfect solution," she'd declared; but what she thought was surely, "He's bringing a strange woman into Louise's house."

What would Lou say? Of course, if Lou were alive there would be no problem, her absence being its crux. It would be nice to think she'd say what Kate had said: "The perfect solution." He might have asked her, back there in the fire, that or any of a dozen more important questions, if indeed it was Lou and not his overheated imagination. At the time he hadn't doubted. Not only because she looked and sounded like herself—hallucinations, he knew, could seem as real as life—but also, and primarily, because the things she said were so utterly Louise. The sense of humor was hers, not his at all. "Pick a bone, any bone." Never in a million years could Sam have joked like that, but it was typical of Lou.

Later doubt set in. Skepticism was his faith, intrinsic to his life and as precious to him as messianism was to Gower's backwoods band of Bible-thumpers. He clung to it still, though his enounter with Louise had perforated his perfect disbelief with a buckshot scattering of hope.

Would she have approved of his offer to Jane, or would she have resented it? No way to know. Sam was not one of those who believe that to love a woman is to know her. Part of what smote him about Louise was her otherness, her autonomy, her constant ability to surprise, to change, to grow. His opinion, based on his marriage, was that no one really knew anyone else's mind; for how can one mind encompass another? People say after a death: "We must do such-and-such because poor so-and-so would want us to." But in his experience, it wasn't the deceased who endorsed that particular action, but rather the survivor who desired it. So in offering Jane shelter, Sam was doing what he wanted to do, for reasons he could only hope were honorable. One thing was clear: whatever unfinished business remained between them could not be resolved now while she was so vulnerable, so wounded, and so grateful. Needlessly grateful: for already it was clear to Sam that whatever good he'd done Peter, the benefit to himself was greater still. At last he had faced his enemy, entered its lair and survived. Had done for Peter what he'd failed to do, so many years ago, for his brother. At the fire and afterward, people kept coming up, pounding his back, calling him a hero. He knew he was no hero. But for the first time in his life, he felt absolved of cowardice.

CHAPTER 22

Entering the room, the doctor did a double take. "Dressed already?" she said.

"If you can call it that," Peter said glumly. They weren't his clothes. He had no clothes any more, if you didn't count the jeans he'd had on when they brought him in, which were all seared and ripped to shreds. He owned nothing now, not one single thing; he was as shorn of possessions as a newborn. At first he told himself it was a good thing—a new beginning, a rebirth, the ultimate break with the past, the very thing he had wished for—which just went to prove the old adage was right on the money. His sister's birthday card, the letters she'd written in answer to his own, the photos of her with her new family and of Carlos with his, the drawings Keisha had made for him, the journal he'd begun to keep, the photo of his real mother that he'd kept hidden beneath his mattress: all those pieces of himself gone up in smoke.

Even the clothes turned out to matter. They defined him, they declared who he was; thus their loss opened him to misinterpretation. The hospital had given him a set of so-called clothes he wouldn't have worn to save his life if he'd had any choice, which clearly he didn't: nubby brown cords, a button-down shirt in a print like old men's boxer shorts, green socks, and a pair of Kmart sneakers: total wuss clothes, kick-me duds. "No way," he'd said when he understood what was expected of him, but the nurse replied tartly, "Beggars can't be choosers," which he supposed was what they were now.

You had to put things in perspective, though. Moses was dead. Jane claimed maybe not, maybe he had just panicked and ran away. But two whole days had passed since the fire and still no sign of him. He was dead, all right. So who gave a rat's fart what clothes Peter wore?

"Let's have a listen," said the doctor, plugging a stethoscope into her ears. That's how they talked here; it was always "Let's do this," and "How are we feeling?" as if they were all in this together, one big happy family or romper room. "Deep breath in," she said, which was easy; exhaling was what hurt. He tried hard not to cough but it couldn't be helped. The doctor frowned.

"Forget it," he said, before she could speak. "I'm outta here."

"Anxious to get home?" she said absently, still listening to his chest.

"What home?" But even as he spoke the answer formed in his mind: home to Jane, home to Keisha and Luz, his variable foster sibs. A revolving door of a family, imperfect, uncertain, but a family nonetheless.

"Sorry," she said. "Still, thank God you all got out."

"Thank Moses," he muttered. The doctor looked at him, wondering perhaps if the smoke had gone to his head, but Peter didn't feel like explaining. The death of his dog was a flat-out kick in the balls from God, who for a guy who was supposed to be dead had a hell of a foot. Peter read the message loud and clear. "You dared to be happy? You dared to love? Take that, fool!"

Whenever he thought about Moses, sorrow possessed him. The dog's heroism coupled with the cruelty of his death was exquisitely painful; and yet in a strange way Peter savored the pain, probing it the way a boy is drawn irresistibly to pick a scab. After his father died, he had felt nothing at all for months and months. Any amount of grief was better than that nothingness.

A few minutes after the doctor left, Jane arrived. She hugged Peter and said, "Let's get out of here before they change their mind."

"Hell, yeah." He turned, stopped, and swallowed hard. Sam Pollak was standing in the doorway.

"Hey, Peter," Sam said.

"Hi."

"Ready to go?"

"Sure. Uh—where?"

"You guys are bunking at my place for a while, till Jane finds a place to rent."

"Cool."

"Peter." Jane looked him up and down. "What exactly are you wearing?"

He winced. "What they gave me. Beggars can't be choosers, they said."

"Idiots." She sniffed. "We're not beggars, and if you think I'd be seen with you dressed like that you better think again. Here." She tossed him a plastic bag.

Inside were sweat socks, underpants, jeans, and a sweatshirt. "Oh, man, you saved my life," he moaned.

"No, actually, Sam did that. I just bought you some clothes."

Thus prodded, Peter couldn't put it off any longer. When Jane first told him who had pulled him out of the fire, he was floored. He was embarrassed, ashamed, grateful of course . . . but he also felt something strangely akin to exultation. During his stay in the hospital, Peter whiled away hours imagining his rescue. He made up a whole story about it, a movie scene with a cast of dozens, dialogue, lights, sirens, the whole works. The climax comes as Sam is being held back by a bunch of firemen yelling, "Get a grip, man! You can't go in there, she's gonna blow!" He nods, seeming to accept what they say, but it's a ruse. The instant they let him go he dashes into the burning house, finds Peter, slings him over his shoulder, and carries him out to safety. (A little music wouldn't hurt here, something along the lines of the *Star Wars* theme.)

Someday he would ask the carpenter what really went down: what he did and saw, what thoughts passed through his mind when he stumbled over Peter's inert body.

Not yet, though. Faced with the man himself, Peter was overcome by embarrassment. He ducked his head at Sam, still hanging by the door. "Hear you hauled my ass out of the fire," he said.

"Wasn't just me."

"You went in first, though. Dumb-ass move, man. Almost as dumb as mine."

"So they told me. Got my wrist slapped good."

"Yeah, well," Peter said. "Thanks anyway. Guess I owe you one."

"You don't owe me a thing," said Sam.

• • •

Not a trace of yellow paint remained. The front of the house was charred black, the roof had collapsed, and the third floor, Peter's aerie, no longer existed. Shards of glass and building debris littered the front lawn.

Peter said, "Why?"

Sam and Jane exchanged looks.

Sam spoke first. "Beats hell outta me."

"Did we do something to him? Did we harm him in some way?"

"No," Jane said.

They stood on the street, their backs to Sam's truck. He hadn't planned to bring them here, had driven out of his way to avoid it. But Peter had asked to see and Jane seconded the request. "Sure?" Sam asked. "If we shut our eyes," she said, "will it go away?"

Now she was sorry she'd insisted. Standing in front of the gutted house, she felt like a ghost. If burglary is akin to rape in the sense of violation experienced by its victims, then losing one's home to arson is surely the material analog of being murdered. People kept saying, "Thank God no one was seriously injured," and good Catholic girl that she once was, Jane replied "Yes, thank God." But they didn't see that she herself was hurt, had suffered a grievous wound to the soul. A thousand choices had gone into the renovating, furnishing, and decorating of that house, every choice a bit of self made manifest. Everything that tied her to her past had been in that house. Now only memory remained; and what was memory but a sieve whose holes grow wider with each passing year?

Jane felt insubstantial, rootless, orphaned anew. She was like the survivor of an earthquake. The very ground beneath her feet felt shaky.

Why? the boy had asked, and asked again. What could she reply? Fertig himself had come to seem insignificant almost as soon as he was identified. The man was nothing: a funneling of malice, an ill-wind tunnel.

"There is no rational explanation," she told Peter. "Just bad luck. Being in the wrong place at the wrong time."

Peter thought about that. There had been a time, not long ago, when he wouldn't have cared why. He'd have danced around the fire and toasted marshmallows in the flames; he'd have sought out Fertig and shook his hand. Now, looking at the ruined house, he was shocked by the anguish he felt inside. Which wasn't all for Moses. Things had changed for him here.

Jane made a strangled sound. He looked at her: rigid, bleak-eyed, pressed against Sam's truck as if it were the edge of the known universe. Sorrow and loss emanated from her like heat from an oven. His own pain suddenly receding, he put his arm around her shoulders. She squeezed his hand and they stood together.

They were turning to go when a voice rang out from down the street. "Yo, city boy!"

Peter recognized Walter Gower's voice and wheeled with clenched fists. Let him say something, he thought. One smirk, one crack; let him just try.

Walter was jogging toward them. Beside him, tied to a length of rope, a huge black mutt trotted on three legs, favoring a bandaged front paw. Peter's first thought was that the dog looked remarkably like Moses. A split second later the mist cleared; he realized it *was* Moses.

Dropping to his knees, he called the dog's name. Moses froze, then leapt forward in giant bounds, jerking the rope out of Walter's hand, galloping toward Peter.

Peter's arms clamped around the dog's neck. He buried his face in thick fur, and the pungent smell of dirty dog penetrated even the burnt smell in his nostrils. Moses whimpered, squirmed ecstatically, nuzzled his ears and neck, mouthed his hands and licked the tears off his cheeks. Walter caught up and stood panting above them, watching with a grin. When Moses turned his attentions to Jane, Peter stood up.

"You found him," he said.

Walter nodded importantly. "Runnin' in the woods behind my house. His paw's burnt pretty bad. I'd of took him to the vet only my old man said no way was he payin'. So I just put some gunk on the burn and bandaged it up. Fed him, too. Thing eats like a horse."

Peter wiped his hand on his pants and stuck it out. "Thanks, man."

After a moment of surprise, Walter shook the hand. "For nothin'."

he said, then stood for a while as if he had something else to say but couldn't quite think what it was. After a while he remembered, and nodded toward the house.

"Sucks about your place, man. What a butthole, Fertig."

"Fuckin' scumbag," Peter said amicably.

"So what you guys gonna do, move back to the city?"

Peter looked at Jane; they all did. She looked at the house and waited with as much interest as they to hear what she would say. There was a longish pause.

"No," she said.

"No?" Peter said.

"Hell, no." She took a cautious step or two away from the truck. The ground held. "Think I'd let a cockroach like Fertig drive me out? This is our home. We tear this place down and rebuild."

"Good for you!" Sam cried. Moses rolled onto his back and waved his paws in the air.

Popular opinion had pivoted around the fire and come to rest squarely behind Jane. Frank Gower kept himself busy, too busy to stop by Whitehill's for his traditional morning cup, but the rest of the back-room chorus was united in support of Jane and condemnation of Lyle Fertig. It seemed, in fact, that everyone had suspected Lyle all along, though they hadn't liked to say so. Clearly, they said, the man had a screw loose, which was no surprise when you considered the well-known fact that every generation of Fertigs produced one maniac. Blood will tell, the women said, and the men nodded sagely. Old tales about Lyle's uncle Leland and his grandfather Caleb Fertig were taken out of mothballs and hung out to air. Remarkable rabble-rousers they'd been, specialists in taking things a step too far, though none had taken them quite so far as Lyle had. The thought that Fertig might have been emboldened, even inspired, by the village's disdain for Jane's family never arose. The accusations against Peter had passed into prehistory.

Old Wickham, not content to let bygones be bygones, preferred to forget there had ever been any bygones.

Practical folk that they were, the villagers did not limit their support to words of sympathy but rather expressed it through giving. Tom Whitehill set out two ten-gallon bins, which quickly filled and refilled with clothing, kitchenware, and sundries. Paul Binder, owner of the Wickham Bookstore, hung a sign by the cash register soliciting donations of used children's books. Within a week he had enough to fill a bookcase. Not to be outdone, the Old Wickham Volunteer Fire Department's Ladies Auxiliary held a toy drive. Even after all the broken dolls and puzzles with missing pieces had been weeded out, Keisha and Luz ended up with more playthings than they had ever owned in their lives. Nor was Peter forgotten: three pairs of lightly used hockey skates and a perfectly good hockey stick were donated anonymously.

Jane's gratitude at this generous outpouring was exceeded only by the self-satisfaction of the donors. Isn't it wonderful, she was asked five times a day, how out of such an evil act so much good can come? Jane *was* touched, she *was* grateful; but she would not partake of the general amnesia. Some people, like the Muellers and Sam Pollak, had proven themselves true friends. As for the rest, she would willingly forgive but never forget the way her family had been received. If getting burned out of her home was the price she had to pay for acceptance, then given her druthers, Jane would have kept the house and forgone the acceptance . . . which did not, in any case, extend so far as to provide her with a place to rent.

"I have a good feeling about this one," Lassiter said, glancing at Jane beside him. He drove fast and one-handed; his freckled left arm rested on the open window well.

"I hope so," Jane replied, though she hadn't much. Tomorrow would be a week since the fire, during which time Earl Lassiter had shown her just about every house available for rent in the area. It wasn't that she was over-particular; her only requirements were that the house be available immediately and located inside the kids' school district. But even within those wide parameters there weren't many possibilities, and most of those were furnished houses intended for the summer-vacation market, too rich for Jane's pocketbook. They'd seen a couple of mobile homes, small and depressing, and a wonderful contemporary in Nassau that turned out to be just outside the school-district boundary. Yesterday Lassiter showed her a three-bedroom, one-bath ranch in a tract of identical houses just north of Wickham. The ranch was dreary and rectangular, the small yard equally regular and featureless. More a warehouse than a house, certainly not a place to heal in; but functional, adequate to their needs, and available.

In the car Jane had said, "I should take it."

Lassiter sniffed.

"I know," she said, "but poor Sam."

"Not so poor. Having you and those kids around's probably just what the doctor ordered."

"A little of us goes a long way. Trust me."

"Wait till tomorrow," Lassiter said. "We've got that Victorian in Wickham to look at. I have a feeling about that one."

"That realtor's instinct," she'd replied, not without affection. Over the past week they'd spent many hours together. A certain unspoken fellow-feeling had evolved. Lassiter was a local boy, but what else he was had changed him in people's eyes and in his own. He was an insider who felt like an outsider; Jane was all outsider.

Having sold her the house and subsequently defended her right to live in it, Lassiter had of all people least cause to feel guilty; yet he was one of the few who seemed to. The day after the fire he ran interference for her with the insurance and mortgage companies, obtaining from the insurer funds for immediate relief and assurances of a prompt settlement, and from the bank a commitment that Jane's mortgage would roll over to the new house. After that, nothing would do but that he personally find her a suitable house to rent while she rebuilt her own. If he hadn't succeeded yet, it was not for lack of trying.

The Victorian was the last house on a dead end. Lassiter wove slowly through a soccer game in progress, the young players parting to let them pass, resuming smoothly in their wake. The owners, a small, nervous couple, showed them rather quickly around a charming doll's house: four tiny idiosyncratic bedrooms upstairs, living room, dining room, parlor, and kitchen down. A deck off the kitchen overlooked a deep backyard. There was a tire swing suspended from a tree, a vegetable garden, a small duck pond surrounded by weeping willows, a cast-iron bench beside the pond. Standing on the deck, Jane pictured herself sitting on that bench on a summer evening, reading and watching the children play.

She nodded once to Lassiter. He smiled and went inside.

Time passed. After a while she went looking. Lassiter wasn't in the kitchen or the dining room. She crossed the hall to the living room and heard his voice coming from the little parlor next door. The paneled door was closed, but the realtor's voice, raised in anger and frustration, penetrated easily.

"Four bedrooms and you don't want kids? Excuse me for asking, but who do you think is looking to rent a four-bedroom house?"

The response, in a woman's tone, was inaudible.

Lassiter said, "What two-year lease? When we talked yesterday you said nothing about a two-year requirement."

A man's voice replied, soft but vehement. Jane heard one word: "Neighbors."

She went outside then, and stood in the driveway watching the game. When she was a kid it was baseball and the faces were darker, but otherwise this game had the same old neighborhood feel to it. The same mix of kids, too: boys, mostly, with a scattering of girls, and one little six-year-old pistol who even now squirted between two defenders and slammed the ball into the net. Then he stood, pounding his chest and Tarzan-yelling in triumph, till his teammates buried him beneath a pile of bodies.

Keisha would have loved it, Jane thought. Keisha loved active games, any kind of sport. She was quick and agile like that little boy, and when she got hurt she didn't fuss. She'd fit right in with this bunch. Luz was a quieter child, content to sit and play with her stuffed animals while Keisha plunged about. But now Jane spotted two little girls, just about Luz's age, pushing doll carriages along the sidewalk.

I could have tended the garden, she thought; I could have walked to the bookstore. We could have healed in this house.

None of it would happen. These people would not rent to her. She'd known it from the moment Lassiter introduced them and a look passed between husband and wife. They knew who she was. Overhearing Lassiter's futile conversation, she'd felt no surprise at all, only a suffocating sadness that started in her chest and radiated outward. As she watched the children play and waited for Lassiter, Jane mourned what would never be: not just the house but also the life that went with it. And though she had never lived that life and knew it was probably full of all kinds of hidden traps and pitfalls, in her heart she still believed they would have been happy here, and she regretted the loss of that happiness as if it were something real, something she already possessed. For there are, of course, two kinds of nostalgia. There is the common or garden-variety nostalgia for what was and is no longer, and there is also its exotic but no less potent cousin: nostalgia for what might have been, the road not taken . . . or the road barred. It's Moses's longing for the Promised Land he will never enter; it's the lingering grief of the woman who loses an unborn child.

With a rattle and a bang Lassiter slammed out of the house, moving like he wanted to hurt someone. The look on his face must have been a throwback to football days. Jane got in the car and he stepped on the gas.

They were halfway to Sam's house before she broke the silence. "I take it we didn't get the house."

"Sometimes," he said through clenched jaws, "I think I'm in the wrong business."

"You're too good at it for it to be wrong," Jane replied. It seemed absurd for her to be comforting him when it was she who just got screwed, but Lassiter's interest in her affairs transcended business. Though her memory of the night of the fire was mercifully blurred, several images stood out like floodlit pictures in a darkened gallery. One of the most vivid was the sight of big Earl in his yellow slicker and fireman's hat, weeping as he sifted through the ashes of her house.

Now he stared straight ahead. "You can take them to court. You have every right and I'll back you up. But it won't get you the house in time."

Jane nodded, way ahead of him. "I'll take the ranch."

He glanced at her. "You hated the ranch."

"I need a place, Earl. It'll do."

"What about the contemporary in Nassau? Now *that* was a house."

"It's out of the district."

"Maybe we should rethink that requirement. Nassau schools are—"

She cut him off. "My kids have gone through enough misery and dislocation, thank you. We'll take the ranch."

He pulled over to the side of the road. Behind a white picket fence, three horses grazed in a grassy paddock, two bays and a pinto. Lassiter leaned over, opened the glove compartment, and took out a thick leather book.

"You sure?"

Her face answered for her. He found the number and reached for the carphone.

"Mrs. Collis? How are you? It's Earl Lassiter . . . Well, I have good news for you. I believe we've found you a tenant . . . Yes, ma'am . . . Jane Goncalves . . . Yes, she is . . . It sure was . . ."

He listened for a minute and his voice changed. "Quite a coincidence. Two takers in twenty-four hours for a house that's been on the market how many months?"

Jane looked at him. Then she turned and fixed her gaze on the pinto mare, who had wandered over for a look at them.

"I see," Lassiter said. "And just out of professional curiosity, which agency was it? . . . Oh, really, *they* found *you.* I see . . . Yeah, you bet. G'bye, Mrs. Collis."

He hung up, winched his head around to look at Jane.

"It's gone," he said.

"Uh-huh."

"They took a deposit."

She nodded politely. "You believe that? 'Cause if you do, I got a bridge I want to sell you."

Lassiter smiled. It wasn't a pretty smile, but it was brief. "They do, however, send their very best wishes. Said to tell you what a terrible thing that young man did."

"That's real white of them."

"Yes, I thought so."

He started the car. They didn't speak again until they got to Sam's house. Lassiter got out and opened the door for Jane. He was particular about things like that.

"I'm going back to the office," he said. "Chin up, dear. I *will* find you a house."

"Maybe I should go back to Brooklyn," Jane said. She was tired, her head hurt, and Portia's voice in her head was drowning out her own. "Maybe this just wasn't meant to be."

Lassiter stuck his hand in his pocket and said, in a fair-to-middling Cagney growl, "Don't even think about it, sweetheart."

Sam had started up the washing machine and poured in detergent. Now he was segregating his laundry. "Whites over here, coloreds there; separate but equal, boys, that's how we do things down here." It occurred to him that talking trash to his socks and underwear was not a good sign. But at least they weren't answering.

It felt good to have his house back, if only for an hour. Sam tried to steer clear when Jane and the kids were in residence. This was partly for their sake—he didn't want to crowd them or make them feel like guests—and partly for his own. It was an unsettling thing, watching Jane inhabit Lou's house, use her dishes, sit in her chair, sleep in her bed like a raven-haired Goldilocks. There was, in this possession, an element of exorcism to which the children, with their wild romping and running about, contributed much. It was as if the house had suffered a stroke and part of it had died, and now the neurons were recombining, forging new pathways, creating alternate routes to perform old functions. The process was necessary but not always easy or pleasant for him to watch. It was a bit like having an impacted tooth removed: it may be unavoidable but you don't necessarily want to be there.

He had another reason for keeping his distance. Before issuing his invitation to Jane, he had vowed to himself that while Jane was a guest under his roof he would not make a pass at her. It was a serious promise, a matter of honor. He also didn't anticipate it being a problem.

He was wrong.

Two days after they moved into his house, Jane had asked him to have dinner with her and the kids. He arrived early and was put to work shucking peas while Jane fixed dinner. Maybe it was the very fact that she was now off-limits that imbued her with a heightened eroticism, or maybe he was simply seeing better these days, but as she moved about the kitchen it seemed to Sam that the light flowed with her, and his eyes followed the light. She talked and he answered, but his thoughts were of her body, the small pert breasts beneath the denim vest, the firm, shapely legs that disappeared beneath her short jean skirt. (Had she dressed to entice him? If so, she'd succeeded.) She was totally different from Louise, who was all lushness and abundance, generous breasts and hips, flowing thighs and sloping belly. Making love to Louise had been like journeying through a luxuriant jungle; there was so much to explore. Whereas Jane was calibrated to a different scale. She had an economical body, brown and nut-hard, built for distance; she was all woman, yet somehow androgynous, like Mary Martin as Peter Pan. It was a whole different kind of sexiness, and Sam found himself responding to it with all the moderation of a fourteen-year-old kid uncovering a stash of *Penthouses.*

She crossed the floor in front of him, opened the pantry and reached up. Her skirt rose, revealing three more inches of tawny thigh. An image of her naked body popped into Sam's head; he didn't seek, but neither did he shun it. He was comparing the image to what he could see of the original when suddenly the object of his reverie, feeling the heat of his eyes on her, happened to glance back—and there was Sam, caught in mid-ogle wearing his heart on his sleeve, his prick on his forehead.

He crossed his legs, he smiled weakly. Jane's eyebrows rose. Her mouth formed itself for laughter, so baldly was he caught. What he wanted was to go to her and stop that laugh with a kiss. What he did was nothing. He forbade himself to stir.

Jane out of pure charity managed not to laugh. Her eyes dropped, then grew wide. She let out a little shriek and said, "Sam, what are you doing!"

For one godawful moment he thought his fly was open. Then he looked down and observed that in his distraction, he had been chucking the peas and depositing the pods in the bowl.

After that he stayed away as much as he could. From his workshop he watched Jane's comings and goings, and when she was out he made such use of the house as he needed. This morning, a Saturday, the three kids left early, scrambling down the hill toward the Muellers' with fishing rods and tackle boxes in their hands. At ten o'clock Lassiter's car pulled up to the house, and Jane came out in her house-hunting clothes. Figuring the coast was clear, Sam went over to do his laundry.

At the same moment Sam was feeding his second load into the washing machine, Earl Lassiter was opening the car door for Jane. With both the washer and dryer running, Sam didn't hear the door open; he had no idea Jane was back until he stepped out of the laundry room and heard the unmistakable sound of a woman weeping.

For one dreadful moment he thought it was Louise, and his heart faltered. Then he pulled himself together and followed the sound down the hall into the living room, where he found Jane sprawled face down on the couch, sobbing in an attitude of utter despair. "Good God," he cried, genuinely frightened, "what's happened now?"

She sprang back into a corner of the sofa, mashing a pillow to her chest. "Jesus, Sam, you scared me."

"Sorry. I came in to do a wash . . . But why were you crying?" He came and sat beside her.

Jane averted her face. "I should have heard the dryer."

"What's wrong?" he said gently. "House no good?"

She got up and walked to the window, keeping her back to Sam. "The house was perfect. We're the ones not good enough."

He went to her: What else could he do? He embraced her as a friend, meaning only to comfort her, or so he told himself. But once she was in his arms he could no more stop himself making love to her than he could command the wind. He'd fantasized this moment idly, a hundred times or more; now the fantasy had exploded, spewing desire like shrapnel.

He bent his lips to her hair, smooth as a crow's wing. He kissed her eyelids, kissed lashes still wet with tears. She hovered in his arms, torn in her feelings, vacillating. He gave her no time to think, but tilted her head back and kissed her lips. His mouth descended to her throat, his hand to the small of her back. Her skin was firm and fragrant, like the skin of a mango. He inhaled her smell, warm and coppery. Her pulse beat against his lips. If Jane didn't stop him now, nothing would.

At the very last moment she did. Two hands against his chest, and "Don't, please don't."

Sam allowed himself be moved back, but kept his hands on her shoulders. She had said no; but he'd felt her stir to his touch, felt her back arch, her nipples harden, her lips part beneath his. He mustered all his persuasiveness.

"Are you sure, Jane? I come in peace."

Her cheeks were flushed, her breath uneven. She said, "It's not the right time."

"I know. I promised myself I wouldn't do this. Didn't want you thinking that's why I offered you the house. But—" here he gave her his most appealing look, a look that had done wonders for him in the old days—"the harder I try not to, the more I keep thinking about you." He ran his fingers down her arm.

He was working her now, he was putting on the moves; he wanted what he wanted, but it wasn't for lack of caring about her. Sam's feelings for Jane now were light-years removed from what they had been when he first tried to bed her, but his immediate goal was the same.

A carpenter to the core, he believed in using the proper tool for each job; and for him the tools of seduction lay close to hand. Like riding a bike, seduction is a skill that once mastered is mastered for life. Sam had always been luckier with women than he deserved. He was no movie star, but he was tall and strong and there was something in his looks that attracted them, which he wasn't above exploiting.

She tried to stave him off with teasing. "You sound like a kid I knew in Brooklyn. 'Ooh, baby, baby, I need you so bad it hoits.'"

"I feel like a kid," he said, undaunted. "I feel like a kid who's frantic to get laid for the very first time."

"I'm supposed to feel flattered?"

"Absolutely. Man hath no greater desire than the desire to lose his virginity."

She laughed. Encouraged, Sam moved closer. The big head told him to lay off, but the little head said push on.

Jane, reading his eyes, moved away from him to stand before the fireplace. She said, "You could have done something about it before."

"I tried."

"Not seriously."

He bowed his head slightly, acknowledging his dereliction. "I didn't feel then that I could give you what you deserve to have."

"And now you do?"

"I'd sure like to try."

His eyes, his voice caressed her. She shuddered at their touch. She too had imagined this moment, but in her fantasy when they came together it was as equals. He wasn't her benefactor, and she wasn't homeless, stressed out, and fraught with tears. Did he like his birds with broken wings, or did they just have the world's worst timing?

"Jane," he said. "Come here."

"I've always been attracted to you. But I can't do this now."

"I won't hurt you."

She shook her head. "I need some ground to stand on. I need to get back what was taken from me. I need a place of my own."

"Ai, Goncalves, you're killing me," he moaned. But that night, as he lay on his cot watching the moon through the skylight, Sam felt remarkably alive, and his thoughts for once were not of the past, nor even the present, but rather of the future.

CHAPTER 23

"I have good news," Jane said, "and I have bad news."

They were walking in the pine forest behind Sam's house, she, Peter, and the dog.

"Good news first," Peter said. "Let me guess: Lyle Fertig hanged himself in his cell."

"No. I found us a place. A nice big apartment in Wickham: three bedrooms, two baths. And the best thing is it's empty now. We can move in this weekend."

If that was the good news, he didn't want to hear the bad. Because even though he'd known from the start this was bound to happen, it still came as a jolt. He liked living at Sam's place. It was great for Moses, who took to the woods like an otter to water. And it was good for Peter, too; because while Sam Pollak was not the world's most genial host, he never seemed to mind Peter hanging out in his workshop. Sam taught him stuff, like how to cane a chair, which wasn't easy—you had to soak the strips and then pull them real tight; but Peter picked the knack up quickly and Sam told him he had good hands, which every time Peter thought of he blushed like a friggin' girl. Last time he finished a chair, Sam slipped him ten bucks.

"What's that for?" he'd asked.

"You did good work. Take it."

"Thought you weren't paying me."

"That ain't pay. That's walking-around money."

First cash Peter ever earned. So naturally, just as things are finally going right, Jane decides to move them into some crummy apartment in town.

"What's the bad news?"

Jane winced. "They don't allow dogs."

Peter stopped and stared. "No fuckin' way. Don't even think about it."

"Don't you be talking that talk to me, boy."

"I'm just sayin' it like it is. If Moses don't go, I don't go."

"I'm not talking about giving him away. I'm talking about six months, till my house is ready. We can find someone—"

"No."

"Peter," Jane said, "I have looked at every damn house in this county. I don't like this any more than you do. But I'm out of options. This place is available. And it's nice, it really is. Three bedrooms, a garden in the back."

"And no dogs. So I don't care if it's the fuckin' Taj Majal."

"I asked them to make an exception. I explained about Moses. They wouldn't budge; it's part of the deal."

"Fuck 'em," he said. "We can stay here."

"That's totally unfair to Sam."

"He doesn't mind."

"Of course he minds! We've put him out of his home. Peter, you've got to work with me on this."

A distinct quaver in that voice. Peter turned his eyes on her. Jane looked gaunt, and there were deep shadows under her eyes, like she hadn't been sleeping well. No wonder, with Luz waking up screaming every night. A stab of guilt pierced his anger. Jane didn't deserve any more grief. But neither did Moses.

Though unleashed, the dog sat between them, turning from one to the other as they spoke. He seemed, if not to understand the conversation, at least to know he was its subject.

"It's just a few months, Peter."

"He wouldn't know that. He'd think we deserted him."

"You can visit him."

"A lot of good that'll do! Jesus, Jane, how can you do this to him?"

Her face hardened. "I am doing what I have to do to keep this family together."

"Moses is part of this family. Without Moses, this 'family' wouldn't exist."

Jane ran both hands through her hair, calling on all the saints she knew. "Peter," she said presently, with tolerable patience, "you can't keep fighting me on this. What's done is done: I gave them a deposit."

Peter couldn't believe it. "You paid a deposit! You agreed to give up Moses without talking to me?"

"Only temporarily. I had to decide. It's very hard to find three-bedroom apartments. I couldn't risk them changing their mind, backing down."

"Oh, man, that sucks. That really, really sucks!" He rushed past her into the woods.

She called his name, but he kept running. There was no path really, nor was any needed, for the forest's thick carpet of pine needles discouraged undergrowth. With Moses keeping pace invisibly, Peter followed the rise of the hill. He ran until he had no breath left; then in a small clearing he slid down to rest against a tree. He whistled, and Moses appeared, panting, with his genie look. *Yes, master, what is your wish?*

Peter said, "Shit, buddy, what are we going to do?"

Moses circled a few times, then plopped down, resting his huge head on Peter's thigh.

"You saved our lives, Moses. I ain't about to desert you, no matter what Jane says. Worst comes to worst we hit the road, buddy, you and me."

He picked up a pine cone and chucked it as far as he could. Moses took off in pursuit.

Sam knew all about the apartment. Jane had stopped by earlier in the day. Stood in the doorway of his workshop and told him the news; wouldn't come in, though he asked her. His fault entirely. What an idiot he'd been the other night, what an adolescent twit. Any fool could see the woman was upset, she was hurting. Sam wasn't proud of himself.

So they were moving. He was pleased for her and told her so. "Now you'll have what you need, a place of your own."

Where, with any luck, they could pick up where they'd left off.

But later, after she'd gone, Sam thought about moving back into the house, how large and comfortable and quiet and empty it would seem, and his pleasure dwindled. And then it occurred to him that with Jane living in town, Peter wouldn't be coming around any more.

Which was absolutely no skin off Sam's back. He never wanted the boy to begin with, never asked him to come. He preferred working alone. In the beginning he kept hoping that Peter would get bored and quit; but the kid must not have had anything else to do, because there he was each afternoon, regular as clockwork, showing up right after school and hanging out till dinner time. Sam got used to having him around. The kid made himself useful, you had to give him that. Didn't jabber, either. When he didn't know something he asked, and you didn't have to explain it twice. And his work was better than you'd expect from a youngster. Peter had the hands of a craftsman, but more importantly, he had the patience to finish one job before moving on to the next.

Sam still didn't like kids. But if he had, he'd have liked Peter Quinn.

He was tapering chair legs when Peter showed up that afternoon, Moses at his heels as usual. Sam didn't look up. He finished drawing the taper onto the leg blank, checked his measurements, laid the leg blank in the tapering jig. Peter came over to watch. The kid was a mess. Pine needles in his hair, dirt on his hands and face.

"You been fighting?" Sam asked.

"Yeah, with Jane." The carpenter looked up sharply, and Peter spread his hands out wide. "Never laid a glove on her."

"Better not." Sam positioned the rip fence and turned on the blade. When the cut was complete, he laid the tapered leg on the bench and put the boy to work smoothing out the saw cuts.

"She tell you?" Peter asked presently.

Sam was plotting another taper and didn't answer right away. "About the apartment? Yeah."

"About Moses."

"She mentioned something. They don't take pets."

"He's not a fucking pet!"

Sam looked at him. Peter's face was all scrunched up, like a kid trying not to cry, and he was sanding the chair leg like he meant to kill it.

"Easy on the leg, son. I said smooth it, not blast it into oblivion."

"Sorry."

They worked in silence for a while.

Sam said, "You can find someone to look after him for a few months. A classmate or something."

"Yeah, right. Like I'd trust any of them. I told her: if he don't go, I don't go."

"Kind of hard on Jane, isn't it?"

"Tough shit. Where's her fucking gratitude? She had no business doing what she did."

Sam shook his head.

"What? You think I'm wrong?"

"You surprise me, kid. What the woman's been through these past couple weeks, she don't need any grief from you."

Peter flushed to the roots of his hair. "I know she's been through shit. Jane's been real good to me; you think I like bustin' her balls? Only it just ain't right, it ain't fair what she's doing to Moses."

It ain't fair! Who but a kid would say that? But of course, Sam thought, Peter was a kid. Boy wasn't even shaving yet. He tended to forget that, treat him older than he was. Losing that dog, even for a while, was a big thing to Peter, and why shouldn't it be? It's not like life's so teeming with love that a man can afford to piss away what he's got.

"It's not Jane that's unfair," Sam said. "That's just life, and you oughtta know it by now. Real life's sloppy; things don't always work out like they should. It ain't like mathematics. Sometimes you run up against a problem doesn't have a solution. The woman's just doing the very best she can under lousy circumstances. You can't punish her for that."

Peter scowled at the floor. Sam watched him struggle. It was like watching a movie alien morph from one form to another. Before his eyes the boy was changing, growing.

After a while Peter looked up. "*If* there was someplace safe, someone I could trust to take him, then maybe I could go along with it."

Sam nodded approval. "How about Billy Mueller?"

"He says he's been wanting a dog for years, but his dad won't have one in the house."

"Must be someone. That girl I've seen you with."

"You gave him to us, Sam," Peter said. "You're the only—"

"Stop right there."

"—one I'd trust. He knows you. He knows this place."

Sam thrust out a hand. "Uh-uh. Forget it."

"Only a few months, isn't that what you said to me? For Jane's sake?"

Sam looked up at the rafters, waiting for some guidance from Louise, but he was on his own. What he wanted was to tell Peter to piss off, he wasn't taking the dog and that's that. What stopped him was the inexorable notion that perhaps he was a tiny bit responsible. If he hadn't tried to jump Jane's bones the other day, maybe she wouldn't have been in such a hurry to get out; maybe she'd have held out longer.

On the other hand, he truly did not want to be saddled with the dog.

An idea came to him.

It was a new idea but it didn't feel new. It felt like something that had been growing for some time, just below the threshold of consciousness. Still, Sam didn't blurt it out. He turned the idea over in his mind, examined all the angles. He rejected, retrieved, and reconsidered it. He saw that it was good.

"Reason I don't want a dog," he said, "is I don't want to look after it. Dog's gotta be walked, fed, played with. I don't have the time or the inclination." The boy's face fell. Sam went on. "Wouldn't mind giving old Moses house space, though, if someone else was to take care of him."

He saw hope dawn in Peter's eyes, and Peter rein it in. The checking reaction was swift and habitual, and it saddened Sam to see it in a face so young.

"What do you mean?" Peter said.

The carpenter had been leaning back on the seed cabinet as they spoke. Now he straightened up. What he had to say next was a business proposal and he meant to present it as such. "You're a capable kid," he said. "I could use another hand around this place. There's plenty of stuff a boy can do if he's willing to work hard. You and Moses'd get your room and board and ten bucks a week. If that's acceptable to you, and *if* Jane and Portia agree, you could stay here with the dog. Just till

Jane's house is ready," he added, so there'd be no misunderstanding on that point.

"Okay," Peter said.

"Okay?" Sam looked around the room, then back at Peter. "That's it? You're not gonna ask what kind of work?"

"What kind of work?"

"Whatever needs doing," Sam said sternly. "Not just in here. House chores, too."

"Okay."

"You don't want to think it over?"

The boy gave him a cocky grin. "You gettin' cold feet?"

"No," Sam lied. Cold feet? He couldn't feel his toes.

"All right then," Peter said. "Who's gonna tell Jane?"

Moving day arrived, and so did two old friends, one expected, the other not.

Portia drove up from the city, emerging limb by limb from Ike's Lincoln in a caftan, turban, and four-inch sling-back heels. She looked around at the bustling yard and the two pickup trucks, and when Jane emerged from the house carrying a carton, Portia went right up to her and pressed a vermillion fingernail into her chest. "Do not think," she declared, "do not imagine for one single moment that just because I have had the misfortune to arrive while you are moving that I am going to help you. Because I'll tell you right now, sugar, I am here in my professional capacity and I am not lifting so much as a feather duster. My moving days are *over*, girl."

"Hello, Portia," Jane said. They kissed.

"Do I know all these people?"

"These are my friends," Jane said, and she introduced them. Earl Lassiter had come to help, with his lover, Mark Hambro. The Muellers were also there. Willem and Billy were helping load the trucks, while Melissa occupied Keisha and Luz with games on the lawn. Kate Mueller had just brewed a fresh pot of strong coffee. She brought a steaming mug out to Portia and made a friend for life.

A chair was produced. Portia sat in the yard, drank her coffee, and observed.

"Jane," she said presently, "I thought you told me everything was destroyed."

"Practically everything. A few odd things survived. An umbrella, a few pots and pans, a load of laundry that was in the washer."

"Then what's all this?" Portia gestured at the two pickup trucks, full of furniture and boxes.

"People from the village gave us things."

"They gave you all this?"

"Yes," Jane said, "they did."

Portia fell uncustomarily silent.

Jane got back to work. Portia finished her coffee, placed the cup on the ground beside her feet, and summoned Sam.

There was no other chair. Sam stood before her, feeling like a kid called into the principal's office.

"A boy," Portia said, "is not a football."

"Thanks," Sam said. "I'd wondered."

Ignoring this feeble attempt at humor, she sailed majestically on. "We do not buy, sell, or barter boys. We do not hand them off, we do not indenture them to carpenters. Peter is a ward of the state, and in everything pertaining to this boy, *l'état, c'est moi*. Do you understand? I am the state."

"Yes ma'am."

"Do you like children, Mr. Pollak?"

"As a class, no. There's a few exceptions, though."

Her eyes glinted. He had no idea whether he'd just scored a point or blown the game.

"What do you want with Peter?" she asked.

"He's a useful kid. It's a business arrangement. Boy helps out, gets room, board, and kibble in return."

Portia's steady gaze cut through his blather like a laser through cheese. She didn't speak. There was an awkward pause.

"I thought," Sam said, in a different tone, "that we might do each other good."

Portia nodded in that way that told him nothing.

"Normally," she said, with extreme neutrality, "we look ten times at any man who wants to take in an adolescent boy."

It took him a moment to understand; then he scowled. "Jesus."

"Just doing my job, Mr. Pollak."

Something in her way of saying his name, the emphasis on "Mister," reminded Sam of the rabbi. Malachi, too, had used that semblance of formality to cloak the most intrusive prying.

He looked away from her. Jane was across the yard, handing a TV up to Lassiter. She was sweating and her T-shirt clung fetchingly to her body, an effect wholly wasted on Lassiter, though not on Sam.

Portia followed his eyes and smiled to herself.

With the packing nearly completed, Jane called them all to take a break on the deck. The day was unseasonably warm for May; the deck thermostat read 85 and the humidity was high. The children came to join them on the deck. Platters of turkey, cheese, and ham sandwiches, chips, and a big bowl of purple grapes were laid out on the picnic table; also pitchers of iced tea and bottles of beer. A modest feast, which Jane had risen at six to prepare. It wasn't much to give back, but it was better than nothing. She took the spoon from her iced tea and tapped it against the glass.

When she had their attention, she said, "Before we leave there's a few things I wanted to say. Sam, I want to thank you for your generosity and your kindness. What you did was above and beyond. You didn't have to be so nice." She paused a beat and held his eye. "I hope you'll come see us soon."

Sam didn't speak, but returned a look of such unconcealed warmth and intensity that those standing nearest him took a step back. It was a rather prolonged and altogether very public kind of look, and among the two acknowledged couples, identical knowing smiles were exchanged.

Jane, blushing, looked away. "Willem, Kate, you got us through a real tough time. Earl, thanks for not giving up. And thanks to all of you for helping us move—except, of course, Portia, who true to her word has not moved so much as a feather duster."

Portia inclined her head in regal acknowledgment.

Earl Lassiter raised his beer bottle. "Here's to the house to come; may it turn out to be everything your heart desires." Amid a general clicking of bottles and glasses, Jane withdrew to join Portia, who had taken a seat to the side.

"Very nice," Portia said. "Very gracious. So this is it? You're really staying up here after they burned you out?"

"*They* didn't burn me out," Jane said. "It was one guy, acting alone."

"That's what the Warren Commission said," Portia said with a sniff, but her heart wasn't in it. Maybe it was seeing the heaps of donated goods, or maybe it was all the people who'd come to help, but quite suddenly she understood that her friend would not be coming home to Brooklyn again. Jane wasn't alone any more. She had people up here; she had the makings of a life.

"Saw you talking to Sam," Jane said. "What do you think?"

"What I always thought. Cute buns."

Jane jabbed her. "Not that."

Portia looked over at the railing where Peter and Sam stood side by side. Sam was pointing at the driveway, making planing motions with his hand, while the boy listened and nodded.

"I think you done good," she said softly.

"Wasn't my doing. Some dick-for-brains burned my house down."

Portia looked at her. "I remember how that boy was when he came to you. You got the healing touch, girl."

"Not me, not this time. I was getting nowhere till he hooked up with Sam. You know," Jane lowered her voice, "he's only talking about six months."

Portia patted the air with her hand. Let it ride, the gesture said. Six months is a long time.

"Peter's been real anxious," Jane said. "Scared you won't let him stay with Sam."

"Tell me somethin' I don't know. Damn kid's called my home so often, Ike's talking about changing our number."

"In fact, I think part of the fuss over the dog was really him not wanting to leave here."

"Wouldn't surprise me. You always said the boy needed a man."

"So? What do you say?"

"Might as well try it," Portia said. (A great *whoosh* of air came out of Jane, who hadn't realized till that moment she'd been holding her breath.) "That boy's growing himself the kind of attitude needs a father. I liked him better when he was living in La-La Land."

"Liar," said Jane.

The second arrival was heralded by a joyous fanfare of barking from Moses, who leapt off the deck to greet him. Sam, looking up at the noise, dropped the ham sandwich he'd been holding.

He descended the steps and met the rabbi halfway across the yard. They shook hands without speaking, like duelists. Sam was amazed at the jolt that shot through him at the touch of Malachi's hand.

"Where have you been?" Sam said.

"Here and there," said the rabbi. "You think you're the only Jew with *tsuris*? Plus a little trouble with my prostate, you shouldn't know. But I see you got guests. I've come at a bad time."

"Kind of your specialty, isn't it?" Sam said. "Come on up."

The rabbi remembered the Muellers and Lassiter from the funeral. When Sam introduced him to Jane, Malachi recognized her name. "You're the lady whose house burned down. What a terrible thing. I read in the newspaper and afterward I wondered what happened to you and the *kinder*."

"We've fallen on our feet, with some help from our friends. Can I get you something to eat, Rabbi? We have turkey, Swiss cheese, and . . . well, I guess ham is out of the question."

"Just a drop of water, *maydeleh;* maybe throw in an ice cube if you got." Jane nodded and moved toward the kitchen door. Malachi turned to Sam. "I see you still got the dog," he said. "Did I hear someone call it Moses?"

"I gave him away. He's Peter's dog now."

"Peter?"

Sam beckoned the boy over and introduced them. "Would you excuse me a minute?" he said.

He followed Jane into the kitchen, cool and pleasant after the heat outdoors. She had turned on the tap and was waiting for the water to stop spurting before holding the glass underneath. Sam leaned against the kitchen table, watching.

"Too much air in the pipes," Jane said without looking around.

"Yeah? How do you know?"

"A woman knows these things."

He laughed but it irked him that he hadn't fixed the damn thing months ago. Lots of other stuff too, he noticed, looking around with eyes sharpened by absence; a lot of basic maintenance he'd neglected. Like the driveway, for instance. He and Louise used to work on it every fall before the first snowfall. Lou was a big strong girl, and between them they'd managed to knock it out in a day. It was a job, though. You had to shift all the rocks and boulders that had sprung up after the last winter, fill in the pits and crannies, adjust the pitch so that rainwater would run off into the gully, not puddle and freeze. Last fall they didn't do it, and now cars had to slalom their way up the drive. Hell of a job fixing it now, but it had to be done. The boy would help.

Jane turned off the faucet, took a handful of cubes from the icemaker, and dropped them into the glass. She held it out to Sam. "Want to give it to him?"

He reached out as if to take the tumbler, but instead closed his fingers lightly on her wrist. He said, "I liked what you said before."

She looked at the hand, then his face. "About coming to see us?"

"That too, but I meant the part about 'You didn't have to be so nice.' It's a song, you know."

"It is?"

"The Lovin' Spoonful." He sang a few bars. "You didn't have to be so nice, I would have liked you anyway." Jane stood with her mouth open. He tipped her a wink and walked out the door.

• • •

Portia came back from the bathroom to find Malachi seated in her chair, drinking a glass of water. He rose as she approached. Portia looked him up and down. "And who are you when you're at home?"

Malachi bowed. "Haim Malachi at your service. Itinerant rabbi; have tallis, will travel."

"Uh-huh," Portia said. "I'll remember that next time I need a hired tallis."

"You never know," said the rabbi.

Peter was handing the last cartons up to Sam when Malachi wandered over to join them. "Are you moving, Mr. Pollak?" he said.

"Not me, no," Sam said. "Jane and the kids." And that was all he meant to say. He knew Malachi; give him an inch, he'd take a mile. But Peter was less discreet, and worse yet he was happy, a dire loosener of tongues. From him the rabbi got the story of how Sam had taken them in after the fire; after which, because Malachi was such a sponge, Peter threw in the part about Sam pulling him from the house.

The rabbi didn't say anything when Peter was through. He just looked at Sam and nodded, the way Sam nodded at a piece of furniture that had come out right.

"Malachi, what are you doing here?" Sam said.

"My job. Following up, making sure."

"Haim Malachi, parole officer of the soul."

The old man laughed till he wheezed. Then he grabbed a carton from the pile beside the truck and lifted it up.

"Jeez," Peter said, alarmed. "Here, let me take that."

"Don't worry, *boychik*," the rabbi said. "I'm stronger than I look. Right, Mr. Pollak?"

Sam looked at Malachi and found him waiting. The rabbi winked.

At last they were all loaded up. Sam and Peter were the last to leave. They stopped the pickup in the parking area to say good-bye to Malachi.

"Wait," said the rabbi. "Aren't you forgetting something?"

"What?" Peter asked.

"Your dog."

"He's not going. We're staying on."

Malachi's eyebrows rose. "You're staying?"

"No dogs allowed in the apartment, so Sam's letting us live here."

"For now," Sam said.

"Very nice," Malachi said. "A man, a boy, and a dog: a whole little *mishpuchah*. You know what's a *mishpuchah*?" he asked the boy.

"Yeah," Peter said, "it's New York for family. Only we ain't about that family shit. We got us a business deal, right, Sam?"

"Right," Sam said. "Shook hands on it and all."

"See," explained Peter, "Sam and me, we're not the family kind."

The rabbi nodded. "Two of a kind, but not the family kind."

"You got it," Peter said. Sam threw the pickup into gear and they headed down the hill.

ABOUT THE AUTHOR

Barbara Rogan was born in New York City and educated at St. John's College. She has lived in New York, Sante Fe, and Tel Aviv, and worked at various times as a horse wrangler, forest ranger, copywriter, book editor, and literary agent. Now a full-time writer, she resides on Long Island with her husband and two sons. Her books have been translated into eight languages. *Rowing in Eden* is her fifth novel.

9 781439 135754